JUST ONE LOOK

Jacquelyn took an involuntary step backward before she was suffocated by his nearness. But she found herself plastered against the wall when Mace bridged the space between them. Now there was no escape. Mace blocked her path like a rock-hard wall. At close range she could detect the brilliant glitter of gold in his eyes, take note of his full, sensuous lips, study the cleft in his chin. . . .

"Is that difficult to shave?" Jacquelyn asked out of the blue, surprising Mace as well as herself.

She could feel the low rumble of laughter vibrating in his massive chest as he inched closer. It was like the shock of an earthquake ricocheting through her, and Jake could feel her fierce reaction to him, all the way to her toes.

"It is a mite tedious." He chuckled before he focused on the curve of her mouth. Their close encounter caused her bottom lip to quiver, and Mace made note of her unconscious mannerism. He was definitely disturbing this bundle of femininity. And he intended to continue this pattern until he had her exactly where he wanted her. . . .

LOVE'S RECKLESS REBEL

Gina Robins

ZEBRA BOOKS
KENSINGTON PUBLISHING CORP.

ZEBRA BOOKS

are published by

Kensington Publishing Corp.
475 Park Avenue South
New York, NY 10016

First printing: September, 1988

Printed in the United States of America

Part I

Man can control everything except a woman and a hurricane. Problems arise when those two impossibilities are one and the same.

Chapter 1

Galveston, Texas, 1849

Jacquelyn Reid's narrowed brown eyes scanned the bustling wharf from her bird's-eye view on the rocking schooner. Impatient annoyance puckered her exquisite features as she searched the crowd for a man who fit the description of her escort, one who had already left her standing for more than an hour. Heaving an agitated sigh, Jacquelyn twirled the mint-green parasol her great-aunt Florence insisted a lady should employ when exposed to the sun.

Damn it all! Why all this pomp and circumstance? Jake asked herself grumpily. She didn't need a frilly parasol, or an escort for that matter. Annoyed, she mopped the perspiration from her brow and inhaled a generous breath of salty sea air. There was no reason for her to be dawdling under an umbrella on this confounded schooner, awaiting an escort who had yet to approach and introduced himself as Jonathan Mason. She didn't need anyone to accompany her home. She could have ridden to her grandfather's cotton plantation blindfolded, and her grandfather damned well knew it!

Frustrated, Jacquelyn tapped a dainty foot and glared

7

at the milling crowd. Tall, dark, handsome, and well-mannered? Jake sniffed cynically at the sketchy description her grandfather had given of Jonathan Mason—whoever and wherever the hell he was! Jake didn't really give a whit who Mason was, only that he was late and she was growing madder by the minute.

For weeks now, the General—as her grandfather preferred to be called—had sent dozens of letters to Jacquelyn in New Orleans, boasting about Jonathan Mason. This phenomenal creature was to meet her in Galveston and accompany her home after her three-year absence. But all the General's glowing accolades had only served to arouse Jacquelyn's darkest suspicions. Even her great-aunt Florence, the General's younger sister, had frowned when she read the letters. With a snort that only Florence could expel with such animated efficiency, she had declared it was matchmaking Harlan Reid had in mind. Obviously, the General was attempting to toss his eligible granddaughter in Jonathan Mason's lap.

Did Mason realize he was being maneuvered? Jacquelyn wondered irritably. Well, if Harlan Reid thought he could coerce Jake into a marriage of his making, he thought wrong! And if Jonathan Mason couldn't keep watch on Galveston Bay to note the arrival of the schooner from New Orleans, she was going to give him a good piece of her mind . . . if the varmint ever showed up!

Jacquelyn had lived for this day for three long-suffering years. And now she was left waiting for the arrival of an escort she didn't want or need! For what had been an eternity, she had been forced to reside with her great-aunt Florence in New Orleans. During that time Jake had been accosted by a cavalry of young men, handpicked by Florence. Jacquelyn had turned up her nose at each aristocrat who had been paraded past her for inspection. Occasionally, Jacquelyn wondered if her

8

Aunt Florence had selected such effeminate dandies just to annoy her. After all, she and her aunt had never been close, even after the length of time they had spent together. In fact, Jacquelyn could safely say they had practiced civilized warfare since the day she'd arrived in New Orleans.

Determinedly, Jacquelyn cast aside her difficulties with her crotchety aunt. She resented the years she had wasted in Louisiana. Jacquelyn had been born a Texan, and she would never have left the state if the General hadn't forcefully uprooted her and sent her off to be properly polished in a finishing school of Aunt Florence's choosing. Why Florence had offered to take her grand-niece in when the General had volunteered his services at the outbreak of the Mexican War, Jake would never know for certain. The woman had never been particularly fond of her oldest brother *or* Jake. She supposed Florence had made the offer out of family obligation, reluctant though it must have been. The General was a dyed-in-the-wool soldier, and had been impatient to match his talents against Mexico's ruthless Santa Anna. Florence had known the General would be itching to fight, and she'd taken Jake in while Texas was battling Mexico for the second time in a decade.

My, but the fur had flown when the General had announced Jake was to take up temporary residence in New Orleans. Jacquelyn had been outraged at the idea, and a trenchant argument had ensued. But the General had ultimately won the debate. It had been a monumental moment in history, Jacquelyn recalled with a bitter smile. Usually she defied the General, and he eventually backed down. But not in that instance. Never had she seen her grandfather in such a snit. In all their years together, she couldn't remember the General being so furious with her, and all because of a careless remark that had . . .

9

Jacquelyn flung aside the unpleasant memory that marred her relationship with her grandfather. Three years had come and gone. The past was behind her, and Jacquelyn refused to allow that blemish to strain her future relations with the General.

After delivering those inspirational platitudes to herself, Jacquelyn resumed her task of searching the faces in the crowd. But she did not possess the patience of Job. By damned, she was not wasting another minute waiting for Jonathan Mason. The man had already forced her to linger on board the schooner, clinging to that ridiculous green parasol, looking like a bundle of unwanted baggage. According to the General's last letter she and her very tardy escort were to spend the night at Galveston's most luxurious hotel before venturing to the plantation. Jacquelyn decided to do her waiting at the hotel, and Mason could rot in hell for all she cared. Surely the inconsiderate dolt had remembered to make the reservations, even if he didn't possess enough intelligence to find his way to the dock.

Determined in her purpose, Jacquelyn grasped her satchel and stamped across the planks to oversee the loading of her other belongings, which had been piled on the wharf. When she had located a man with a wagon who agreed to assist her for a reasonable price, Jacquelyn sent him and her luggage to the hotel. Although she entrusted her luggage to the man, who smelled like a brewery, she was not about to climb up beside him on the wagon.

Still fuming at Jonathan Mason, a man she deplored sight unseen, Jake stomped down the street. Silently, she formulated a tirade of insults to hurl at Mason . . . if she ever caught up with the lout. Dozens of degrading comments danced in her head. After she raked Mason over the coals for his tardiness, she would let it be known that she would not be a party to the General's matchmaking. And by the time Jake had stretched her

10

legs and made the brisk jaunt to the hotel, she would be armed with a score of suitably nasty remarks to fling at Mason.

Now, there are some individuals who are prone to take a stroll to quell their frustrations. And there are those who walk to permit their irritation to fester. Jacquelyn belonged to the latter group. Walking fanned her volatile temper, and Jonathan Mason was going to be sorry he'd left Jacquelyn standing in the sun. She would hold it over him for the rest of his life. . . .

"Well, ain't we got us a perty lady here in Galveston," Daniel Johnson said, snickering, as he watched the graceful sway of Jacquelyn's hips.

Another pair of leering eyes assessed Jacquelyn's well-sculptured physique. "Mmmm . . . might perty indeed," Frank Norman growled suggestively.

Jacquelyn's back stiffened when she caught wind of the two foul-smelling men who were following all too closely in her footsteps. Although it was her intention to ignore them, each man latched onto an elbow of hers. The instant they passed a secluded alley they herded her off the street. Although Jacquelyn had been sent to New Orleans to be polished in the ways of a full-fledged lady, she had not forgotten the self-preservation techniques she had acquired in her first seventeen years while she was running wild in Texas. In fact, she had relied upon many of her survival tactics when dealing with over-zealous beaux. The General had seen to it that Jake could fight like a soldier. She was adept with a pistol and knife, but unfortunately she had neither at her disposal at that crucial moment.

When Daniel Johnson attempted to clamp his hand over Jake's mouth to muffle the scream she intended to expel, he was the one who yelped in surprise. Using makeshift tactics, Jacquelyn bit into his hand and simultaneously kicked at Frank Norman, who stood

11

directly in front of her. Daniel shrank back to inspect his throbbing hand, Frank doubled over to protect his vital parts from another painful attack, and Jacquelyn came uncoiled like a disturbed rattlesnake.

Employing her parasol as an improvised rapier, Jacquelyn gouged Frank in the ribs, and then whacked him over the head with her satchel. Wheeling about, she used the same effective tactics on Daniel, who was fumbling for his pistol with his wounded hand. Spouting curses that would have sent Aunt Florence into a dead faint, Jacquelyn physically and verbally attacked her assailants. Daniel did not have the opportunity to squeeze the trigger of his pistol before Jake stabbed him in the midsection with her parasol-sword. The Colt .45 went flying when Jake's satchel swished through the air to collide with Daniel's already injured hand.

Neither man had anticipated the beating they were receiving from Jacquelyn. Although she looked to be dainty and delicate, her appearance was deceiving. This human wildcat came at them with claws bared, intent on doing unto them before they did unto her. It was as if Jake had sprouted another set of arms and legs with which to kick and claw—not to mention the painful blows from her satchel and parasol.

Cursing and growling, the two men made one last attempt to subdue the resourceful spitfire before they were poked and jabbed yet again. But Jacquelyn was poised and waiting. With lightning quickness she pounced, ramming her parasol into each man's belly. With her enemies buckling beneath her fierce attacks, Jacquelyn shot from the alley like an exploding cannon ball. She ran as fast as her legs would carry her, and she didn't slow her pace until she was surrounded by the passel of citizens who meandered through the streets of Galveston.

Renegade strands of silky brown hair tumbled from what had been an immaculate bun beneath her plumed hat—one that no longer sat regally atop her head. Jacquelyn shrugged off the loss of her silk bonnet. She detested the frilly headgear. It was a gift from Aunt Florence. A rather spiteful gift, Jake thought as she elbowed her way through the crowd. Florence knew how Jake disliked such frivolous paraphernalia. Indeed, that was why Florence delighted in wasting the monthly allowance the General sent for Jake on such distasteful purchases. The only gift that served a practical purpose was the parasol, Jake mused as she stomped toward her destination. No doubt Florence would have complained about using the umbrella as a weapon of defense. . . . But Jake would not have been forced to resort to such drastic measures if Jonathan Mason had arrived on time. Damn the man!

Jacquelyn silently seethed as she gobbled up the distance to the grand hotel in unladylike strides. This was all Mason's fault. If she hadn't waited around for her irresponsible, inconsiderate escort, she wouldn't have found herself assaulted by the riffraff on the wharf. She could have taken the coach, along with the other passengers from the schooner. And she had no inclination to crawl onto a wagon with the stubble-faced, whiskey-saturated man she had hired to transport her luggage! Double damn that Mason! When Jake got her hands on him she was going to have him poisoned, stabbed, shot, and hung. . . .

Inhaling a ragged breath, Jacquelyn composed herself. Glancing down, she realized she was still clutching her parasol in a stranglehold. A reluctant smile pursed her lips. She would have to remember to compliment Aunt Florence for buying this umbrella. It had saved Jake's life and the compliment would annoy Florence, whose intent it had been to buy her grandniece a gift she wouldn't appreciate.

Tossing the spiteful thought aside, Jake concentrated on Mason—the man who was entirely responsible for her inconvenience and her tussle with two foul-smelling assailants. If Mason thought to impress her upon their first encounter, he had certainly gotten off to a miserable start. Jacquelyn had her heart set on hating the scoundrel.

Veering through the main entrance of the hotel, Jacquelyn aimed herself toward the registration desk. "Has a man named Mason made reservations for the night?" she asked, striving to contain her aggravation.

The bald-headed innkeeper's eyes brightened and he broke into a cordial smile. Mason was a familiar name to him. In fact, if not for Mason, Henry Boswell might not have enjoyed such a thriving business. Mason recommended the hotel to all his friends and associates, and he had granted a loan when Henry was suffering hard times.

"Yes, miss," Henry enthused. "Mason has reserved the best suite in the hotel—the first door on the second floor."

Jake gnashed her teeth. It infuriated her to note the innkeeper's apparent affection for a man who obviously couldn't tell time. "I would like the key to Mason's rooms," she managed to say without barking out the words.

"That won't be necessary, miss," Henry informed her with another cheerful smile. "Mason is in his room and you can—"

Jacquelyn was seeing various shades of red as she stomped toward the staircase, leaving Henry in midsentence. Blast it, while she was baking in the sun and fending off those two disgusting scalawags, Mason was dawdling in his suite—one rented at the General's expense, no doubt!

14

Although Jake had already fought one intense battle that afternoon, she was spoiling for another. She was outraged to think Mason had been sitting in the lap of luxury while she'd single-handedly struggled to preserve her life. The nerve of Jonathan Mason! Just wait until she got her hands on that irresponsible, inconsiderate rascal. He would rue the day he was born.

Chapter 2

After rearranging her tattered gown, Jacquelyn drew herself up in front of Jonathan Mason's hotel suite. She pounded her parasol against the door with the vigor of a carpenter driving nails. "Mason!" she yelled for all she was worth.

"Yes?" a deep voice responded.

Jacquelyn didn't bother with the courtesy of waiting to be invited inside. She barreled into the room, craving to tear Mason limb from limb. But the scene before her eyes brought her to a skidding halt. There, lounging in a brass bathtub, was the dark and handsome Mason. Jake couldn't determine if he was "tall" (as the General's letters stated), but she was learning things about the man—things her grandfather had not dared describe. The display of masculine flesh took the wind out of Jake's sails and placed a crimson blush on her cheeks. Helplessly, she gawked at the man, who hadn't batted an eyelash at being caught in the buff.

Raven hair that shined blue-black in the afternoon sunlight capped Mason's head. From beneath a thick fan of lashes, twinkling golden eyes stared back at Jacquelyn with a mixture of curiosity and wry amusement. Full, sensuous lips curved into a rakish smile as Mason

17

assessed the ruffled bundle of femininity who had breezed into his suite like a flying carpet.

Jacquelyn shoved the unruly strands of dark hair from her face and clamped her sagging jaw shut. Despite her attempt to glare disapprovingly at the dashingly handsome rake who was sprawled in his bath, her eyes descended from his arresting facial features to land on the broad expanse of his bronzed chest. A dark matting of hair covered his bare flesh (and all the rest of him as near as Jake could tell). The rim of the tub concealed the private parts of his anatomy from her gawking gaze, but Jake had received a full view of hair-roughened arms, legs, and chest.

Long, tapered fingers were curled around a goblet of brandy. The other large hand held a half-smoked cigarillo. Whipcord muscles bulged and relaxed as Mason propped himself against the back of the tub and lifted a heavy brow.

Bold though she had always been, Jake took a retreating step and gulped over the lump that had collected in her throat. Masculinity emanated from this magnificent specimen like heat radiating from the summer sun. Jacquelyn felt another warm blush stain her cheeks when Mason drew his long, muscular legs against his chest and leaned out to set his goblet aside. Like magnets, her brown eyes were helplessly drawn to the corded tendons and wide muscles that wrapped sensuously around Mason's back. The man had the shoulders of a bull and the legs of a thoroughbred, she decided, giving him a thorough appraisal.

The bright pink flush on the lady's face and her ruffled appearance provoked Mason to chuckle softly. "I would rise to make a proper greeting bow, my dear, if you—"

Mason was interrupted by Jacquelyn's shocked gasp. Before the scoundrel dared to expose himself completely,

18

Jacquelyn spun around to stare at the wall. But it didn't relieve her frustration. Mason's arousing physique materialized on the wall as if an artist had painted his portrait to further fluster her.

"How dare you even suggest I would wish to see more of you than I already have!" Jake gritted out between clenched teeth.

Squaring her shoulders, Jake drew herself up proudly and rattled off the sizzling remarks she had mentally rehearsed while she stormed toward the hotel. But it annoyed her that she didn't have enough nerve to shout them into Mason's grinning face. She did, however, allow her booming remarks to bounce off the wall and rebound onto the handsome rake who was negligently lounging in his bath.

"The Gen'ral hailed you as a saint, but I consider you an irresponsible rake!" she snapped at the tormenting image on the wall. "I stood on that damned ship for an hour and a half, waiting for you to escort me to the hotel. When I found a man to haul my trunks to the hotel, I decided to walk rather than ride with the inebriated cur. I thought perhaps I might run across the gentleman the Gen'ral sent to accompany me. But instead, I ran headlong into two hooligans who would have killed me . . . or worse, if I hadn't been capable of defending myself!"

Jacquelyn paused just long enough to fling a glare of irksome disgust over her shoulder. It galled her no end that Mason was sitting in his bath, studying her with casual amusement. "I did not need an escort in the first place," she ranted on. "I know Texas like the back of my own hand. But obviously the Gen'ral thought to throw us together for his own purposes." Her voice grew brittle with irritation. "And if either of you are harboring any notions that I might become romantically involved with you because the Gen'ral has been bragging about you in

19

all his letters, you can both discard such distasteful ideas. You, Mr. Mason, have made a very poor showing during our first encounter."

One thick brow arched to a teasing angle. "Does that imply that you didn't like what you saw before you turned like a coward to face the wall?" he drawled in a husky voice that glided across Jake's flesh like a lingering caress. "I rather thought you took your Texas time about looking me over."

Jacquelyn jerked her head around to glare holes in his roguish grin. Angrily, she tugged at the wild sable strands of hair that blocked her vision. "What I see is a rude excuse of a man who has obviously been catering to the Gen'ral for his own selfish purposes and who is not deserving of even a smidgen of the praise that has been bestowed on him." Her head swiveled back around to glower at the wall when she realized she did like what she saw and that she was ogling him again, damn it all!

Mason's perceptive gaze flooded over Jake's enchanting profile. Although she did indeed appear the worse for wear after her confrontation with the local riffraff, her unruly hair and torn gown could not detract from her radiant beauty. She had the face of a cherub, the body of an angel, and the disposition of the devil himself.

So this was Harlan Reid's feisty granddaughter. Mason had heard stories about this legendary firebrand who ran as wild as the Comanche renegades who terrorized Texas. Rumor had it that the General had packed his granddaughter off to Louisiana before the outbreak of war. Rumor also had it that Harlan had had a bona-fide battle on his hands long before he'd taken command of the Texas troops. According to the stories Mason had heard, the chit had fought tooth and nail to prevent being uprooted from her homeland and shuffled away from the fighting.

Mason knew for a fact that General Harlan Reid was a

stickler for method and order. But the old buzzard had obviously run amuck when he was left with the awesome responsibility of raising his granddaughter. From what Mason had previously heard and recently seen, he deemed Jacquelyn Reid to be a full-fledged hellion.

Although the General demanded that the world and all those in it behave in military fashion, he had been unsuccessful in teaching this she-cat to march in procession. This firebrand looked to be a rebel without pause, a troublesome, contrary bundle of femininity who was accustomed to having her way.

Poor General Reid, Mason mused with wicked delight. The old coot had a renegade in his nest. No wonder the General wanted strict discipline and close adherence to military protocol. This fiery minx contradicted all the General represented. She was his cross to bear, his one defeat in life.

A pensive frown creased Mason's brow. Now what was this chit's name? He had heard it on several occasions. Mason racked his brain trying to attach a name to the wild tales that had been related to him during the war. Damn, he had to remember this shapely firebrand's name. This situation was too delightful to bypass.

Obviously, the General's granddaughter had mistaken him for *Jonathan* Mason, the General's obedient over-seer. What she didn't know was that she had interrupted Mason *Gallagher's* bath. It was also apparent that the young lady was unaware of the feud and rivalry that had developed between Mason and the General during and after the Mexican War.

An ornery grin tugged at one side of Mason's mouth. If the old goat knew his precious granddaughter was in his business competitor's hands, he would be hopping up and down in fury. Grappling with that mischievous thought, Mason puffed on his cheroot and studied the fascinating

21

assets of . . . Blast it, he had to remember her name!

Perhaps he should assume Jonathan Mason's identity. He knew enough about the General to play the charade. He could field most questions without difficulty . . . if only he could recall this shapely bundle of beauty's name. He must have heard it a half-dozen times. If he had known how arrestingly attractive the General's granddaughter was, he would have paid closer attention.

The silence between them fell like stones. Finally, Jacquelyn composed herself enough to face her companion without turning all the colors of a rainbow. "Well, have you nothing to say in defense, Mason?" she inquired smartly.

"In the first place, my friends call me Mace," he informed her as his roving eyes made another critical sweep of her curvaceous figure, missing not even one alluring detail.

Jake stamped her foot in a burst of temper. It still unnerved her that this man could sit casually in his bath and fling suggestive glances at a woman he had only met. "I'm reasonably certain you have little occasion to answer to your nickname," she sniped. "You couldn't have many friends with your blatant lack of punctuality and your total disregard for responsibility!"

Egad, what was she saying! If Jacquelyn hadn't known better, she would have sworn it was Aunt Florence standing here delivering this scathing lecture, the very kind Jake had been forced to endure on numerous occasions.

Although Jacquelyn was dismayed to realize she sounded like her aunt, she was silently cursing her betraying eyes. While she was spouting her sermon on the importance of punctuality, her gaze had wandered over Mace's well-proportioned physique, finding not one flaw except the jagged scar on his left side. And damnit, she shouldn't even have known about that scar. Mace was a total stranger, and she had already seen him without a stitch of clothes. Their relationship had begun backwards, and he was having a staggering effect on her composure.

Mace smiled to himself when he noticed the appreciative, but reluctant, attention he was receiving. The lady's behavior indicated that she was unnerved by the sight of bare flesh. Her perfect features flooded with color when Mace elevated a dark brow to indicate that he knew where her eyes and mind had strayed. Jake was obviously curious about those of the male persuasion, and yet she was uncomfortable in this situation. For all the girl's wild shenanigans that had been the topic of gossip, Mace had the sneaking suspicion she was a stranger to passion.

Concentrating on his first and foremost task, learning the chit's name, Mace took a long draw on his cigarillo and then blew a lopsided halo above his head. "Since we are to be traveling companions I would appreciate knowing what name you prefer. Do you also have a nickname, my dear?" he queried, subtly prying for information to aid him in his ploy.

The nerve of this man! She silently seethed. There he sat soaking and smoking, behaving as if nothing extraordinary had occurred. She had chastised him for his lack of consideration, and he had the audacity to bypass an apology and demand to know her nickname.

"My friends call me Jake, but you may refer to me as Miss Reid, if you must speak to me at all," she bit off.

Jake . . . Jack . . . Jackie . . . Jacquelyn . . . that was it, Mace recalled. Ah yes, Miss Jacquelyn Reid. Mason's golden eyes slid over her pink cheeks to focus on her heart-shaped lips. Like an artist scrutinizing his subject before painting a portrait, Mace studied every enticing asset of Jake's perfectly constructed figure. He had always been appreciative of well-endowed women. Jacquelyn Reid had been graced with a body that would

23

stop a stampede. It was little wonder she had come dangerously close to being molested the moment she sashayed off the schooner. As a matter of fact, Mace was contemplating committing a few crimes himself. This minx was an intriguing combination of flawless beauty and fiery spirit.

Attentively, Mace focused on the wild mane of dark hair that glistened with golden highlights. The unbound strands lay in natural waves that tumbled helter-skelter from what was left of the bun atop her head. Her hair was so lustrous that a translucent halo seemed to encircle her head.

There was something of the sun in her lively facial features—a radiance that burned from within. Her beguiling eyes had incredibly dark centers that were surrounded by lustrous whites. A fringe of thick, curly lashes rimmed those spellbinding eyes, which dominated her pixie-like face. Finely etched, beautifully shaped brows arched above those shimmering ebony pools. Flawless olive skin curved over high cheekbones, making Mace yearn to reach out and touch this statue of rumpled but ravishing beauty.

"I'm sorry I wasn't at the dock to meet you, Jake," Mace murmured, too distracted by his visual explorations to sound the least bit apologetic. "I was unavoidably detained."

Jacquelyn had been anxiously awaiting this rapscallion's apology so she could curtly refuse it. Her chin tilted to an aloof angle that allowed her to look down her nose at Mace. "You were unavoidably detained in the tub?" she scoffed sarcastically. "Next I suppose you are going to tell me this tub of brass is glued to your a—"

Mace's burst of laughter drowned Jake's last word and she was forced to wait until his merriment subsided before continuing with her usual amount of candor. "You realize, of course, that I will hold this incident over you for the rest of your natural life, Mace. Indeed, I will be better satisfied if the Gen'ral fires you for your lack of responsibility. It wouldn't surprise me to learn you have been cavorting in this room with some shameless whore. And if I discover my suspicions are correct, I will insure the Gen'ral tosses you out on your . . . brass tub." She finished with a scalding glare.

My, what a sassy little thing she was! Mace mused while he puffed on his cheroot, surrounding himself with a cloud of smoke. Jake probably gave the General hell. Probably? Mace chuckled to himself. There was no doubt about it. Jake was a handful. That speculation delighted Mace since he and Harlan Reid got on like a cobra and mongoose. The General detested Mace's casual air, his disregard of military authority. Mace had ridden with the Texas Rangers, who cared not a tittle for military protocol.

Although Harlan deplored the Rangers, referring to them as a rough-edged band of cutthroat horsemen who could easily ride on both sides of the law, he called upon them when he needed scouts or capable men to run reconnaissance missions for him. But Harlan wanted nothing to do with the "uncivilized, half-men, half-devils" before *or* after battle. The Mexicans were terrified of the *Los Diablos Tejanos,* and Harlan only approved of the unruly Texas Devils when they were winning battles for him. The fact that Captain Mace Gallagher had never once saluted a lifelong military officer irritated the General no end.

"Well, are you going to sit there stewing in your own juice for the rest of the evening?" Jacquelyn wanted to know. "My arms are burned from standing overly long in the sun. My gown has suffered irreparable damage, and I'm famished from fighting my way to the hotel. I have my heart set on a thick, juicy steak."

Jacquelyn always ate when she was frustrated or upset.

25

It calmed her nerves and soothed her explosive anger. She wanted to sink her teeth into a succulent cut of beef. There were none better than the steaks served in Texas. Beef was an abundant commodity, and it had been three years since Jacquelyn had enjoyed a steak Texas style.

"Very well then. I will treat you to the best meal money can buy," Mace graciously offered as he unfolded himself from the tub.

The sound of splashing water and the further display of masculine flesh incited Jacquelyn's shocked squawk. Like a spinning top, she whirled around to glare at the wall. "You could have given notice before you stood up!" she squeaked, her voice two octaves higher than normal.

Mace broke into a devilish smile. Grasping his towel, he draped it around his hips. "You didn't bother to give notice before you burst into the room," he countered airily. "For a woman who demands consideration, you certainly don't return the courtesy. It appears the Gen'ral wasted his time and money toting you off to Louisiana to receive instruction in the proper social graces."

Jacquelyn puffed up with indignation. "I went because I was forced," she defended sourly. "The Gen'ral has these odd notions about what constitutes a proper lady and I have mine. I'm sure he has mentioned that we disagree on a myriad of issues."

Mace was prepared to bet his self-made fortune this firebrand was as stubborn and independent as they came. Harlan Reid may have demanded that the soldiers under his command toe the line, but Mace felt sure the General had gotten nowhere with this rebellious spitfire. She was not easily intimidated, and she didn't appear to have a submissive bone in her gorgeous body. Mace liked her spunk, especially since most of it had been directed toward the General.

While Mace fastened himself into his garments, Jake

continued to stare at the wall, wondering why Mason rattled her so much. Jacquelyn had always prided herself in her ability to handle adversity, no matter what its magnitude. When she had been accosted by ruffians she'd defended herself with swift efficiency. She had been motivated more by fury than fear. But when Mace assaulted her with that smile that oozed with charm, and exposed far more flesh than she needed to see, Jake melted into senseless mush.

Mace was not at all what she expected of the General's overseer. In fact, Mace was the exact opposite of what her grandfather usually expected of his friends and companions. To the General, the world was a huge military drill field, and subordinate officers were expected to take orders without question. Mace didn't seem the General's type. Indeed, she doubted Mace called any man his master. There was an arrogance about Mace, an impenetrable shell of self-esteem and inner confidence that was not easily cracked. Jake also sensed his virility and sensuality, that dynamic, compelling quality that separated him from ordinary men. He was cool and calm and unrattled by even the most awkward of situations.

Unwillingly, Jake admired the man she had her heart set on disliking. If her grandfather had selected this man as her possible mate, it should follow that she rebel against Harlan's scheme. She always had. It was second nature. The General had been born with a soldier's soul and Jake possessed a rebel's heart. They rarely agreed on anything, except that Aunt Florence was crabby and cranky and—

"You can turn around now, Jake," Mace announced, dragging her from her pensive deliberations.

The soft, sexy voice so close to her ear caused Jacquelyn to leap out of her skin. The man disturbed her. Indeed, he relished shocking and startling her. Jake pivoted to find this powerful package of masculinity looming over her.

Mace was tall, all right. He towered over her like Goliath. The fresh, clean scent of him swarmed in her senses and constricted her breathing. The teasing twinkle in his amber eyes sent her heart tumbling pell-mell around in her chest. He had charm galore, and Jake disliked the fact that she was so aware of him as a man.

Jacquelyn took an involuntary step backward before she was suffocated by his nearness. But she found herself plastered against the wall when Mace bridged the space between them. Now there was no escape. Mace blocked her path like a rock-hard wall. At close range she could detect the brilliant glitter of gold in his eyes, take note of his full, sensuous lips, study the cleft in his chin. . . .

"Is that difficult to shave?" Jacquelyn asked out of the blue, surprising Mace as well as herself.

She could feel the low rumble of laughter vibrating in his massive chest as he inched closer. It was like the shock of an earthquake ricocheting through her, and Jake could feel her fierce reaction to him, all the way to her toes.

"It is a mite tedious." He chuckled before he focused on the appetizing curve of her mouth. Their close encounter caused her bottom lip to quiver and Mace made note of her unconscious mannerism. He was definitely disturbing this bundle of femininity. Her breathing had altered to emit short, shallow gasps of air. Her full breasts heaved, brushing lightly against his chest, and her dark eyes were as wide as saucers.

Mace was baffled when he realized he was also suffering from lack of oxygen. He had intended to tease and intimidate Jacquelyn, but his ploy had backfired, just as his charade might do if he didn't watch his step. Mace was living dangerously. But then, he always had. His association with the General's granddaughter could work for or against him, depending on how he handled the situation. But Mace was willing to accept the risk since he had always been a bit of a daredevil.

It had been a long time since Mace had found himself captivated by a female. And Jake definitely fascinated him. How had she grown up to be so strong and willful after she had spent so many years under the General's domineering rule? How could she have defied a man who could transform a passel of unruly men into obedient soldiers? And why did she have to have such an irresistible mouth? This dark-eyed fairy made a man want to waltz right up and kiss her without contemplating the repercussions of such impulsive actions.

"Since you insist upon knowing what I'm going to do before I do it . . ." Mace braced his hands on the wall instead of placing them where he really wanted to put them—on Jacquelyn's curvaceous hips. "I'm going to end our curiosity about each other by kissing you."

Jake would have protested if she could have located her tongue. She had inadvertently swallowed it, along with a mouthful of air that lodged like an inflated balloon in her chest. Her brain broke down when his moist lips courted hers with unrivaled expertise. Instead of punching Mace in the midsection, as she should have done, she simply stood there enjoying their embrace and cursing her feminine curiosity.

Jacquelyn had increased her knowledge of men these past years, experimenting with various kinds of kisses. She had determined which techniques she preferred. For the most part, she had been unimpressed with men. But the feel of Mace's warm lips whispering over hers with such compelling tenderness—something she hadn't expected from such a large, overpowering man—was an entirely new experience. She had been kissed by bungling fops, masterful rogues, and a few young men who'd had even less practice than she'd had. But this kiss in no way resembled anything in her somewhat limited repertoire

29

of romantic encounters. Mace looked like a lion, but his arousing embrace contradicted his apparent strength and potential forcefulness.

A flood of tingling sensations splashed over Jacquelyn as Mace's muscled chest molded itself to her breasts. She could feel the heat of his body setting fire to her senses, bringing each of them to life. She could feel him, taste him, touch him. His masculine aroma was slowly becoming a part of her, attaching itself to the tantalizing memory he was creating.

Jacquelyn assured herself that she would have been outraged by his boldness if his touch had not been embroidered with such unbelievable tenderness. Mace was cherishing her lips, subtly persuading her to surrender to the sensual pleasure he could offer. As his kiss deepened to explore the soft recesses of her mouth, Jacquelyn swore her bones had been boiled down into the consistency of strawberry jam. If Mace had not been supporting her, she feared she would have dripped down the wall.

Mace had waded through various dimensions of hell and defied death on dozens of occasions. And he had seduced more than his fair share of lovely damsels in his thirty-one years. But he couldn't recall feeling quite so helpless and disoriented. This was only a kiss, his malfunctioning brain tried to reassure him. But if that was all it was, it was the strangest phenomenon Mace had ever encountered. Warning signals were clanging in his ears. His strength and energy were seeping from his body into hers like a current of heat flowing from one location to another. All that was left of Mace was a smoky residue of burnt ashes that would have been scattered to kingdom come by the slightest breath of wind. And before that happened, Mace inhaled a shuddering breath and retreated a shaky step.

If he had any sense left he would immediately confess

that he wasn't who Jacquelyn thought he was. He should end this charade before he found himself entangled in complications he didn't need. The words stampeded to the tip of his tongue, but they toppled backward when Mace peered down into that bewitching face, those expressive brown eyes, and those soft, kissable lips that were as intoxicating as cherry wine.

For what seemed forever, Jacquelyn remained paralyzed. She stood there returning Mace's bewildered stare, memorizing his craggy features and the arousing way his expensive garments hugged his masculine physique. Her body was still blazing with unfamiliar sensations, ones that provoked longings she wasn't aware existed.

Jacquelyn had always been an uninhibited creature who followed her instincts, even after Aunt Florence constantly nagged her about the necessity of restraining herself. All those lectures hadn't changed Jacquelyn's impulsiveness. Holding true to form, Jacquelyn did what she felt like doing. She reached up on tiptoe to press her lips to Mace's sensuous mouth. Why? She couldn't say for certain. It just seemed the natural thing to do, so she did it.

Mace responded without thinking. His sinewy arms slid around the trim indentation of Jacquelyn's waist, molding her voluptuous curves into his hard contours. The fragrance of violets engulfed his senses, transporting him to a meadow of sunshine and wild flowers. He was drifting like a butterfly, his heart fluttering like velvet wings skimming the wind-blown grasses.

Lord-a-mercy, what was the matter with him? He was reacting to Jacquelyn like a naive schoolboy. First kisses weren't supposed to be like this! They were supposed to be an inquisition, a simple test of reactions, an appeasement of male curiosity. And sex was supposed to be second nature, a reflexive response, just as it had always been, he reminded himself. But what had been

31

was no more. When their lips met, internal combustion took place and Mace went up in flames. His ears weren't supposed to be peeling like a mission bell. His pulse wasn't supposed to be racing like the mustangs that thundered across the wild Texas prairie.

Now it was Mace's turn to gape incredulously at this vivacious beauty. Suddenly, he knew why General Reid couldn't control his vibrant granddaughter. There was no such thing as "controlling" Jake. She did as she pleased. She did what she felt because it came naturally. To demand this minx to contain the dozens of emotions that were bottled up inside her would be like requesting the sun not to shine while it was hanging in the midday sky. Jacquelyn did because she was, because she . . .

A perplexed frown clouded Mace's brow as he awkwardly shifted from one foot to the other. *She did because she was?* What the hell kind of mumbo jumbo was that?

While Mace was stepping around as if he were standing on hot coals, struggling to untangle the jungle of thoughts that cluttered his head, Jacquelyn moved gracefully toward her satchel. "Give me a moment to freshen up," she chirped, her voice rattling with the aftereffects of their heart-shattering kiss.

Dumbfounded, Mace watched Jacquelyn rearrange the renegade curls into a neat bun. Finally, he managed to encourage his feet to stride toward the door. He felt like a convict who had been shackled with iron ankle bracelets. His reflexes were sluggish, and walking had suddenly become a tedious task.

Grasping the door knob for support, Mace shook his head to shatter the strange spell that had enveloped him. "I'll hail a carriage while you are changing clothes," he offered in a strangled voice.

It was not until Mace had weaved down the hall to tackle the mountain of steps that rational thought returned. Sweet merciful heavens! Had he lost the good sense he had been born with? Didn't he have enough trouble with the General without toying with the man's spirited granddaughter? That female could bring him nothing but trouble, especially if she could rattle him with one kiss! That wild-haired vixen had barged into his suite and the walls had come tumbling down. Mace had dared to kiss her, and she had kissed him senseless! Lord, what did he think he was doing?

Resolutely, Mace squared his shoulders and descended the stairs. There was a logical explanation for his reaction, of course. He had been burning the candle at both ends, as well as the middle. He had met himself coming and going these past few months. Since he had been so busy building his own empire in postwar Texas, he had rushed through women like a man gobbling down his meal on his way to another task. The General's granddaughter had simply thrown him off balance, that was all. She was different from the other women he had bedded and left without a second thought.

Mace missed a step and clutched the banister to prevent tumbling topsy-turvy. Good gawd, I am actually contemplating accompanying Jacquelyn to Harlan's plantation! he realized. Hell, he didn't have time to go traipsing off from Galveston during cotton harvest. He had arrangements to make with incoming steamers that were heaped with bales from plantations upriver. They were expecting more than fifty thousand bales, loaded on scores of flatboats and steamers, to reach the port of Galveston this season. He had to coordinate the transfer of crops to schooners that were bound for clothes-manufacturing centers in eastern seaports, for Chrissake! This was his busiest season and he couldn't spare the time for reckless amusement.

A low peal of laughter tripped from Mace's lips when he regained his footing. Composing himself, he swaggered down the remainder of the steps. He owned the commission company and he had surrounded himself with competent men. All he had to do was delegate authority. Maybe a short vacation is just what I need, he rationalized. After all, someone had to keep a watchful eye on that dark-haired beauty. Jake had attracted trouble the moment she stepped ashore. The town was teeming with lusty men who might wish to do more than steal a glance at that shapely minx.

Mace found himself yearning to learn the many facets of Jacquelyn's complicated personality. She was an intriguing creature who had defied her grandfather's rule and had managed to keep eager beaux at a safe distance. By the time he and Jake reached the General's plantation Mace's infatuation for the high-spirited sprite would fade. He would see her as only a woman, one of the many he had known in his lifetime. And perhaps Harlan would forgive Mace's transgressions if he safely returned Jacquelyn home.

Why, the General might even find it in his military heart to like Mace. No, Mace thought, giving the whimsical notion a moment's consideration. Mace and Harlan were as different as dawn and midnight. In the General's eyes, Mace would always be a renegade, even after he had assumed a respectable profession. Besides, Mace had become Harlan's competition in the commission business. It would take a miracle to soften Harlan. The man was made of military bricks.

Chapter 3

While Mace was locating a carriage and arranging to have Jacquelyn's trunks carted to the suite, Jacquelyn was staring at her reflection in the mirror. She certainly looked like the same person she had always been. But she felt as if her emotions were held together by a single thread. Perhaps her startling reaction to Mace was provoked by her scuffle with those two disgusting ruffians. It was only that her confrontation with Mace, compounded by the fracas with those hooligans, had left her a mite rattled. If Mace had met her at the wharf as he was supposed to have done, she wouldn't have been exposed to the sight of his bare flesh. And she most certainly wouldn't have responded to what should have been no more than a harmless kiss to appease their curiosity!

After inhaling a steadying breath, Jake delivered herself an inspirational lecture on keeping all men at a respectable distance. From here on out, she would hold herself aloof from Mace. She would broach safe topics of conversation and maintain what little dignity she had left after she'd practically thrown herself in his arms. And when she arrived at the plantation she would inform the General that she would not be a party to his matchmaking. She wanted nothing to do with contrived marriages. Jacquelyn was not about to marry anyone until she was good and ready (which, of course, she wasn't).

No man had ever caught and held her interest for any length of time. Most men held certain expectations of what a woman should be and Jacquelyn had never conformed to any of their standards. As a matter of fact, she had spent a lifetime defying the General's rules and regulations, and she would probably react the same way to a demanding husband. And yes, she was contrary. Jacquelyn readily admitted to her faults—stubborn, temperamental, impatient, to name a few. She had been born and bred a Texan and had grown up wild and free, despite the General's attempt to conform her to a dignified, orderly life. Perhaps she had too much zest for living, but after a full dose of Aunt Florence and the sophisticated aristocrats in New Orleans, Jake knew she could never survive as a man's puppet. She wanted to enjoy life rather than parade through a mundane existence.

Jake was Jake, and she wasn't changing her ways for any man. Men could accept her for what she was or leave her alone. She didn't give a whit, one way or another. She was satisfied with her unconventionality and was determined to be herself. Operating on that philosophy, Jacquelyn made a quick inspection of the bright pink gown she had donned to replace the tattered emerald-green dress.

Jacquelyn inhaled a deep breath and stared out the window to savor the sight of the thriving island city. She was in Texas again, and she was anxious to note the changes that had taken place in the bustling seaport of Galveston. If Mace wasn't interested in sightseeing, she would go alone.

A mischievous smile pursed Jacquelyn's lips as she

veered around the trunks that had been deposited in front of the door. She might even go out of her way to be herself—just to set Mace back on his heels. The truth was, Jake found herself liking Mace a bit more than she should. And, being rebellious by nature, Jake had a tendency to battle feelings she didn't understand. She didn't want to find herself attracted to the man her grandfather had selected as her suitor. Nor did she wish to cope with the peculiar sensations that burned deep inside her when she came within ten feet of a man who was packed with devilish charm and irresistible sensuality. These feelings were unnatural, and Jake was wary of them. She sensed the rise of vulnerability when she encountered that darkly handsome rake with the twinkling golden eyes. The best defense was a strong offense, the General always said. Jacquelyn heeded that advice, and mentally prepared to put it to good use.

As Jacquelyn descended the stairs, the rotund innkeeper waddled toward her. "Mason said for you to await his return," Henry informed her courteously. "He had urgent business to attend to, and he assures you he will return as soon as possible."

Jacquelyn nodded politely, but she continued on her way. It irked her that Mace thought to keep her waiting like an attendant to a king. He was going to learn, and quickly, that she would not be put off!

Simmering brown eyes swept the street. When she spied the waiting carriage, she marched toward it. "Did a man named Mason hire you, sir?" she inquired. When the driver nodded confirmation, Jake lifted her skirts and seated herself in the coach. After she had given directions to her favorite restaurant, the groom opened his mouth to protest leaving without Mason.

"Mason reserved the carriage for me," she declared in a no-nonsense tone. "If he cannot return on time he can walk for all I care."

Biting back a grin, the driver grabbed the reins and popped them on the horse's rump. A triumphant smile tugged at the corner of Jacquelyn's mouth as the coach careened around the corner. She hoped Mace stood waiting for an hour before he realized she had taken the carriage and left him to do whatever he was doing at the moment. It would serve that rascal right!

Cursing the fact that he had been detained at the custom house longer than he anticipated, Mace strode down the boardwalk at a fast clip. Jacquelyn was going to be annoyed with him, sure as hell. He could expect to be on the receiving end of another lecture on punctuality. Of course he hadn't met her at the dock because he wasn't Jonathan Mason, and he was ever so thankful he wasn't! But he couldn't explain that to that feisty beauty if he wanted to assume Jonathan's identity.

Jonathan Mason—what a sniveling excuse for a man, Mace mused with a derisive snort. He had met Jonathan while they were both serving with General Reid along the route from Matamoros to Mexico City. Mace had seen exactly what Jonathan was made of when they'd launched their crucial assault on the Bishop's Palace at Monterrey. The man was born without a spine, and he'd followed orders like an obedient puppy until his life was threatened. In that instance, Jonathan had frozen up like an icicle. But with all his faults, Jonathan was perfectly suited to be the General's lackey and plantation overseer. Harlan Reid had only to say, "Jump," and Jonathan saluted and then politely inquired, "How high?" Mace, on the other hand, was prone to tell the General and any other officer who was regular army where they could stash their orders—

Mace's wandering thoughts and his feet screeched to a

38

halt when he noticed the carriage he had hired was no longer sitting in front of the hotel. Blast it, was no one dependable these days? he asked himself cynically. Mace had paid the man in advance, and the varmint had lit out without earning his wages!

Muttering to himself, Mace stomped into the hotel, aggravated that Jacquelyn was not waiting in the lobby. Women! It took females forever to fuss with their coiffure and garments, even the highly unusual Jacquelyn Reid. She was probably still upstairs primping while he was stewing about arriving too late to please her. The fact that he was worried about what Jake thought at all had Mace grumbling under his breath.

Just as Mace stormed toward the stairs to retrieve the dawdling female, Henry called to him. "Mason, if you are looking for the lady, she left without you, long ago."

Mace glared daggers at the innkeeper's wide smile. "I told you to give her my message. Is this the thanks I get for patronizing your place of business each time I frequent Galveston?" he snorted caustically.

Henry Boswell's smile remained intact. "The fault lies with the lovely young lady," he calmly explained. "I delivered your message, and then I watched her step into your rented coach without so much as a backward glance. Unless I miss my guess, I'd say the young lady does not take orders from anyone."

The news had Mace growling all over again. Damn that defiant little snip. Grumbling a few unprintable obscenities, Mace stamped outside, looking in all directions at once. Where the hell could she have gone? There were several fine restaurants in the city and Jake could have selected any one of them. A pensive frown knitted Mace's brow as he recalled that Jacquelyn had declared she craved steak. Grappling with that thought, Mace hurried down the street.

After scanning the crowd in the first restaurant with

no success, Mace spun on his heels and aimed himself toward the second eating establishment. The moment he barreled through the door of the quaint dining hall, he knew he had located the elusive Miss Reid. A congregation of men had collected in a candlelit corner of the room. Although Mace couldn't see who was the object of so much attention, he ventured a guess. An unescorted young lady, especially one with Jacquelyn's dazzling beauty, would certainly draw a crowd. He was willing to bet his right arm that independent minx was amidst that clump of men.

Inhaling an annoyed breath, Mace shoved bodies out of his way to find Jacquelyn carving into a juicy cut of steak. Draped on either side of her were two men who were bending her ear with flattery and idle chatter. Mace suspected as much, confound that woman!

When a long shadow fell over her, Jacquelyn's long lashes swept up to meet Mace's disapproving scowl. After swallowing a morsel of succulent steak, Jake blessed him with a nonchalant smile.

"Thank you for waiting," Mace sniped sarcastically.

The jibe slid off Jacquelyn like beads of water rolling down a duck's back. Primly, she touched her napkin to her lips and countered with an impish grin. "Time awaits no man, Mace," she declared. "And neither do I. This is my stamping ground. I hardly need an escort now that I am back in Texas, and I refuse to twiddle my thumbs while you are gadding about town." One tapered finger indicated the unoccupied chair across from her. "You can join me or you can be on your way. It makes little difference to me so long as I am allowed to enjoy my steak."

If Mace could have clamped her swanlike neck in a stranglehold without being dragged away by Jake's endless rabble of admirers, he would have. Damn her indifference!

40

Mace had never boasted about being a ladies' man, but neither had he been without a woman when he wanted one. Most women came to him with very little encouragement and, even more often, without invitation. But this brown-eyed vixen behaved as if he were only another face in the crowd. Blast her! He had been racing around the city for three quarters of an hour searching for her, wondering if she had met with disaster. This was not the type of reception he'd anticipated for his efforts. The nerve of this little witch!

When Mace abruptly dismissed her admirers with words that were punctuation in themselves, Jake arched a perfectly etched brow. To her amazement the gruff demand caused the men to fade into the woodwork. Perhaps it was the menacing growl in Mace's voice or their visualization of Mace as a crouching cougar that prompted them to flee from harm's way. Jacquelyn couldn't say for certain, but she too was startled by this new facet of Mace's personality.

Mace had appeared easygoing and good-natured. But it was evident there was a fierce, dangerous side to this man. His very size and the graceful masculine poise with which he carried himself demanded respect. When those tawny eyes glittered and his features turned to granite, she wouldn't have wanted to cross him either! But she would have, of course, for the mere challenge of determining if Mace would allow her to get away with it.

As Mace dropped into the vacant chair, Jacquelyn studied him with a curious smile. Mace intrigued her. He wasn't what she expected from one of her grandfather's devoted servants. She had the feeling Mace could transform from saint to devil, depending upon his mood or his situation. If this awesome man meekly obeyed the General's orders, she would eat her steak, plate and all!

"I don't know what you expected," Jacquelyn remarked, flinging her contemplative deliberations aside.

Leisurely, she picked up her knife and fork and carved a bite of steak. "If you envisoned me as a helpless, dependent female who couldn't find her way out of a feed sack, you have sorely misjudged me."

"I expected you to await my return," Mace grumbled crankily. "Ladies without escorts are an open invitation for trouble. You have apparently forgotten your scuffle with the dock riffraff."

"I have not forgotten someone tried to kill me," she assured him saucily. "But I survived the ordeal quite satisfactorily . . . no thanks to your tardiness. If I were not confident of my abilities I wouldn't venture off unchaperoned."

"Someone was trying to kill you?" Mace mimicked sarcastically. "My dear, you exaggerate. I'm sure your assailants were more interested in your body than your life."

Sizzling brown eyes fried him to a crisp. "I was there," she reminded him curtly. "I ought to know if my life was in danger. It was!"

Mace expelled an exasperated breath. Suddenly he was stung by the realization that he had bitten off more than he could chew when he'd decided to woo this fiery chit. She would argue with a wall. She was stubborn, independent, and impulsive. Jacquelyn Reid, despite her compelling beauty, was trouble with a capital T. And not only that, she attracted people who attracted trouble! For the second time that day, Mace seriously contemplated blurting out the truth about his identity. There was no reason why he should take a browbeating from this sassy sprite. And it was for damned certain a man would have to remain on his toes to keep himself one step ahead of this lively nymph. She was an incorrigible adventuress, and controlling her would be a full-time job—if not virtually impossible!

Mace could list two dozen reasons why he should wash

his hands of the General's granddaughter and go about his business. But the moment he gazed into those dark, shimmering eyes that brimmed with mischief, he was overwhelmed by an illogical craving to enjoy whatever scraps of affection Jake might offer him. She was like spring rain and summer sunshine, a refreshing change from the women he had known. Jake intrigued him in ways he had never experienced.

"I promise to be more punctual if you will, in the future, allow me a grace period of at least five minutes before you go tearing off by yourself," he bartered in a businesslike tone.

Jacquelyn's lighthearted laughter was sweet music to his ears. Her radiant smile was contagious, and Mace smiled in spite of himself.

"Agreed. And I won't ignore you if you don't take me for granted," she offered in a soft, raspy tone that sent a fleet of goose gumps cruising across his flesh. "Now, tell me about yourself, Jonathan Mason. How did you meet the Gen'ral? I must confess, you are nothing like the other men Grandfather counts among his friends."

After ordering his meal, Mace offered a sketchy and modest rendition of his association with General Harlan Reid. He discussed their association during the war, their gruelling trek from Texas to capture Mexico's capital. Mace didn't bother with the gory details, nor did he admit that the General disliked him with a passion. Jake would discover that soon enough, Mace reminded himself. He could only hope his association with Jacquelyn would permit her to form her own impression, one that wouldn't be altered or influenced by the General.

In truth, Mace was strategically bargaining for Jacquelyn's friendship. Twice in the past four months, Mace had suggested a merger between the General's faltering cotton commission company and the one owned and operated by Mace Gallagher. Pride and past resentment had prevented General Reid from accepting the business arrangement. Mace hoped to endear Jacquelyn to him. As strong and willful as she was, she might be able to convince the General to ignore the advice of his nephew and accept a merger that would benefit the Reids as well as Mace Gallagher.

All right, so my tactics are a bit unscrupulous, Mace acknowledged as he munched on his meal. But General Reid was stubborn to the core. And for some reason, Malcolm Reid (Harlan's nephew) was adamantly against the business proposition. Perhaps it was because Malcolm had been left in control of the business while Harlan was battling his way across Mexico. Malcolm thrived on tossing his authority around and feeding his self-importance. No doubt, Malcolm viewed the merger as a threat to his position as financial advisor and manager of the commission company. Mace had heard rumors of the propaganda Malcolm had been spreading, labelling the Gallagher Company a hindrance rather than a help to Texas plantation owners.

Whatever Malcolm's reasons for resisting, he had insured that the General wouldn't budge. Mace would actually be doing both companies a favor, but Malcolm and Harlan refused to see that. With the General's reputation and influential name and Mace's numerous contacts, they could form a strong company that would insure top prices for all cotton planters in Texas. Their combined efforts could boost the sagging economy of the new state.

While politicians were battling with Congress over the admission of Texas as a slave state, Mace was striving to solidify economic conditions from within. Since Mace's arrival the previous decade, he had come to consider Texas his home. Indeed, he had tried to block out the formative years of his life, ones that were brimming with tragic memories. When he'd run away from home he'd drifted where the wind had taken him, learning to survive with weapons and his wits. He and the other soldiers of fortune who'd wound up in Texas to serve as Rangers had been paid in land grants. Through the years Mace had acquired eight thousand acres of fertile land, and he had established a prospering plantation. In his attempt to obtain fair prices for his cotton crops he had ventured into the commission business when he'd returned from the war. Many of his friends and acquaintances had become his clients, depending on him to make the arrangements to sell their produce in eastern seaports. Mace's time-consuming dedication had paid off. His company had mushroomed into the largest buying house in the state, leaving Malcolm and Harlan Reid standing in his shadow.

And yet, with all his success, there was a vacuum in Mace's life, an emptiness wealth couldn't fill. Only when the Rangers were called back to service did Mace feel the stirring in his heart. He missed those days of reckless daring when he'd survived by his instincts, when every moment had been crucial. Now Mace only returned to service when Governor Wood needed reinforcements against the brown-skinned vaqueros and raiding Comanches who harassed settlers in the western sectors of the state. The United States Army could not quell the disturbances, and settlers often cried out for the rough-edged band of light horsemen who had once been the only law and order Texas knew. Although the struggling state government had little money, its politicians appropriated funds for the Rangers when the situation demanded immediate attention.

Jacquelyn's small hand folded over Mace's, jostling him from his pensive contemplations. "Forgive me for dredging up unpleasant memories. I was only curious to know how you and the Gen'ral met," she murmured.

45

Mace's thoughts scattered when Jacquelyn graced him with an apologetic smile. It was like breath of fresh air and the warmth of sunshine. In some ways, this dark-haired hoyden reminded Mace of himself—or at least the way he had been ten years earlier. She was young, vibrant, and eager to pursue adventure. But now, at thirty-one, Mace had put those reckless days behind him to settle into a respectable profession.

"Now that I have offered you the condensed chronicles of my life, it's your turn," he announced. "How did you fare in New Orleans society?"

A sheepish smile caught the corners of Jacquelyn's heart-shaped mouth. "Do I have your word you won't convey my confessions to the Gen'ral?"

Melodramatically, Mace placed his hand over his heart. "I will take your admissions to the grave," he promised.

"I was dismissed from finishing schools thrice for my . . ." Jake paused to formulate a suitable description of her expulsions. "For my indiscrete behavior and lack of social propriety."

One thick brow rose to a teasing angle. "Too many wild shenanigans?" He chuckled. "Now, why doesn't that surprise me?"

Jacquelyn released a sigh and plunged on. "The first time I was asked to leave because I told the schoolmaster that I was certain I would have no practical use for the . . . facts . . . he insisted on drilling into my head."

Mace snickered. "I'm sure you chose a more colorful term than *facts*," he declared. "Would you, perchance, have referred to your formal education as something resembling manure?"

A becoming blush stained Jake's flawless cheeks and she giggled impishly. "I don't think he was as offended by my description of his brand of education as he was by my references to his person. He declared that I was a pain in

46

the neck, and I suggested that he was a pain in a lower part of the anatomy."

Mace attempted to bite back a snicker, but it was not to be contained. "And what, pray tell, prompted your second dismissal?" Mace had to know.

Jacquelyn's head dropped as if she were fascinated by the silverware. "I punched a fellow student in the mouth," she quietly confessed.

"Male or female?" Mace interrogated.

"A viper-tongued female," Jacquelyn declared bitterly. "She lost her two front teeth, and her father was a generous contributor to the school. Aunt Florence begged and pleaded every day for a month before I was readmitted to classes." An impish smile replaced her somber expression. "I do believe the only reason my great-aunt came to my defense was to insure that I wouldn't be underfoot for the remainder of my stay in New Orleans. She isn't that fond of me either."

Mace chuckled out loud. Oddly enough, he could envision this she-cat with claws bared. "Were you having words over a man, perhaps?" he pried.

Jacquelyn favored him with an owlish stare. "How did you know?"

His broad shoulders lifted in a shrug. "You are a very lovely young lady. I rather suspect jealousy runs rampant among your female rivals."

A resentful frown puckered Jacquelyn's face. "Anna Marie had the nerve to suggest that I stole her beau by spreading myself beneath him like a common whore," she blurted out, and then cursed her runaway tongue.

One thick brow quirked in amusement. "Well? Did you?"

Jacquelyn presented him with a glare that cut like a double-edged dagger. "How many women have you bedded in your lifetime, Mace?" She countered his question with a question. "Can you count your affairs on two hands or is it necessary for you to peel off your socks and calculate the number on your toes?"

Mace bowed from his chair. "Touché." He chuckled good-naturedly, and then broached another topic. "What of your third dismissal?"

She looked him squarely in the eye and said unrepentantly, "I defended my honor in a duel against a man who thought to take privileges after he heard Anna Marie's vicious lies. The schoolmaster got wind of the incident and promptly booted me out of school for conduct unbecoming a lady."

Her confession did not meet with the response she anticipated. Mace burst into merry laughter. Her remark assured him that this feisty minx was as pure as twenty-four-karat gold, even if she had all but told him to mind his own business a few moments earlier. No doubt the man Jake had duelled was one of her frustrated beaux who'd sought to appease his lust.

"It doesn't shock you that I shot a man in the knee with a pistol at twenty paces?" she queried incredulously.

Still chuckling, Mace clasped her hand and drew her to her feet. "I have no doubt that you were justified in doing what you did," he assured her. "I would have done the same thing."

"Do you have any virtuous honor left to defend?" she teased with an impish smile.

Mace tilted her bewitching face to his. Sparkling golden eyes flooded over her comely features and then dropped to the bright pink gown that complimented her arresting assets. "What do you think, my dear Jacquelyn?"

The touch of his hand was like a sizzling lightning bolt. Shock waves rippled down her spine. "To be honest, I don't quite know what to make of you, Jonathan Mason," she murmured shakily.

As Mace led her through the maze of tables, a demure smile drifted across Jacquelyn's lips. Although she wasn't certain what she thought of this rakish devil, it relieved her to know that Mace accepted her for what she was without passing judgment on her behavior. A new respect for Mace dawned in her eyes. Maybe he wasn't the womanizer she suspected he was. But she was not foolish enough to think he was no more worldly than she. He kissed far too superbly to be a novice.

"I am a bit bumfuzzled by today's double standards," Jake declared as she fished into her purse to pay for her meal. "If a woman does enjoy variety in men, as I was accused of doing, she is disrespectfully labeled a whore. But if a man dallies with scores of women, he is envied and idolized by the rest of his species. Perhaps I have been too cautious. Maybe I should shop around to determine which man would best—"

Before Jake could complete her philosophical sentence and offer money for her meal, Mace produced sufficient funds for the both of them. "I invited you to supper and I intend to pay. I am trying to redeem myself after I kept you waiting."

Her perfectly arched brow elevated to a taunting angle. "Are you also being compensated from the Gen'ral's expense account?"

Damn but this vixen had a knack for needling a man until his pride resembled a leaking colander. "You are dining at my expense, Jake," he clarified. "You may have assumed that I am at Harlan's beck and call and that he is my source of income, but nothing could be further from the truth."

She had indeed leaped to that conclusion, and she was surprised to learn that Mace was not the General's shadow or the extension of her grandfather's will. "And what about my room at the hotel?" she couldn't help but ask. Surely Mace had not taken it upon himself to cover that expense for a woman he hadn't even met!

A cryptic smile tugged at Mace's lips as he steered Jacquelyn toward the street. Now here was an interesting matter. Mace hadn't the faintest notion he would be entertaining an unexpected guest in his suite—one that contained only one double bed. There were no other rooms available at the hotel, not in the height of cotton season. He couldn't wait to see the expression on Jacquelyn's exquisite features when she was confronted with the possibility of sharing a bed with him. That would put a bee in her bonnet, Mace speculated with an inward snicker.

"The hotel suite was rented with my money, not your grandfather's," he stated matter-of-factly.

A muddled frown creased Jacquelyn's brow. "Then you did not travel to Galveston in hopes of courting me? I felt certain my grandfather was trying to make a match of us and that you were eager to gain control of the family fortune."

Glittering golden eyes locked with those dark pools of lively curiosity. This chit's candor was a refreshing change from the maneuvering, scheming women Mace had encountered since his rise to wealth. Jake spoke her mind and there was no speculation about what she thought of a man. No doubt, if she disliked an individual, she would make that clear with her words and deeds. And the real Jonathan Mason would probably hold true to Jake's darkest suspicions. Jon would undoubtedly leap at the chance of inheriting the General's holdings through marriage to this fascinating creature.

For another fleeting moment Mace's conscience nagged him for deceiving this dark-haired hoyden. Yet the possibility of spending a few days with Jake and winning her affection was too tempting to ignore. The General would probably have a conniption when he discovered who'd accompanied his granddaughter home.

50

But then again, Harlan might appreciate the courtesy, especially since the real Jonathan Mason had yet to show his face in Galveston.

What do I have to lose? Mace asked himself. Nothing, the logical side of his brain replied. If the General cursed Mace, it certainly wouldn't be the first time in their strained acquaintance. Jacquelyn might be the buffer needed between them.

Mulling over that thought, Mace guided Jacquelyn back into the street, envisioning their return to the hotel. Mace couldn't remember when he had anticipated an evening quite so much. It was going to be delightful watching this minx's self-confidence crack when she was faced with the dilemma of sleeping with him or curling up on the narrow couch beside Henry's registration desk.

Chapter 4

Above the lamplighted streets of Galveston a gray haze began to swallow the winking stars. Mace absently reminded himself that the mass of approaching clouds was typical of the stormy season, but he was too preoccupied with the bewitching lady by his side to pay much attention when he was drifting on a cloud of his own making. Ah, this was going to be an enchanting evening, Mace assured himself as he strided along the boardwalk—

Jacquelyn's feline growl interrupted Mace's lusty fantasy. A surprised grunt erupted from Mace's lips when Jake stuffed her purse in his belly and clawed at the Colt that hung beneath his waistcoat.

"What the hell—" was all Mace could get out before Jacquelyn snatched his pistol and turned it on two darkly clad men who had suddenly reversed direction and were clomping along the boardwalk in search of an alley.

With lightning quickness, Mace's hand snaked out to retrieve his weapon. But Jacquelyn was as agile as he was. Before Mace could recover his Colt, Jake's trigger finger contracted. Two rapid-fire shots screamed through the night air. The first bullet caught Daniel Johnson in the shoulder just before he swerved around the corner. The

53

second shot parted Frank Norman's hair and sent his hat flipping end over end in the dirt. Two startled yelps erupted in the stony silence that followed the exploding Colt.

While a dozen bystanders stood with mouths gaping, Mace ripped his pistol from Jake's fingertips. "Gimme that!" he growled furiously. "What the sweet loving hell were you trying to—"

Leaving Mace in midsentence, Jacquelyn sped off like a launched rocket. The instant she had realized her assailants were following her she'd been stung with thoughts of vengeance. Since it would have spoiled the element of surprise by floundering to retrieve the small handgun she had stashed in her purse, Jacquelyn had tugged Mace's pistol from its holster and fired before her assailants knew what she was about. And if Mace's brawny body hadn't partially blocked the line of fire, Daniel and Frank would have taken their last steps. Jacquelyn was certain of that. Her aim was as good as her eyesight.

Mace was so startled by the entire incident that he remained paralyzed while Jake sprinted toward the alley. When his frozen brain thawed, he realized Jake had every intention of giving chase. Like a pouncing lion Mace sprang into action, momentarily delayed by disbelief though he had been.

While Jake was leaping off the boardwalk like a mountain goat, Mace raced toward the alley. When he skidded around the corner he found Jacquelyn fumbling in her purse for her derringer. Just as Mace seized her arm, she unloaded her weapon at the two scalawags who were running for their lives. The misdirected shot ricocheted off the garbage cans that lined the alley, followed by Jacquelyn's burst of expletives.

Anger and exasperation assaulted Mace as he held Jake to him, preventing her from scampering after the men.

Mace had found himself in dozens of battles while he rode with the Texas Rangers, but never in his life had he expected to encounter a war while he was escorting a lovely young lady back to a respectable hotel in Galveston! Lord, Texas had survived the Revolution and its war with Mexico, but this struggling new state was unprepared for this five-foot-two-inch terrorist in pink silk!

"What the devil did you think to accomplish with your shooting spree?" Mace's question began as a low, breathless growl and ended in an eardrum-shattering roar. He couldn't believe the panache with which this firebrand had thrust herself into danger. This female was a daredevil in every sense of the word.

With breasts heaving, Jake jerked her arm from his viselike grasp and glared into his annoyed scowl. "Those were the same two men who tried to kill me this afternoon," she snapped. "And if you hadn't gotten in the way, I would have dropped them in their tracks!"

"No one is trying to kill you, for Chrissake!" Mace bellowed, his voice echoing through the alley like rolling thunder. "Texas may have been a mite wild and lawless when you departed for New Orleans. But that was three years ago, damnit. We are more civilized these days, and you are supposed to be. That veneer of sophistication you acquired at finishing school has already begun to crack." Mace thrust his sneering face into hers. "And ladies do not instigate gunfights in the street!"

"You thought it was perfectly all right for me to challenge a man for taking privileges with me," Jacquelyn shouted at him as if he were deaf and stupid. Mostly stupid, she silently added before ranting on. "How can you possibly condemn me for retaliating against two men who physically attacked me?"

Mace reeled in the reins of his temper and sucked in a steadying breath. Roughly, he clamped a grip on Jake's elbow and whisked her back to the street. "I'm taking you

55

back to the hotel," he informed her through gritted teeth. "You have caused more than enough trouble for one night."

Jake wormed her arm from his grasp and tilted a defiant chin. "I have every intention of enjoying a tour of this city," she exclaimed in a tone that brooked no argument. "It has been a long time since I was here, and I wish to view the progress of civilization."

Mace was frustrated as hell. Never in his life had he known a woman who could put him in such a turmoil and keep him there indefinitely. Somewhere along the way he had lost control. As if I have ever had control of this sprite, Mace thought with a resentful snort. Jake was like a misdirected hurricane, and the passersby who had witnessed her bold antics were still staring curiously at her. If Jake were aware of the attention she was receiving, she wouldn't have cared, Mace realized. This termagent had already assured him that she did as she pleased. She was most certainly living up to her reputation as a hellion.

As Mace stared down at the colorfully dressed minx, it occurred to him that her attire was shouting things about her personality that he had neglected to notice when distracted by her curvaceous body. Some people wore garments that suggested they were aloof and unapproachable. Meek and modest individuals selected drab apparel that called little attention to themselves. There were also those who donned bright fabrics to call attention to themselves because their God-given features did not. But there were those rare, unique individuals who dressed in flamboyant colors to warn the world of their approach. Jacquelyn Reid was one of the select few whose clothing served as a flashing light to warn of danger. If the citizens of Galveston knew what was good for them, they would stand aside and allow trouble to pass without throwing themselves in harm's way.

56

Mace had always prided himself in being strong-willed. He hadn't gotten where he was in this world by being a mealymouthed mouse dressed in glay flannel. But when he compared himself to this fiery bundle of pink silk and lace, he wondered if he hadn't met his match. It finally dawned on him why the staunch, stolid General Reid had wound up with a granddaughter who was his direct opposite. Jacquelyn was an unstoppable force who teemed with undaunted spirit. She might give out occasionally, but she would never give up. She might retreat, but only to regroup. This chit did not know the meaning of defeat. She rebelled against barked orders and rigid rules and regulations. No doubt Jake had heard her fair share of them while she was living under Harlan's roof. For all the good it had done for the General to dictate to Jake, Mace mused with a reluctant chuckle. This young woman was the personification of incorrigible spirit and determined will.

Despite his exasperation, Mace felt a smile tugging at the taut corners of his mouth. How could any man stay angry with this feisty beauty? Jacquelyn's dark, sultry eyes drew him like magnets. The heart-shaped curve of her lips lured him like a bee to nectar.

Jacquelyn blinked in surprise when Mace's raven head moved deliberately toward hers. They had been involved in a heated debate, and suddenly Mace looked as if he meant to kiss her. What sort of tactic was that?

Her answer came in the form of a slow, burning kiss that created a fire in the core of her being—one which channeled out in all directions. When his sensuous lips rolled over hers and his muscled arms stole around her waist to bring her into intimate contact with his sinewy body, Jake's brain broke down. For the life of her she couldn't remember what issue they were debating.

The crowd of onlookers faded from the perimeters of her vision. The world shrank to the space Mace occupied.

Jake had been kissed, but never quite like this. There was something sweet and compelling in the way Mace savored the taste of her, the gentle way he held her to him. For such a large, brawny man he seemed capable of extraordinary tenderness. The paradox of overpowering virility and persuasive gentleness crumbled Jacquelyn's defenses as if she had not one iota of willpower.

The simple truth was she instinctively responded when Mace kissed her. It just seemed the natural thing to do. Jacquelyn knew it was outrageous to be caught kissing in public. Why, Aunt Florence would have fainted dead away if she observed this clinging embrace. But Jacquelyn couldn't have pulled away if her life depended on it.

When Mace finally had the decency to withdraw, Jacquelyn half-collapsed. Clutching his supporting arm, she composed herself and ordered her knees to cease clanging together like cymbals. "Why did you do that?" she questioned. Her voice was not as steady as she had hoped. Indeed, Jake rather thought she sounded like a sick cricket.

Mace curled his hand beneath her chin, marveling at the soft texture of her skin and the kaleidoscope of sensations that were tumbling through him. "Just because I felt like it," he answered honestly. "You of all people should be able to identify with that."

His voice was a caress in itself, and Jacquelyn came dangerously close to wilting at his feet. It was a rare man who could cause her to lose composure. Mace hadn't plied her with long-winded phrases of flattery. He didn't attempt to dazzle her with eloquently spoken compliments. He was straightforward, and she liked that in a man.

Ah, it was so nice to meet an honest man, she thought to herself. In the past, she had been wary of males. Men would connive and lie to lure a woman into their arms.

58

They were devious creatures who sought to employ any methods at their disposal to take what they wanted from a woman. But Jonathan Mason was different. He wasn't her grandfather's puppet. He was his own man and he respected Jacquelyn for what she was, even if he didn't always approve of her shenanigans. But most importantly, Mace had been honest with her . . . or so she thought.

While Jacquelyn was listing all of Mace's redeeming qualities, he was falling deeper into a trap of his own making. Mace had preyed upon this case of mistaken identity, unwittingly building walls that would eventually stand like mountains between them. Unfortunately, Mace was too entranced by this bewitching misfit to notice his blunder and the unforeseen problems he was creating. What had begun as a harmless prank to needle the General had developed into the type of fascination that made Mace long for more than casual friendship. Mace perceived Jake as a challenge. She was his equal in all facets except one. Primal desire roared through him as he speculated on what it would be like to teach this nymph about the finer pleasures in life.

"Uh . . . well . . . about that sightseeing tour," Jacquelyn stammered awkwardly as she rearranged her twisted gown.

With a flair of sophistication, Mace dropped into a bow and then offered Jake his arm. "If it is a tour you want, it is a tour you shall have, my dear Jacquelyn. Shall we walk or ride?"

Jacquelyn's lively features blossomed into a dazzling smile. With sylphlike grace she laid her hand on Mace's proffered arm. "I prefer to walk," she declared, her voice throaty with a myriad of unanalyzed emotions. "And I would be most happy to share my walk with you, Mr. Mason."

Mace broke stride for a split second, but he quickly

recovered to match Jacquelyn's graceful gait. A twinge of guilt tapped at his conscience. In all fairness to Jacquelyn he should explain who he really was. But Mace didn't want to spoil the mood of the moment. He was too absorbed in Jacquelyn's words and the soft resonance of her voice. And worse, he was mesmerized by this walking contradiction of fiery spirit and unmatched beauty.

"Do you know what it's like to be dragged away from the land you love and then return to it after a long absence?" Jacquelyn smiled contentedly as they strolled down the avenue that was bathed in the golden light of gas street lanterns. "I feel as if I have repossessed a special part of me that has been missing for years on end. Ah . . . it's so nice to be back in Texas . . . away from my great-aunt."

The glow of satisfaction in her dark, expressive eyes tugged at the strings of Mace's heart. Impulsively, he moved closer to slip his arm around her small waist. No words formed on his lips. Mace merely listened as Jacquelyn reminisced about her life in Texas . . . before she was forcefully carted to Louisiana.

"I suppose the General told you of the full-scale war we fought when he demanded that I travel to New Orleans to live with Aunt Florence," Jacquelyn grumbled.

Mace frowned curiously at the undertone of bitterness in her voice. "I have heard bits and pieces of the incident," he murmured, neglecting to say that it was not the General who conveyed the tale. Indeed, the General refused to speak to Mace unless it was absolutely necessary. The General avoided Mace like the plague until he was cornered at a social function or business conference. "I would like to hear your rendition of the story."

Jacquelyn inwardly flinched as the bitter memories poured from the corners of her mind. "It was the only time in my life that my grandfather ever struck me, at least that I can remember." Jake expelled a frustrated breath. "As you well know, my grandfather is usually a self-reserved individual. He is regular army from the tip of his gray head to the toes of his polished boots. Duty and obligation have always been foremost with him. But I have known no other family besides the General.

"I have little recollection of my parents, and my grandfather's brother Jesse perished in the Texas Revolution. That left only his son Malcolm and my great-aunt Florence." A quiet sigh escaped her lips as her lashes fluttered up to meet Mace's unblinking gaze. "All I had was the General and the family plantation where I grew up. I know my grandfather thought I was being more sentimental than sensible, but I did not wish to leave home while he took command of the Texas forces. I was certain that leaving home would be worse than tearing off an arm."

"Was it?" Mace queried, gauging her reaction by her change of expression.

"At first it was living hell," she admitted. "Aunt Florence had it in mind to smooth my rough edges. She maintained that I had grown up like a wildflower. She delighted in declaring that I was my grandfather's one failing in life. Florence refused to allow me to do all those things I had done at home." Humorless laughter bubbled from her lips. "Each time I felt the walls closing in on me and sneaked off to ride, I faced a tirade of insults and ultimatums when I returned. All I heard the first year of my stay in New Orleans was, 'Ladies do not.'" Jacquelyn's shoulders slumped momentarily. "Everything I did or wanted to do was Aunt Florence's list of 'Ladies do not.'"

"And I would guess conformity is not among your virtues," Mace interjected with a teasing chuckle.

Unoffended by the taunt, Jacquelyn nodded affirmatively. "According to Aunt Florence, I have very few saving graces. She referred to me as the Gen'ral's misfit." Her eyes took on a solemn glow. "After my trenchant argument with the Gen'ral, I was hustled off to New Orleans by three servants who were ordered to consider me a criminal who might attempt escape. I suppose my tantrum provoked my grandfather's precaution. He wanted to make certain I did not jump ship and come flying back to Texas like a homing pigeon.

"There was war in the wind and the Gen'ral meant to be a part of it. Commanding is in his blood, and he has been marching off to war since he was old enough to handle a rifle. He had been hither and yon, fighting for one cause or another, since I can remember. When I was a child, he left me in the care of Emma, the housekeeper, and other trustworthy servants. I could not understand why he would send me away when that had never been his policy before."

Mace sympathized with Jacquelyn. To her, it must have seemed as if the world were coming to an end. Her closest relative was sending her away while he answered the call of patriotism. Perhaps the General, in his later years of life, was not so confident that he would return from battle. Maybe, in his own way, he was hoping Jake would also come to consider her great-aunt's house as her second home. And if the Mexicans had been successful in taking control of the land that had once been a part of their vast holdings, perhaps the General feared marauding soldiers would abuse his granddaughter.

Mace didn't envy Jacquelyn's childhood or her past few years under Florence's strict rule, even if his own childhood had been nothing short of a nightmare. Jake could not have grown up in an atmosphere of love. Mace doubted Harlan Reid had an affectionate bone in his body. Jacquelyn was a handful, and Harlan probably treated her like one of his soldiers. Hell, the old buzzard probably demanded that she salute him each time they crossed paths in the house!

"I know I sound as if I dislike my grandfather." Jacquelyn sighed and then stared down the shadowed street. "When he forced me to leave I swore I hated him for being so cruel and heartless. But in time I came to realize that he was only doing what he thought was best. I love him for caring for me when there was no one else to look after me. The Gen'ral and I don't always see eye to eye, but he is a brilliant military strategist and an enthusiastic patriot. When politicians hounded him to seek office, assuring him he would be elected because he had made such a name for himself on the battlefield, he declined. Grandfather declared that he was a soldier of the field and had no taste for the verbal wars waged in Congress."

A faint smile brimmed her lips when she realized Mace was scrutinizing her with unspoken questions. "I suppose you are wondering how I maintained my individuality with a hardened general looming over me."

Mace returned her grin as he steered her in the direction of the hotel. "I didn't realize I was so transparent." He chortled. "But yes, I was grappling with that question."

"The Gen'ral grumbles about my independent nature, misdirected as he considers it to be. But beneath the uniform and polished brass lies a warm, caring heart." A confident smile rippled across her lips. "Despite our private war of wills, I know the Gen'ral loves me in his own special way. I merely accept what he is able to give. He complains about my willfulness and my contrariness, but I think deep down inside he admires my strength. After all, that is why we clash. We are a great deal alike."

Her insight into the General's personality surprised Mace. Rowdy and impulsive though Jacquelyn was at times, she also possessed perceptive intuition. Mace had taken the General at face value during their dealings on the battle field and in business competition. He had never taken the time to analyze what made the old bird tick. Mace's association with Jacquelyn had aided him in ways he had never imagined. . . .

Before Mace realized it they were staring at the entrance of the hotel. Mace was standing on a shaky threshold and wasn't certain how to proceed. He and Jake had enjoyed a companionable evening. Well, for the most part, Mace hastily amended. He hadn't been pleased with her when she'd stolen his pistol and spirited off like a one-man posse. Although he had been furious with her earlier, he was stung by an entirely different emotion now. And if Jake knew what lusty thoughts were dancing in his head, she might not be so congenial toward him. Mace knew what he wanted from this bewitching nymph, but he reminded himself that Jake was not the kind of woman who was accustomed to one-night affairs.

Jacquelyn's dark eyes lifted curiously when Mace refused to stir another step. "Aren't you coming in?"

"I . . . I have a few arrangements to make," Mace explained.

And he did. He had called a conference with his associates at the custom house. There were dozens of instructions to be given to insure that business ran smoothly during his absence with Jacquelyn. Many of his associates were the same competent men who had served under him as Texas Rangers. When reinforcements were needed, the Rangers returned to a few months of active duty. And when Indian uprisings and outlaw raids were at a lull, the men carried on their duties in the commission business. Mace had answered the call for assistance on numerous occasions. Of course, his current responsibility was not the kind he normally assumed during difficult times in Texas. But he quickly reminded himself that nothing was more difficult than

Jacquelyn Reid. This firebrand would try the patience of a saint.

Mace had intended to remain in Galveston for a fortnight, wrapping up loose ends. And yet he didn't want to turn this high-spirited minx lose on unprepared Texas. There was no telling what kind of trouble Jake would brew if she were left to her own devices. Why, come to think of it, this *was* a job for a Texas Ranger. He was sworn to uphold law and order, and there wasn't much of it while this spitfire was running loose.

A skeptical frown knitted Jacquelyn's brow when Mace regarded her with an indecipherable smile. She had the sneaking feeling Mace was holding something from her. It was not her nature to place blind faith in men, and the fact that she liked Mace more than she should have triggered an unfamiliar brand of jealousy. Was he tactfully trying to take his leave to rendezvous with one of his lovers?

"These arrangements . . . are they business or personal?" she wanted to know. "A lady perhaps?" She could have bitten off her tongue for being so obvious!

Even in the dim light cast by a distant lantern Mace could detect the blush that rose in her cheeks. "Would you honestly care if there was another woman waiting in the wings?" He chuckled.

"That depends on whether or not she provides you with services I cannot," came another swift reply that Jake wished she had kept to herself.

Mace's golden eyes made a slow, deliberate sweep of Jacquelyn's assets, of which there were plenty. The lady had delicious curves and tantalizing swells in all the right places. Mace had tried not to concentrate on her arousing figure, but staring too long at this luscious bundle of beauty whetted a man's appetite.

"Cannot?" A deep skirl of laughter rumbled in his massive chest. "Or will not?" Mace inquired with a rakish grin that sent dimples diving into his craggy features.

"What do you think?" she countered with a saucy smile.

For a long moment Mace peered into those brown eyes that glistened with living fire. "I think I am already late for my business meeting. If my associates are also sticklers for punctuality, I may find myself conferring with empty chairs."

When Mace pivoted and strode away, Jacquelyn's eyes followed him until his footsteps faded into silence. It startled her to realize that for the first time in her life she was actually wondering what it would be like to join a man in bed—not just any man, but rather Jonathan Mason—the very man her grandfather had shoved at her the moment she'd arrived in Texas!

Mechanically, Jacquelyn mounted the steps to the elegantly furnished suite. Her thoughts transported her back to her first encounter with Mace. She could visualize the bulging muscles of his arms, the long, sinewy columns of his legs, the thick matting of hair that descended down his broad, masculine chest. . . .

Stop that! Jake scolded herself brusquely. It was suicide to even imagine how it would feel to caress what her betraying eyes had touched earlier that afternoon. And why on earth would a man like Mace want an inexperienced woman when he could probably pick and chose his lovers . . . scores of them?

For God's sake! Jake was jealous of women she had never even met and didn't want to meet. Mace had indicated that he had agreed to escort her to the plantation, but that he had not come with courting in mind. He wasn't interested in her. He had said as much. He was probably a dedicated bachelor. Well, of course he was, she told herself sensibly. A man with Mace's dashing good looks and abundance of masculine charm wouldn't remain footloose and fancy free if he had any inclination to settle down with one woman. He would have selected a worthy mate long ago if he truly wanted to marry.

To Mace, she was only a temporary diversion who . . . A pained grunt erupted from Jacquelyn's lips when she opened the door and plowed into the forgotten trunks that blocked her path. Cursing a blue streak that would have provoked Aunt Florence's scathing lectures, Jacquelyn rammed her heel into one of the trunks, shoving it aside. After pushing the other heavy trunk out of her way, she cautiously inched across the dark room to light the lantern.

When the suite was bathed in flickering light, Jacquelyn rifled through her satchel to retrieve her nightgown, and then had a change of heart. She was back in Texas, out from under her great-aunt's condescending gaze. Jake had never batted an eyelash at sleeping in the buff before her forced migration to Louisiana. Now she was free to return to her old habits, and that was exactly what she intended to do.

Recklessly flinging the gown aside, Jake crawled beneath the silk sheets. For a few moments she lay there, lost to a fantasy that shouldn't even have entered her mind. The sensations Mace had evoked while he was lounging in his bath, the unexplainable twinges that assaulted her when he kissed her, came back to torment her.

"Cannot or will not?" His teasing remark echoed through her thoughts as her lashes fluttered against her cheeks. Jake stared into the darkness behind her eyelids. Would she be a passionate woman who could please and arouse a man? Or would she be cold and unreceptive when it came to intimacy? Would she turn such a dynamic man like Mace away because she feared she couldn't live up to his expectations or because she simply didn't want him in her bed?

Jacquelyn had confidence in her abilities and her resourcefulness. But for all her varied education there was one subject that was sorely lacking—the topic of birds and bees—and not in the scientific sense!

Grappling with the unsettling thought that she was virtually ignorant of passion, and shaken by her outrageous speculations about how it would feel to lie naked with a man, Jacquelyn drifted off to sleep. Her overactive imagination pursued the erotic possibilities into dreams even when she had consciously denied herself the speculations of what it would be like to lie in Mace's powerful arms.

Hub MacIntosh stared at his timepiece and then tossed Mace a mocking smile. "I thought you called this meet for a quarter past nine, Captain." His blue eyes sparkled with deviltry. "I hope whoever she was was worth our wait."

A wry grin dangled from the corner of Mace's mouth as he nodded a greeting to the group of men who had served under his command. "Actually, the lady I have been escorting about town was Gen'ral Reid's granddaughter."

Several pair of eyebrows elevated in surprise and Hub chuckled heartily. "Did she have you marching in military precision like the Gen'ral would have you do? No doubt the chit is cut from the same chunk of granite."

Mace dropped into his chair at the conference table. "On the contrary," he declared. "Jacquelyn Reid could have ridden with the Rangers. She bears all the characteristics of a reckless, undisciplined renegade."

The remark provoked several skeptical glances and contemplative stares, but Mace refused to elaborate when assaulted with a barrage of questions. If he had offered a rendition of the episode in which Jake took the law into her own hands, the men would have trampled over him to meet the feisty young lady who had taken Galveston by storm. Jacquelyn Reid had assumed command of Galveston Island, just as Jean Laffite and his crew of pirates had done when they arrived three decades earlier, setting up headquarters on the island and causing a stir.

Mace flung his comparisons aside and focused on Hub. "Have you learned anything about Malcolm's reasons for refusing the merger?"

Hub's broad shoulders lifted in a shrug. "Not much. Malcolm just seems to have his heart set on disliking you. I would think he would be eager to increase his profits. Since the man has been in control of the Gen'ral's commission company, business has declined." A perplexed frown creased Hub's blond brow. "Damned if I know why Malcolm is reinforcing the Gen'ral's low opinion of you."

Mace drummed his fingers on the table. "Have you spoken personally with Malcolm?"

"Hell, he won't even answer my messages!" Hub snorted disgustedly. "The man has blockaded himself in his office and refuses to meet with me."

The news caused Mace's brows to flatten over his golden eyes. Why did Malcolm dislike him so? They had never clashed. And yet Malcolm stood behind the General at each business conference, allowing Harlan to voice all the objections. Malcolm was a weasel, Mace assured himself. Never once had Mace threatened the man or spoken a harsh word to him. Mace could understand the General's stubborn stand, one provoked by unreasonable pride and a refusal to let bygones be bygones. But why was Malcolm dead set against a merger? He had everything to gain except complete control of a floundering company.

Shifting the topic of discussion, Mace announced his

intentions of escorting Jacquelyn to her plantation and then listed the duties to be performed during his absence. Most of their clients had unloaded or were in the process of unloading the cotton crops they had shipped down the Brazos and Colorado Rivers by steamers. Produce was arriving daily and Mace wanted to insure that the transactions and transport of bales to awaiting schooners proceeded without incident.

Although Mace did not consider himself indispensable, he wanted no mishaps while he was negotiating the merger of the Gallagher Commission Company with the Reid Commission Company. If there was the slightest complication, Malcolm would tattle to the General and Mace would never get anywhere with Harlan.

After Mace dismissed the meeting, Hub lingered by the door. His scrutinizing gaze pinned Mace to the wall. "Are you planning to use the Gen'ral's granddaughter to get to him?" he asked point-blank.

Mace swaggered toward the door, pausing long enough to regard his sturdy friend with a wry smile. "I hardly think I could sabotage the Gen'ral through Jake. She thinks I'm Jon Mason, come to accompany her home."

"Jonathan Ma—" Hub choked on his breath. That was ridiculous. "How could the chit confuse the two of you? Jon is built like a flagpole and he was born saluting!"

"Jake hadn't met either of us before her return to Texas," he explained nonchalantly as he ambled out the door.

Hub hurried to catch up to Mace. "Why would you let her think you were the Gen'ral's overseer? That's crazy!"

Mace broke stride. Despite his attempt to conceal his emotions, a rakish smile hovered on his lips. "When you chance to meet Jake, I would imagine you would permit her to call you anything she wanted, just to . . ." Mace bit into the cigar that protruded from his mouth at a jaunty angle and left the sentence dangling in midair, allowing

Hub to form his own conclusions.

Blue eyes twinkled with sly amusement. "A pretty lady, is she, Captain?" Hub didn't know why he bothered to ask. Mace was a connoisseur of women. He was never without one when he wanted one, and he always had the loveliest of females on his arm. "Well, if endearing the lady to you doesn't soften the Gen'ral, you could always marry her—with or without Harlan's consent," he said, kidding Mace. "Surely that old goat wouldn't cast out his grandson-in-law."

A peal of laughter rang through the warehouse. "I hadn't planned on marrying during this lifetime," Mace reminded Hub. "I want the merger, but I'm not sure a marriage to the extraordinary Jacquelyn Reid would be worth all the trials and tribulations. Wedlock is a four-letter word!"

As Mace disappeared around the corner, Hub heaved a quiet sigh. Not many people knew of Mace's troubled past, of the bleak shadows that haunted him. But the tragic memories clouded Mace's opinion of love and marriage. It wasn't something Mace freely discussed. Hub had learned of it quite by accident while they were riding together during the siege of Mexico. After the Rangers had sent Mexico's General Woll retreating across the Rio Grande, he and Mace had lingered in a dusty border town to celebrate. Liquor was flowing freely and Mace had divulged the bitter secrets of his past over many a glass of whiskey. Hub wasn't even certain Mace remembered spilling out the story, and he had kept it in the strictest confidence out of respect for the Ranger captain.

Pushing away from the wall, Hub exited the warehouse on the wharf. It was little wonder Mace was so cynical when it came to wedlock. But it was also a shame to see a man like Mace shun his chance at lasting happiness. Ah well, maybe one day the right woman would come along,

Hub thought wistfully. But it was going to take someone very unique to intrigue Captain Mason Gallagher.

A curious smile etched Hub's lips as he recalled the expression on Mace's face when he mentioned Jacquelyn Reid. It made Hub wonder. . . .

Seizing that delicious thought, Hub set off to indulge in some private detective work. A man never knew when a little snooping might prove beneficial. Hub had as much experience tracking Mexican guerrilla bands and Comanche raiding parties as Mace had. Maybe it was time Hub polished his techniques and investigated the return of Miss Jacquelyn Reid before he began snooping around Malcolm's office, as Mace had suggested.

Chapter 5

Mace contemplated the brandy that sat before him—
his third. The tavern held few occupants. Mace could
count all of them on his right hand if it hadn't been
wrapped around his glass. He had been grappling with his
alternatives for well over two hours and still hadn't
arrived at a decision.

Even while he discussed business arrangements with
his associates he kept seeing enormous brown eyes and
an impish smile. And even three glasses of liquor hadn't
erased the taste of Jacquelyn's explosive kisses. . . .

Hell's bells, Mace growled at himself. He had only
known that lively misfit for one day and already she had
taken up residence inside his head. He had attempted to
regard that bundle of spirit in a strictly platonic sense.
But the tactic hadn't worked worth a tittle. Mace was left
wanting things Jake wouldn't give. If he didn't watch his
step that minx would wind up despising him as much as
her grandfather did. And then where would he be? But
yet, what did he have to lose? Malcolm and Harlan Reid
already disliked him. Why not Jake as well?

The battle between common sense and primal desire
waged on while Mace downed his drink and poured
another. Oh what the hell, he thought as he inhaled his

brandy. He enjoyed Jacquelyn's company. Why should he deprive himself? She was sleeping in his room, after all. Why not allow fate to follow its own course? Mace would simply roll with the flow. He would permit Jacquelyn to make the decision as to how their relationship proceeded. . . .

A roguish grin tripped across Mace's lips as he aimed himself toward the hotel. He was anticipating Jacquelyn's reaction to the possibility of sharing a room with a man. The lady was admirably bold when it came to confronting her nemeses. Mace was curious to see how deep her courage ran when she encountered this awkward situation.

Mace tripped over his own feet when he recalled how swiftly and efficiently Jake had dealt with those two hooligans in the street. Perhaps it would be wise to keep his right hand on his Colt. His lightning-quick draw was legendary with the Rangers. And if he was lucky, he could get the drop on Jake before she blew him to smithereens.

As cautiously as a lion tamer enters a cage of starving cats, Mace slipped the key into the lock and eased open the door. To his relief, Jacquelyn was already asleep. On tiptoe, Mace crept across the room to survey the sleeping beauty.

Jacquelyn had neglected to douse the lantern. Pale golden light sprayed across the wind tangle of sable hair that streamed across the pillow. Bare arms glowed like honey in the flickering light. Mystical shadows caressed her perfect features, ones that were soft in repose. The sagging sheet revealed the swanlike column of her neck and the creamy smoothness of her shoulders to his devouring gaze.

Mace felt a tingling ache in his loins as his eyes swept over the display of satiny flesh. Here lay an angel, the stuff dreams were made of, he thought with an

74

appreciative sigh. For another indecisive moment Mace towered over Jake, ogling every tantalizing inch of her, speculating on how she would look without the concealing sheet.

Well, here I am, he mused, pulling himself together. Now what am I going to do? Mace had planned to let fate lead him, but fate was stalling, waiting for him to make the first move. A muddled frown creased his brow. Had Jacquelyn realized there was only one room rented for the night? Had she gone to bed, naked as the day she was born, expecting his arrival? Was this her subtle invitation?

Jacquelyn stirred slightly. The unfamiliar bed and surroundings prevented her from enjoying uninterrupted sleep. Moaning softly, Jake lifted heavy eyelids and squirmed onto her side. Mace's heart very nearly jumped from his chest when the sheet dipped over her bare back to display the curve of her hip. The room suddenly seemed as hot as a sweltering oven and Mace's blood threatened to boil.

As Jake snuggled beneath the sheet, she caught a brief glimpse of the darkly handsome man who loomed over her bed like a stone statue. "Hello, Mace . . ." she murmured groggily as she closed her eyes to pursue her arousing dreams. Suddenly the haze of sleep lifted from her brain and her eyes popped open. She wasn't dreaming that Mace was standing over her while she lay beneath the sheet without a stitch! This was no figment of her imagination. He was here . . . in her room . . . beside her bed . . . !

With a shocked squawk, Jacquelyn twisted to lie flat on her back. The sheet was clamped in her fists, which were poised just beneath her chin—the one sitting directly beneath her gaping mouth. "What are you doing in here?" she croaked.

Judging by the bewildered look on her sleep-drugged

features, Jake had not realized they might be sharing the same bed. Lord-a-mercy, did she always sleep in the nude? He wouldn't be the least bit surprised to learn a hundred Peeping Toms had been arrested in New Orleans—all of them apprehended outside this seductive beauty's bedroom window!

Mace dropped down on the edge of the bed as if he belonged there—which of course he did. It was his room, after all. Involuntarily, his hand drifted over the lustrous waves that shimmered with golden highlights in the lantern light. Her hair was like silk, he thought as he met her astonished gaze.

"This is the only room available, Jake," he told her, his voice husky with unfulfilled desire.

Jacquelyn eyed him with wary trepidation. "Why didn't you tell me that when I first arrived?" she wanted to know.

His broad shoulders lifted in a reckless shrug. "I decided it best to cross this bridge when we came to it."

"Well, this is a fine time to inform me!" Jacquelyn snapped huffily.

She had never felt so vulnerable in all her life. Her nightgown might as well have been ten miles away for all the good it would do her. If Mace made a grab for her, she could stay and fight or she could flee. And if she battled to keep the sheet between them, she wouldn't have so much as a prayer of fending off this muscular giant. And if she took flight, Mace would receive an eyeful before she could snatch up her nightgown. Damn, what was she to do?

When Mace braced his arms on either side of her bare shoulders and leaned closer, Jake flinched as if she had been stabbed in the back. Mace was all too close, and the smell of whiskey was on his breath. "You've been drinking," she accused harshly. "What have you been doing? Lounging in some dingy tavern, scheming to seduce me?"

Low laughter vibrated in his chest. Jacquelyn re-minded him of a defenseless rabbit which expected to be attacked from every direction at once. She may have been a tigress when she faced her foe, but her confidence drooped several notches when she confronted a man in this unfamiliar situation.

"Did you discard your gown in hopes I would return?" he teased mercilessly.

Jacquelyn puffed up with so much indignation she would have popped the buttons on her nightgown if she had been wearing one. (And she sorely wished she had been!) "I didn't have the foggiest notion you would appear to interrupt my sleep!" she protested hotly. "And if you think I'm going to welcome you with open arms, you had better think again, Jonathan Mason!"

Again it was on the tip of his tongue to confess his true identity. But the words died into silence when his eyes lingered on the taut peaks of her breasts that were pressed to the sheet. Gawd, he was aching with the want of a woman—not just any woman, but rather this sassy, sexy pixie. And yet, Mace couldn't bring himself to resort to force. He wanted Jake in his arms without a preliminary battle. Calling upon his dwindling willpower, Mace climbed to his feet. As calmly as you please, he peeled off his black waistcoat and shrugged off his white linen shirt.

Jacquelyn's eyes were as round as dinner plates. "What are you doing?" she squeaked, cursing her failing voice. The moment Mace exposed his bare chest she was reminded of the arousing vision that had chased across her dreams.

"I'm preparing for bed," Mace told her matter-of-factly. "This is how a man undresses himself. First his jacket comes off and then his shirt. . . ." Mace sank to the edge of the bed. "Next he removes his stockings and boots and then . . ."

"I can guess what then!" Jake all but shouted. "I do not need a running description."

Mace laid a tanned finger on her lips to shush her. "Keep your voice down, honey. We don't want to disturb the other guests."

"Why the hell not?" she sniffed sarcastically. "You are most certainly disturbing me."

A roguish grin captured his bronzed features as he unfolded his long, muscular frame to unfasten his breeches. "Do I?"

"Do you what?" Jake piped, her voice two octaves higher than normal. Her eyes were as round as globes as she watched Mace's fingertips glide along the band of his breeches.

Mace smiled a seductive smile when Jake's face flushed beet red. "Do I disturb you?"

She ignored that incriminating question. But it didn't matter that she refused to answer. *Yes* was printed on her face in bold letters. "Don't you dare remove your trousers in my presence!" she hissed up at him. "I have seen enough of you already."

"And if I dare?" One heavy brow lifted to a challenging angle. "What do you intend to do? Leap from bed, stark naked, wrestle me to the floor, and forcefully put me back in my breeches?"

Her breath came out in an exasperated rush. "How can you be so casual about this? You seem so . . . so . . ."

"Uninhibited?" he supplied. A teasing grin hung on the corner of his sensuous lips.

"Damn you!" she growled mutinously. Jacquelyn hated herself for staring at his swarthy physique. And she was infuriated that Mace was putting her through this embarrassment. She thought he was different from the rest of the male species. Oh, how wrong she had been. He was just like the rest of his annoying breed.

78

Mace tucked his thumbs in the sagging band of his trousers and regarded her scarlet face with an amused grin. "Did Aunt Florence approve of your cursing?"

Jake couldn't believe Mace could conduct a nonchalant conversation while he was undressing in front of a woman. He must have done this sort of thing so often that he possessed not an ounce of modesty. "Aunt Florence would wash my mouth with soap if she could hear me," she managed to say without her voice cracking completely. "And she would have you lynched for exposing yourself to me."

A startled gasp exploded from Jacquelyn's lips when Mace loosed the last button on his breeches and pushed them low on his hips. He really was going to strip naked before her naive eyes! Double damn him.

Jake expelled a flustered shriek when his bare hips were revealed to her innocent gaze. Blast it, she was learning more about Jonathan Mason that she wanted to know. "D . . . d . . . don't do that!" she pleaded shakily.

"If you don't want to watch, then don't," Mace suggested.

Like a turtle crawling into its protective shell, Jake covered her head with the sheet. She lay as stiff and immobile as a block of wood while the bed creaked and sagged with Mace's heavy weight. Her heart was thumping so wildly she feared it would beat her to death. What was she going to do when Mace reached for her, when he laid those lean fingers on her bare flesh? No doubt he would mock her inexperience, and that would humiliate her to no end.

Her mind raced with alternatives. Finally, Jacquelyn decided to be open and honest in her dealings with Mace. She could only hope his conscience would get the best of him and he would leave her alone.

After Mace settled into his niche beside her and covered himself, Jake withdrew her head from beneath the sheet. Uncomfortably, she glanced at the ruggedly handsome face that was cushioned on the linked fingers clasped behind his head. It galled her that Mace appeared so nonchalant, so unaffected. The man possessed nerves of steel while hers were quivering like leaves besieged by a windstorm.

"Mace, I'm going to be totally honest with you," she began. After swallowing the oversized lump that clogged her throat, she licked her bone-dry lips. "Despite the various rumors buzzing around New Orleans, I have never before slept with a man."

His raven head shifted to peer into her enormous brown eyes. Mace noticed that her knuckles had turned white from clutching the hem of the sheet that protected her from his devouring gaze. He knew he was amusing himself at Jacquelyn's expense, but he couldn't help himself. This firebrand had few inhibitions. For the most part, she came and went like a hurricane. But for once in their brief acquaintance, this sassy minx was out of her element and it did his heart good to see her rattled.

"And despite my vast and varied experiences in this life, this is a first for me too," Mace declared, straight-faced.

Jacquelyn's jaw dropped off its hinges. She couldn't believe what she was hearing. "You've never slept with a woman before?"

Mace levered himself upon his elbow and the sheet dropped to expose the wide expanse of his chest to Jake's observant gaze. "I've never slept with a woman who has never slept with a man before," he clarified, flashing her a wry smile.

His lips were poised directly above hers. She could feel the warm draft of his brandy-scented breath on her flaming cheeks. She remembered the alluring taste of his kiss, the exciting tingles his embrace evoked. How would she respond if he sidled closer, molding his sinewy flesh

80

to her innocent body?

Her train of thought derailed when he hypnotized her with those piercing golden eyes. They seemed to look right through her to pluck out her private thoughts. His penetrating gaze was so intense Jake trembled involuntarily. Mace was staring at her mouth as if it were the first one he had seen at close range, as if he were bewitched by it.

His handsome face was only a hairbreadth away. Their closeness sent her pulse leapfrogging through her blood stream. Her breathing was shallow and erratic and her mouth was dry as cotton. The wait was agonizing torment. Jake wanted his kiss and yet she was frightened of where it would lead, afraid she couldn't please a man with Mace's experience with women. Why that mattered so much Jacquelyn hadn't puzzled out, but it did matter. She didn't want to look the naive fool to this brawny mass of masculinity. It would be like admitting she was not his equal.

The silence stretched into eternity. Jake could hear the vibrations of her heart pounding in her ears, feel the warmth of Mace's body radiating onto hers, even when he had yet to make physical contact. Lord, the anticipation was killing her. Jacquelyn swore her overworked heart would beat her senseless before Mace did whatever it was he had in mind to do.

"Good night, Jake." Her nickname rolled off his tongue in a rumbling purr that heightened the tautness of her nerves. "Pleasant dreams . . ." His index finger sketched her heart-shaped lips as he blessed her with a smile. "First thing in the morning, I'll make arrangements to have your luggage shipped home and we'll take the stagecoach. All those heaping trunks will never fit on the stage if there are other passengers scheduled to join us."

To Jacquelyn's utter amazement, Mace twisted around

to reach for the lantern. Her wide eyes scanned his back, noting the jagged scar that wrapped around his ribs. The whipcord muscles of his arms and shoulders bunched and relaxed beneath his bronzed skin as he extinguished the lantern.

The world faded into silent darkness and Jake lay there in perplexed bemusement. While Mace sank onto his pillow and stretched out beside her, Jake stared at the moonlit shadows that drifted across the ceiling.

That was it? *Good night? I'll fetch a wagon in the morning?* Jacquelyn was bewildered by Mace's actions and startled by the feeling of disappointment that splashed over her. What the devil was the matter with her? She should have been relieved that Mace had no intention of doing anything except sleeping in the same bed with her. But that was not the emotion that mastered the myriad of feelings that were sizzling through her. She felt rejected, for crying out loud. Apparently she wasn't woman enough to attract Mace.

Just exactly what was there about her that provoked this man to turn his back without giving her a second thought? One glance in the mirror assured Jake that she wasn't exactly homely. She didn't consider herself a raving beauty, but she had never been without a man's attention if she desired it. Why, there had been dozens of suitors lined up on Aunt Florence's doorstep. Jacquelyn had warded off the advances of scores of men in the past. And the one time she found herself abed with a man, he settled down to sleep as if he were lying beside a pile of quilts! She wasn't relieved; she was downright insulted!

A contemplative frown knitted her brow. Mace had never come right out and said he had seduced scores of women. As a matter of fact, *she* was the one who suggested his worldliness. He hadn't denied it, but neither had he admitted to his sexual prowess. Was he only protecting his male pride? After all, wouldn't a sexually active man have at least attempted to seduce a woman who was lying naked in his bed, even if he got his face soundly slapped? Maybe Mace wasn't married because he . . .

"Do you prefer men?" Jacquelyn clamped her mouth shut so quickly she bit her tongue. She couldn't believe she had actually put her darkest suspicions into words!

There was a long, brittle silence, leaving Jake to wonder if she had leaped to the right conclusion after all.

Mace rather thought he deserved an award for his performance. He'd managed to lie beside this tempting minx without physically attacking her. And he also deserved a medal for stifling the bubble of laughter that ached to burst free. *Prefer men? Not hardly!*

"In what capacity are you referring?" he asked without snickering. I truly should pursue a career in the theater, he thought arrogantly. He was giving a most convincing performance.

Jacquelyn peered at his shadowed form. "Don't pretend ignorance, Mace. You know exactly what I mean."

The bed vibrated when Mace heaved a heavy sigh. "No, Jake. I like loving women," he assured her. If Jake could have viewed the ornery smile that claimed his features, she would have retrieved her derringer and shot him on the spot.

"Then what is the matter with me? I'm a woman . . . or hadn't you noticed we aren't built alike." Damn her wagging tongue! It had a mind of its own and it was rattling off sentences that were better left unspoken.

"I've noticed," he declared with a bored yawn. (At least it sounded that way to Jake, who found herself hanging on his every word and gesture.) "You are a very attractive young lady. Is that what you wanted to hear?"

The taunt brought her into an upright position beside him. Clutching the sheet over her breasts, Jake glowered poison arrows at the back of Mace's head.

"No, that is not what I wanted to hear!" she growled crossly. "I want to know why you didn't try to seduce me when opportunity was staring you in the face!"

"We really should get some sleep," Mace murmured drowsily. "Tomorrow will be a long day."

My, I'm handling this superbly, he complimented himself. Before long, Jake would be begging him to kiss her.

How dare he shrug her off like a discarded bundle of laundry. He might as well have come right out and said she was as appealing as a damp mop!

While Jacquelyn was nursing her wounded pride and Mace was inwardly giggling at his ornery prank, the man who had been eavesdropping for the past quarter of an hour inched away from the door. His footsteps receded down the hall, and the occupants of the suite never knew he had come and gone.

"You could at least behave as if you found me mildly attractive," Jacquelyn burst out in annoyance.

Like a rousing lion, Mace sat up beside her in bed and crossed his arms over his hair-matted chest. His amusement was masked behind a carefully blank stare, one Jacquelyn would have had difficulty interpreting in the darkness in any case. Mace could have been grinning outrageously and she wouldn't have known it.

"I have never forced myself on a woman," Mace informed her blandly. "I see no reason to begin now. You appear offended that I would want to enjoy a decent night's sleep before a long, grueling ride over Texas roads, roads with deep ruts that are notorious for flinging the occupants of stagecoaches from one seat to another. If you will recall, this is my room, rented with my hard-earned money. I am sorry we cannot enjoy privacy, but there are no other rooms available. Yet, at the same time, I see no reason to change my custom of sleeping in the nude, especially since you are equally undressed," he pointed out. "We are two mature adults, caught up in circumstances beyond our control. We have only one bed and we both need sleep. I did not—"

Jacquelyn's impatient sniff interrupted his soliloquy. She had grown tired of Mace's diplomatic prattle. "Just answer the question, damnit. Why didn't you make any advances toward me? Don't I appeal to you?"

Biting back his laughter, Mace stared into her shadowed face. "If I kiss you, will it make you feel better, Jake?"

"Yes, if you want to know!" she spewed out resentfully. "Do you have any conception of what I'm feeling? Are you so insensitive? For the first time in my life I find myself abed with a man and he completely ignores me, even when I'm lying beside him without a stitch of clothing. It leaves me to wonder if, even on my wedding night—should I ever experience one," she added in a bitter tone, "if my husband will be snoring the moment his head hits the pillow. I thought something was supposed to happen when a man and woman climbed into bed together." Jake inhaled a hasty breath and rattled on. "And if nothing really happens, why were all the gabbing young ladies in finishing school whispering and giggling in speculation? What exactly does—"

Mace fumbled to clamp his hand over her mouth. Jacquelyn was ranting as if she were conversing with someone at the other end of the hall instead of the man who was sitting beside her in bed.

"If I kiss you will you please be quiet and go to sleep?" Mace queried tartly. "You caught a nap before I arrived, but I'm dead tired."

When Jacquelyn nodded agreeably, Mace's hand glided to her neck, feeling the rapid pulsations beneath his inquiring fingertips. Gently, he tilted her face to his kiss. It was sweet torture to take her lips under his, to

85

force himself to keep a respectable distance when his hands ached to discover every inch of her feminine flesh, when his male body craved to mold itself to her irresistible curves. Mace muffled a groan of torment when her untutored hands slid over his chest to rest on his shoulders. The sheet had fallen away and the tips of her breasts lightly caressed his flesh, igniting fires that all the water in Galveston Bay couldn't extinguish.

Sweet mercy! How could he stop what he was doing when his body was on fire for this spirited enchantress? How could he be satisfied with one good-night kiss when he wanted to make wild, sweet love to Jacquelyn until dawn? And yet, how could he seduce this naive imp and live with his conscience, one that had already been sorely put upon during the course of the day? He had deceived Jake by passing himself off as Jon Mason. Now he was feeding her this nonsense about not wanting her the way a man lusts after a beautiful woman. Damn, he was getting himself in deeper and deeper!

Mace might have paused to contemplate the repercussions of this encounter with Jacquelyn if he could have maintained rational thought. Unfortunately, he couldn't. Jacquelyn kissed him back and his brain melted. The heat of desire was burning through him like a crownfire.

Calling upon the last shred of willpower, Mace pried himself away from the tempting package. Lord, this prank had backfired in his face. He would spend the remainder of the night on a slow burn. "Are you satisfied now?" he questioned more gruffly than he intended.

Jacquelyn stared owlishly at the man who had untangled himself from her arms long before she was inclined to let him go. "Should I be?" Her tone was raspy with unfulfilled passion, an emotion she was only beginning to understanding. Her body was trembling with many sensations. She felt hot and cold and shaky, all in the same moment. Was this a normal reaction to intimacy or was she coming down with the grippe?

"You should be satisfied if you prefer to remain innocent of men," Mace grumbled, hating himself for carrying this dangerous game to such perilous extents. Damnation, didn't she know how difficult it was for him to offer one kiss when he was aching to devour all of her?

Jacquelyn strained to decipher the expression on Mace's handsome face in the concealing shadows. "Would you make love to me if I asked you to?"

Mace felt like a man strung out on a medieval torture rack. His conscience and his male desires were being twisted and stretched until he was completely bent out of shape. Finally, he expelled a frustrated breath. "Yes, I suppose I would, so don't ask," he snapped gruffly. "If we did, you would rouse in the morning hating me and probably yourself as well." Egad, he detested himself for being so sensible, so noble! He had maneuvered this inexperienced minx into his hands and he was graciously letting her go, knowing it was going to kill him if he were forced to sleep with her without satisfying his male desires. Exasperated, Mace punched his pillow and slammed his head onto it.

"Mace?" Jake chewed on her bottom lip, debating whether or not to pose such an intimate question. But demons of curiosity were dancing in her head and she couldn't contain her inquisitiveness. It was another of her numerous faults. "Wouldn't I enjoy lovemaking? Is that why you said I would hate both of us in the morning?"

Mace rolled his eyes and growled into his pillow. He should have known better than to get mixed up with this naive pixie. He'd known she was a unique brand of woman since the moment she barged in his room to interrupt his bath. Lord, it seemed eons ago that he had been sitting in his tub, minding his own business, drifting in harmless thoughts.

"With the right man, lovemaking would be one of the most satisfying experiences you could imagine," he replied, striving to control the fire that was burning him inside and out.

Jacquelyn contemplated the ceiling. "Solving a complicated mathematical problem is satisfying, no matter what type of paper one is calculating on. Different paper, same satisfaction," she stated thoughtfully.

Mace couldn't help himself. His laughter erupted like a volcano. How could she reduce lovemaking to mathematical equations? Because she knew nothing about sexual encounters, he quickly reminded himself. And Mace had religiously avoided virgins . . . until now. It appeared he should have made no exceptions to that hard and fast rule.

"You needn't ridicule me," Jacquelyn grumbled as the bed shook from Mace's laughing spasms. "I'm only trying to reason this out."

Mace struggled to compose himself as he eased onto his back to toss Jake a hasty glance. "I'm sorry, but your comparison struck me funny, little imp," he said, his voice rattling with barely restrained laughter. "There is a vast difference between lovemaking and addition problems. One and one do occasionally make three instead of two. But there is a vast difference between simply adding to the population and enjoying doing so."

There was a long pause. "Do you suppose I would find pleasure with a man like you, Mace?"

The inquisition was uttered with such genuine innocence that Mace actually winced. Egad, he couldn't believe they were having this conversation. What the devil did she think he was anyway? One of her school professors? It was difficult enough to go on pretending her presence beside him wasn't disturbing, without discussing what he ached to be doing!

"There is only one way to determine the answer to that question, Jacquelyn," he murmured hoarsely. "That decision must lie with you and I think it wise to sleep on it. Good night."

Now Mace was absolutely certain he deserved an award for his theatrical performance and his noble self-restraint. Male desire was silently cursing him for being so damned honorable. This dazzling beauty might have submitted to his embrace if he had employed his powers of persuasion. Damn, wasn't he turning out to be quite the gentleman? Who would have thought it? Certainly not General Reid. Harlan had Mace pegged as a scoundrel and a renegade. Why, the General would be saluting Mace if he knew how noble Mace had been when faced with this incredible temptation.

You are doing the right thing, his better judgment consoled him. If he wanted to appease his lust, he should have sought out a female who would demand no more than a moment of his time. If he tampered with this high-spirited sprite, he would be asking for serious trouble.

Mace bitterly accepted his own good advice, but it didn't stop the ache that channeled into every fiber of his being. Denying himself was torture, pure and simple, and his sleep was interrupted by recurring dreams, which caused him to awake at irregular intervals in a cold sweat.

While Mace was lying beside her, stiff as a statue, Jacquelyn was frowning pensively. Had she lost her mind? Why was she even entertaining thoughts of experimenting with passion? She had just met Jonathan Mason, for heaven's sake! The fact that this man bore the General's stamp of approval should be reason enough to avoid him. She could not become involved with Mace, just on general principles. She had always defied her grandfather's wishes, if only to irritate him.

Why are you even stewing over this man? Jake asked

89

herself sourly. The General might have schemed to match her with Mace, but Mace assured her he did not have marriage in mind. He didn't even want her body all that much, she thought dejectedly. If he had, he wouldn't have fallen asleep while they were sharing the same bed!

For what seemed forever, Jacquelyn wrestled with a maelstrom of emotions. She was shocked to find herself so physically attracted to Mace. She had spent three years saying no to men's advances. For the first time in her life she had deliberated saying yes. Now was that crazy? she asked herself seriously. Why, of course it was! And yet . . . what kind of man would refuse opportunity? What sort of man would leave the decision to her? Jake wasn't certain how to proceed. In the past, men had chased her. But Mace didn't have to chase women. They followed him like ants on the trail of a picnic. Obviously, she hadn't made much of an impression on Mace. If she had, he wouldn't be so indifferent.

The fault must surely lie with me, Jacquelyn told herself sadly. She did not appeal to this breed of man. Perhaps this was her deserved punishment for rejecting her eager suitors. Now she knew how it felt to be cast aside. And now that the shoe was on the other foot, she was feeling the pinch of humiliation. Mace had her questioning her femininity—or rather her lack of it. She found herself wanting to be more alluring, for Mace's sake.

Stop this nonsense, she scolded herself. She cared nothing for pretense. She was the way she was, and if Mace didn't find her stimulating company she must accept that. Jacquelyn had resolved long ago that she would never put on airs to attract a man. And she was going to continue following that practical guideline. She was Jacquelyn Reid and she would behave as she always had. If Mace didn't like her enough to be interested in the woman she was, she was not about to pretend to be something she was not!

With that positive thought, Jacquelyn closed her eyes and opened her arms to sleep. But it was difficult to pursue slumber when a naked man occupied her bed. As long as she lived she would never forget this night and this riptide of emotions that swamped her. She hadn't wanted her grandfather's protégé to make such a strong impression on her, but he had. Confound it, he had!

Chapter 6

"How could a mere slip of a girl overpower and assault two grown men!" came the booming voice of Frank Norman and Daniel Johnson's employer.

Frank and Daniel shrugged noncommittally when their employer glowered at them.

Impatient fingers drummed on the arm of the chair. "I paid you good money to dispose of the chit and you bungled both attempts!" he raged.

Frank massaged his throbbing head, the one Jacquelyn had come dangerously close to separating from his shoulders. He glanced quickly at Daniel, who had sustained a shot in the arm. "We know where she's stayin'," he assured his irate employer. "Me an' Dan'l followed her. We'll see to the matter the moment she takes to the open road."

A venomous snarl curled the man's mouth. "You should have exterminated the wench this afternoon."

"We tried," Frank defended hotly. "But she took us by surprise. And tonight she had that giant of a bodyguard with her." As if that had really mattered, Frank thought disconcertedly. The dark-haired hoyden had very nearly gunned down Daniel and him all by herself!

"I want you to make her death appear the result of a robbery," the man growled at them. "And you had best not bungle this attempt or I will do more than take potshots at *you!*"

Nodding mutely, Frank and Daniel slinked out of the room into the darkness.

"I thought this would be easy money," Daniel grumbled as he massaged his aching shoulder. "That ain't no normal woman. She's a wildcat, and that bodyguard of hers is nothing to sneeze at either!"

"Now that we know what kind of chit we're dealin' with, we'll be prepared," Frank replied encouragingly. "I won't have that girl making a laughingstock of me. And when I git my hands on her, she'll pay for this humiliation."

"*If* you git yer hands on her." Frank smirked disgustedly. "I ain't so sure she can be got, except from a distance!"

Those were Frank's sentiments exactly. But he wasn't about to voice those discouraging words. He still had his pride, after all. And thanks to that feisty firebrand, he also had a new part in his hair!

Sullenly, Mace made his way back to the hotel. He had awakened from a fitful night's sleep, stung by the insane desire to rouse the gorgeous minx beside him and introduce her to a world of sensual passion. Growling at his failing willpower, Mace had dragged himself from bed at the break of dawn. But when the sheet dipped low over the swells of Jacquelyn's breasts and the sun sprayed through the window to sparkle on that wild mane of golden-brown hair, Mace's knees had buckled beneath him.

Damn, she had looked ravishing in the morning light, lying there like a serene angel. Pulling himself together,

94

Mace had dressed in record time and fled the chamber without bothering to shave the stubble from his face. After securing transportation for Jacquelyn's luggage, Mace attended to his last-minute tasks at the commission company. With business in order, he aimed himself toward the hotel to retrieve Jacquelyn. But he wondered how he could ever again stare at that desirable nymph without seeing her as she had been that morning.

I can't, Mace thought grumpily. He was doomed to hallucinate about that bewitching temptress for the rest of his natural life. . . .

A curious frown creased Mace's brow when he noticed the crowd of men who had collected around the entrance of the hotel. A snake of apprehension uncoiled on his spine as he wondered if the two hooligans who had been pestering Jake had somehow managed to attack her. Was she lying there in a pool of blood? Had those maniacs spitefully disfigured her?

Panic-stricken, Mace shoved bodies out of his way to locate the source of the commotion. His apprehension evolved into irritation when he heard Jacquelyn's carefree laughter wafting its way toward him. There, amid another endless rabble of admirers, stood Jacquelyn, looking all too healthy to have been set upon by muggers and thieves. Healthy? Mace scowled at his poor choice of words. The minx appeared more than healthy. She looked absolutely enticing and seductive, damn her!

A long braid of dark hair dangled over Jacquelyn's shoulder and descended to her waist. She had discarded her bright, colorful gowns and had stepped into a pair of tight blue breeches that looked as if they had been stitched directly to her skin. A bright red shirt accented her shapely curves and swells. Black boots extended up her calves, drawing attention to her well-proportioned legs and completing her outlandish attire.

Mace could have strangled her for dressing so

outrageously and drawing such a crowd—all of them eager males. Her striking appearance reminded him of the theory he had formulated the previous evening—the one about plain women dressing in colorful wardrobes to draw attention to themselves. Mace still maintained that Jacquelyn's costume was a posted warning that announced, "Step aside, world, here comes trouble." Indeed, Jake was doing the world a favor by offering a forewarning. Unfortunately, men were too busy ogling her arresting assets to recognize trouble at a glance! Damnit, he should have had more sense than to agree to accompany Jake home. Hell, she didn't need him when she was surrounded by an army of admirers!

Expelling a wordless growl, Mace elbowed his way toward Jake. Blast it, why couldn't she have waited in their suite instead of sashaying into the street? Mace heaved a frustrated sigh. Damn, that woman beat anything he ever saw. She looked like a female but she certainly didn't behave like one!

It suddenly occurred to Mace that this fiery vixen truly was a first time for him. He had always confronted other women in one-dimensional relationships—the kind that entailed leapfrogging in and out of bed without concern for the past or future. But dealing with Jacquelyn Reid was an altogether different matter. It was like waking up in a new world every day without a clue as to how the hours would unfold. Mace couldn't flash Jake a come-hither glance and expect her to fetch and heel the way other women did. He was the one left to chase after her. Mace was constantly fighting for male domination when it should have come with the territory. But, put quite simply, that brown-eyed spitfire defied the laws of nature and refused to recognize her place.

As Mace watched Jake charm a half-dozen men out of the boots, he almost pitied General Reid. The man prided himself in maintaining order, in establishing military obedience among his troops and his associates. Harlan Reid must have suffered scores of conniption fits while raising this inexhaustible bundle of spirit and energy. . . .

Mace's rambling thoughts dissipated when Jacquelyn glanced in his direction to rake him with her own astute gaze. There was living fire dancing in those enormous brown eyes. The resentment and frustration fell away and Mace's brain froze as he too admired this exquisite, vibrant beauty. Mace couldn't help himself. He broke into an appreciative smile and allowed his eyes to take an arousing tour of her tantalizing figure.

Jacquelyn had planned to face the day, behaving as if nothing out of the ordinary had occurred the previous night. But the moment she laid eyes on this darkly handsome rogue, the forbidden memories came rushing back, provoking her heart to patter like a pounding rain on a tin roof. Mace had set aside the fancy trappings of a gentleman. He was garbed in a cream-colored shirt that stretched sensuously across his thick chest. A wide-brimmed felt hat capped his raven head. His long, muscular legs (which Jake had admired the previous day) were clad in form-fitting buckskin breeches. Around his waist lay a wide leather belt, and attached to it were two Colt revolvers and a Bowie knife. The rugged frontiersman appealed to Jacquelyn far more than the gentleman who garbed himself in a velvet waistcoat and breeches. It made her all the more aware that Mace was every inch a man.

Regaining his composure, Mace swallowed his lovesick smile. He was annoyed with Jake, and he wasn't going to be sidetracked by his lust. Growling, Mace grabbed Jake's arm and herded her back into the hotel lobby.

Jacquelyn was amazed at the sudden change in Mace's mood. He looked like black thunder, and she was at a loss to explain what had soured his disposition.

"What the hell did you intend to prove by gallivanting into the streets dressed like that?" Mace snarled, struggling to prevent his voice from rising to a roar.

He was in a snit because of her clothes? Calmly, Jacquelyn glanced down her torso. There was nothing indecent about her attire. The way Mace was carrying on, one would have thought she had strolled into the street naked.

"I'm dressed like you," she argued. "I don't know why you are making such a fuss."

"Perhaps," he gritted out resentfully. "But that garb is highly improper for a supposedly civilized young lady."

One delicately carved brow rose to a challenging angle. She thought Mace had accepted her as she was. Apparently, he wasn't as tolerant as she had assumed. "Are you suggesting that clothes make the lady?" she inquired.

"I am suggesting that your attire displays more of the lady than the rest of the male population needs to see," Mace parried, struggling to regain his temper. By God, he was jealous because that crowd of men had been leering at this voluptuous misfit! Jealous? Mace Gallagher? Christ! What was he saying?

Jake crossed her arms beneath her breasts and stared Mace squarely in the eye, oblivious to the fact that she had begun to draw a crowd inside the hotel. Mace noticed, and it rankled him more than ever.

His misplaced feelings of possession and his attempt to dictate to her irritated Jake. "Make no mistake, Mace. I will do what I please and dress as I please," she told him matter-of-factly. "I fully intend to ride to the plantation, and I cannot do that if I'm tangled in those hindering dresses and undergarments some buffoon designed for women. Their practical purpose escapes me. Indeed, I doubt there is one except to differentiate women's

98

clothes from men's clothes. And it wouldn't surprise me if it were a man who first designed long, entangling skirts for women. If a man had to wear such constricting garb, he would be complaining as loudly as I am!''

Mace stomped a step closer, looming over Jake's defiant stance. "I told you we were taking the stagecoach," he growled as quietly as he could. His tone brooked no argument, but that didn't mean he was able to avoid one. He was quickly learning this spirited minx would argue with a stone wall.

"You take the stage," she suggested flippantly. "I just purchased a mount from one of the gentlemen in the street and I am riding astride—a pleasure of which I have been deprived unless I sneaked away to the stables when Aunt Florence wasn't looking."

Without further ado, Jake performed an about-face that would have done her grandfather proud. In precise strides she marched back outside to retrieve her newly purchased gelding. Mace expelled the breath he had been holding, and then stiffened in annoyance when he heard Henry's goading laughter behind him. Mace wheeled to glare daggers at the hotel proprietor.

"What's so damned funny?" Mace demanded to know.

Henry's eyes twinkled with merriment. "You are," he said with a snicker. "You may be twice as big and three times as strong as that female, but she ultimately won the debate." Henry cocked a questioning brow. "Shall I have my errand boy fetch your horse? It looks as if you will be riding."

Muttering several uncomplimentary epithets about Henry and Jacquelyn, Mace stalked toward the door. "I'll fetch Diego myself. You send your errand boy to retrieve our luggage and load it on the wagon."

With that, Mace disappeared outside to manacle Jake's arm in a bone-crushing grip.

Jacquelyn sucked in her breath when Mace clamped

onto her elbow. "You're hurting me," she hissed as Mace propelled her and her steed down the congested street.

"Your consolation is that this crowd is preventing me from turning you over my knee and throttling you," he bit off.

"You are not my father, Jonathan Mason," she sassed, futilely squirming for release. "I will not have you ordering me about and you will never lay a hand on me!"

"Never?" Mace mocked spitefully. "We'll see about that. . . ."

His voice trailed off when he glanced up to note the man who stood in the shadows of the livery stable. Of all the rotten luck, he growled under his breath. The last thing Mace wanted was to encounter Hub MacIntosh, who had an eye for ladies. No doubt this particular bundle of femininity in men's clothes would bewitch Hub in a matter of seconds. Mace's prediction proved correct. The moment Hub's blue eyes fastened on Jake, he was ogling her comely figure.

Jacquelyn found their path blocked by a brawny blond who equalled Mace's size and stature. He was as handsome with his glistening blue eyes and light features as Mace was with his dark, swarthy characteristics.

"The Gen'ral's granddaughter, I presume," Hub drawled, his eyes still wandering at will, liking everything they saw. Sweeping his gray Stetson from his sandy blond head, Hub honored Jake with a sweeping bow. "Hub MacIntosh at your service, for now and evermore."

"Thank you," Jacquelyn replied, and then indicated the oversized brute who was clamped on her arm, which at the moment was without circulation. "You can do me a great service by unloosening this rabid dog from my person. He has practically wrenched my arm from its socket."

Two thick brows jackknifed when Hub got around to noticing that Mace was indeed pinching the lady's arm.

"The Gen'ral won't be at all pleased if you deliver the young lady with various parts of her body broken or missing," Hub teased.

Reluctantly, Mace released Jake's arm and forced the semblance of a smile. "Hub, may I present Jacquelyn Reid, the terror of Texas." His voice carried the same amount of bite as the remark itself.

"I think you do the lady an injustice," Hub murmured, distracted. His keen gaze made another thorough sweep of Jake's well-sculptured figure. "Nothing so attractive could possibly terrorize the countryside. Mmm . . . I think I'm in love. . . ."

Mace rolled his eyes in disgust. "You never met a woman you didn't love," he scoffed sarcastically.

Just to spite the grumbling Mace, Jacquelyn presented Hub with an angelic smile. When her dark eyes sparkled like ebony, Hub sighed melodramatically, swearing the dazzling beauty required only a pair of wings and a halo to achieve sainthood.

"Don't be fooled by first impressions," Mace advised his drooling friend, and then stomped off to retrieve Diego from his stall before Jake's sticky-sweet smile gave him a toothache.

To Mace's dismay, Jacquelyn seemed taken by Hub. Enthusiastically, she dived into conversation. Indeed, she behaved as if she wouldn't have cared if Mace ever returned.

A disappointed frown crossed Hub's brow when Mace reappeared to shuffle Jake on her way. "We were just getting acquainted," Hub complained. Hurriedly, Hub strode up beside Mace, but his eyes were still lingering on the graceful sway of Jake's hips in those form-fitting breeches. Damn, but this curvaceous beauty gave new meaning to trousers! "How long are you going to be gone?" Hub inquired as Mace swung into the saddle.

"Until I return," Mace grumbled cryptically. "I intend to use the time contacting clients upriver."

"I'll just bet you are." Hub smirked caustically.

Mace leveled him a glare that would have knocked a lesser man to his knees. However, giant that Hub was, he managed to keep his feet beneath him. "You keep business in mind while I'm gone."

"What am I supposed to tell Governor Wood if he sends another courier?" Hub questioned suddenly.

"Tell him I'm still contemplating his request," Mace snapped impatiently.

"Give my best to Raoul when you see him," Hub called as Mace reined into the street.

As Mace escorted Jacquelyn back to the hotel to insure that their luggage had been loaded, she frowned curiously. "Is the governor a personal friend of yours?"

"Wood occasionally requests my services," he said evasively, annoyed at Hub for bringing up the subject in Jake's presence.

"What kind of services?" Jake pried.

Mace's scant smile implied the topic was none of her business, which of course it wasn't. But Jake had the curiosity of a cat and she was relentless in her pursuit of knowledge.

"Are you his eyes in Galveston?"

"Nope."

"His ears then?" she prodded, but to no avail.

Mace frowned at the bank of clouds that clogged the southeastern sky. Gesturing his raven head, he called her attention to the approaching storm. "I suggest we begin our trip before inclement weather befalls us. You can question me later, for all the good it will do you."

Jake pulled a face at his broad back, but her excitement of riding home after her three-year absence soon overshadowed her irritation. She was going home at last! Nothing could spoil her elation, not even Mace's evasiveness and his domineering attitude. Jacquelyn

102

consoled herself by recalling she had softened her staunch grandfather. Mace couldn't be as difficult as Harlan Reid. And besides, she decided, it was best if she and Mace were slightly crosswise of each other. Jake didn't trust herself where he was concerned. Mace made her feel vulnerable, and she was far too aware of the man in form-fitting buckskin.

If the subject of conversation they discussed the previous night never cropped up again, Jake would be relieved. Things had very nearly gotten out of hand and it would have been all her fault. Mace had discouraged her from involving herself in a situation she might later regret. Yes, it was better if she and Mace weren't on the best of terms. It would save her from herself!

After being ferried across from Galveston to the mainland, Jacquelyn sighed appreciatively at the familiar landmarks that unfolded before her. She was on native soil again, inhaling the fragrant wildflowers that spilled across the plain, adding to the radiant color of the scenery. Impulsively, Jake dug her heels into the rose-gray gelding's flanks, sending him into a canter. The feel of the wind caressing her cheeks filled her spirits to overflowing. She was home now, and no one would ever send her away again. She would run wild and free on the sprawling meadows, living life to the fullest.

A smile rippled across Mace's lips as he held his fidgety chestnut stallion to a walk. Diego itched to race the gelding, but Mace preferred to study the uninhibited nymph from a safe distance. Thus far, Mace had been stung by such varying emotions that he couldn't quite master his feelings. Jacquelyn was turning him wrong side out. Mace had ridden the emotional seesaw since the moment this ebony-eyed hellion burst into his life. She was a walking contradiction, an unstoppable force, the essence of femininity, and yet the epitome of adventurous spirit.

103

A man shouldn't permit a woman to disturb him so, Mace lectured himself sternly. He recalled the strange jealousy that had overcome him when he'd returned to the hotel to find Jake surrounded by her swarm of admirers. Why, men trotted after her like kittens in pursuit of fresh milk. Possessive jealousy burned through him, the fierce, uncontrollable kind that had . . . Mace squelched the tormenting thought. Those bitter, nightmarish memories were a closed chapter from his past and he had resolved never to dwell on or speculate about them. Damnit, he didn't want to remember or compare, not when those recollections cut like a knife, leaving his soul to bleed.

In an attempt to outrun a past that wouldn't die, Mace gouged Diego in the ribs and trailed after the reckless hoyden who was thundering across the meadow. By the time Mace caught up to Jacquelyn her face was aflame with the colors of pleasure. The exuberant smile that claimed her exquisite features melted Mace into mush.

"Is something amiss?" Jake questioned, puzzled by the odd expression on Mace's face.

Mace regained his composure. He was certain Jake wouldn't approve of what he was thinking of doing to her. And for the sake of argument, he lied convincingly. "No, I was only admiring your excellent horsemanship. You ride very well."

Lighthearted laughter bubbled from her lips. "When I was younger my one ambition in life was to ride with the Texas Rangers," she confessed. "I practiced riding all over my horse like the Comanches are said to do. I even pleaded with my grandfather to teach me to become proficient with a pistol and knife."

"Did he?" Mace queried curiously. Someone had taught this minx to be deadly with weapons. She knew exactly what she was doing when she took aim at her assailants. But Mace couldn't imagine Harlan Reid having the patience to teach his granddaughter to do much of anything. The man had a short fuse on his temper.

Jacquelyn nodded positively. "The Gen'ral deemed it important that I learn to defend myself." An impish grin caused her dark eyes to shine like the sun, even if it had been swallowed by the overcast sky. "Of course, I didn't tell him of my ambition. The Gen'ral dislikes the Rangers. Many a time I have heard him say that that band of renegades were appropriately named by the Mexicans —*Los Diablos Tejanos*, the Texas Devils."

Mace bit back an amused grin. "Dislikes? I think you put it too mildly," he countered. "Harlan deplores the Rangers. If he had his way they would be disbanded and placed before a firing squad."

"I think deep down inside the Gen'ral admires that breed of men," Jake contradicted. "He says they can ride and track like Comanches, shoot like Kentuckians, and fight like the devil. His only complaint is that they lack military discipline. It is only that he resents the fact that he couldn't exert any control over them."

The General certainly had failed in that department, Mace recalled. He could remember seeing the General hopping up and down with indignation on several occasions when the Rangers refused to treat Harlan with the respect he thought he deserved.

The smile slid off Jake's lips and she focused on some distant point. Glancing back through the window of time, she found herself trapped in the memory of her argument with Harlan. "It was my frantic declaration that I would prefer to remain in Texas and join the ranks of the Rangers that provoked my grandfather to strike me and insist that I would be carted to New Orleans against my wishes."

A muddled frown creased Mace's brow. He knew the General hated the Rangers because of their lack of respect for military authority, but he couldn't fathom why Harlan would strike Jake for stating she wanted to be like them. After all, she could never become one of them. She was a female.

Her gaze swung back to meet Mace's contemplative stare. "You think the Gen'ral a bit mad, I suppose," she speculated. "I thought so too at the time. It wasn't until I revealed the bitter incident to Aunt Florence that I came to understand my grandfather's sensitivity where the Rangers are concerned. My mother ran away with one of Texas's legendary heroes. Because of it, my father drank himself to death. For years my grandfather led me to believe that cholera had taken my parents' lives. He detested my mother for what she did to my father and he refused to speak of it. It was Florence who delighted in exposing the skeletons in her brother's family closet."

Mace didn't know what to say so he said nothing at all. But it did help him understand the man who spited him at every turn. The Rangers represented frustration and bitterness to Harlan. He had disliked that breed of men long before he laid eyes on Mace. . . .

"And what about you?" Jake inquired as she stood in the stirrups to give her backside a rest. "Thus far, you have revealed very little about your past. Were you hatched from an egg or did you come unassembled?"

Mace's irrepressible laughter split the damp air that had surged up from the Gulf with the thick mass of clouds. "I thought you had defined the propagation of the species in mathematical equations," he teased. "And no, I was neither hatched from an egg nor assembled from the contents of a box." Golden eyes glistened as they lingered on her arresting curves and swells. "Perhaps you do need to be instructed on subjects that were obviously avoided at finishing school."

Jacquelyn watched his tawny eyes devour her in ways no other man had ever been able to do without insulting her. Mace was trying to distract her. She knew it. He was the master of evasion and, as of yet, she had pried very little information from this elusive rogue.

"You didn't answer my question," she reminded him pointedly. "Are you afraid to speak of your past?"

"No," Mace grumbled as he stared straight ahead.

"Then where do you call home?"

"Texas."

"You were born here?" she quizzed.

"No."

Jacquelyn expelled an exasperated breath. She would need a crowbar to pry information from that tight-lipped clam.

Her exaggerated pout drew Mace's amused chuckle. He was playing havoc with her inquisitive nature, and either he revealed bits and pieces of his past or Jake would hound him every step of the journey.

"I hail from Louisiana," Mace finally confessed. "I have lived in Texas for twelve years. I am not married and I never have been and I definitely prefer women. Even if I do not prefer wedlock," he added in reminder of her probing question the previous night. "And I do not enjoy being cross-examined about my past."

"Was it a lover who has embittered you against marriage and your past?" Jacquelyn delighted in needling Mace, especially since he had badgered her with such relish.

"You don't know when to quit, do you, minx?" he muttered, glaring at her ornery grin.

"If I did, the Gen'ral would have had me marching in military formation and saluting my life away," she said breezily. "I have never had aspirations of conforming to my grandfather's regulations or to anyone else's for that matter."

"Truly?" Mace blessed her with a mock-innocent smile. "I never would have guessed it—"

Their conversation was interrupted by the thunder of rifles that exploded from the skirting of trees that lined the meadow. Instinctively Mace ducked, and then glanced toward the grove of trees and underbrush. To his amazement, Jacquelyn slid off the saddle, using her mount as a shield. With one boot in the stirrup and one hand on the reins, Jake plastered herself against the gelding's left side and took off like the wind.

Mace performed the same maneuver and aimed himself toward the underbrush that crowded the creek. Together they spirited away from danger, serenaded by the scream of bullets. Only after Mace dropped down into the tall weeds beside Jake did he notice the bloodstain that saturated the shoulder of her shirt. His expression testified to the extent of his concern and amazement. Jake had not uttered even the faintest cry when the first bullet found its mark. Instead she had sprawled against the side of her rose-gray gelding and reined him toward cover.

"I told you someone was trying to kill me," she hissed as Mace's fingertips investigated the edge of the wound.

"I thought you had exaggerated the situation," he mumbled absently. "Peel off your shirt and let me have a look."

"I most certainly will not!" Jake declared emphatically. "It's only a scratch."

"I should like to determine that for myself, if you don't mind." Mace scowled, disgusted with himself for being so unattentive of their surroundings and the possibility of trouble. As always, Jake distracted him.

"I do mind." She sat up cross-legged, cradling her injured arm against her ribs.

Another rumble shook the silence. But this time it was a clap of thunder. Mace muttered sourly as he glared at the threatening sky. This was a fine time for a tropical storm to come sweeping up from the Gulf. He could only hope Hub had taken precautions on the wharf. The last hurricane that blew ashore in Galveston had resulted in devastation. Mace had no desire to return to the dock to see the commission company and its investments lying in tangled heaps. Nor was he thrilled with the possibility of fighting the elements and unseen enemies during their journey.

As the black clouds scraped across the meadow, huge raindrops splattered against the ground. Carefully, Mace set Jake on her feet. "There is an abandoned shack a few miles west. Do you think you can make it?"

Jake forced a courageous smile. "Of course. As I said, it's only a flesh wound."

But once the numbness wore off, the pain in her arm became an agonizing throb. She had never sustained a gunshot wound, and it left her feeling a bit dizzy and nauseous. Blinking through the rain, Jacquelyn stared west, hoping to catch sight of the hut. Every minute that ticked by seemed like an hour. It was as if some unseen force was steadily draining her strength, making it virtually impossible to remain upright in the saddle.

Forcing Jacquelyn into the lead, Mace kept glancing over his shoulder, wondering if the snipers intended to give chase. Had Jake incited the wrath of her assailants? Or had they been surprised by thieves whose intent it had been to lift their coins?

His silent speculations gave way to a muted scowl when Jacquelyn slumped in the saddle. Damned female, she was injured worse than she was willing to admit. Mace jabbed Diego in the flanks, urging him beside the gelding before Jake slid to the ground in an unconscious heap. Leaning out, Mace hooked an arm around Jacquelyn and dragged her onto his lap.

"Just a scratch?" he snorted derisively. "I admire your bravery, but not your foolishness!"

Jacquelyn heard the rumble so close to her ear, but she

wasn't certain if it were Mace's gruff voice or the echo of thunder. A fuzzy haze had crept onto the perimeters of her vision, enshrouding her in a suffocating cloud. Jake didn't know what clever rejoinder she had intended to fling at Mace. But whatever it was, the words died on her lips. Unwillingly, Jacquelyn surrendered to the approaching darkness that accompanied the storm.

Mace muttered a string of curses when Jake's wet head rolled against his shoulder. The carefully woven braid was now a mass of tangles that spilled over his arm. Straining, Mace situated Jake across his thighs and hugged her close.

Blast it, who had taken those shots at them? he wondered as he rode toward the shack. Could it truly have been the two men Jacquelyn had encountered in Galveston? Or had someone trailed her all the way from New Orleans? A vengeful beau perhaps? Or were these hoodlums hired by Anna Marie, the jealous rival? If Jake's problems hadn't arisen from conflicts in New Orleans, how could she have made such bitter enemies in Galveston in such a short time? Giving the matter careful consideration, Mace supposed that was the way it was with a firebrand like Jacquelyn. Men either hated her or adored her. There could be no in-between where she was concerned. Jake was the pure essence of fiery spirit. If she rejected a man, he could easily become jealous and resentful. If she countered an attack, men could easily become humiliated and vindictive. No man appreciated being bested by a woman. It could very well have been the hooligans from the wharf who had trailed Jacquelyn to finish the deed they had begun in the alley. And if someone had hired them, it was anybody's guess who might have been responsible.

Mace winced when he peered down into Jacquelyn's blanched face. It seemed unnatural for her to be lying in his arms like a rag doll. She was usually a bundle of nervous energy seeking release. Damnit, why hadn't she told him she was seriously injured? This was no time to play the martyr!

Casting aside his contemplations, Mace nudged the stallion west, cursing the fact that the sky had opened to dump buckets of rain. Grumbling, Mace paused before the dilapidated hut. Once he dragged Jacquelyn from the saddle, he deposited her on a damp blanket inside the shack. After hobbling the horses beneath the canopy of trees, Mace returned to the hut to survey Jake's wound.

Mace hurriedly unbuttoned her shirt and scowled when he spied the jagged wound that marred her perfect flesh. He knew his eyes shouldn't be lingering on the creamy swells of her breasts when she needed medical attention. But Mace felt like a schoolboy on the threshold of sexual discovery. Fumbling with makeshift bandages, Mace continued to assess Jacquelyn's olive skin, fantasizing about how it would feel to caress those roseate buds with his lips and fingertips. . . .

"Damned lecher," Mace scolded himself as he tore his eyes away to fish into his saddlebag for a bottle of brandy. After employing the whiskey as an antiseptic, Mace helped himself to a drink to steady his hands. He had performed primitive surgery during his service with the Rangers but he suddenly lacked confidence in his abilities. He hated the bastard who'd forced him to take a knife to Jacquelyn's flawless flesh. She would bear a scar, one Mace might have prevented if he hadn't been so busy drooling over this bewitching beauty.

Inhaling a deep breath, Mace poised the knife above her shoulder. Jacquelyn flinched as the blade cut into her flesh to seek out the bullet. Her dark eyes flew open instantaneously and a doleful whimper trickled from her lips. The tormenting look on her face slashed across Mace's heart. Jacquelyn was staring at him without seeing him, as if she were barely cognizant of what

111

transpired, as if she were trapped somewhere just beyond reality. When she collapsed, Mace dragged in another deep breath and sought the bullet that had lodged next to the bone.

The steady drip from the leaking roof continued while Mace attended his patient. Mace swore he had labored for hours to remove the bullet and stitch the wound. When he finally completed his task and covered Jacquelyn, he strolled to the window to stare across the soggy meadow. Torrents of rain still spilled from the sky, transforming the grassy pasture into a swamp. . . .

A disgusted growl erupted from his lips when he realized he had failed to gather firewood before beginning surgery. There were only a few logs in the hearth to ward off the chill. Now it would be difficult to secure dry kindling. And food . . . Mace groaned. He had packed very few supplies since he had intended to take the stage and purchase meals at the roadside inns.

After rifling through his bags, Mace shrugged on his long rain slicker and ventured outside to collect wood, rain-soaked though it was. He had never made it a habit of hunting during a downpour, but he had no intention of forcing Jacquelyn to choke down dry pemmican during her recovery.

By the time Mace returned with a turkey and rabbit, a cold dampness had engulfed the shack. Jacquelyn had yet to rouse, and Mace set about to build a fire. Being a seasoned soldier who was accustomed to small conveniences, Mace prepared a meal and made the best of their meager accommodations. He reminded himself that this dilapidated shack would seem a palace compared to the conditions he and Hub and Raoul had endured six months earlier while they were chasing a Comanche raiding party. Obviously, he was becoming spoiled during his sojourns in civilization. There were worse places to be during a tropical storm, he consoled himself. This leaky shack provided far more protection than they might have found.

Even after delivering several inspirational platitudes to himself, Mace still found himself restlessly pacing the confines of the cabin. God, he wished Jacquelyn would rouse, assuring him that his surgical techniques had saved her life rather than killed her. Listening to her taunt him and attempt to pry out information about his past was better than hearing the drumming of rain and the incessant drip from the roof! But Mace wasn't granted his wish. Jake simply lay there like a corpse while the cloudburst transformed creeks into flooding rivers.

Chapter 7

A burning pain brought Jacquelyn from the depths of sleep. Her tangled lashes fluttered up to see the golden fingers of the fire flickering around the logs. A cloud of smoke hovered over the damp timber and drifted upward from the blackened hearth.

A bemused frown knitted Jacquelyn's brow. Where was she? All she remembered was galloping through the rain, fighting to maintain an upright position on her mount.

"Mace?" Her voice sounded as if it were echoing through a long, winding tunnel.

A darkly handsome face appeared from the leaping shadows. Relief washed over Jake's waxen features when Mace smiled down at her.

"I'm here, little imp," Mace murmured affectionately. "Feeling better?" It had been two days since he had heard her voice. It was sweet music to his ears.

"Worse, I think." She sighed heavily. Her eyes dipped to her throbbing shoulder and she gasped when she noticed the stained bandages lying against her bare skin. The implication put a blush on her otherwise ashen face.

A quiet chuckle resounded in Mace's chest. Gently, he cupped her chin, lifting her gaze to his wry smile. "You needn't be embarrassed. I did what had to be done. The bullet lay against the bone and it had to come out. The Gen'ral would never forgive me if I permitted you to die of blood poisoning."

Jacquelyn jerked her head away. "You removed my shirt!"

"There was no time for modesty," he defended. "Besides, we should be past all that by now. We slept naked together in Galveston." A rakish grin cut dimples in his stubbled cheeks. "And may I say, you have a very lovely body, at least what I have seen of it."

Crimson red flooded up her neck to the roots of her hair. "Doctors are not supposed to take time to leer at their patients' anatomy," she spouted indignantly.

"I'm not a certified physician," Mace reminded her with another roguish grin. "I'm allowed to leer when I confront an enticing patient."

In a huff, Jacquelyn squirmed to her side. A groan burst from her lips when she landed on her tender shoulder. Carefully, Mace turned her back to face him, even when she had her heart set on giving him the silent treatment.

"It's time to change the dressing," Mace declared in a no-nonsense tone.

Jacquelyn clamped her hand over the quilt and raised a determined chin. "I will see to the task myself."

Mace flung the defiant minx a withering glance. "Stop being so childish, Jake."

"Childish?" she parroted, her tone crackling with sarcasm. "You consider it childish if I refuse to disrobe in front of you?"

"Very childish," he insisted as he unclamped her fingers to effortlessly capture her small hand in his callused one. "You know damned well you can't bandage your own arm without bungling the job. And it's not as if I have never seen a woman in the flesh before. . . ."

116

Mace should have carefully formulated his thoughts instead of allowing the words to topple off his tongue. His remark served to make Jake more irritated and humiliated than she already was.

Before Jacquelyn could sputter a nasty rejoinder, the quilt was ripped from her clenched fists. Her face throbbed with color and an outraged gasp erupted from her lips. Shielding herself as best she could with her good arm, Jacquelyn glared poison arrows at Mace's ornery smile.

"Damn you to hell and back, Jonathan Mason!" she spat out.

It took concerted effort not to dwell on the luscious swells that were barely concealed by her arm. Focusing on her shoulder, Mace meticulously unwrapped the bandage to inspect the seeping wound. Twisting around, Mace snatched up the brandy.

"Grit your teeth, sweetheart. This is going to burn like fire."

Sure enough, it did. Jacquelyn bit into her lip until it bled. Flames shot across her shoulder, leaving her lightheaded. Instinctively, her left arm moved toward her right shoulder, as if touching the wound could somehow make the pain go away.

Mace's eyes fell to the full mounds, and then drifted to the trim indention of her waist. When Jake's face turned another shade of red, Mace forced himself to meet her embarrassed gaze. He could have spent the evening admiring her with masculine appreciation, allowing his eyes to traverse her olive skin, memorizing each delicious inch of her.

Inhaling a determined breath, Mace changed the dressing on the wound and then gently replaced the bandage. By the time he completed his ministrations he could list dozens of things he would rather have been doing with his hands. None of them were remotely associated with nursing duties, mind you.

Lord, did Jacquelyn have any idea how difficult it was for him to ignore the bonfire that was raging within him? Did she have the foggiest notion how her bewitching beauty affected a man? Did she realize the incredible willpower required to stare at her without caressing what his eyes beheld?

Jacquelyn's wide brown eyes were glued to Mace's profile, one that was enhanced by firelight and flitting shadows. The shock of having him see her in this state of undress slowly ebbed to be replaced by an emotion Jake labeled as something akin to rejection.

First he had ignored her while they slept together in Galveston, and now this! Her feminine pride was bruised and bleeding. Wasn't a man supposed to be slightly aroused by the sight of a partially naked woman? Or was it just that she in particular didn't stir Jonathan Mason? Wasn't she woman enough to ignite Mace's male desires? He seemed so untouched, so casual about it all. Twice opportunity lay at Mace's feet. He could have reached out to touch her and she would have been too weak and vulnerable to resist him. But did Mace try? Hell no. He hadn't given her the satisfaction of attempting to stop him from making improper advances. She appreciated his respect, but, after a while, his consideration rather resembled an insult!

Damn my ridiculous vanity! Jacquelyn shouted at herself. She had spent twenty years fending off men. Her retribution for refusing other men was to find herself jilted by this cold, unemotional giant. What goes around comes around, Jacquelyn reminded herself philosophically. She was receiving a taste of what she had been dishing out for three years. Her confidence sagged. Confound it, she could probably strip off all her clothes and Mace would be more interested in determining the amount of rain that had gushed from the sky!

118

"Here, drink this. It will ease the pain," Mace ordered.

God, Jacquelyn was gorgeous and this pretended nonchalance was eating him alive! But Mace would be damned if he wallowed at her feet like the rest of her lovestruck admirers who showered her with praise and begged for affection.

Jake dutifully swallowed the brandy. (Yes, dutifully. She was so demolished by his apparent lack of interest that she obeyed without protest.) With fumbling fingers, Mace tucked the quilt beneath Jacquelyn's chin. On legs that felt unsteady, Mace wobbled toward the hearth.

"Do you feel up to some broth? I can't guarantee this weak soup will tantalize your palate, but it is fit for human consumption." Mace mentally congratulated himself for regaining his composure. In truth, he felt like the little boy who attempted to hold back raging flood waters by stuffing his index finger in the hole of a crumbling dam. Sweet mercy, he didn't want to want this appetizing beauty in all the ways he was wanting her, but he did. It was like enduring the worst tortures of hell without permitting himself to scream in pain.

"I suppose I could stomach a little broth," Jacquelyn murmured, deflated. What did it take to melt a man like Mace? Was sex so familiar to him that it required an experienced seductress to even turn this man's head? "That is none of your concern." She answered her own question without realizing she had done more than silently mouth the words.

Mace had ears like a fox. He twisted to peer curiously at the bundle of quilts from which Jacquelyn's head protruded. "What is none of my concern?" Cautiously, he retrieved the steaming pot of soup and dipped out a cupful.

"Nothing," she grumbled grouchily. "I was talking to myself." Not only did she feel as desirable as a wet mop, but she looked like one with this scraggly mane of hair plastered against the sides of her face.

When Mace squatted down on his haunches to tip the cup to her lips, Jake grudgingly permitted his mothering. She might as well, she mused. Mace had no interest in her as a possible lover, even if she openly invited intimacy.

"Men don't appreciate independent women, do they?" Jacquelyn heard herself say.

Mace's brows shot upward and then slid back to their normal arch. "What the devil brought that on?"

Jacquelyn shrugged her good shoulder. "The pain must have numbed my inhibitions. The question just leaped to my tongue."

A low rumble rattled in his massive chest as he tipped the cup back to her lips. "I don't think it fair to blame your lack of inhibition on your pain. Injury may have compounded your candor, but it definitely isn't the cause of it."

Jake pulled a sour face at his teasing remark. She shoved the cup away. "I prefer the brandy," she announced. "At least it doesn't taste like skunk stew!"

"I wouldn't advise—" Mace began, only to be cut off by Jacquelyn's sarcastic sniff.

"Good. I detest being advised. Hand me the damned bottle," she ordered curtly.

Mace sank down to survey Jacquelyn for a long, deliberate moment. "Are you planning to drink to ease the pain or to forget that I didn't take advantage of you when I could have?" he had the gall to ask.

Jacquelyn glared holes in his tight-fitting shirt, and Mace deflected the maiming glower with a beaming smile. "The latter, I think."

"You derive excessive pleasure in humiliating me," she growled as she reached for the bottle, only to have it snatched from her fingertips.

Mace lifted the flask to guzzle a drink. Grinning outrageously, he offered her the liquor she sought . . .

120

but in the most arousing way. The taste of brandy was in his kiss, one that could melt bone and muscle. Jacquelyn swore she would become intoxicated with just one sip. The feel of his sensuous mouth whispering over hers made her ache in places she didn't know she had. She longed for a dozen more kisses, just like the one Mace was bestowing on her. The tension seeped out of her, leaving her warm and trembling inside, leaving her throbbing with forbidden hunger.

No one kissed quite like Mace, she mused in a daze. This raven-haired rogue gave new dimensions to the word. He made her ache for things she didn't understand, things she suddenly wanted to learn from this incredibly appealing man.

When Mace eased away, Jacquelyn was left gasping to restore her heart to a slower pace. Her breathing came in ragged spurts and her blood simmered as if *she* were dangling above the fire instead of the stew.

I shouldn't look down while I'm dangling from this perilous perch, he realized too late. But Mace did look down—down into eyes like melting chocolate. Those spellbinding pools were dark and shimmering with emotion. He had kissed the color back into her lips, lips that were still parted in an invitation he was hard pressed not to accept.

"Believe me, little siren," he rasped hoarsely. "I was tempted to teach you things about yourself that would surprise you. . . ." Slowly, his hand glided down the pulsating column of her throat to tease the peak of her breast through the concealing quilt. "When I look at you, it arouses me far more than it should. I see a very lovely, desirable woman, and with each passing moment it becomes painfully difficult to remember who you are."

Jacquelyn's heart nearly popped out of her chest when Mace's moist lips followed the arousing flight of his hands. But this time, the protective quilt was drawn away without her protest. A shuddering sigh tripped from Jacquelyn's lips when Mace's worshipping kisses touched the unclaimed territory of her quivering flesh. Giddy sensations flowed through her naive body when his tongue flicked at each taut peak. And when his adventurous hand followed the sloping terrain of her breasts to caress the other dusky bud, Jacquelyn melted into a puddle of liquid desire.

His gentle touch was like a tide rolling to shore, lightly drifting over her and then receding. His caresses washed away all that had come before, leaving her craving an end to this maddening ache that burned in the core of her being. Her thick lashes swept up to see his amber eyes radiating down upon her exposed flesh like warm beams of summer sunshine. Entranced, Jacquelyn reached up to trace his commanding features, to follow the dark stubble that lined his jaws. Her untutored hands wandered over the corded tendons of his neck to map the expanse of his chest before dipping beneath the buttons of his shift to arouse and explore.

Emitting a shuddering moan, Mace struggled for self-control. Her gentle touch was driving him mad with wanting. And caressing her was burning him alive. Grimacing at the side effects caused by this tug-of-war of emotions, Mace forced his hands back to his sides instead of permitting them to sail over Jacquelyn's silky skin.

Damnit, he should have himself shot! Jacquelyn was weak and defenseless and he was trying to seduce her, even after he'd resolved to keep his distance. Didn't he possess a smidgen of conscience these days? Jacquelyn was wounded, for heaven's sake! What kind of man took advantage of an injured woman, especially one who had no experience with men? A good-for-nothing, low-down scoundrel, Mace told himself bitterly.

"Go to sleep," Mace demanded, his tone gruff. Frustrated passion was frying him alive. "You need to regain your strength."

Fighting the magnetic field that lured him ever closer, Mace gathered his legs beneath him and marched toward the door. What he needed right now was a walk in the cold rain. Surely it would extinguish the fires that blazed beneath his flesh. If it didn't, he was going to go up in smoke.

"Where are you going?" Jacquelyn questioned, clutching the drooping quilt. She was so rattled by what had transpired between them that the words flooded from her tongue in a stammering rush.

Mace didn't dare look back for fear of reversing direction to finish what he shouldn't have begun in the first place. "I had better check on the horses," he mumbled in excuse.

When the door banged shut behind him, Jacquelyn sagged onto her pallet. Her body felt like putty that had been shaped to fit Mace's masterful hands. Her skin still tingled from his titillating caresses and kisses. A choked sob clogged her throat. She was ashamed of herself for permitting Mace to touch her so familiarly. But even her shame couldn't overshadow that ever-lingering feeling of rejection. Their encounter had only served to assure her that it would take more of a woman than she was to force Mace past the point of no return. He could have done whatever he wished and Jacquelyn wasn't sure she could have stopped him or even wanted to stop him.

Was something in his past restraining him from making love to her? Did he look at her and see another woman's face? Did she resemble some vicious female who had betrayed him? Or was it the fact that she was General Reid's granddaughter that prevented him from seducing her? Or was it as she had first suspected? Mace was simply satisfied with their casual friendship and had no true inclination for them to be as close as two people could get.

123

"Stop analyzing the situation," Jacquelyn scolded herself. "You'll give yourself a headache."

When the aftereffects of Mace's magical touch wore off, Jacquelyn was besieged by exhaustion. She wanted to remain awake, but her eyes kept slamming shut, leaving her to chase her arousing dreams. Finally she slept, unaware that Mace had returned to the shack.

With the silence of a cat, Mace crossed the room to stand beside his pallet. Quietly, he peeled off his soggy clothes and draped them beside the fire. He had been in such a rush to put a safe distance between him and temptation that he had neglected to don his rain slicker. Now he was chilled to the bone.

Once Mace had wiggled into his cocoon of quilts he cursed himself all over again for getting entangled with a virgin—General Reid's granddaughter no less! He should have his head examined. He should have told Jake he wasn't Jonathan Mason. If he had, he wouldn't have found himself sharing a bed and now a secluded cabin with Jacquelyn. Was this ornery prank on Harlan Reid worth this emotional turmoil he was putting himself through? Would it work for or against him in his dealings with the General?

Scowling at himself, Mace closed his eyes and tried not to think of how close he had come to disregarding his common sense. How long did he think he could pretend he didn't ache for this curvaceous vixen? How long would it be before he yielded to the lusting beast within him? Jacquelyn was an impossible temptation. With each encounter, Mace felt another corner of the foundation of his willpower crumbling. The more he dared to take, the more he wanted from Jacquelyn.

"You certainly waded in over your head this time, Gallagher," Mace reprimanded himself. He had wandered into a sea of fire, knowing full well he would be burned, knowing he couldn't resist the lure of enormous

124

brown eyes and a smile that radiated with the brilliance of the sun. Lord, how much more of this celibacy can I endure? he asked himself grimly. Having Jacquelyn so close, learning her moods, wanting her . . . Mace clenched his fist in his quilt and gnashed his teeth. Sweet mercy, just thinking of the pleasure he derived from kissing her, from touching her silky skin, made him ache up to his eyebrows!

"Get hold of yourself," Mace demanded sternly. He was not giving into his primal needs. Jacquelyn was just another woman. He could resist her tantalizing charms and hold himself at bay.

Mace wondered how many times he would have to convince himself of his monumental self-control before his body began believing his brain. It was for damned certain his body and brain were presently working against each other. One was left wanting what the other was struggling to deny.

Heaving a tired sigh, Mace yanked the quilts around his shoulders and pretended he needed nothing more than a decent night's sleep.

Chapter 8

Heavily lidded eyes swept up to survey the gloomy shack. The cloudy dawn provided little light, and the incessant tap of rain still drummed on the roof and seeped through its many cracks. Wincing at the streak of pain that plagued her shoulder, Jacquelyn pushed herself into an upright position and glanced groggily around the cabin. The unexpected crack of thunder caused Jake to flinch. Her abrupt movement initiated another sharp stab of pain and she cursed her carelessness.

Wrapping the quilt around her, Jacquelyn struggled to her feet and ambled toward the warmth of the fire. The second boom of thunder heralded Mace's swift entrance into the shack. His brawny frame filled the portal. Game birds of all sizes dangled from his hand and a condescending frown puckered his brow.

"You shouldn't be up and moving just yet," he scolded her, bypassing a morning greeting.

"I'm fine." To emphasize her declaration, Jacquelyn mustered a sunny smile.

"Of course, you are," Mace grunted, his tone implying he didn't believe her for a minute. "That's why your face is as white as a sheet."

Jacquelyn shrugged recklessly, and then knelt to toss

another rain-soaked log on the dwindling fire. She felt awkward in Mace's presence, especially after what had occurred the previous night. Things were drastically changing between them, and Jacquelyn found it impossible to remain indifferent to a man who had touched her familiarly, who had aroused her feminine desires and left her wanting. . . .

The whistling wind besieged the shack, jostling Jacquelyn from her frustrated musings. It howled through the cracks in the walls like a banshee's doleful wailing. Shafts of piercing silver light stabbed through the shadowy confines of the cabin, pursued by another deafening roll of thunder. It seemed they had yet to endure the brunt of the tropical storm that had blown ashore.

Jacquelyn wasn't terrified of the tornadoes that often accompanied such storms, but she maintained a wary respect for them. Being inside this swaying shack did nothing to ease her apprehension. A grimace settled on her pale features when she glanced out the window to see the trees bowing to the forces of raging winds.

Lord, what if . . . Jake forced herself not to contemplate "what if." It was too unsettling and Mace's presence already had her rattled.

"Come lie down," Mace instructed. "Judging by the look of the sky, we're in for a rough morning."

In swift strides, Mace closed the distance between them and herded Jacquelyn toward their pallets. His morning excursion of hunting had been interrupted by the approach of another threatening bank of clouds, and Mace had beaten a hasty retreat to the hut. The swirling clouds that scraped the meadows indicated turbulent weather. Mace had spent enough days out in devastating storms to know he much preferred a roof over his head, flimsy though it was.

"Storms make me nervous," Jacquelyn felt obliged

to confess.

"I'm not too crazy about them myself," Mace mumbled as he urged Jacquelyn to her pallet and promptly joined her. "I don't wish to alarm you, but this storm looks a mite grisly."

That was not what Jake needed to hear. In most situations she felt in firm control. There were, however, three stumbling blocks in the way of her self-confidence. One was this violent storm; another was the vulnerability provoked by suffering a gunshot wound; and last but hardly least was having this powerfully built man lying beside her. Jacquelyn suddenly felt as nervous as a caged cat, and the roaring wind did nothing to curb her anxiety.

"I need something to chew on," Jacquelyn insisted as she attempted to untangle herself from the quilts.

Mace's strong hand folded around her good arm and a wry smile tugged at one corner of his mouth. "Do you make it a habit of feeding your apprehensions?" His amber eyes focused on her quivering bottom lip—a dead giveaway that her emotions were in turmoil. "Which is it that drives you to eating, having me cuddled up to you or the threat of this storm?"

Jacquelyn didn't want to discuss it, not when she was shaking all over. "What's to eat?" she questioned impatiently.

"I'll see what I can find," Mace offered as he gently pushed her back to the pallet.

When Mace had retrieved the pemmican, Jacquelyn munched silently upon it, fighting the insane need to snuggle up to the warm strength of the man who lay beside her.

Thunder crashed like the roll of a gigantic cymbal, followed by a fierce gust of wind that caused the flimsy shack to shudder and groan. Before Jacquelyn realized what she had done, her good arm fastened around the

129

taut tendons of Mace's neck. Her head buried itself against his sturdy shoulder, and the discarded pemmican lay in the folds of the quilts. She concentrated on the steady thud of Mace's heart, inhaled the manly scent that filled her senses. Her attempt to protect herself from one source of anxiety only served to make her more aware of the other. Jon Mason had a devastating effect on her, one just as unnerving as the storm that threatened to swallow them alive.

When one corner of the roof flapped in the wind, Jacquelyn expelled a startled gasp and plastered her body against Mace's muscled length. She knew the wobbling shack would collapse upon them, that there was nowhere to run. If she were to die, she was going to be transported to a higher sphere—via Mace's comforting arms. There was nowhere she would rather be.

Mace was assaulted by contradicting emotions when Jacquelyn molded her tempting body to his. He hungered to appease a need that had gnawed at him for five days. And yet, he was stung by the premonition that they were about to be engulfed in one of the most devastating storms to besiege the coast. Although driving rain pelleted against the shack like a regiment of soldiers storming the enemy's walls of defense, Mace was far more aware of the ache in his loins. His brain was shouting at him to beware of the swirling winds, but his male instincts were urging him closer, encouraging him to lose himself in distraction.

Jacquelyn nearly leaped out of her skin when a tree branch broke loose and crashed against the far wall, splintering planks. "Kiss me!" she shrieked, pressing herself closer. "And don't stop kissing me until it's over or we perish . . . whichever comes first!"

The impulsive request was hastily given and quickly accepted. Mace levered himself up on one arm to stare down into Jacquelyn's haunted eyes. Her lips trembled, but this time Mace couldn't tell for certain if the noticeable quaking stemmed from fear of the storm or anticipation of his embrace. All he knew was that this bewitching sprite was impossible to resist and he had grown weary of trying to deprive himself of the pleasure he knew she could provide. The previous night had been a foretaste of heaven. And when a man faced a destructive storm that offered no guarantees of survival, he had a tendency to clutch at one moment of pleasure before the world collapsed around him.

Golden eyes burned down upon her animated features. Eagerly, his raven head moved toward her quivering lips. The flash of silver that illuminated the shadows was like a spark igniting a fire. It triggered emotions that both Mace and Jacquelyn had had difficulty holding in check since they met. The tension between them had intensified until it was as taut as a tightly strung cable.

Jacquelyn didn't wait for Mace to come to her; she went to him like a homing pigeon returning to roost. Her mouth opened on his, savoring and devouring the taste of him. Her tangled lashes fluttered down to block out the careening world of wind and rain. She didn't want to think. She didn't want to feel anything except the sinewy warmth of Mace's masculine strength enveloping her. She didn't want to inhale the smell of rain, only the heady fragrance of the man who held her so expertly in his arms.

As his darting tongue probed the recesses of her mouth, Jacquelyn arched closer, concentrating solely on a kiss that sent her heart thudding as loudly as the wind-driven rain. Hailstones pattered against the roof, but Jacquelyn was becoming less conscious of impending doom. Her body was ablaze with a wild longing Mace had instilled in her. She ached to have his skillful hands upon her flesh, to feel the magical fires of caresses that could ward off the deadly storm's chill.

131

Mace was far past contemplating what was right or wrong. His male body was consumed with a monstrous need that refused to be denied. Whatever else happened, he would have satisfied this obsessive craving, this maddening desire to become a part of Jacquelyn's lively spirit, to appease his curiosity and his fantasies. This shapely nymph was the stuff dreams were made of, and Mace yearned to introduce her to the world of sensuous passion before he perished from the earth.

His questing hands possessed a will of their own. They longed to set out upon an intimate journey of discovery that encompassed every titillating inch of Jacquelyn's exquisite body, giving and taking pleasure along the way. Gently, Mace pushed aside the quilt that hindered the flight of his fingertips. A contented sigh toppled from his lips when he felt warm, satiny flesh quivering beneath his exploring touch. His lips abandoned hers to fan the trail of fire that spilled over the slope of her shoulder. His hot kisses discovered the texture of her skin. He suckled at the rigid peaks of her breasts until Jacquelyn moaned in sweet torment.

Vaguely, Mace remembered hearing the roar of the storm, but he was far too entranced by his explorations to care what damage befell the shack. He ached to know this enchanting beauty by touch. He longed to seek out each sensitive point on her delicious body, to bring her sleeping passions to life. He wanted to weave a protective cocoon about them, to submit to their own private storm of desire. He yearned to make Jacquelyn forget there was a world beyond the unending circle of his arms.

Jacquelyn gasped for breath when Mace's bold caresses and kisses skimmed her quaking flesh, sending her heart into triple time. Never had she experienced such a flood of sensations. It was as if a flame had begun to burn deep inside her. It spread into every fiber of her being, consuming her—body, mind, and soul. His skillful touch branded her as it followed the flatness of her stomach. His lips fed the flames that sizzled across her and through her until she was ablaze, inside and out. It seemed Mace had suddenly acquired an extra set of hands. They were roaming everywhere, caressing, teasing, arousing her to unfamiliar plateaus of rapture.

So skillfully had he removed her breeches that Jacquelyn swore the garment had simply fallen apart at the seams. All that covered her naive flesh were practiced hands that glided to and fro, that set off multiple reactions inside her. A moan of total surrender tripped from Jacquelyn's lips as Mace's fingertips skimmed the sensitive flesh of her thighs. Her body involuntarily arched when his teasing caresses receded to track along her hip and ribs and then encircled the thrusting buds of her breasts.

Jacquelyn swore she was dying when his tongue teased the throbbing peaks and his hands flowed downward to retrace their enticing path to her thighs. Her breath lodged in her throat when his probing fingertips aroused her to the limits of sanity. The intimacy of his touch sent her pulse leapfrogging. Breathing was next to impossible when he was doing such incredible things to her body. Jacquelyn yearned to satisfy the maddening craving he had evoked, and yet she wasn't sure anything could appease this ineffable need that engulfed her.

Over and over again, Mace mapped the curvaceous flesh that seemed to melt beneath his inquiring caresses. He adored touching her silken skin, learning what pleasured this innocent maiden. He marveled at the power he held over her, the satisfaction he derived from merely touching her. His eyes toured her luscious body as if he had unwrapped a precious gift. He reveled in the sight and feel of her satiny skin beneath his fingertips.

In the past, lovemaking had been no more than the assuagement of sexual needs. Mace never had much consideration for the woman in his arms. But with Jacquelyn it was a new experience. It was as if he had accepted a tremendous responsibility that had been nonexistent in previous relationships with women. He was not simply taking from Jacquelyn, but he was giving in return. And his giving had become satisfaction in itself. He wanted no regrets when his body took possession of this perfectly formed angel. He wanted this ebony-eyed nymph to want him as wildly and completely as he ached for her.

"Mace . . . ?" Jacquelyn's ragged voice was barely discernible above the roaring storm.

While his hands continued to work their sweet, hypnotic magic, his lips drifted back to make a slow, lazy descent onto hers. "Do you want me to stop what I'm doing to you?" he questioned huskily.

Passion flared in his golden eyes, eyes that were surrounded by thick, black lashes, eyes that could look through her to unlock the precious secrets in her soul. Jacquelyn was spellbound by the rapturous sensations that spilled her, mesmerized by the expression that claimed Mace's ruggedly handsome face.

"I want you, minx," Mace admitted in a seductive growl. "But you have to want me just as much. You have to consent to let me love you in all the glorious ways a man and woman can express their emotions."

The intimate promises of his words and the provocative tone of his voice sent another round of tingling sensations surging through her. Although common sense warned her to reject him, her body cried out to discover where these mystical feelings ultimately led. Denying Mace would be denying herself. She would be left aching with a need that would never know fulfillment.

Jacquelyn reached up to comb her fingers through the ruffled coal-black hair that framed his craggy face. A quiet moan echoed beneath her breasts as his straying hand stroked and aroused. Her eyes darkened with unmistakable desire as she focused on his full lips. "Love me, Mace. . . . I want you. . . ." she whispered brokenly.

Her body trembled with anticipation when Mace braced his arms beside her and lowered himself to her. She felt the velvet warmth of him against her before the haze of pleasure split asunder. Another kind of pain stabbed through the trancelike dream that cradled her. Jacquelyn instinctively braced her good hand against Mace's hair-roughened chest, holding him at bay when he would have swallowed her in his hard, masculine strength.

Reluctantly, Mace raised his head to peer into her lovely face. Her brown eyes were filled with unanswered questions. Mace knew he could easily destroy the trust Jacquelyn had placed in him. And yet, he couldn't stop now, not when frustrated passion demanded release. With deliberate gentleness, Mace bent to brush his lips over hers while he slowly glided over her quaking body. Carefully, he came to her, taking care not to hurt her. His tongue probed into her mouth as he moved against her, gradually luring her over the hurdle of initiation.

A warm tide of rapture crested upon Jacquelyn. She could feel herself slipping deeper into Mace's wondrous spell of lovemaking. He was making her want him, despite the initial pain. She could feel his muscular body brushing provocatively against hers. He was weaving a web of silken pleasure that rivaled nothing she had experienced. He had become the flame that burned within her—intensifying, engulfing, consuming her.

Jacquelyn heard Mace's muffled groan against her cheek and felt the sound vibrate in his devouring kiss. Her arm tightened about him, her fingertips digging into the whipcord muscles of his back. Breathlessly, she clung to him as he drove into her, sending her soaring on a wild, dizzying orbit through time and space. Even the roar of the storm could not match the whirlwind of sensations that assaulted her while she sailed in motionless flight. The sweet pleasure built into a soul-shattering crescendo that left Jacquelyn wondering if she would survive. She was oblivious to the pain in her shoulder, mindless of the howling gale that snapped gigantic tree limbs and sent them crashing into the soggy ground. Mace had touched each and every one of her emotions, magnifying them until she could not think past this glorious moment of ecstasy.

Her astonished gasp mingled with the angry winds that raged outside the shack. Mace thrust against her, over and over again, striving to satisfy their breathless need for each other. He couldn't seem to get close enough to the craving that obsessed him. And then suddenly, passion spilled from him like flood waters churning down a river channel. Wave upon wave of numbing pleasure swamped and buffeted him until his mind and body were bathed in indescribable ecstasy. . . .

When the storm unleashed its full fury on the shack, it took Mace a moment to respond to imminent danger. He felt as if he were moving in slow motion. But there was no place to hide from the cyclonic winds that sucked at the rafters and caved in the far wall. Mace grabbed the nearby table and dragged it over them, certain the flapping hut was about to avalanche upon them. He could feel Jacquelyn clutching at him and they clung together, awaiting their destiny.

In that frantic moment that held them suspended between life and death, Mace bore no resentment. He was in the circle of an angel's arms, awaiting the arrival of a heavenly chariot . . . at least he hoped his ultimate destination would be up, as opposed to down.

Timbers strained and cracked beneath the pressure of the churning winds. Debris scattered hither and yon.

Jacquelyn squeezed her eyes shut and prepared herself to face her final moments of life. Her knuckle clenched against Mace's arm. Gritting her teeth, she waited for the dark silence to engulf her.

The deafening roar did recede, but only into the distance. The calm that followed the storm was interrupted by the light patter of raindrops on what was left of the demolished shack. Gloomy daylight spilled through the wide opening in the roof and wall, but Jake was reasonably certain she was still alive. She could feel Mace's warm length upon her, feel his hair-matted flesh clinging to her quivering skin. The thought brought a quick rise of color to her cheeks. Mace was still lying intimately above her, shielding her from the fallen debris.

One dark brow elevated when Mace noticed the embarrassed flush on her face. Dragging his eyes from the expression of coy innocence, Mace surveyed the damage of the tornadic winds. The path of the storm had obviously tracked close to their abode. If it had raged directly above them, Mace doubted they would have been there at all.

When Mace rolled away to prevent crushing her and causing more pain to her mending wound, Jacquelyn nervously chewed on her bottom lip. She felt awkward and self-conscious. "Am I supposed to say something after we—"

Mace's explosive laugh cracked the silence. This naive little imp was a constant source of amusement and pleasure. (When she wasn't driving him crazy with her impulsive antics, that is.) "No, actually, I think we pretty much said it all without voicing a single word." He chortled as he helped himself to another honeyed kiss. Lord, how quickly he had become addicted to the taste of this vivacious elf.

A radiant smile blossomed on Jacquelyn's face.

Guilelessly, she stared into those twinkling amber eyes. "Do you know, I was under the impression that sex was a rather distasteful experience women were supposed to endure. . . ."

Another irrepressible gurgle of laughter sliced the silence. "Who the devil told you that?"

"Aunt Florence," she replied as her eyes traveled across the broad expanse of his chest and drifted down to his tapered waist. "She said a dutiful wife was to submit to her husband's demands, even if she would prefer to sleep the night away." A muddled frown knitted Jacquelyn's brow. "Why would she lie to me?"

A roguish smile pursed Mace's lips as he unfolded himself to fetch his discarded breeches. Jacquelyn studied the unhindered view of bronzed skin and steel-hard muscles and then blushed two more shades of red. Damn her shameless soul for staring at him. But it was impossible not to gawk at the man's well-sculptured physique. He was built like a Roman god!

"For some women, sex is no more than dutiful obligation. For others, it is the fulfillment of life's most wondrous pleasure. That is what separates sex from lovemaking. You might not find the encounter satisfactory if you were in another man's arms," he had the audacity to tell her.

They had been getting along just fine until Mace made that remark. His arrogance rubbed Jacquelyn the wrong way. Did he think he was God's gift to woman and that she should be thanking him for stealing her virginity? Well, perhaps lovemaking would not be so magical with another man. She couldn't say for certain, having never slept with anyone else of the male persuasion. But she would rather die than blurt out a compliment to a man who had just patted himself on the back! The haughty ogre.

"Sex is sex," Jacquelyn declared in a matter-of-fact

138

tone. "I hardly think you deserve all the credit. Indeed, I would hazard a guess that there are at least a dozen men of my acquaintance who could provide satisfactory results."

Mace fastened himself into his breeches and then wheeled around to glare at her ridiculing smile. Damn her hide. She didn't know how careful, how loving he had been with her. It didn't have to be that way. If she knew the difference, she wouldn't have made those ludicrous remarks. Lovemaking and sex were two entirely different matters. Unfortunately, Jake was too innocent of men to understand. "I suppose you plan to do some experimental bed-hopping to determine if your theory proves correct," he snorted, wondering why he was so upset by the possibility of sending this feisty minx into another man's bed. It had never bothered him when the other women in his life wound up with other men. Why was this minx so confoundedly different from the others?

"I might," Jake commented as she made a one-armed attempt to shrug on her clothes. "Men don't bat an eye at hopping from one bed to another. Women deserve the same privilege. I found lovemaking to be . . . enjoyable . . ." Jacquelyn was cautious not to ply him with superlative compliments. Mace's male pride was over-inflated enough as it was. "But who is to say I won't find more pleasure in someone else's arms?" Let him stuff that possibility in his cheroot and smoke it, she thought spitefully.

Damn that ornery minx! She could cut his male pride to pieces with her goading remarks. If anyone was going to teach Jake the numerous skills involved in love-making, it was going to be him! She was not going to gallivant about the countryside (or whatever was left of it after this destructive storm) polishing techniques *he* had taught her! And how dare she even suggest cavorting with other men in the first place! The General would have

139

a seizure if he knew Jake was experimenting with love to broaden the scope of her horizons.

Stalking forward, Mace took up the chore of fastening the buttons on Jake's clean shirt. None too gently did he press her injured arm against her ribs and tie her into a sling. "You'll get yourself into trouble if you attempt to pursue this ridiculous theory of yours," he growled into her face.

Jacquelyn was sure Mace had a full set of teeth. She had seen all of them when he practically bit her head off. But his surly demeanor didn't faze her. Jacquelyn was delighting in getting Mace's goat. Usually he was the one who was calm and nonchalant, but suddenly he was bulging at the seams. It was a refreshing change.

"What happened between us just happened," she said sensibly. "Our emotions were in turmoil and we were countering the threat of the storm by preoccupying ourselves. I expect nothing from you because of what transpired between us. And you can expect nothing of me. I am hardly inclined to run to the Gen'ral, crying that I have been deflowered, demanding marriage because of what occurred in a reckless moment."

Mace visualized, and quite vividly, how this sassy hellion would look with her swanlike throat clamped in a necklace of clenched fingers—his. The women in Mace's past had showered him with flowery compliments in the aftermath of love. They'd hinted at permanence and maneuvered to entrap him, but he had become as slippery as an eel. Now this sable-haired misfit was shrugging off their tête-à-tête as if it were nothing special. Well, it was, damnit, only she hadn't been around enough to know it!

Nonplussed, Mace stood as stiff as a rail. He opened and closed his mouth like the damper of a chimney, but no words came out. Satisfied that she had managed to leave Mace speechless, Jacquelyn ambled over to the door to inspect the damage. When she exited, he expelled the breath he had been holding in an exasperated rush. Mace was beginning to sympathize with General Reid. That shapely hoyden could turn a man inside out so quickly he was at a loss to counter her sharp remarks. Mace was left chomping on thoughts he was unable to put into words before Jake breezed off like a cyclone. Damn her! What she needed was an iron-willed man to keep her toeing the mark. But it would take a courageous man to control that feisty sprite, a man who possessed relentless determination, a headstrong, domineering man who refused to give in to her, even when it would be easier just to let her have her way.

It was most fortunate for that saucy termagant that Mace Gallagher wasn't the marrying kind or he would have wed Jake just for spite. Jacquelyn Reid would quickly learn who wore the breeches in their marriage! Why, within two months he would have that she-cat purring like a kitten.

Humming that confident tune, Mace stepped outside to see that he wasn't the only one upended up a tempest. Oak and pine trees that had once towered into the sky were now gnarled and twisted and sprawled on the ground. Grass that once stood knee high was flattened against the soupy earth. To make matters worse, the horses had galloped off to only God knew where.

After barking a gruff order for Jake to stay put, Mace stalked off to locate the horses. It took two hours to round up the frightened mounts and return to the shack. Mace was sure he would be in better control of his emotions by the time he faced that frustrating female again. But he thought wrong. The split second before he entered the hut he was still entertaining the thought of grabbing her and shaking her until her teeth rattled. But when Jacquelyn turned to present him with a greeting smile, Mace couldn't remember what had put him in a snit. One look at that curvaceous seductress and Mace

141

recalled all the remarkable sensations that had spilled through him earlier that morning. He was back to wanting her in the worst way, even when he knew it would be suicide to become emotionally involved with Jake. *To become?* Mace grudgingly laughed at his poor choice of words. He was already involved with that minx and it would require surgery to remove her memory from his mind!

Chapter 9

The last rays of hazy sunlight splintered from the puffy clouds that loomed on the horizon as the weary travelers plodded through the mud to reach the roadside inn. Jacquelyn was exhausted from the ride and the nagging pain in her shoulder. Although Mace had protested against traveling at all, Jacquelyn was driven by the insatiable urge to reach home as soon as possible. But by the end of the day she regretted her foolish decision to trek cross-country when she lacked her usual stamina. When Mace pulled her from the saddle and laid a supporting arm around her, she made no protest.

"I told you so," Mace muttered into her peaked face. "If you suffer a relapse you have no one to blame but yourself."

Jacquelyn, too weary to argue, breathed a heavy sigh and massaged her aching arm. "Be sure to have those words etched on my tombstone in the event of my death," she insisted flippantly. "I know you'll want them to stand over me for all eternity."

Mace rolled his eyes skyward. What had he said that afternoon about taking this stubborn minx in hand? Famous last words, he thought sourly. He had allowed Jake to persuade him to travel when he knew damned good and well she needed rest. But would she listen to reason? Hell no! This ebony-eyed wildcat had pulled herself into the saddle and announced she was leaving the collapsed shack. She had further decreed that Mace could accompany her or remain behind in that dilapidated hut. The choice was his.

Mace shepherded Jacquelyn upstairs, practically carrying her when her legs folded up like an accordion and the color seeped from her hollowed features. Mace scowled disgustedly as he eased Jake onto the bed. "This time you are going to do exactly what I tell you, woman!" he all but shouted at her.

Jacquelyn, undaunted by his tirade intended to establish male supremacy, stretched out on the lumpy mattress. "Whatever you say your highness," she murmured in mock obedience. She didn't possess the strength to do anything except collapse, so it was relatively simple to follow Mace's barked orders. Indeed, resting was what she had planned to do anyway.

"I want you to stay put," Mace demanded as he shook a lean finger in her face. "I'll fetch some food from the tavern. And if you are not flat on your back when I return, I'm tying you to the cussed bedpost! Do you hear me, Jake?"

"Who can't?" She smirked after his booming voice completed its second orbit around the walls. "I'm wounded, not deaf." The tiniest hint of a smile tugged at her pale lips as she watched Mace stamp across the modestly furnished quarters to retrieve his razor. Had he counted on locating a female to occupy his evening? she wondered. Shaving was not a prerequisite for eating. Why else would he bother with the task unless he had intentions of tomcatting? "If you find a wench to appease your male appetite, be sure to rent an extra room. There isn't space for three of us in this narrow bed."

"I ought to tumble some wench," Mace grumbled

144

spitefully. "Since you have declared that variety is the spice of life, I ought to let you lie here and mildew while I follow your theory."

Thoughtfully, Jacquelyn surveyed Mace while he shaved the stubble from his face and struggled with the cleft in his chin. It would never do to permit a man like Mace to know she cared about him. It would kill her to have him learn their first encounter had tugged on the strings of her heart. Jacquelyn prided herself in being honest and straightforward. But when it came to expressing her private emotions, it was an altogether different matter. Her head bade her to be cautious. She wanted Mace to feel something special for her, but choking him with possessive demands would never accomplish anything. Mace had to come to her on his own accord and without reservations. Jacquelyn would never settle for tying any man to her if he couldn't return her affection.

"It is my firm conviction that every individual should be entitled to his own choices," she said with a yawn. Did she sound casual enough? She certainly hoped so. It would never do to have Mace think she cared one way or another about his dalliances with other women. "Never let it be said that I approve or disapprove of your actions. If you want another woman I certainly see no reason why you shouldn't have one. After all, we have made no commitment to each other."

Jacquelyn tossed Mace a fleeting glance, surprised to see that his back was as rigid as a fence post. "I intend to follow the same policy," she went on to say. "Indeed, I don't know why I've kept men at an arm's length all these years. They are capable of providing pleasures I have foolishly denied myself."

Mace jerked his head around so quickly that he nearly sliced a second cleft in his chin with his razor. Swearing under his breath, he pressed his index finger to the wound to stop the bleeding. Jacquelyn's remark sounded like something *he* would have said to some clinging female who had ideas about limiting his encounters with other women. Gnashing his teeth in irritation, Mace completed the task of shaving and then stuffed his arms into a fresh shirt. When he turned back to fling Jake the snide remark that waited on the tip of his tongue she was sound asleep.

Damnit, why was he so exasperated? He thrived on unbounded freedom. Indeed, he wanted it no other way. So why was he so frustrated when this feisty female graciously suggested that he do whatever he pleased with whomever he pleased? She was showing him the door, making absolutely no demands on him. What man could ask for more?

She could have at least acted a mite jealous, Mace thought sourly. Did he mean so little to her that she didn't give a fig what he did? Was his illogical fascination for this elusive beauty one-sided? Now wouldn't that be the crowning glory, Mace mused as he strided down the hall. What if he found himself falling in love with a woman who didn't want him, one who couldn't return his affection . . . if in fact he felt anything for her . . .

"Stop all this hypothetical nonsense," Mace growled at himself. He had agreed to escort this fiery vixen home in hopes of softening the General's attitude toward him. All he had wanted was Jake's respect, the opportunity to get to know her before Harlan could turn her against the idea of a merger and against Mace Gallagher himself.

Okay, so they had become intimate in a reckless moment when they feared the world was about to disintegrate. There would be no repercussions to hound him. Jacquelyn had taken their encounter in stride, reading nothing into it that wasn't there. As a matter of fact, she took it a little too well, his male pride resentfully reminded him. He was the one who had made more of the

146

moment than Jacquelyn had!

The instant Mace ambled into the adjoining tavern, he shoved his rambling thoughts aside. The most efficient way to forget the frustrations caused by one female was to locate another. And it didn't take Mace long to do just that. The moment he approached a vacant table and parked himself in a chair, a voluptuous blond was hovering over him.

Mace had passed this way on numerous occasions during his journeys from his plantation to the customs house in Galveston. And more than once he had found this particular wench eager to accommodate him. But to Mace's disgust he was instantly comparing the buxom blonde to the feisty, dark-haired beauty who was asleep in his room.

Women were women, Mace reminded himself cynically. They served their purpose in a man's life. Just because Tess Harrington's lips weren't as soft and inviting as Jake's was no reason not to engage them in a kiss. Just because Tess was showing signs of losing her youthful figure did not mean she wasn't a skillful lover. So what if Tess's pale blue eyes didn't possess the living fire that flamed in those fathomless pools of ebony?

It was better that way, Mace assured himself. Jake's eyes could easily entrance him while Tess's did not. Tess was safe and Mace felt no attachment to her. But Jacquelyn Reid was a dangerous breed of woman who defied the norm. If Mace knew what was good for him he would avoid Jake like the plague. There was no reason for him to feel the slightest twinge of guilt about dallying with Tess. Jake had encouraged him, Mace recalled with unfamiliar bitterness. She had made their affair seem so . . . so meaningless.

Confound that woman! She didn't give a whit about him. She may as well have said so because she was damned sure thinking it. He saw her thinking it!

Mace swallowed his second drink and cast Tess a speculative glance. Damnation, it galled him that Jake's parting remark still stuck like a barb. "If you want another woman I see no reason why you shouldn't have one," she had said unemotionally. But that didn't rankle him as much as her final comment about sampling other men's charms when she was back on her feet. Hell, she was casting Mace off like a worn shirt! Him! Mace Gallagher, for Chrissake! Jacquelyn had somehow managed to exchange roles with him, uttering declarations that should have come from *his* mouth. Mace wasn't comfortable with his new role of the man shunned. His male pride was still smarting from swallowing a dose of the medicine he was accustomed to spooning out to the women in his life.

Muttering an inventive string of obscenities, Mace inbibed two more drinks to take the edge off his irritation. But the longer he sat there, the more annoyed he became. He should vent his irritation by attempting to make that wild-spirited tigress fall in love with him. That should be a new experience for her. Jacquelyn was accustomed to trampling all over men's hearts. She should learn how it felt to have her heart stomped on as if it were a doormat. And besides, if Mace won Jacquelyn's affection, she would be less likely to be influenced by Harlan Reid. She might even persuade the old buzzard to agree to a merger. With the General's influence and Mace's ability to manage business they could monopolize imports and exports and bolster the economy of Texas.

The young state could use all the help it could get. Since Texas had entered the Union as a slave state, the North was up in arms because the South held the majority of power. The clash between free and slave state sent threats of secession undulating through the country. The South was outraged over the North's constant propaganda against slavery. At present the boundaries of Texas stretched along the Rio Grande to Sante Fe. The federal government was studying the proposal of creating a free state from New Mexico Territory, one that included land claimed by Texas. And Texas was being tugged on by political and economical unrest. Mace longed to bring his adopted homeland credibility and peace. If Texas were to battle Indians and Mexicans, not to mention the turmoil of having its boundaries annexed by future states, its citizens needed to band together once again to regain strength. Mace felt he had done his share to solidify the state. He had extended credit to his clients and friends, hoping to hoist them back on their feet. The merger with the Reid Commission Company could double his abilities and power for the good of the state and its citizens. . . .

A heavy sigh escaped Mace's lips. Gorging himself with brandy and mulling over two of the most exasperating issues known to man—politics and women—was idiocy. Already he couldn't think clearly, and he was wading into deep topics which, contemplated separately, were enough to boggle the mind. He should stick to cotton and leave politics to Governor Wood and Senator Sam Houston. He should also ignore the hellion who was sleeping in his bed by distracting himself. He needed to accompany Tess Harrington to her cottage and forget the complex world even existed.

Mace only had to look as if he were interested and Tess sashayed back to him, wearing a willing smile. Unfolding himself from the chair, Mace slipped his arm around Tess's waist and propelled her toward the door. In an hour, Mace wouldn't even remember what that ebony-eyed, wild-haired temptress looked like. Visions of a shapely blonde would be swimming in his head. Tess could cure this insane craving for Jake, Mace consoled himself. After he spent some time with another woman he could see Jacquelyn Reid in the proper perspective.

149

She meant nothing to him, nothing at all!

Jacquelyn was jostled from her sleep by loud voices in the hall. It sounded as if a herd of drunken elephants had come clomping into the inn. When the disturbing noise died down, Jacquelyn threw her legs over the edge of the bed and glanced around the dark room. Her rumbling stomach provoked her to question Mace's whereabouts. He had promised to return, bearing food and drink, but there was no sign of nourishment awaiting her.

The inconsiderate lout, she grumbled crossly. Mace's tardiness had become her pet peeve. She might never be able to earn the man's affection, but she would teach him a thing or two about proper regard for punctuality and about promises made to be kept!

Pulling her sling into place, Jacquelyn arose to run a quick comb through the mass of tangled tendrils. Inhaling a deep breath, Jacquelyn marched through the hall to locate the tavern. It was her misfortune to step outside just as Mace and his paramour were strolling toward one of the dozen cottages in the small rural community.

Jacquelyn had pretended nonchalance in Mace's presence, but viewing his indiscretion cut her to the quick. She was stung by the impulsive urge to stamp over and unload her pistol at Mace's chest for cavorting with another woman, even if she had been the one to suggest it. But blast it, she hadn't truly meant what she said! She had only tried to protect her pride, hoping to project an image that suggested she was just as much the rogue as he was. Apparently her strategy hadn't worked worth a whit. It was obvious that Mace liked women—the more the better. Jacquelyn was hurt to see Mace with the comely blonde. The sight provoked a peculiar ache in the pit of her stomach, one that was already tied in knots from lack

150

of food—and that was Mace's fault too!

Hastily, her eyes darted about her, eager to latch on to a man—any man. Her gaze landed on the man who had swung from his steed to quench his thirst in the tavern. A wide-brimmed sombrero hid his features and a colorful serape concealed his physique. A bandoleer, brimming with ammunition, was draped across his wide chest, giving him a rather formidable appearance. But Jake didn't have time to be particular. She needed a man and quickly. With determined strides, Jacquelyn closed the distance between them. Upon offering a greeting, one loud enough to catch Mace's attention before he locked himself in the cottage with his consort, Jacquelyn plunged into a conversation.

The gas lantern that illuminated the entrance of the tavern provided enough light to set the stage, just as Jake hoped it would. The man she had randomly selected for a companion seemed well acquainted with the tactic of picking up stray women. In an instant he was offering suggestive overtures that would have earned him a slap on the cheek if Jake hadn't required his assistance in this ploy.

Jacquelyn voiced no protest when Gilbert Davis stole his arm around her waist and broke into a leering smile. Indeed, she wanted Mace to see for himself that she had no aversion to cavorting with other men. She would rather suffer a beating than allow Mace to know she was jealous. That would be like aiding and abetting one's enemy!

Gil had not expected to find such a curvaceous beauty when he stopped over on his long day's ride. He had planned to continue on to Galveston to meet with his associate before pleasuring himself. But this dark-eyed minx was much too atractive to dismiss.

While Jacquelyn permitted Gil to wrap her in his arms and fielded his questions about her injured shoulder,

Mace stood silently seething. The gas lantern bathed the entangled couple in golden light, and Mace watched with mounting irritation as Gil planted a kiss on Jacquelyn's lips. Gil's hands were never still for a moment. They were wandering along Jake's waist and venturing along her ribs. . . .

"Mace? Aren't you coming inside?" Tess questioned as she surveyed his rigid stance. To her amazement, Mace reversed direction and left her standing on the stoop.

Jacquelyn endured Gil's ravishing kiss and the flight of his adventurous hands for about as long as she could stand. The shaggy-haired hombre, though mildly appealing to the eye, did not possess Mace's unique brand of gentleness. It annoyed Jake to realize she was making comparisons. She never had before. But nothing had been the same since she'd crossed paths with Mace.

"Let her go," Mace growled threateningly.

The rumbling purr in Mace's voice startled Jacquelyn. There was a deadly undertone she had never noticed on the occasions she had stirred Mace to anger. Gil slowly raised his head to glare at the intruder. His body tensed when he met Mace's glittering gold eyes and menacing sneer. But Gil was not a man to be cowed by verbal threats. Boldly, he laid his left arm around Jacquelyn's shoulder. His right hand hovered just above the revolver that hung on his hip.

"The lady doesn't seem to have any complaints, *amigo*. I don't know why you think you should," he taunted.

"Because she's with me," Mace bit off, uncertain which one of them aggravated him the most at the moment, the rugged hombre or the troublesome minx.

A mocking smile dangled from the corner of Gil's mouth. "Not any more she isn't."

Jacquelyn was not the type of woman who stood aside when two rutting stags were about to do battle. But the venomous snarl on Mace's face held her frozen to the spot. She was seeing the dangerous, almost inhuman side of Mace for the first time in their acquaintance. It was as if the sophisticated veneer had warped to reveal the savage virility beneath it. Jacquelyn had learned nothing about Mace's past, but intuition told her this brawny mass of masculinity could handle himself in the face of adversity. There was a strange calmness about Mace, one that suggested he had tested himself to the limits of his abilities. He hadn't batted an eye at reinforcing his threats with drastic actions.

The tension was so thick it could have been stirred with a stick. Jacquelyn could feel the tautness of Gil's body as it brushed against hers. Out of the corner of her eyes, she detected the slight movement of Gil's gun hand. Instinctively, she elbowed him in the midsection and then wondered why she had bothered to come to Mace's defense. He certainly didn't need her assistance.

Jacquelyn's jaw fell when Mace came uncoiled like a raven-haired rattlesnake. She wasn't sure she could believe what she thought she saw with her eyes. Indeed, it required more time to formulate the thought of what Mace had done than for him to accomplish the incredible feat. He moved faster than a disembodied spirit! she mused in astonishment.

Never in her life had she seen a man display such lightning-swift efficiency when disarming his worthy competitor. Mace's booted foot struck Gil's holster, causing the pistol to twirl over Gil's knuckles. In that split second, while the Colt was skidding across the dirt, Mace's leg recoiled. Simultaneously, Mace snatched his Bowie knife from its sheath. Before Gil could react, or even think to retrieve the fallen pistol, Mace had sliced the neck of Gil's serape and laid the blade to his throat.

Jacquelyn's eyes bulged from their sockets and her mouth gaped open wide enough for a covey of quail to nest. Good gawd! How could Mace move so quickly? The

153

entire motion had been a blur and the fight was over before it began. Mace Gallagher was not what he seemed. If he were an ordinary man, she was Cleopatra, Queen of Egypt!

Gil Davis prided himself in his quick draw, but he'd never had the opportunity to display his expertise. The Colt went sailing from his fingers before he could grasp it. His astonished gaze fell to the cold steel blade that lay beside his jugular vein.

While Gil stood staring incredulously, Mace roughly yanked Jacquelyn to his side. "Like I said, *amigo*, the lady is with me." The words rolled off his tongue in a slow, deliberate drawl that anticipated no further argument.

Placing Jacquelyn behind him, Mace backed away, his eyes intently focused on Gil's right hand—the one that knotted and uncurled indecisively. Mace didn't dare turn his back on his challenger until he had herded Jacquelyn into the inn. There was no telling how many weapons Gil was carrying under tha concealing serape, and Mace was not about to present the hombre with the opportunity of retrieving another pistol or knife.

Before Jacquelyn could fire the barrage of questions that flocked to her tongue, Mace shoved her toward the steps. After rapping out the order for the proprietor to fetch food from the tavern, Mace prodded Jacquelyn up the stairs to their room.

"Where did you learn to fight like that?" she demanded to know after the door slammed shut behind them.

"Like what?" Mace questioned in mock innocence.

Jacquelyn tossed him a withering glance. "Why don't you just tell me it's none of my business if you don't want me to know," she said, pouting.

An ornery smile pursed Mace's lips. "It's none of your business." The grin evaporated as quickly as it appeared. With narrowed eyes, Mace indicated the chair, silently demanding that Jake plant herself in it. "I hope you are satisfied with yourself, minx." His annoyed gaze drilled into her and there was a distinctly unpleasant edge on his voice. "Had you intended to include rape on your list of misadventures with men?"

Jacquelyn puffed up with indignation and her chin tilted to that defiant angle Mace had come to recognize at a glance. "I didn't ask you to interrupt us," she snapped. "I am perfectly capable of fending for myself."

"Of course you are." Mace smirked sarcastically.

Jacquelyn was already beginning to detest that mocking rejoinder. Mace could take a harmless comment and transform it into a needling jibe with the merest fluctutation of his voice.

"If I need saving I'll let you know. Until then, I will thank you to keep your nose out of my affairs."

One thick brow arched over his laughing golden eyes. "Is that what you intended to have with whoever-the-hell-he-was?" Mace frowned curiously. "What's his name anyway?"

A sheepish blush tainted her features. "Actually, I hadn't gotten around to asking that particular question."

Mace dropped into his chair and nodded thoughtfully. "Ah yes, I forgot. Your first question is whether a man enjoys female companionship. Once you have established his preference you proceed accordingly."

His taunting tone caused Jake to stiffen like an arched-backed cat. "I haven't ridiculed you for carousing with that blonde-haired strumpet who was wrapped around you like a twining vine," she sniped. "You handle your affairs your way and I'll take care of mine!" Jake had only begun her tirade, anxious to air the frustration of this ill-founded jealousy. But before she could let loose with both barrels, Mace stalked toward her, casting his ominous shadow upon her.

It infuriated Mace that this shapely hellion had spoiled

155

what would have been a much-needed distraction. But what irked him most was knowing Jacquelyn would have been experiencing the same diversion. Confound her. How could he have enjoyed Tess's company, knowing Jake was doing the same thing with someone else?

"For a woman who claims to have duelled a man for attempting to take intimate privileges, you have certainly turned over a new leaf!" Mace grumbled bitterly.

Undaunted, Jake flung him a goading smile. "Perhaps I was a harlot in another lifetime and I only just realized it." She was delighting in watching Mace grind his teeth in annoyance. Usually, he had complete control of himself. Now that she had located a raw nerve she intended to prey upon it. "You may have been my first experience with passion, but surely you aren't so arrogant to think you will be the last."

Mace's fingers involuntarily curled, itching to squeeze the stuffing out of her. Jacquelyn kept his emotions in constant turmoil. He was perpetually tossed back and forth between anger, amusement, frustration, and desire. Jake was so unpredictable that Mace never knew which sensation would inflame him until the moment was upon him. His even disposition and his long-fused temper had been twisted and stretched until they were dangerously close to snapping.

The rap at the door interrupted Mace's vindictive thoughts, and he glared at the portal before leveling Jake a glower that was meant to maim. "Troublesome wench, I'd like to choke you within an inch of your life," he muttered spitefully as he sidestepped to grasp the latch. "Be warned. All that saved you this time was the arrival of our meal."

"Oh, thank you for sparing me," Jacquelyn breathed, clutching her bosom as if overcome by relief. "I shall be forever grateful that someone has brought food for you to chew on instead of me."

Mace grumbled several unprintable curses before swinging open the door. Did nothing rattle this daring vixen? Lord-a-mercy, it was a wonder the General had kept his sanity during his granddaughter's upbringing. This misfit could drive a sane man mad with her rapier tongue and her unpredictable shenanigans.

Biting back a mischievous grin, Jake watched Mace stab his steak and slice it into bite-sized pieces. No doubt he was visualizing her body lying on his plate. He was the fire-breathing dragon who gobbled his victim alive. The comparison evoked Jake's irrepressible snicker.

Mace glared flaming arrows at her impish grin. "What's so damned funny?" he demanded to know.

Her good shoulder lifted and dropped evasively, and Mace resorted to counting to ten to control his temper. He was allowing this termagant to creep beneath his skin, even when he knew the hazards of being too conscious of all she said and did. Jake was toying with him, just as she preyed on her staunch grandfather. This minx was relentless. She pushed and pulled until a man finally threw up his hands in exasperation. Making demands on this dark-eyed hoyden accomplished nothing, Mace reminded himself. Jake had spent a lifetime countering the General's iron will and she was an expert at defying forceful commands. Armed with that knowledge, Mace decided to try a different approach, one to which Jake had yet to develop a countertactic.

Deliberately, he rose from the table and walked around to assist Jacquelyn from her chair. A wary frown knitted her brow. All of a sudden, Mace was calm and composed. The feathers she had ruffled minutes before had resettled into place and she was left to deal with that part of his personality she wasn't sure she could handle.

"What are you doing?" she queried as his patient hands traced her finely etched features.

Without pausing to respond, Mace sketched her

157

perfectly arched brows, her elegant cheekbones, and her heart-shaped lips. His eyes held her hostage while his roaming hands, ever so slowly, glided down the swanlike column of her neck. Avoiding her tender shoulder, Mace's light caress traced her collarbone, and then ventured across the swell of her breasts. He saw her bottom lip quiver the way it always did when he had awakened her desire. It was a sure sign that he had crumbled her defenses to unlock emotions that were still wildly unfamiliar to her.

Jacquelyn flinched when his roaming hands teased and aroused. Danger she could face without buckling beneath paralyzing fear. Groping men she could control without difficulty. But Jacquelyn's self-preservation instincts were thrown into a turmoil when Mace assaulted her with such persuasive tenderness.

A tiny gasp of pleasure shattered the silence when his fingertips caressed the taut peaks of her breasts. She could feel the knot of desire uncoiling deep inside, expanding and swelling like a wave upon the ocean. Her legs turned to rubber and she was stung by the oddest notion that invisible hands were tripping down her spine, setting each nerve and muscle to tingling.

Mace's exploring hand descended across her abdomen and glided beneath the band of her breeches. Attentively, he monitored her reaction in those expressive pools of ebony. As his lips slanted across hers, drinking in the sweet taste of her kiss, his caresses swirled over the bare flesh of her inner thigh. Tenderly, his hand receded to retrace the titillating path he had blazed across her responsive body. His fingertips investigated and aroused until Jacquelyn's breathing was erratic, until she arched toward him in hopeless abandon.

There was a certain satisfaction, an undefinable pleasure, that came with unchaining the wildly passionate woman who lurked beneath Jacquelyn's fiery exterior. Mace felt his heart slam against his ribs when her delicious body pressed eagerly into his. He could feel the throbbing tips of her breasts boring into his chest, feel her soft, feminine curves melting against his sinewy length.

Ah, there was but one way to control a woman who was brimming with stubborn independence. A man had to love her, to gently delve beneath the protective barriers to touch her passions, to teach her the wondrous pleasures that awaited her, to earn her affection without demanding it.

Their first experience in lovemaking had been born of desperation. They had clung to each other when the tempestuous winds threatened to destroy them. The pleasure had been laced with a frantic need spurred by the raging storm. But this time their loving would be unhurried. It would be a slow, gradual ascent into ecstasy. Mace vowed to teach this curvaceous creature to arouse him as fully as he aroused her. He would brand his memory on her mind, whether she wanted it there or not.

Perhaps it was male pride that spurred his need to leave Jacquelyn with a sweet memory she would not soon forget. Mace wasn't sure why he was so obsessed with carving his initials on her wild heart. But it mattered to him, too damned much!

"Touch me, nymph. . . ." he whispered as he raised his raven head to peer into her shimmering brown eyes. "I want to feel your hands on my skin. . . ."

As if she were entranced, Jacquelyn obeyed. Her trembling fingertips drifted over the buttons of his shirt, but it was difficult to concentrate when his hands were rediscovering the feel of her skin and spreading flames that burned like wildfire. Her eyes swept down from the angular features of his face to focus on the dark matting of hair that covered his muscled chest. Suddenly Jake resented her injured arm all the more. She longed to set

159

both hands on his hard contours, to discover every masculine inch of him.

In the back of her mind, Jacquelyn wondered if she would later regret learning all there was to know about this powerfully built man. Common sense reminded her that there could never be anything lasting and permanent between them. Mace wasn't the kind of man who could be content with only one woman. And despite what she had told Mace in hopes of protecting her pride, Jacquelyn would never be satisfied to share him. Maybe she was being vain and foolish, but she wanted to experience that rare and special brand of love that was granted to only a select few. And if she found herself falling in love with this brawny giant who fought like an Indian as well as a scrappy mountain lion, she wanted him to return every ounce of her affection.

If she allowed Mace too close and was then forced to watch him waltz away, she would wither and die inside. It would crush her to lose her heart to a man who cared nothing for the precious gift of love. And yet, Jacquelyn could not resist caressing Mace's masculine body, learning to make him respond to her untutored techniques.

Mace sucked in his breath when her hand followed the thick furring of hair that descended down his belly. Her touch sensitized his flesh and sent his pulse leapfrogging through his blood. Her caresses became bolder when she viewed his responses. She felt a strange sense of power over this invincible warrior. Somehow she had evoked the same shuddering responses, the same monstrous cravings he had aroused in her.

When her warm lips hovered over each male nipple, Mace swore he had melted into a puddle of liquid desire. He ached to clutch Jacquelyn to him but he could not risk bruising her tender shoulder. A groan of unholy torment bubbled in his laboring chest when her seeking hands

160

dived beneath the band of his breeches and her lips drifted off to purse the exciting flight of her fingertips.

Why the devil am I granting her privileges that I have allowed no other lover? he asked himself shakily. It wasn't at all like him to permit a woman to take the initiative in lovemaking. And it was dangerous to teach such an inventive female to take possession of a man's body. This unique nymph already had been blessed with magical powers that he was helpless to resist.

With trembling hands, Mace drew Jacquelyn to him, aching to take her lips beneath his, to regain some semblance of self-reserve. But her roaming caresses had unleashed his savage passion, creating maddening cravings. Groaning hungrily, Mace bent Jacquelyn into his hard contours, allowing her to feel his ardent need for her. But even while they were molded tightly to each other she was still agonizingly far away. It demanded monumental self-control for Mace to gently remove Jake's hindering garments. He ached to rip away the clothes that separated them, to clutch her to him as if the world were about to end . . . as it almost had that morning during the storm. The thought left Mace to wonder if desperation were only an excuse he had created to explain the wild, obsessive feelings that assaulted him when Jake was lying in his arms. Mace wanted to believe the storm had provoked his reckless response to Jake. But he had the sinking feeling that he had been desperate with *wanting* rather than desperate to forget the threat of cyclonic winds.

Mace reassured himself that the time taken to disrobe and stretch out on the bed would serve to hold his raging desires in check. But he soon discovered those moments only aggravated the ache that came dangerously close to consuming him. His golden eyes flooded over Jacquelyn's perfect figure as she stepped away to shrug the shirt from her shoulders. Mace gulped down his heart,

161

one that had climbed the ladder of his ribs to clog his throat. When Jake provocatively pushed her trim-fitting breeches from her hips, Mace stiffened to prevent his legs from collapsing beneath him. The mere sight of her did incredible things to his body. Devouring her shapely contours with only his eyes was another kind of frustrated torment. He resented the dancing shadows and beams of lantern light that molded themselves to Jacquelyn's magnificently sculptured figure. He silently cursed the man who had enveloped this enticing beauty the previous hour.

A strange possessiveness channeled through Mace as he studied Jacquelyn with his all-consuming gaze. No other man had been granted this breathtaking view. He was her first experience with passion and he had sole rights to her. And before this night was out Jacquelyn would come to realize their first encounter had been only one of the many avenues that led into the dark, sensuous world of desire. She would drift into dreams with the taste of his kisses on her lips. She would remember the gentle touch of his hands upon her satiny skin. She would recall the feel of his hair-matted flesh merging with hers. Theirs would be a memory time couldn't erase, an emotion that lingered long after the loving was over.

"Do you know how very beautiful you are?" Mace rasped as Jacquelyn shook out her hair, allowing the golden-brown tendrils to cascade over her shoulders in a waterfall of lustrous waves.

His knees buckled when the dim light formed a shiny halo above her lustrous hair. Mace had always been attracted to fair-skinned beauties with blonde features. But the sight of this goddess, who possessed a smooth olive complexion and the body of an angel, left him to wonder at his previous preferences. Jacquelyn was like no other woman he had ever known. She was vibrant and alive, a spirited adventuress. Not once had she catered to him the way most women did. She was like a wild, free bird that he longed to capture and claim as his own.

Mace knew Jacquelyn was an instinctive creature who responded to what she felt inside. She was an inexperienced woman who reacted to her own innate needs, so freely, so naturally. She felt emotion without taking time to analyze it. She allowed the flow of sensations to channel through her naive body and she was curious about the source of her feelings. She was the pure, sweet essence of passion, beauty, and spirit and Mace was completely bewitched by her.

Reverently, he approached this shapely sprite to caress what his eyes had worshipped. Jacquelyn was surprised by her lack of modesty. Mace must have cast a black-magic spell upon her, one that dissolved all her inhibitions. She had wanted his eyes upon her. Now she ached to have his hands and lips upon her skin. He made her feel special, totally alive. When she was responding to Mace all seemed right. There was no past or future, only the sweet, hypnotic moment that burned away time.

When Mace gently laid her on the bed, Jacquelyn stared up into those spellbinding golden eyes, watching emotion pour from them. A quiet sigh escaped her lips when Mace's tender caresses melted bone and muscle. He had perfect recall, as if it had been seconds instead of hours since he had touched her. He remembered the location of each sensitive point on her flesh. He knew how and where to touch, how to make her feel every ounce a woman.

Sensation upon exquisite sensation spilled over her as Mace's hands and lips swirled across her skin. Pleasure beyond bearing flooded over her, erasing thought, replacing it with ineffable rapture. Her senses, ones that were filled with the taste, feel, and fragrance of him, took flight when his powerful body moved upon hers. Jacquelyn hungered to become his possession, to

163

reexperience all the wondrous sensations she had discovered the first time she had lain in the magical circle of his arms.

Shamelessly, her hand folded around him, urging him intimately closer. She was wild with the want of him. She yearned to feel the pulsating flames of passion engulfing her—body, mind, and soul.

Mace had intended to display the epitome of patience and gentleness. But Jacquelyn's ardent response freed his primitive desires, leaving him a creature of need, releasing cravings that were as ancient as time itself. He came to her in wild abandon, taking possession, only to find himself a slave to this sweet, inexperienced enchantress. There was no hope for self-restraint when he was one with this spirited nymph. Jacquelyn could make Mace feel things he had never experienced, even when he swore he had previously explored the heights and depths of passion.

A kaleidoscope of colors fanned before him. And each shade of brilliant color was entangled with triplets of emotions, ones that had never become entangled until he'd encountered this rare, beautiful creature. Mace felt himself tumbling pell-mell through the maelstrom of sensations. He was reaching upward to grasp at some unexplainable feeling that lured him closer and closer. Mindlessly, he drove into her, striving to satisfy the incredible craving that threatened to consume him long before he understood its meaning.

And then it came, that wild budding of pleasure that burst inside him and then spilled forth, creating another mystical rainbow of colors and complex emotions. Mace felt like a bird in flight—dipping, diving, soaring on outstretched wings, traversing through a pastel hue of sunbeams. Ever so slowly, he made his descent through time and space to see the fringe of reality stretching out before him.

Jacquelyn was besieged by one delicious tremor after another. Sensations defied description. She wanted to let go, and yet she was paralyzed by the intense pleasure of lovemaking. It is odd how the course of five days has turned my life around, she mused as she drifted back to reality. She had been courted and pursued by scores of men from all walks of life. In a few of her suitors she had discovered endearing traits. But never had one man possessed so many admirable characteristics that blinded her to his flaws. In some ways Mace remained an enigma and mystery to her. And yet, with this awesomely built man of many intriguing moods Jacquelyn had discovered that vital flame that set fire to her heart and burned brands on her soul.

Jacquelyn knew what she wanted in a man, but until now she had been unable to locate the perfect combination that moved her to deep emotion. There were some women who needed time to analyze what they felt for a man. But Jacquelyn recognized the wondrous feelings that had eluded her until now. Mace was the long-awaited vision of her dreams. This was love, she assured herself. She knew it as well as she knew her own name. *How* she knew it she couldn't explain, even to herself. But she just knew it and that was as simple as that.

That realization was overshadowed by a sense of regret that came in knowing Mace would never be able to return her heartfelt affection. Ah, the irony of it, Jacquelyn thought with a remorseful smile. Dozens of times she had listened to confessions of love from men who could not stir her to feel anything more than casual friendship. And the one time she was inclined to voice her emotions she knew they would fall on insensitive ears.

I love you. It was such a simple phrase, but it encompassed such large areas of emotion. *I love you. . . .* It expressed feeling that blossomed in every fiber of her being.

Mace winced when he heard Jacquelyn's soft utterance. "What did you say?" Surely his ringing ears had deceived him. He must not have heard Jacquelyn correctly.

Jacquelyn's wide-eyed gaze flew to Mace's curious smile. "Did I say something?" she chirped. Had her tongue located the betraying thoughts and translated what lay in her heart?

Gingerly, Mace tunneled his fingers through the tangled tendrils that sprayed across his pillow. "I could have sworn you said you loved me," he whispered as he stared into those chocolate brown eyes.

Jacquelyn chewed indecisively on her bottom lip. She would be every kind of fool to offer her heart so carelessly after she had spent twenty years protecting it. But the overflowing emotions freed the words that were trapped in her throat.

"I do love you. . . ." she heard herself say.

Mace eased away, stung by a riptide of feelings entangled with tormenting memories from his past. Dark images leaped from the shadowed corners of his mind, haunting him. What if he accepted her love, and what if history repeated itself? Would his reaction be the same? Would he be consumed by that same maddening, mindless . . .

Frantically, Mace blocked out the ghastly vision and the soul-splitting emotions associated with it. He couldn't fall in love with this spirited beauty, knowing how fate could twist a man's life and his mind. Already he was meeting himself coming and going. He had spread himself too thin. There was the plantation to manage and the commission business in Galveston. There was his obligation to old friends, some who were like family, some who would call upon him at unexpected moments and plead with him to respond to their requests. He had squeezed a week's interlude into his hectic schedule, but he didn't have a lifetime to spare.

Hell, he couldn't wedge love into this maze he called his life. Jacquelyn was the kind of woman who would monopolize a man's time as well as his thoughts. It would take a lifetime in itself to learn all her moods, to love her the way she needed to be loved. She was a complex creature who, left to her own devices once too often, might respond the same way. . . .

Again the bitter memories stabbed like a knife. Damnit, he was never going to get that close to a woman, to become weakened by love's vulnerability. He'd sworn on dozens of occasions that he would not allow himself to become possessed by the powers of love. Mace didn't want to be the one left clinging to emotions that would wither in time, emotions *he* would probably be responsible for killing. . . .

God, how could he explain the turmoil he was experiencing without disclosing that bitter chapter of his past to Jacquelyn? She was too young and innocent to understand, and Mace wasn't even certain he could force out the confession even if he wanted to. After all these years, he could still remember sitting there, watching in agonized torment, listening to the . . .

A tremor shook the roots of his soul. Sweet mercy, he didn't want to find himself hissing out the words he had heard that tragic afternoon. God, as long as he lived he would never forget that horrible nightmare.

Jacquelyn's heart felt like a ton of lead weighting down her chest. The indecipherable emotions that chased each other across Mace's ruggedly handsome face assured her that he hadn't wanted to hear her confession. What she felt for him was one-sided. Though she had suspected as much, it hurt no less to be the one rejected. Rarely had Jacquelyn succumbed to tears, but they welled up in her eyes, threatening to trickle down her cheeks. It took incredible willpower to compose herself and muster a misty smile.

Levering herself up on an elbow, she pressed one last kiss to Mace's lips. "Good night."

"Jake?" Mace murmured as she turned her back on him. "I . . ." Mace didn't know exactly what to say in this awkward moment. When he accepted confessions from other women he had always managed to rattle off some tactful phrase. But now the words stuck in his throat and clung to the roof of his mouth like glue.

Silly fool! Jacquelyn scolded herself as she stared at the shadows through a haze of tears. She had known better than to reveal her heart. She had expected to have it trampled on one day. And that day had inevitably come. She might as well have sprawled on the ground and invited a herd of wild mustangs to stampede over the top of her. She couldn't be hurting worse than she was now.

Mace had only been satisfying his male lust. It was a perfectly normal response for the male of the species, Jacquelyn reminded herself bitterly. She had practically invited Mace to make love to her on both occasions, and he had only accommodated her. Mace was not gentleman enough to say no. Indeed, it was that wild nobility in him, that reckless nonchalance, that attracted her in the first place. She had never been partial to proper gentlemen. And she had found the one man who stirred her to great emotion, only to realize she wanted what she could never truly have. Mace would accept what she offered, but he had nothing to give in return.

From this moment forward, Jacquelyn resolved never again to look upon Mace as a lover. He would be no more than a friend. If there was any loving to be done, she would have to do it from afar. There would be no obligations, no strings attached. It was her fault that they had become intimate. *Her fault!* Jacquelyn laughed humorlessly at herself. Oh, she was a fool, all right. She had offered Mace what no man had taken from her. Offered, mind you. She had lost her virginity, but she was not about to go crying to the General, demanding that Mace do the right thing by her. The blame lay squarely on her shoulders and there it would stay. Jake would not become like those simpering women who sought to entrap a man by giving him her body and then expecting him to pay the price by giving them a wedding ring.

Clinging to that noble thought, Jacquelyn surrendered to exhaustion. But Mace was not so fortunate. Sleep eluded him until the dark hour before dawn. Damnit, he really hadn't wanted Jacquelyn to fall in love with him. It had crossed his mind as a spiteful whim. But he truly hadn't meant to hurt this wild, windswept sprite. He had nothing to give her except material wealth. That would never be enough to satisfy a woman with Jake's zest for living. He couldn't bear to watch her affection for him seep away, to watch her turn to another man. And she would, Mace prophesied. Hadn't she done just that with whoever-he-was this very evening?

Lord, it had all seemed so innocent, so uncomplicated when he'd decided to escort this dazzling beauty home. But the amusement was gone. And even if the situation worked to his advantage, Mace wasn't going to like living with his deceit. Damnation, why couldn't the General's granddaughter have been a simpering little twit who provoked his sympathy instead of his admiration? Mace hadn't counted on liking Jacquelyn quite so much.

Well, I am doing the right thing by rejecting her confession, he consoled himself. He might as well forget about the merger. After all, the Reid Company wasn't as stable as his own business. In fact, Mace had been trying to do the General a favor by joining efforts. Granted, the General's name lured clients, but Harlan did not possess a head for business and Malcolm barely kept the company afloat. But Mace held a certain respect for General Reid. The old buzzard was an institution and Mace didn't want to see the General humiliated by failing in business. Hell, it was the least Mace could do after all the frustration he and Hub had dealt the General during their confrontations near the battlefield.

But now Mace would have to turn his back on the General and his floundering company. Mace's affair with Jacquelyn had spoiled any chance of reconciliation instead of serving to heal a wound. All that was left to do was to deliver Jake to Harlan's doorstep and fade into oblivion. Not that Harlan Reid would object to that, Mace thought with a deflated sigh. They were incompatible, and the General only had use for Mace when he was cutting the ranks of Mexican soldiers to pieces.

Hesitantly, Mace reached over to brush his hand across the wild spray of wavy hair that lay beside him. This impulsive beauty was every man's dream. Every man's but one, Mace amended. There was no time in his life for entangling affairs. Jacquelyn would further complicate his already complex life. Gawd, if he hadn't surrounded himself with competent men he could never keep the frantic pace required of him. And to make matters worse, Governor Wood was again requesting that he and Hub and Raoul accept a short tour of duty with the Rangers. Indian and Mexican uprisings were prevalent along the border. Renegades were harassing Texas citizens and stealing their livestock. "Rip" Ford and his company of Rangers were already patrolling the area between Corpus Christi and Laredo to quell disturbances.

Hell, Mace knew he couldn't spare the time to join "Rip" Ford right now. And yet, battling banditos and Comanches would be no less exhausting than warring with the emotions this sable-haired pixie evoked from him. When he looked into those big brown eyes that could melt a man's heart, he felt the whirlpool of desire towing him under. But before he could surrender to the whims Jake aroused in him, he was tormented by a past that refused to die. Jake would never understand why he was so cautious of affairs of the heart, and he couldn't bring himself to explain. Even time couldn't heal this wound that still festered in his soul.

Mace eased onto his side, begging for sleep, wanting to mold Jacquelyn's sweet, innocent body to his, aching to hold her all through the night. But if he couldn't hold her forever, he didn't dare hold her at all. If she knew what a great favor he was doing for her, she most surely would have thanked him for caring enough to let her go before he hurt her more than he had already.

Chapter 10

The moment the splinters of sunlight stabbed into the dark room, Jacquelyn quietly eased from bed. Ruefully, she stared down at the brawny form of the man who could bring her both pleasure and pain. Although it hurt to be rejected, Jake resolved not to behave like the woman scorned.

There were those females of her acquaintance who allowed themselves to become embittered by unrequited love. They countered their affection for the man who rejected them by mustering a spiteful hatred. Jacquelyn promised herself she was above such pettiness. If Mace could not return her affection, she was going to accept that which she couldn't change and get on with the rest of her life. After all, there was no hard and fast rule that stated a man had to love the woman who loved him. Jacquelyn was going to be sensible and mature about this ill-fated affair. Mace had made no confessions of affection, nor had he made any promises. She would expect nothing from him. She would cherish the sweet memories they had made together, memories that were now a closed chapter of her past.

After delivering that inspirational sermon to herself, along with several consoling platitudes, Jacquelyn slipped from the room to tend their horses. Even though she felt empty and dead inside, she was anxious to return home. Nothing is going to spoil my homecoming, she vowed to herself. She could still enjoy a normal life, even if she had fallen in love with a dedicated bachelor.

While Jake was preparing the horses for travel, Mace was slowly fighting his way through the drugging effects of a short night's sleep. With a doleful groan, he squirmed on his back and pried open one puffy eyelid. Lord, it couldn't be morning already, he thought dismally. He felt as if he had only dozed for a quarter of an hour.

Memories of the previous night unfolded themselves from the closet of his mind. Mace could almost feel that bold nymph's hands caressing his skin, setting his nerves to quivering. Jacquelyn's softly spoken confession whispered through his thoughts, causing Mace to wince as if he were lying on a scorpion.

How am I to handle Jacquelyn "the morning after?" he asked himself pensively. No doubt she would be hurt and angry. Women always were. They were such flighty, emotional creatures. What could he say to ease her suffering, to let her down gently?

Reluctantly, Mace turned his head to survey the curvaceous beauty who stirred crosscurrents of emotions within him. His eyes popped from their sockets when he spied the empty space beside him. Damn! Jake had been so upset that she had spirited away, too humiliated to face him. Surely she wouldn't do herself bodily harm because her first bout with love hadn't met her whimsical expectations. He had spoiled a young maiden's dream, her hope of everlasting love. God, he had ended affairs dozens of times before but he had never felt quite so guilty, so unwilling to terminate a relationship that he knew had no future. I am doing the right thing, Mace reassured himself. It was best for both of them. He only hoped Jake hadn't become so distraught that she'd run off and done something crazy. . . .

Mace's imagination ran wild. Had Jake decided to end it all by thrusting a knife into her wounded heart? Or had she sought out the man she'd encountered the previous night, hoping to forget the pain of rejection in another man's arms? Or perhaps she had been so upset that she'd thrown herself into the river to drown her troubles. . . .

The thought had Mace leaping out of bed like a mountain goat. He climbed into his clothes and scooped up his belongings on his way to the door. Cursing the fact that Jake had taken her satchel with her, Mace bounded down the steps two at a time to give chase. Obviously, Jacquelyn had no intention of returning. If she had, she would have left her satchel behind. She was planning to take herself and her belongings out of his life, never to be seen or heard from again. The poor little nymph, Mace mused compassionately. He had broken Jacquelyn's spirit. If she killed herself because of him he would never be able to live with his conscience. Her death would become another nightmare that haunted his dreams. . . .

Mace came to a skidding halt when he spied Jacquelyn leading their horses from the blacksmith's barn. A radiant smile curved her mouth upward while she chatted with the smithy, who was having difficulty keeping his eyes focused on her exquisite face instead of on her arresting curves, where his gaze was prone to stray. If the rotund little man with frizzy red hair and a generous splattering of freckles had missed one alluring detail of Jake's body, Mace would eat his saddlebag!

The fact that another man was devouring this reckless minx with his hawkish stare irritated Mace. But what truly got his dander up was Jacquelyn's calm, carefree demeanor. He had worried himself sick, wondering if Jacquelyn had taken her life because he couldn't return her love. But, judging by her dry eyes and sunny smile, she had taken it all in stride. The speed with which she'd recovered from their affair was incredible. Damn her!

Mace's male pride had been stabbed from all directions at once. If Jacquelyn cared as much as she said she did, she certainly hid her rejection well! And the one time Mace honestly cared enough not to hurt his lover any more than necessary, she didn't even need a shoulder to cry on!

A smoldering frown swallowed Mace's handsome features. It was obvious that Jacquelyn wasn't in love with him at all. She had said the words but they were meaningless. Why aren't I surprised? Mace quizzed himself as he stalked toward the barn. This flighty, fickle, daring sprite didn't know beans about love. She, like he, had never spent enough time developing a deep attachment for the opposite sex. And to compound that flaw, Jacquelyn was too independent to ever need a man the way a woman should truly need and depend on a husband. Forlorn and distraught? Mace scoffed cynically. The day that brown-eyed hellion needed a man would be the same day the Sahara was besieged by a blizzard!

Jacquelyn glanced up to see Mace stamping toward her. At that moment it was difficult to tell if Mace still had a mouth. The slit on the lower portion of his face was so taut it looked as if it might snap under the pressure. What the blazes was the matter with him? If anyone should have appeared as sour as a green apple it should have been her! Just seeing him again after what had transpired the previous night was an exercise in self-control. Her wounded heart was bleeding all over her ribs, and her smile served only to disguise the ache of wanting a man she couldn't have.

"Thanks a helluva lot for waiting for me," Mace growled sarcastically. Flinging her a contemptuous glare, Mace snatched Diego's reins from her fingertips and slung the saddlebags over the steed's hips. "Say your last goodbye to your new friend, honey. We're wasting daylight."

Baffled by Mace's irascible mood, Jacquelyn bid farewell to the smithy, who graciously helped her into the saddle. As they rode southwest Jacquelyn surveyed Mace's hollow-eyed scowl from a new angle, but he looked just as surly and unapproachable as before.

"My, we certainly got up on the wrong side of the bed, didn't we?" she said saucily.

Glittering golden eyes drilled into her like porcupine quills. Her cheerfulness was nauseating. Her eyes should have been swollen and red from crying. But not Jake, he observed resentfully. Nothing fazed that spirited hoyden. "I was worried about you, afraid you had thundered off after what was said last night. . . ."

The arrogant cur! Jacquelyn felt steam boiling from her collar. Mace thought she had left him to find a private place to fall apart. Or had he expected her to commit suicide because he couldn't return her affection? Ha! No man was worth that drastic price.

Now Jacquelyn was all the more determined to pretend indifference. As far as she was concerned, the previous night never happened and she had not uttered that foolish confession. Why, it was ludicrous to imagine herself in love with a man who derived sadistic pleasure from collecting a necklace of broken hearts. Mace would soon realize that she may have surrendered her body to his brand of passion, but she would not crack and crumble just because she found herself an object of his lust. Mace didn't really want her. And come to think of it, she wasn't all that sure she wanted him either! He may have thought himself God's gift to woman, but as far as she was concerned, Jonathan Mason wasn't such a prize. Why, there probably wasn't a loyal bone in the man's body. If a woman ever dragged him to the altar, he would still practice infidelity any time he felt like it.

"Really, Mace," she scoffed, sending him a withering glance. "You are the one who took the incident too seriously. I forgot it the moment I fell asleep. It's a pity you didn't." Her eyes noted his unkempt appearance and the dark circles around those watery pools of amber. "You look awful. I'm sorry you stayed awake worrying about how I would react. As you can plainly see, I survived quite nicely."

As Jake galloped off, cradling her wounded arm against her ribs, Mace ground his teeth until they were smooth. Damn her! He wouldn't have been such a bad catch if he were inclined toward matrimony—which of course he wasn't—and especially not to that unmanageable bundle of trouble! The way that termagant was behaving, one would have thought she would have rejected his marriage proposal if he had offered one (which of course he wouldn't have).

Gouging his heels into Diego's flanks, Mace took off like a flying arrow. When he caught up with Jake his hand snaked out to grab her reins, slowing the rose-gray gelding to a walk.

"What would you have said last night if I claimed to love you in return and that I wanted to marry you?" he blurted out huffily.

Jacquelyn suppressed a mischievous smile. Mace was getting exactly what he deserved and she relished watching him get it. "I would have called you a liar and I would have declined the offer," she told him flatly.

Mace's shirt, one that had been haphazardly buttoned in haste, strained across his overinflated chest. "I can certainly see how you might have given the Gen'ral fits," he bit off in a resentful tone. "Your moods change so quickly it is impossible to keep up with them." Mace glared shadows on her sunny smile. "And I swear your heart is encased in a block of ice! Talk about insensitive!"

178

Jacquelyn yanked the reins from his hand. There was nothing wrong with her sensitivity. His was the one at fault and she was going to be as unfeeling and calloused as he was. "I had hoped to enjoy a pleasurable ride home. The journey was not to include a long-distance argument about who is guilty of the most peccadilloes." Jacquelyn flung her dainty nose in the air and presented Mace with the cold shoulder, complete with icicles. "If you can't put that reckless moment in the proper perspective and accept the fact that passion spurred my confession, then you can follow your own route to the plantation. I wish to speak no more of it. The incident is over and done and forgotten, as well it should be."

Mace's jaw swung from its hinges. A passion-provoked confession? Hell's bells, that sounded like something *he* would have said. And damnit, he was the one feeling like the spurned and rejected lover! Somewhere along the way he had completely lost control of the situation. But then I have never been in control of this firebrand, he reminded himself sourly.

Well, he was going to have the last laugh on this fickle chit. Mace no longer felt guilty about deceiving Jacquelyn. Just wait until she discovered that he wasn't the mealy-mouthed Jonathan Mason, come to fetch her home at the General's request. Then they would see if she could maintain her infuriating nonchalance. Give Mace Gallagher the brush-off, would she? In a few hours she would realize she had been bamboozled, and Mace was going to grace her with a goading grin she would not soon forget!

Much to Mace's chagrin, Jacquelyn was the epitome of gaiety during the remainder of their journey to the plantation. She had long ago forgiven the General for dragging her off to Louisiana and she was anticipating their reunion. Jake rattled on about her eagerness to see Lancelot, the magnificent buckskin stallion her grand-

179

father had given her for her seventeenth birthday, and how anxious she was to exercise the steed herself. With fond affection, she spoke of Emma, the Negress who had cared for her while the General was coming and going during her childhood. Indeed, Jacquelyn sounded as happy as a lark as she narrowed the distance to the stately plantation southwest of Galveston.

As of yet, Mace had had no opportunity to sit himself down and determine why he was so frustrated with Jake. But he was, so much so that he was sulking like a sourpuss. It irked him to realize how easily he could be forgotten. Nothing truly upset this sable-haired vixen. Jacquelyn easily adapted to any situation. She was like a cat who always landed on her feet to breeze into another of her nine lives. Her spirited nature sustained her when a blow to anyone else's pride would have rendered that person bitter and spiteful. Jacquelyn could have had revenge on Mace because he had taken her virginity. She could have threatened to blackmail him. She could have vowed to deprive him of his freedom by forcing him to marry her. But she had followed none of those vindictive courses of action Mace might have expected from another woman.

Damn but this minx beat anything he had ever seen! Mace had the feeling no man would ever tame this wild-hearted woman. She was destined to break a score of hearts during her quest for adventure. Any affection she might feel for a man would not be the deep-rooted, lasting kind. Indeed, Mace was fortunate he wasn't foolish enough to fall head over heels in love with a woman like Jacquelyn Reid. A man could easily be burned by this saucy spitfire who had bounced back from their reckless affair without sustaining so much as a bruise!

A wave of nostalgia swept over Jacquelyn when she spied the sprawling cotton plantation her grandfather had built from this wild, lawless land. The two-story mansion stood as a stately monument to civilization. The elegantly furnished rooms that boasted imported furniture opened to broad verandas which completely surrounded the house. The grounds that encircled the picturesque structure blossomed with colorful flowers and bulged with thick green vegetation. Huge plastered-brick colonnades supported the upper galleries, and had served as a means of escape when Jacquelyn sneaked from her upstairs room to satisfy her craving for nocturnal prowling. Many a time she had climbed over the ornamental cast-iron rails and slid down the columns to become one of the evening shadows.

Sighing appreciatively, Jacquelyn swung her gaze to the stables that graced the flower-dappled meadows. She couldn't wait to greet the servants who had been her dear friends. The very thought provoked Jake to nudge her steed into a swifter pace. She flew like the wind, her dark hair undulating like a flag waving in the breeze.

She was home again! Neither the nagging throb in her shoulder nor her bittersweet affair with Mace could spoil her happiness. She belonged to this land. It was a part of her. Jake had every intention of thrusting herself into the family business and the management of the plantation. The General would be pleased with her enthusiasm, her acceptance of responsibility. Although Aunt Florence had discouraged her from cluttering her mind with business, Jacquelyn was determined to assume her place and become a productive member of the Reid family.

A reluctant smile pursed Mace's lips as he watched the lovely sprite wing her way across the gentle slope of the meadow. It stole his breath to watch her flow with the movement of her rose-gray gelding. They moved as one, like a mythical centaur, gobbling up the distance that separated them from the enchanting plantation.

Fighting his way through a jungle of contradicting

181

thoughts, Mace spurred Diego into a faster clip. He was anxious to view the reaction provoked by Jake's arrival and to determine how well received this feisty minx would be. Would the servants view her homecoming as the return of trouble, or had the slaves actually missed this vibrant misfit?

His answer came in the form of a booming cry, one that erupted from an elderly black woman who was the first to recognize the wild-haired beauty. Within seconds, a flood of humanity poured from the stables and the surrounding outbuildings. The moment Jake hopped to the ground she was swarmed by smiling servants.

As troublesome as Jake was, Mace expected her to meet with a cool reception. But that wasn't the case. Mace hadn't heard such whooping and hollering since he and the Rangers had clashed with a Comanche war party.

After Jake had the stuffing squeezed out of her, she turned toward the house. Had her grandfather changed these past three years? Would he look the same? Behave the same? Had he softened during her absence? Had he too set aside the heated argument that had occurred the day she was spirited way from Texas?

With swift, precise strides, Jacquelyn marched through the central foyer. Her gaze flowed appreciatively over the spiraling staircase that led to her boudoir on the second floor. Her eyes swung back to the mahogany door that opened into the General's study. Without knocking, Jacquelyn burst into the room, wearing a beaming smile that could have replaced the sun, should it ever burn itself out.

Harlan Reid glanced up, intending to level a glare at the rude intruder. When he spied his wind-blown granddaughter, a smile twitched his lips. Lord, she had blossomed into a full-fledged woman since he had seen her. No doubt Jonathan Mason had been astounded when he laid eyes on this dazzling beauty. Even if her

182

outlandish attire of breeches and her rambuctiousness were not becoming for a lady, there wasn't a man who wouldn't be stirred by her mere presence. Jacquelyn radiated lively spirit. Harlan could feel it the moment she bounded into the study. She was like sunshine flooding through an open window.

"Jake . . ." His voice trembled with emotion, even though he attempted to mask his sentiment. Struggling, Harlan pushed himself out of his chair and grasped his cane.

"Gen'ral!" Jake giggled with giddy pleasure. She had noted the pleased expression that touched Harlan's wrinkled features before he disguised his emotion behind his stoic demeanor. "I'm ever so glad to see you!" she enthused.

Neither Jacquelyn nor Harlan took time to quiz each other about their injuries. They simply flew to each other, murmuring greetings while they hugged each other close.

"Lord, it's been a long time," Harlan whispered as he placed a kiss to her sunburned brow. "Louisiana must have agreed with you after all." A teasing grin broke loose and one twinkling brown eye dropped into a teasing wink behind wire-rimmed glasses. "When you left, kicking and biting and screaming, you swore it was the last time I would ever lay eyes on you, that you would shrivel up and die in that muggy New Orleans climate."

"I was upset." Jacquelyn shrugged off the taunt. "But I did not return bearing a grudge. I'm only thankful to be home again."

A wry smile again found the corner of the General's mouth. It amazed him that he felt rejuvenated just hugging this delightful bundle of spirit. He hadn't realized what a great space Jake had filled in his life until she was gone. Indeed, the sun seemed to blaze a few degrees brighter when Jake was underfoot. Harlan had every intention of keeping Jake with him forevermore. He prayed the time Jake had spent alone with Jonathan Mason would evolve into a marriage proposal. Jonathan had become Harlan's overseer after the war, assisting Harlan, who was recovering from a painful wound in the knee. Jonathan responded to orders as efficiently as any junior officer under his command and he had become Harlan's legs, his strength. If Harlan could match his granddaughter with Jonathan, he could insure that the plantation would remain in proper working order and that Jacquelyn would always be here to liven up his days.

"Were you impressed with my man Jonathan Mason?" Harlan inquired, cutting to the heart of the matter.

That rascal. Harlan had indeed planned the whole scheme, Jacquelyn assured herself. Her grandfather had conveniently thrown Mace and her together, just as she suspected. "Of course he impressed me," she declared saucily. "Isn't that what you intended?"

The General fairly beamed. "I had hoped the two of you would become good friends. But you can be contrary at times, Jake. I feared you would second-guess my intentions and you would decide to dislike Jonathan, just to spite me." His voice trailed off when his dark eyes fell to Jake's injured arm. "When did this happen?"

"Someone tried to kill me on the way home," she informed her grandfather matter-of-factly. She waited for Harlan to explode. He did.

"What?" he boomed in disbelief. "Who did?"

"Probably the same two men who tried to attack me in the streets of Galveston," she explained.

Harlan looked as if he had swallowed a mushmelon and was about to choke on it. "Where was Mason while all this was going on?"

"Which time?" Her brow arched at the ambiguity of his question.

The color evaporated from Harlan's weather-beaten

184

features. "There was more than one?" he croaked, aghast.

Jacquelyn nodded affirmatively. "The first time I was dragged into the alley by two burly men and the second time I was bushwhacked on the road to the plantation."

"Twice?" Harlan crowed like a disturbed rooster. "Damnit, I sent him to protect you from harm, and it appears he did a miserable job of seeing you safely home!"

Frustration provoked Harlan to resort to the loud voice he employed on the battlefield. But in close quarters, the sound ricocheted off the walls like the thunder of bass drums.

"We failed to make connections," Jake declared in a much calmer tone than her bellowing grandfather. "He could not have foreseen the danger on the road since it was virtually impossible to detect snipers in the concealing trees and underbrush."

Harlan sat down before he fell down. His face bleached white as flour. "Who the devil would want to kill you?" His rounded eyes lifted to peer incredulously at Jacquelyn. "Could you have made mortal enemies in New Orleans who followed you back to Texas to exterminate you on your native soil?"

Her good shoulder lifted and dropped. The thought had occurred to her. The beau she had wounded during the duel now hated her with a vengeance, and Anna Marie was spiteful and wealthy enough to hire a mercenary to settle the score for her. "I have considered that possibility. But then it could also be that I have attracted new enemies since I dropped anchor in Galveston." Her dark eyes glistened with mischief. "This may come as a shock to you, Gen'ral, but not everyone who knows me likes me. But the important thing is I'm home and I am not going away again," she added with a contented smile.

"Indeed." Harlan snorted in exasperation. "I am thankful for your return, but I have a few words to say to Mason. Apparently, he is not as capable and dependable as I thought."

The last thing Jake wanted was for Mace to think she had belittled him in front of the General. What was between her and Mace was a private matter. She no longer held Mace responsible for her misfortune and she refused to be the cause of conflict between Mace and the General.

"Despite what happened, Mace was a dependable escort. In fact, I cannot name another man who has earned my respect without demanding it. Mace proved himself to be—"

The color drained from Harlan's features and disappeared beneath the collar of his shirt. "Mace?" he chirped like a sick sparrow. "Mace!" Harlan regained his voice to growl out the name.

Jacquelyn couldn't imagine what had put a sour expression on her grandfather's features. He looked like an erupting volcano. "He said his friends called him Mace," she replied, and then flinched when Harlan did indeed erupt from his chair like spewing lava. "For heaven's sake, Gen'ral, what is wrong with you?"

"That sneaky sidewinder!" Harlan ground his cane into the carpet. "You haven't spent the past few days with Jonathan Mason. You've been cavorting with Mason *Gallagher*—the man who has been pressing me to merge with his commission company—the man who should have been court-martialed for insubordination during the war." His voice had grown higher and wilder until he was practically yelling into Jake's shocked face. "Captain Mace Gallagher is one of those deplorable renegades who rode with the Texas Rangers. I had the displeasure of sharing a command with him in the field. Captain Gallagher constantly disobeyed my orders.

Mine!" Harlan tapped his chest, one that was inflated like a balloon. "I was the high-ranking officer, the commander of the troops. I had more brass on my chest than he has in his house and yet he refused to obey my orders as an army officer." His mouth twisted in a scowl. "Damn that unscrupulous rapscallion. Did he think to play up to you, hoping I would be swayed by this misdirected respect you feel for him?"

Jacquelyn felt her knees buckling beneath her. Sweet mercy, no wonder Mace didn't fit the personality of the man Jake had pictured as the match her grandfather selected for her lifelong mate. Mace had allowed her to think he was Jonathan Mason, knowing he would have the last laugh on her. Double damn him! Did he think she would still come to his defense after she learned the truth? How dare he play such a rotten prank on her unsuspecting person!

Speak of the devil and he appeared, Jacquelyn mused bitterly. And sure enough, Mace materialized from behind the door that stood ajar. Negligently, he propped himself against the wall. His eyes glittered like gold nuggets as he regarded the Reids. "I believe I heard my name mentioned," he remarked with a smile that was as wide and cocky as ever.

Jacquelyn clenched her fists, itching to beat him to a pulp. It was one thing to make a fool of herself, but it was infuriating to have someone else do it for her. Curse the man!

"Good afternoon, Gen'ral. It's a pleasure to see you again," Mace purred in all too civil a tone.

Wearing an outraged scowl, Harlan limped over to confront Mace face to face. "How dare you waltz into my home unannounced," he blustered in offended dignity. "How dare you deceive my granddaughter! And what have you done with Jonathan?"

Mace crossed his arms and legs in front of him,

undaunted by Harlan's less than cordial greeting. "Instead of consigning me to the fires of hell for deceiving your lovely granddaughter, you should be thanking me." A wry smile pursed his lips as he watched the General display furious gestures and contemptuous glowers. "But then, you never were one to express your gratitude for my efforts, were you, Harlan?"

Jacquelyn didn't have the faintest notion what that remark meant, but apparently Harlan did. His face was suddenly pulsating with bright red splotches.

While Harlan's mouth opened and closed at irregular intervals, Mace took advantage of the silence. "The fact is your devoted lackey Jon Mason never showed up at all. I was kind enough to take time from my hectic schedule to accompany Jake home before she got herself into more trouble than she already had. . . ."

His keen gaze shifted to Jacquelyn, who had bolted out of her chair to storm toward him. When the palm of her hand circled through the air, Mace caught her wrist before she could deliver the vicious blow.

"Damn you to hell and back, Mace Gallagher," she shouted into his amused face.

"Mind your tongue, Granddaughter," Harlan growled without unpinning his smoldering brown eyes from Mace's ornery grin. If looks could kill Mace would have been pushing up daisies. (Not that he wasn't fond of the fragrant flowers, but he had no inclination to stare at them from the roots up.)

"I am minding my tongue," Jake hissed venomously. "I wanted to call him a son of a bitch, but I doubted you would approve."

"You just did and I'm inclined to agree with you," Harlan sputtered angrily.

Before Harlan clubbed Mace with his cane and Jake kicked him in places that would now and forever render him useless to any other woman, Mace pushed away from the wall and stepped aside. After dropping into a mocking bow, Mace flashed Jake a wide smile that displayed pearly white teeth. "Despite your indignation, I found our journey to be an enjoyable interlude, my dear. The pleasure was all mine, even if you don't feel obliged to thank me. And I shall remain your humble servant."

Oh, how she would have loved to get her hands on that haughty scoundrel. But after witnessing the fracas the previous evening at the inn, Jacquelyn knew Mace could tear her to pieces before she could kick him into splinters. "Humble?" She sniffed caustically. "Never! Servant?" Her glare sparkled with contempt. "Not hardly!"

"Get out of my house, Gallagher," Harlan sneered, brandishing his cane at the unwelcomed intruder. "It will be a cold day in hell when I accept a business merger with the likes of you. I may have had to tolerate your insolence and disrespect on the battlefield, but I do not have to endure your presence in civilian life." His eyes burned fire and brimstone. "You stay away from me and my granddaughter. Do you hear me, Gallagher?"

How could Mace help not hearing the General? Harlan's explosive voice very nearly burst Mace's eardrums. Mace drew himself up as if he were awaiting military inspection. Bypassing the salute he had never once bestowed on the General, Mace performed a perfectly executed about-face and swaggered across the hall. He paused to glance over his shoulder at the shapely brunette who, like her grandfather, looked as if she were poised for a portrait of fury.

"I was flattered by what you said to me last night, my dear Jacquelyn," he drawled, and then paused to await the flush of color in her cheeks. "I was hoping you would accept me for what I am, not what the Gen'ral would have you think of me. But I suppose even a free-spirit like you can be swayed by external influences. I, on the other hand, appreciate you for what you are without—"

Jacquelyn snatched up the imported figurine that stood beside the door. The projectile sailed through the foyer and would have found its mark if Mace hadn't been quick as a jungle cat. To Jake's dismay, Mace ducked and the statue crashed against the wall instead of cracking against his thick skull.

"Here try this one," Harlan insisted as he thrust an expensive vase into her empty hand.

"I thought this was a valuable relic," Jacquelyn commented.

"It isn't as priceless as watching you clobber that wily viper. And blast it, aim lower this time!" Harlan snapped.

She did. The missile collided with Mace's shoulder the split second before he scampered out the front door. Jacquelyn assured herself that she could have hit Mace right between the eyes on her first attempt if she could have used her throwing arm. But since her right arm lay in a sling she had been forced to resort to her left arm. At least the vase had struck some part of his arrogant body, she consoled herself. She only wished she could have hurled a boulder at the blackguard.

"That ornery rakehell," Harlan grumbled as he limped over to pour himself a stiff drink. "Mace Gallagher will never change. I swear, his greatest aspiration in life is to harass me."

"I can certainly see why you dislike him," Jacquelyn muttered resentfully. "He never overlooks the opportunity to badger a person to the limits of his self-restraint."

Harlan collapsed at his desk to rest his aching leg. His speculative glance wandered over Jacquelyn's animated features. "What did you say to flatter Mace Gallagher?" he wanted to know.

Damn that Mace. He had purposely left a trail of insinuations behind him when he disappeared, with which Jake was forced to contend. Drawing herself up proudly, Jacquelyn looked the General squarely in the eye. "I confessed that I was falling in love with him." That was about all she could say without incriminating herself any further, and was far too much the way it was.

Harlan clutched his chest as if his heart were about to leap out and then he groaned disgustedly, "Lord, no, not him!"

Jacquelyn had anticipated his reaction and rushed on before Harlan had a seizure. "I realize now that it was only a silly infatuation. Mace is different from the men who courted me in New Orleans. I detested being pampered and coddled as if I were a dim-witted female. For the most part, Mace treated me as his equal, not a senseless mule who needed to be led around on a halter."

"Now don't you go getting any crazy ideas about that man," Harlan warned, wagging a stubby finger at her. "Mace Gallagher is everything I'm not. I cringe at the very idea of having him as a member of my family. It was bad enough that I had to tolerate him on the same side of the war!"

"You are worrying for naught, Gen'ral," she said with great conviction. "My fascination for Mace is over as quickly as it began. I do not appreciate being the brunt of his cruel jokes."

The timid rap at the door interrupted their conversation. Jacquelyn spun around to see Emma's dark, round face appear from behind the door, followed by her even rounder body. Emma's eyes shone like ebony when she spied the young woman she had raised as one of her own.

"Emma!" Jacquelyn rushed forward to bestow a one-armed hug on the Negress. "Ah, how I've missed you!"

Emma held Jacquelyn at arm's length. "Will you look at dis chile, Gen'ral. Why, she's all growed up and filled out! A reg'lar young lady." Her eyes narrowed disapprovingly as they swept down Jake's unfeminine attire.

"'Cept fer dis gawdawful garb, dat is," she added with a distasteful sniff. "I thought shore we'd git you outa them britches after fussy Miz Florence sent you off to dat uppity school in New Orleans."

Jacquelyn stared fondly at the old woman whose figure had always reminded her of St. Nicholas. Her gray hair was swept up in a bun, and the white-collared uniform the General demanded his servants wear contributed to the vision of a jolly elf.

"I haven't changed all that much, Emma," Jacquelyn assured her saucily. "All I can say about that uppity finishing school is that I'm finished with it."

"Or perhaps it was finished with you," Harlan interjected with an explosive snort. "Knowing you as I do, I cannot help but wonder who was the most relieved to see you go, you or your schoolmaster. Judging by the progress reports and the letters I received from Flo, you did not conform to their strict regulations."

"'Scuse me for saying so, Gen'ral." Emma tittered. "But you knew she wouldn't when you had her toted off. Dis girl's got a wild streak in her that even military discipline can't correct. If it could've, Jake woulda been marchin' like a trooper years ago."

Harlan's brows flattened over his brown eyes. "Don't you have chores to attend to?" he grunted. "I do not expect this house to be ignored just because Jake has come home. And from the looks of my granddaughter, she could do with a scrubbing and another set of clothes as well."

"Yes, sir!" Emma snapped to attention and presented him with a salute. "I'll see to her bathin' right away."

When Emma waddled off in what was to have been a high-stepping march, Jacquelyn burst into a smile. It seemed she was back in the regular army and the Gen'ral was still spouting orders to his servants as if they were

192

soldiers. Slowly she turned to survey her grandfather. A wave of sentimentality splashed over her. The General could bark commands at her all day if it would insure that she was never forced to leave home again. She wouldn't obey them, of course. But she would allow Harlan the personal satisfaction of rattling off his brisk orders nonetheless.

"Gen'ral, it's good to be home. . . ." she murmured with genuine sincerity.

Harlan nearly melted in his chair when Jacquelyn blessed him with that heart-stopping smile of hers. "It's good to have you back, child." The low rumble in his voice hinted at too much emotion. Harlan quickly composed himself before Jacquelyn pegged him as a tender-hearted softy. "Now you march yourself up to your room and make yourself presentable for dinner. I have no desire to be seated at the table with a filthy ragamuffin who smells more like a horse than a woman!"

Jacquelyn sailed toward the door and then broke stride. "My luggage has yet to arrive," she informed the General. "And I'm not sure I can squeeze into the gowns I left behind."

Harlan frowned. "Where the devil is your luggage? One would presume it would have accompanied you home in the stage."

"I rode horseback," she announced, confirming Harlan's suspicion that she had been close enough to a horse to absorb its aroma instead of perched on the seat of a stage.

"Confound it, Jacquelyn. Did you learn nothing of proper behavior in that finishing school? I think I wasted a fortune when I paid your tuition."

For a long moment Jacquelyn examined her brooding grandfather. "Did you truly expect me to change these past three years?" she questioned curiously.

Harlan's chest fell and his shoulders slumped. "I honestly didn't think you would change a whit," he confessed. "But your Aunt Flo insisted that I send you to New Orleans to receive a formal education. She had been after me for years. She and I never got on that well together, and I was surprised she would even offer to take in my grandchild. I suppose the living expenses I've been sending have helped her make ends meet."

Harlan leaned back in his chair and sighed. "I don't know why I even fretted over Flo. Geoffrey, that imbecile she married, never was worth a damn. I tried to tell her that in the beginning, but she wouldn't listen and she sorely resented my meddling. But apparently she has forgiven me for my faults. Otherwise, I would not have expected her to take you under her wing."

Harlan was annoyed with himself for rambling. He had not intended to fly off on a tangent about his younger sister. Florence had opened her home to Jacquelyn when the threat of war hung heavy in Texas. There was no reason for him to belittle Florence because she had not met his expectations. Neither was it his place to question Florence's motives for inviting Jake to New Orleans. They were, after all, family. And yet, Harlan knew his sister too well to blindly assume her generous invitation was not without purpose. Florence had probably seen the opportunity of rooming and boarding Jacquelyn as a boost to her monthly income. Ah well, Harlan thought to himself. He and Florence had done each other a favor. He should accept it for its worth. At least they had corresponded through letters after too many years of little or no association with each other. Jacquelyn had become the liaison between them.

"There will be time enough for talking later," he insisted, indicating the door. "I have duties to attend to during Jonathan's absence. And when that man comes dragging home, he damned well better be quick with a believable excuse as to why he didn't meet your ship!"

While Jacquelyn headed toward her bedroom, Harlan struggled from his chair. Harlan's leg was plagued with a steady throb because of all the extra physical activity he was forced to endure while Jon was in Galveston, or wherever the hell he was. Age and Harlan's war wound were taking their toll. But if Harlan was successful in his matchmaking, it would be worth aggravating his injury. Soon he would place the business of the plantation in Jon and Jacquelyn's hands. And with his nephew managing the customs house in Galveston, there should be a generous inheritance to support his granddaughter in the decades to come.

Harlan was thankful he had Malcolm to assume some of the headaches of unloading incoming cargo and transporting it to outgoing ships. If Harlan had attempted to manage the business and his plantation, his gimpy leg would have completely folded up beneath him.

Mace Gallagher had accomplished the feat of commuting to Galveston and back to handle both his business interests and his plantation with amazing success, Harlan mused resentfully. Mace's commission company had grown so large so quickly that the Reid Commission Company stood in its shadow. And that galled Harlan to no end.

"Damn that man," Harlan grunted as he hobbled outside. Mace had been a thorn in his side for years. It irritated Harlan that beneath his dislike of Mace that he could not help but respect the renegade's capabilities and resourcefulness. Hell, there is nothing wrong with admitting I face a worthy opponent in Mace Gallagher, Harlan reminded himself. It was far better to be overshadowed by a giant than a dim-witted weakling. But if that rascal had any designs on Jacquelyn, he had better think again! Mace was not gaining control of the Reid Commission Company, not through a merger and certainly not through a convenient marriage to Jacquelyn. And that was all there was to it! Harlan vowed as he pulled himself onto his mount to check the tilling of the fields for the upcoming year's planting of cotton.

Part II

The most lonely place in the world is the human heart when love is absent.

Chapter 11

Wearily, Mace trudged up the steps to his plantation home, which lay to the northeast of Harlan's. Mace's lack of sleep the previous night had caught up with him. That, compounded with the fact that he had missed that spitfire's company on the last leg of his journey, served to sour Mace's sweet disposition.

He had wanted to have the last laugh on that insensitive minx, hadn't he? If that were true, why did he feel so lost without her, so disgruntled with the way he had handled the situation?

When Raoul lumbered into the study to greet him, Mace managed a weary smile. "Well, at least someone is glad to see me." After planting himself in his chair, Mace indicated the bottle of brandy that sat on the edge of his marble-topped desk. "Fetch the whiskey, Raoul. I could use a drink . . . or six."

Obediently, Raoul did as he was told. When he had completed the task requested of him, Raoul sank into the tuft chair across from Mace and studied the master of the house with fondness.

Mace uncorked the bottle and took a long swallow. For a pensive moment he stared into Raoul's dark, penetrating eyes. Mace's gaze drifted to the black whiskers and straight black hair that surrounded Raoul's harsh, intimidating features. Raoul was a far cry from handsome. In fact there were those who considered Raoul an ugly, oversized beast. Raoul was the strong, silent type if ever there was one. Although he was mute, he possessed a keen sense of sight and hearing. Raoul's companionship provided a great deal of satisfaction for Mace. Raoul was awesome in size and strength, and if Mace ever needed a bodyguard, Raoul would intimidate the fiercest of foes. Even if Raoul wasn't much to look at, the two of them had been friends for so long that Mace saw past the oversized nose, pointed jaw, dark, probing eyes, and noticeably long ears that protruded from the sides of his face.

Mace and Raoul had become traveling companions after they'd met in one of the desolate areas of Mexico during the first months of the war. Both of them had suffered wounds, and they'd nursed each other back to health. Since Raoul could not speak, read, or write, and had no means of communicating, Mace had given him the name, based on the fact that Raoul's appearance suggested Spanish breeding somewhere in his family tree. When Hub MacIntosh was reassigned to ride with Mace, the threesome had become inseparable. Like the three musketeers they had become friends and confidants during the war. And despite Harlan Reid's dislike for them and their undisciplined ways, they had proved their worth during several difficult reconnaissance missions.

"Hub sends his best," Mace murmured before he took another guzzle of brandy. "You know, Raoul, I envy you."

Raoul, of course, said nothing. He merely peered intently at Mace, doing what he did best—listening while Mace unburdened himself of troubled thoughts.

"Your inability to speak is a blessing in disguise,

whereas my tongue gets me into a helluva lot of trouble."
Mace downed another drink and squirmed in his chair.
"And as far as Jake is concerned . . ."

Raoul cocked his head in bemusement.

"That's the Gen'ral's granddaughter," Mace elaborated. "She is a hellion from head to toe and all parts in between. And speak of your viperous tongues!" Mace scowled under his breath. "I thought to amuse myself with that shapely nymph and to deliver her home. It seemed harmless enough at the time."

Raoul expelled a muted sound and Mace nodded repentantly. "Hell, I know it was underhanded to deceive her, but she would have stomped out of my room, thinking I was no better than that bungling dolt Jonathan Mason. Mason of all people!" He snorted disgustedly. "I'd bet my right arm the Gen'ral still intends to match Jake up with that spindly-legged goose!"

Raoul breathed a heavy sigh and glanced speculatively at Mace before settling more comfortably in his chair.

Mace knew that look. Raoul was patronizing him. "I didn't say I was interested in marrying her," he protested. "So don't assume the idea crossed my mind. I just don't happen to think a free spirit like Jacquelyn Reid could be satisfied with Jon Mason. The man follows after Harlan like a lowly private seeking promotion. And if you ask me, Jon would marry that minx just to get his hands on the Reid fortune!"

Raoul's eyes dropped when Mace paused to take another swallow of whiskey and twist in his chair. But they popped wide open again when Mace demanded he pay attention. Despite his drowsiness, Raoul listened to Mace rattle off several more remarks.

"I'm well rid of that troublesome vixen," Mace grumbled, wondering if he were trying to convince Raoul or himself. Damn, he was so frustrated he couldn't sit still. "I don't know which of us played the other for the bigger fool."

He glared at Raoul, who gave every indication of dozing off. "One night she said she loved me and the next morning you would have thought I didn't matter a tittle! How is a man supposed to know where he stands with a woman like Jake? She doesn't think she needs any man, the independent little snip," Mace added bitterly before he polished off the remainder of the brandy. Heaving an exasperated sigh, he slumped in his chair. "Well, I don't need Jake either. I have enough headaches without importing one. That chit measures five feet, two inches of constant trouble."

Slowly, Mace unfolded himself and ambled toward the door. When Raoul didn't stir, Mace frowned at him. "Aren't you coming?"

Raoul looked as if he preferred to remain where he was, but Mace's question brought him to his feet. Silently, they trudged up the steps. Although Raoul was delighted to have the master of the house back in residence, he had the feeling Mace intended to bend his ear for the next several hours while he soaked in his tub. It seemed Mace planned to eradicate Jacquelyn Reid from his mind by *talking* her away. But, from the sound of things, Jake's memory refused to be neatly folded and stashed in some forgotten corner.

"Women! Who needs them!" Mace snorted cynically. "Especially that one." There were at least a dozen females hereabouts who claimed to want and need him. So why was he so frustrated by that wild-haired hellion? Why was he hounded by this irrational possessiveness for a woman who had constantly assured him she could manage quite nicely without him? Damned if Mace knew the answer to those questions. He wanted to forget that saucy temptress but he couldn't let go, even when he knew for a fact it was the wisest thing to do.

*   *   *

When Emma finished fussing over Jake's appearance she circled the young beauty in final inspection. With an approving nod, Emma waddled from the room to insure the evening meal would meet with the General's specifications.

Jacquelyn peered at her reflection in the mirror and then pulled a face at the image that materialized in her looking glass. She had vowed not to become bitter and spiteful because Mace couldn't return her affection. But that was before that deceitful scoundrel had divulged his true identity. The nerve of that man! He had known from the very beginning that she had mistaken him for Jon Mason. But did that ornery varmint admit that an error had been made? Hell no, he had played her for a bungling idiot, silently laughing at her during their journey. Well, never again would a man hear those three little words tumble from her lips! She had been successfully cured of her romantic notions of love.

With determined thought, Jake hiked up the plunging neckline of her burgundy gown. The garment had fit her perfectly before she left for New Orleans. But now it appeared she was poured into the dress and pouring *out* of the bodice! No doubt the General would comment on the indecent display of bosom. To avoid a clash, Jacquelyn wrapped a shawl around her neck and proceeded downstairs.

A proud smile tugged at Harlan's lips when he spied his granddaughter floating gracefully down the steps. Lord, he had missed this vibrant little pixie. When Jacquelyn was underfoot things just naturally happened. She kept the plantation hopping, and it had been since she'd arrived three days earlier.

"I swear you grow more lovely with each passing day," Harlan declared in his matter-of-fact voice. Formally offering Jacquelyn his arm, Harlan escorted her into the dining hall.

Jacquelyn sighed appreciatively at the candlelit

Federal table and the delicate lace tablecloth that protected the intricately carved rosewood. Above the table hung a gilded bronze chandelier. Hazy shadows paraded along the sixteen-foot-high ceiling and added a soft hue to the smoked blue walls. A French clock sat regally upon the mantel, which was bookended by huge mirrors that were encased in gold-leafed frames.

When Harlan clanged the bell that sat beside his left hand, a military procession of servants filed from the kitchen to place steaming bowls of food on the table. After a formal bow to the General and a discreet smile to Jake, the servants retreated, leaving Jake and Harlan to savor their succulent meal.

"You have yet to tell me how you were wounded," Jacquelyn reminded her grandfather. As a matter of fact, each time she broached the subject, Harlan had veered to another topic of conversation. "And don't try to distract me this time. I want to know what happened."

Jacquelyn's pointed glance provoked Harlan's frown. "I was struck by a mortar shell during our march into Mexico City." Harlan indicated the cane that lay over the arm of his chair. "It seems I'm to spend the rest of my days leaning on this stick of wood. My knee was shattered and Mace . . ." He muttered under his breath and wolfed down a forkful of mashed potatoes.

One perfectly arched brow elevated. "Mace?" she prodded.

"Yes, Mace." Harlan snorted disgustedly, wishing his tongue hadn't outdistanced his brain. He really hadn't intended to mention the man's name ever again if it could be avoided. "That rascal never followed an order in his life! When I fell, I ordered him to assume command and charge the enemy. In flagrant disregard of the order, Mace scooped me off the ground and had me carted to the army surgeon for immediate attention. And then . . ." Harlan grumbled several disrespectful epithets. "Mace decided the enemy's strenght posed too great a threat to our troops and he sounded the retreat."

"He saved your life?" Jacquelyn chirped in surprise.

"Yes, damnit!" Harlan did not appear happy about it. "But it was the way he did it that infuriated me. The moment I was incapacitated he took over as if *he* were the General in charge of Texas troops!"

Jake suppressed an impish smile. "It sounds as if you and your men might have faced a slaughter if you hadn't regrouped."

"It was my opinion that we could have held our ground until reinforcements arrived. And if we hadn't, at least I would have died a hero instead of being a cripple." Harlan scowled. "But Mace deprived me of that honor. While our infantry was licking its wounds, Mace took his unruly band of Rangers and circled the Mexican forces who had gathered to celebrate our retreat. Like arrogant fools, the enemy had tucked themselves at the back of a canyon for a fiesta. Mace surprised them with a barrage of fire and turned our retreat into victory." Harlan let out his breath in a rush. "And then that renegade had the gall to hand me his medal of honor, reminding me that I was the one who was fond of brass and that he had no practical use for it."

Jacquelyn eased back in her chair, watching Harlan's face change from mortified red to the color of raw liver. As much as she now disliked the conniving Mace Gallagher, she couldn't help but be amused by her grandfather's indignant attitude toward the man who had saved his life. The General was too proud and stubborn to admit Mace was a man of sturdy character and keen intelligence. It wasn't so much what Mace had done that offended Harlan; it was the way Mace had gone about it with his lack of military protocol and his disregard for higher authority.

Now she understood how and when Mace had learned

to fight with such skillful efficiency. He fought like a Texan, a Comanche, and a Mexican vaquero all rolled into one. Commanding a band of rough-edged Rangers was a strike against Mace, as far as Harlan was concerned. Mace symbolized the rowdy, unruly, undisciplined breed of men the General was forced to tolerate, men he disliked on mere principle. Mace could have been a saint (which of course he wasn't, the scoundrel!), but Harlan would have still detested him simply because of the company he kept, because Jacquelyn's mother had betrayed her father by running off with that same breed of man.

"It seems you should be praising Gallagher's capabilities instead of condemning him," Jacquelyn taunted, lifting her glass to peer at her grandfather from over the rim.

Harlan slammed his fist on the table, sloshing wine on the lace tablecloth. "How can you defend the man after he deceived you? Don't tell me you are still harboring affection for that lout!"

Her brown eyes lanced off Harlan's decorated uniform, the one he saved for special occasions—the one he had worn to dinner each evening since her return to the plantation. "Despite my personal feelings for the man, I cannot deny that I respect his ability to handle himself in the face of adversity. I am also thankful he saved your life as well as mine."

Harlan released an annoyed grunt. "You like his style because you are two of a kind, as much as I hate to admit it. My own granddaughter, my own flesh and blood." He sighed dramatically. "She has denied her military upbringing to become as much the renegade as Mace Gallagher!"

After counting to ten to prevent the eruption of her temper, Jacquelyn vigorously carved her steak. She and Mace may be two of a kind, but she did not appreciate the

General calling attention to that fact.

The brittle silence was shattered by Harlan's grumbling. "I owe Mace Gallagher my life, although it galls me to say so since I was prepared to die the honorable death of a soldier. But I will admit my gratitude to him in only one instance," he resentfully admitted. "The army surgeon in our division determined that my leg needed to be removed. Mace refused to permit the man to lay a saw to me. Defying another order from a superior officer, the surgeon, he and his cohort, Hub MacIntosh, carted me to another camp where there was a physician they respected."

Intuition told Jacquelyn that deep down inside, beneath that stoic veneer of military protocol, Harlan admired Mace Gallagher's gumption. Although the two men were as different as night and day and would probably never agree on any issue, Mace had earned Harlan's grudging respect. Harlan knew a merger between them would never work. These two war-horses would constantly butt heads, each one confident that his decision was correct. In Harlan's estimation, there was a right way and a wrong way. Harlan's was the right way. Her own dealings with the General had proved that theory. As far as her grandfather was concerned, Jacquelyn had never been right in her life, even if Harlan had let her get away with being wrong.

"I think it best to dismiss this subject of conversation before it spoils my appetite," Harlan insisted as he masked his emotions behind a blank stare. "And in honor of your return, I have planned a grand ball. Now that you're home you can see to the guest list and select suitable refreshments for our party."

Jacquelyn calmly set her eating utensils aside and met the General's somber countenance. "I have not returned to serve only in the capacity of mistress of this house," she informed him firmly. "You know I was never content with merely overseeing domestic affairs." Her chin tilted to that determined angle Harlan had come to know all too well. "I wish to take an active part in business matters and acquaint myself with the financial workings of this plantation, as well as the commission company."

His wrinkled face registered surprise. "Blast it, girl, there is no need for that." Harlan sniffed in a tone that squelched argument. Holding true to form, Jacquelyn ignored it. "Your cousin Malcolm," he went on, "has been managing the commission company since I marched off to war. And Jon Mason has been overseeing the plantation quite satisfactorily. A woman's place is . . ."

When Jacquelyn's brow elevated to an even higher angle, Harlan swallowed the remainder of his sentence.

"A woman's place is wherever a woman wishes to be, Gen'ral," she declared, her dark eyes flickering rebelliously. "I did not spend hours laboring over the mastery of mathematics just to count the stacks of dishes in the kitchen and the linen in the closet!"

Harlan glared at his stubbornly independent granddaughter. "You haven't changed one whit, have you?"

A mischievous smile pursed her lips. "Come now, Gen'ral, you said you were certain I wouldn't," she reminded him saucily.

Her grandfather let out his breath in a rush. "Yes, I did, but I had hoped—"

"Only last year a convention was held in New York to deliver a general declaration of women's rights," Jacquelyn informed him between bites. "Not the least of the demands was to allow women to vote and to enter careers that have been restricted only to men. I have been reading Sarah Grimke's *Letters on the Equality of the Sexes and the Conditions of Women* and—"

"And I think it's time to change the subject," Harlan muttered, fighting to contain his temper.

"We already have once," she reminded him with a

teasing grin.

Harlan's graying brows narrowed over his glittering brown eyes. "Don't badger me, Jake," he warned in a gruff tone that indicated her taunting was not well received.

Their dark eyes locked and clashed.

"I want the right to assume at least partial control of the family business. Malcolm is only your nephew and I am your granddaughter. I should think close relatives should be entitled—"

"No!" he spouted.

"Yes!" she contradicted just as loudly.

"No, you are a wom—"

"I am a Reid, a chip off the block, *your* block," Jacquelyn cut in. "I am willing and capable and I wish to do my part," she declared firmly.

Harlan threw up his hands in a gesture of futility. Jacquelyn had that look about her—one that suggested she had dug in her heels and would not turn from this topic of conversation until she had been granted her way. "Oh, very well, I'll send a message to Malcolm, ordering him to tote home the ledgers so you can acquaint yourself with the company. And when you puzzle it all out you can explain it to me."

"What about the plantation ledgers?" Jake pressed, biting back a victorious smile.

"They are at your disposal. If Jon Mason ever returns from Galveston, and after I finish raking him over the coals for not meeting your ship, he can answer your questions." Harlan gouged his steak and glared at his potatoes. Damnit, he had done it again. He had yielded to Jacquelyn's demands, even when he hadn't intended to back down from his stand. "I don't know why I always put up such a fuss," he grumbled. "You always could poke and prod me until I depleted my patience and gave into your whims."

209

Gracefully, Jacquelyn rose from her chair and sailed around the table to plant a kiss on Harlan's knitted brow. "I thought we had an understanding, you and I." Her eyes twinkled with a radiance that melted Harlan's resentment. "I love you for what you are—beneath all that military brass and polish. And you love me for what I am, flaws and all."

"Including headstrong, relentless, unruly, opinionated . . ." Harlan rattled off her peccadilloes with ease and then broke into a crooked smile. "And in return for my permission to thrust yourself into family affairs, I ask that you give Jonathan Mason a chance to court you."

"A military officer suggesting a bribe?" Jacquelyn feigned astonishment. "The army would strip you of your medals of honor and toss you out on your . . . brass."

Her grin was contagious. Despite Harlan's attempt to maintain a blank expression, he broke into a reluctant smile. "I have only your best interests at heart," he defended himself. "Jon Mason and I are compatible. But any romantic notions you have for that rapscallion Mace Gallagher will only cause conflict. He delights in needling me as much as you do."

Jacquelyn felt her wounded heart lurch in her chest. The mere mention of Mace's name still had the power to hurt her. She was vulnerable where he was concerned. And yet she possessed the intelligence to know she was not woman enough to tame a man like Mace. He cherished his freedom and he had too many other females at his beck and call to settle for one lasting relationship.

"I know on which side of the Reid-Gallagher feud I belong," she assured her grandfather with more conviction than she felt at the moment.

Harlan fondly squeezed her hand. "Then you will consider Jon Mason as a suitor, just to please me?" he said hopefully.

Jacquelyn nodded her consent, not enthusiastically, but at least graciously.

"And you won't contemplate blowing Jon to smithereens the way you did that young man in New Orleans?" he questioned with a disapproving glare.

Uncomfortably, Jacquelyn shifted from one foot to the other and toyed with the sling that cradled her right arm. Confound it, why had Aunt Florence disclosed that incident to Harlan? Probably to harass him, Jake speculated. Florence derived wicked delight in cutting her older brother down to her size, and she did it every chance she got. And no doubt Harlan knew of all the other unladylike shenanigans Jake had failed to mention in her letters.

"No duels," Jacquelyn promised grudgingly. "I will give Jon Mason a sporting chance to prove himself worthy of my admiration and respect."

"I ask no more than that," Harlan declared. "And despite my gruffness and brisk demands, I do not wish to see you wed to a man you can't love. I would wish for you the same happiness I shared with your grandmother. I wanted your father . . ." His voice trailed off and his eyes took on a bitter glow.

"I know the truth about my mother," Jacquelyn confided quietly. "Aunt Florence told me."

"Damn that woman!" Harlan snapped. "I didn't want you to know."

"Nor did I wish you to learn of my antics in New Orleans," Jacquelyn countered.

"Despite her scant good qualities, that sister of mine has a bit of the devil in her," Harlan muttered crossly. "She always did have the knack for brewing trouble."

After Jacquelyn swept out of the room, Harlan sat staring at the far wall. Had Florence ever really forgiven him for objecting to her marriage to that irresponsible tumbleweed? Was this her way of reciprocating? Harlan

211

expelled a heavy sigh. There was no way of knowing what was on Florence's mind. She may have been his sister but sometimes she behaved more like his enemy. What had possessed Florence to tell Jacquelyn about her mother's infidelity to her father? Damned Rangers anyway, Harlan growled to himself. They were sworn to uphold justice and squelch trouble, but they were also notorious hell-raisers who could cause their own set of problems. In Harlan's opinion there was an incredibly fine line between Texas Rangers and outlaws. They could be ruthless, insolent, and impossible to deal with.

Harlan shoved aside that thought and frowned pensively. Maybe it was best that Jacquelyn knew the truth about her mother. Now she was old enough to accept it. Perhaps Jacquelyn could see the bitter past as a valuable lesson for the future. Surely she understood that any feelings she was harboring for Mace Gallagher would be wasteful thought. The man had a reputation with women, and if Mace had dared to take advantage of Jacquelyn during their journey, Harlan swore he would . . .

A disgusted growl shattered the silence. Harlan didn't know exactly what he would do, but Mace would definitely pay for taking liberties. Digesting that vengeful thought, Harlan limped outside, hoping Jon Mason would quickly return to assume his duties as overseer of the plantation. All this extra walking and riding was playing havoc with Harlan's crippled leg. And although Jacquelyn had thrust herself into many of the duties, Harlan still maintained that some tasks were designed for men. That had instigated another argument, which Harlan had cut short by ordering his granddaughter to change the subject.

Chapter 12

Seated beside her grandfather at the desk, Jacquelyn concentrated on the ledgers she had been laboring over for the past hour. The General had attempted to explain Jonathan's bookkeeping methods, but it was difficult to tell exactly what Jon had been doing. He had devised his own unique technique of calculation and it compared to nothing Jacquelyn had learned in finishing school. In exasperation, Jacquelyn had referred to Jonathan's methods as incompetent hen scratchings, while Harlan had preferred to diplomatically label the man's methods as unique and creative.

The murmur of voices interrupted what would surely have become an argument over Jon's ability to keep books, and Harlan was relieved to have a distraction.

"I wonder who that could be." Harlan didn't have long to wonder. Within a few moments the battered and haggared Jonathan Mason wobbled into the study.

Without introduction, Jacquelyn knew who this bedraggled specimen was. She supposed he could be described as tall, dark, and handsome—if one stretched one's imagination. Jacquelyn would have referred to Jon Mason as tall, thin, spindly-legged, and mildly pleasing to the eye. Although Jon wasn't exactly homely, his features and physique could never compare to the well-sculptured, brawny Mace Gal—

Jacquelyn's mind skidded to a halt. The last thing she wanted was to compare her grandfather's overseer to that raven-haired devil who had stripped her of her innocence. Mace was out of sight, and she was determined to keep him out of mind.

"What the Hades has happened to you?" Harlan growled in question. "And where have you been for over two weeks?"

Jonathan drew his thin frame up to full stature and squared his narrow shoulders as if he were standing at attention. His ragged clothes hung off of him in an uncomplimentary fashion. The ruffled appearance of his hair and the smudges on his face suggested that he had endured one hellacious fortnight.

"Forgive me, Gen'ral. I was set upon by thieves during my trek to Galveston." His pale gray eyes shifted to the lovely vision who was poised beside Harlan. Courteously, Jon dropped into a bow and murmured a greeting to the bewitching young lady in bright yellow silk. "I received a blow to the back of the head that scrambled my brain. It was two full days before I could see or think straight. By the time I got my bearings and reached Galveston, a tropical storm had hit the coast. I learned that Miss Jacquelyn had come and gone from the hotel, but it was impossible to track her during the inclement weather." A relieved smile spread across his lips. "I assume this lovely angel is Jacquelyn, and I am most thankful she found her way home without suffering unnecessarily."

Since Jacquelyn had shed the hampering sling that had cradled her arm, Jon had no way of knowing her journey had been far from easy or eventless. But Harlan was not about to permit his granddaughter's trials to go unnoticed. Jonathan may have received a bump on the

214

skull, but Jacquelyn had been dragged into an alley and ambushed, and the General proceeded to tell him so!

"My granddaughter was dragged into an alley and then ambushed on the road." Harlan snorted disdainfully. "She was shot in the shoulder by snipers—perhaps by the same scalawags who attacked you." His graying brows flattened over his flashing brown eyes. "I am not at all pleased that I was foolish enough to send a boy to do a man's job!"

The insult caused Jonathan to duck his ruffled head in silent apology. In that instant Jacquelyn knew her grandfather's lackey would never suit her. Jon responded to Harlan as if he were a private in the military ranks. Jacquelyn had promised to give Jon a sporting chance, but it would be no more than pretense. Jon was too meek to suit her tastes. There was no challenge in matching will and wit against the meek Jon Mason.

"I am truly sorry to hear of your misfortune, Miss Jacquelyn," Jon replied apologetically. "I hold myself totally responsible for your perilous plight and I will do all I can to compensate."

"The first order of business is to make yourself presentable," Harlan insisted. "See that you are starched and pressed before you join us for supper."

With a humble salute, Jon slinked from the room, leaving Jacquelyn staring thoughtfully after him. She wasn't so certain of the man's abilities to manage the plantation, judging by his entries in the ledgers. And she was even less impressed with Jon as a man. He may have been capable of carrying out orders but Jacquelyn was skeptical of his mentality.

"Well, what do you think of him?" the General demanded abruptly.

"Compared to what?" Jake countered with a teasing smile.

Harlan glared at her over the top of his wire-rimmed glasses. "Don't taunt me, Jake. Do you suppose you could find yourself attracted to Jon once he has improved his appearance?"

Jacquelyn had always held firm to the theory that clothes did not make a man. But in Jon's case, she doubted he could do anything to alter her first impression of him. There was a long pause while Jacquelyn debated whether to lie through her teeth in order to pacify Harlan or to blurt out the truth.

"Well?" Harlan drummed his blunt fingertips on the desk.

"I will permit his courtship if he is so inclined," Jacquelyn promised, her voice lacking enthusiasm. "But surely you must realize Jonathan Mason is not my type."

Harlan sank back in his chair and eyed his granddaughter with a dubious frown. "I'm not at all sure you have a type." He sniffed caustically. "From what I learned from Flo's letters, you rejected beaux from all walks of life . . . and for reasons that sounded a mite flimsy."

"I know exactly what I want in a man," Jacquelyn said defensively, her dark eyes flickering in mild irritation.

"What you want and what you need are two entirely different matters," Harlan declared with stern conviction.

"I do not need a man at all," Jacquelyn snapped, her voice rising to match Harlan's. "I am perfectly capable of taking care of myself."

"I think you and Jon would make suitable mates. He is well bred, well mannered, and most importantly, I can tolerate him in my house."

"If Jon possesses all the traits you consider noteworthy, perhaps you should marry him." Her pleasant

216

voice eased the sting of her words and her impish smile made it difficult to take offense.

Harlan grinned in spite of himself. "I suppose you think I am being pushy and domineering, as always."

"I do," she agreed without hesitation.

"Oh hell, I guess I am," he reluctantly admitted. "But before the heavenly chariot comes to fetch me I wish to see you happy and married."

"Couldn't you settle for just happy?" she inquired as she took her seat beside him. "You have always been the only man in my life. I should think you—"

Harlan's scowl interrupted her. "Don't try to flatter me, Jake. This is a serious matter. I want to see you married to an honorable, trustworthy man who can assume the responsibilities of the family plantation and business." When Jake opened her mouth to protest his comment, Harlan rushed on. "That is not to say you are not capable. Only that it is right and proper for you to wed and to share the responsibility with your husband," he added emphatically.

"I will marry when the right man comes along and not a moment before." Her chin tilted to a stubborn angle.

"I can only hope I live long enough to meet the right man . . . if and when he comes along," Harlan muttered sourly.

"We had better change the subject," Jacquelyn suggested. "Our arguments tend to spoil your appetite and increase mine."

Harlan eased back in his chair, amused that his granddaughter had resorted to this tactic of avoiding conflicts. "Very well, let's scan these confounded ledgers to see if we can make sense of them. Later Jon can explain what we have read."

A slight frown knitted her brow as she stared at the scribbling in the ledgers. "In my estimation the expenditures are too great in comparison to the profit. It seems to be that your man Jon might have cut a few corners."

"Balderdash!" Harlan spouted. "Jon is frugal to a fault."

"Not according to these entries," Jacquelyn pointed out.

Harlan leaned forward to stare at the scribblings Jake had indicated. "You are quibbling over the purchase of the latest farming equipment? Machinery often breaks down and must be replaced. That is a fact of life!"

"There is such a thing as repairs," Jacquelyn contended. "I think dear Jon has been a mite wasteful and frivolous. If he cannot repair machinery, he should seek out someone who can."

"He most certainly is not!" Harlan grumbled indignantly. "You are purposely contesting his decisions, just to be contrary. You don't want to like the man because I do!"

"Balderdash!" Jacquelyn shouted, tossing Harlan's favorite expletive back in his face.

The argument continued for several more minutes. Finally, Harlan snatched the ledger from beneath Jacquelyn's nose and slammed the book shut. "You and Jon can labor over these financial statements later. You are indeed going to give me indigestion if you continue with your accusations."

"Fine, Jon can speak for himself—if he can justify these wasteful purchases," she gritted out.

As Jacquelyn sailed out of the study, her skirts swishing around her, Harlan rolled his eyes upward. Confound it, why was Jake taking such an interest in business management? She seemed determined to throw herself into the workings of both the commission company and the plantation. Was it a method of distraction? Was she still being tormented by her infatuation for that renegade Mace Gallagher?

Harlan grumbled under his breath. Of all the men for Jake to stumble onto in Galveston! Well, she had best rout any foolish notions about Mace from her mind. Mace wasn't good enough for Jacquelyn. The man could be a scoundrel when it suited his whims. Malcolm had informed Harlan that Mace was undermining their business by offering higher prices for cotton to their clients, encouraging planters to abandon the Reid Commission Company. No wonder that varmint had become a giant in the commission business, Harlan thought resentfuilly. Reid's profits had steadily declined the past three years and he had Mace Gallagher to thank for it. Mace didn't seem to care whose toes he stepped on during his ascent to the top.

Damn that man. First he'd preyed on Harlan's clients, and now he had cast his spell on Jake. But Harlan would never agree to a merger or a marriage between Mace and Jacquelyn. Hell would be dripping with icicles long before Harlan consented to tying his name to that wily rascal's. Mace may have found a way to obtain all he wanted financially, but he wasn't going to take control of this family!

While Harlan was cursing Mace for his skullduggery, Jacquelyn was denouncing the lingering memories that followed her like her own shadow. Hurriedly, she changed into her breeches and shirt. What she needed was to ride astride her buckskin stallion, to allow the wind to clear the clutter from her mind. She hadn't seen Mace for over a week, and yet his vision colored all conversation and spoiled every thought. How long would it take to free herself from his spell? Heaven only knew, she mused with a dispirited sigh.

God, what a fool she had been to fall beneath his seductive charm. Mace had toyed with her to ease his lusts and to annoy the General. To Mace, she was a conquered prize, an object of pleasure, the brunt of his jokes. Lord, if her grandfather ever discovered that she had slept in Mace's arms . . .

Grimly, Jacquelyn stalked into the stable, veering around one of the many oversized anthills that plagued the plantation. In irritation, she stamped on a few of the pesky insects on her way into the barn to retrieve Lancelot.

She was not going to spare Mace Gallagher another thought. He was like a severe case of the grippe, but she had survived the affliction. It wasn't like her to dawdle over a man, especially one who could never return her affection. The sooner she accepted the fact that Mace was a page from her past, the happier she would be.

Clinging to that sensible thought, Jacquelyn thundered off on her steed with no particular destination in mind. All she wanted was to outrun those laughing amber eyes and that disarming smile, to forget the moments of splendor that had no place in her life.

After galloping across the meadow at breakneck speed, Jacquelyn reined Lancelot to a halt beside the river. Impulsively, Jacquelyn bounded from the saddle and peeled off her clothes. She had often taken to the stream as a child, even when Harlan had ordered her not to swim alone. But there was something pacifying about this spot at the bend of the river. The quiet cove lured her; it always had. She needed time to sort out her emotions, to spread them before her and analyze them one at a time.

With a contented sigh, Jacquelyn glided across the sparkling blue water, allowing the sun to beat down on her bare skin. Ah, this was heaven, she mused with a sigh. It was as if she were alone in the world, as if the tranquil cove had been created just for her. And like a playful child, Jacquelyn dived beneath the surface, exploring the underwater world that was untainted by memories of Mace Gallagher. He had not left his mark here. This haven was free of his spell, and Jacquelyn could venture back through time without being entrapped by the darkly handsome vision which had haunted her for seven frustrating days.

Before her lungs burst, Jacquelyn resurfaced. Absently she shoved the wet tendrils of dark hair away from her face and wiped the water from her eyes. When her vision cleared, a startled gasp erupted from her lips. There, lounging leisurely on the river bank, was the last man she wanted to see. Mace Gallagher was grinning rakishly, his golden eyes making a meal of her.

"Are you enjoying your swim, little mermaid?" he inquired casually.

"What are you doing here?" she snapped. "This is private property and you are trespassing. The Gen'ral would have a conniption fit if he knew you were spying on me."

Mace's tawny eyes drank in the bewitching sight of diamond water droplets glistening on her satiny flesh. Desire inflamed his wandering thoughts. Mace instantly recalled every exquisite inch of her body, remembering the feel of her luscious curves beneath his exploring hands. It was difficult to sit on the bank when he ached to tear off his clothes and mold himself to her tempting body.

Mace wasn't sure why he had ridden toward the Reid plantation, but it really hadn't mattered what excuse he dreamed up. The moment he noticed this daredevil hoyden sailing across the pasture on her winged stallion, Mace had followed in her tracks. He hadn't even scolded himself once when he crouched in the underbrush to watch her strip from her garments. He had spied on this shapely minx like a Peeping Tom and had relished every tantalizing moment of it.

After Jacquelyn had dived into the river, Mace had told himself it would be best if he sneaked quietly away. But his legs had refused to beat a hasty retreat. His betraying appendages had brought him to the river's edge and deposited him beside Jake's discarded clothes.

"You truly are a sight to behold," Mace complimented, his voice ragged with mounting passion. It was a mark of heroism that he was still sitting on the ground instead of swimming toward this enchanting nymph. Heaven knew he wanted to join her for a swim and then . . .

"And you are a scoundrel of the worst sort, Mace Gallagher," she declared frostily. It annoyed her that Mace merely smiled as if she had blessed him with a compliment rather than the insult he so richly deserved.

For a long, brittle moment they stared at each other. Mace offered intimate promises with his eyes, while Jacquelyn's glower spoke volumes, none of which he dared to ask her to translate into words. Mace was fantasizing about the splendorous things they could do together, and Jacquelyn was visualizing how Mace would look while he was roasting over his private barbecue pit in hell. Finally deciding it was useless to attempt to outstare the rake, Jacquelyn expelled an exasperated breath.

"Kindly turn your back so I can come ashore." Her tone brooked no argument, but it didn't faze Mace. He was still all eyes.

"No," he told her matter-of-factly. When Jake's face turned furious red, Mace flashed her a grin of roguish anticipation. "There is no need to pretend modesty. We have been as close as two people can get."

His eyes slid down her body in total possession, provoking Jacquelyn's notorious temper. "Damn you! There is not one gentlemanly bone in your body!" she spewed at him. Her accompanying glare was as hot as the hinges on hell's door.

"Nor a ladylike ligament in your delicious body, my

dear," Mace purred with a mocking smile. "And if you want your clothes you'll have to come and get them. I'm not leaving until I'm damned good and ready."

Oh, she would love to march ashore and beat the tar out of him. Perhaps that was exactly what she should do. Her modesty was not as important as her eagerness for revenge. Besides, it would be best if Mace disliked her as much as she wanted to dislike him. Then he would never come near her again and she could forget this ridiculous fascination for this conniving, two-legged rat.

"Very well then, since you leave me no choice . . ." Jacquelyn sighed melodramatically as she glided toward shore.

When Jacquelyn found solid footing and rose from the water, Mace's keen gaze sketched every luscious inch of her exposed flesh. Lord, he hadn't forgotten even one minute detail of her alluring figure. She was as he remembered—the essence of feminine beauty. Her damp hair clung to her wet skin, skin that danced with sunshine and diamond droplets. Mace ached to reach out and touch what his eyes consumed, to map her well-formed body and bring it into intimate contact with his.

Even after a week of self-inspiring sermons Mace was still wrestling with the memories of their days together. He had even attempted to find distraction in another woman's arms. But his torment came in seeing Jacquelyn's flawless features the moment he closed his eyes to lose himself in passion. The woman he had sought out to ease his longings had thought him crazed when he'd suddenly pulled away from her and bounded from the bed. Mace had muttered some silly excuse while he dressed. He had ridden back home to unload his frustration on Raoul, his faithful but mute confidant, who had listened without passing judgment.

Like a fool Mace had believed he wouldn't give this feisty sprite another thought after he'd deposited her on the General's doorstep. But Mace had thought wrong. He'd kept envisioning this dazzling beauty pouncing on him to retrieve his pistol so she could blow her assailants to kingdom come. He'd rememberered how she'd balanced on the side of her steed after the ambush. He'd felt the sensations of having her exquisite body molded against his. And he'd recalled the dejected expression that had claimed her features when she'd discovered he had deceived her by pretending to be Jon Mason. But what haunted Mace most, even more than wanting to recreate those memroies of unrivaled passion, was . . .

His thoughts dispersed when Jacquelyn approached him. Mace wanted to make quick comparisons, to assure himself that this dark-haired goddess was just another woman. But Mace couldn't conjure up even one other female who could match Jacquelyn's grace, poise, and unsurpassed beauty. This misfit was in a league all by herself, as much as he hated to admit it.

When Jacquelyn knelt to scoop up her garments, Mace was granted the heart-stopping view of her profile. She was so perfectly formed, so delicately boned, so . . . His mind lurched to seek an appropriate description while his eyes wandered at will.

A disappointed frown crossed Mace's brow when Jake climbed into her boyish clothes, depriving him of the enticing view. Desire gnawed at his insides and his breathing became erratic when Jacquelyn sashayed toward him, wearing that mischievous smile of hers.

"Again it seems you have enjoyed yourself at my expense," she said, striving for a pleasant tone that wouldn't betray her intentions. "Do you make it a habit of sneaking up on defenseless women and forcing them to submit to having your eyes roam all over them?"

"Actually this is my first time," Mace confessed unrepentantly.

His golden eyes dropped to the damp fabric that

hugged her high-thrusting breasts and trim waist, just as he ached to do. The intensity of his gaze made Jacquelyn flinch. It unnerved her that this rapscallion could look at her in that unique way of his and make her want what he was contemplating doing to her.

But when I'm finished with Mace, he won't come within ten feet of me again, she assured herself. It had to be this way. She would always be vulnerable to this lion of a man. All that would save her from humiliating herself was to build walls between them, to incite his anger.

As Jacquelyn paused in front of him, Mace unfolded himself from the ground. He loomed over Jacquelyn with his towering height, yearning to envelop her in his arms, to remove the hindering garments she had just climbed into.

A surprised yelp erupted from Mace's lips when Jacquelyn came uncoiled. She was no longer the alluring temptress but rather the vengeful she-cat. Her boot collided with his shin. Before Mace could think to counter the painful attack on his person, Jacquelyn planted her fist in his jaw. The blow rattled Mace's teeth, but he recovered in time to catch the boot that was aimed at his loins.

It was Jacquelyn's turn to shriek in surprise. Mace's hand clamped around her ankle, uplifting her leg. With a quick snap of his wrist he knocked her off balance and sent her sprawling backward. Pronouncing every curse word in her vocabulary, Jacquelyn rolled to her feet and sprang at him. Mace was caught in mid-laughter when Jacquelyn used her head as a battering ram in his belly. The force of her forward momentum sent him stumbling back in an attempt to catch his balance. Before he could steady himself, he was toppling into the mud with Jacquelyn straddling his hips.

Mace's next maneuver would have been to twist

sideways, dragging this wildcat beneath him. But Jacquelyn scooped up a handful of mud and mashed it into his face. Blindly, Mace groped to clamp his fingers into her waist and shove her face down in the gooey mud. But Jacquelyn was lightning quick. She vaulted to her feet and jabbed her boot heel in his belly. A pained grunt burst from Mace's muddy lips, and Jacquelyn chuckled triumphantly.

"There is nothing so satisfying as felling a giant," she taunted unmercifully. "That makes us even . . . almost." Adding insult to injury, Jake scooped up another glob of mud and flung it in Mace's eyes before he could wipe away the first clump.

"I advise you to keep your distance, Mace Gallagher. As you can see, your attention is unwanted. What you and I once shared is over and done." Pride demanded that she curtly dismiss him, and so she did. "We had a frivolous affair, but it will not be repeated. I retract every nice thing I ever said or thought about you. You, sir, can go straight to hell!"

Flinging her nose in the air, Jacquelyn stomped toward Lancelot. My, she felt ever so much better after she'd satisfied her thirst for revenge. Hating Mace comppensated for all the hurt and disappointment she had suffered after he had deceived and dismissed her. So much for graciously accepting rejection, she thought to herself. Ah well, she never claimed to be perfect.

Mace was furious with himself for permitting that firebrand to best him. He had faced far worthier opponents and emerged victorious. But to be knocked down by a mere wisp of a woman burned his male pride to a crisp!

Wiping the mud from his eyes, Mace launched himself off the ground and charged like a buffalo. Jacquelyn barely had time to notice his approach before she was flat on her back, staring up into Mace's mud-caked face, one that was frozen in an agitated glare. Damn her foolishness, she should have known better than to turn her back on Mace. She knew how dangerous he could be when he was angered. She had witnessed his fighting techniques that night at the inn. And now it seemed she was to be on the receiving end of his effective attack.

"Go ahead, hit a woman," Jacquelyn sneered contemptuously. "I would expect no less from the likes of you."

A wry smile appeared from the cracks in his muddy mask. Holding her pinned on the ground, Mace lowered his head. "I would derive no pleasure from pounding you flat, my little she-wolf." His voice rattled with mischievous laughter when Jacquelyn squirmed beneath him, making him all the more aware of her ripe body brushing against his. "If you are so fond of this muddy mask, maybe you would like to wear it. . . ."

Jacquelyn half-expected Mace to grasp a wad of mud and smear it on her face. Indeed, she would have preferred it. But Mace's retaliation was far worse than she anticipated. He kissed mud onto her features as his powerful body slid down hers. His knee situated itself between her thighs, allowing him to lie familiarly upon her. His skillful hand traversed the curvaceous terrain of her breasts and then roamed across her hips, starting fires Jacquelyn had never wanted to experience again. But experience them she did. Her betraying body tingled beneath his exploring touch and her pounding heart catapulted to her throat.

Oh, why hadn't he plied her with rough abuse, granting her one more reason to hate him? Why did he have to arouse her with a breath-stealing kiss that crumbled her defenses? And how on earth could she possibly like this man when she was striving to despise him? It wasn't fair, damnit! She shouldn't be enjoying

227

the feel of his muscled body pressing intimately against hers. She shouldn't be returning his kiss as if she were hungry for the taste of him, mud and all.

When Mace finally raised his head, Jacquelyn lay entranced. She stared bewilderedly at the smudged face that hovered a hairbreadth away from hers. "You said it was over between us, but that's a lie and you know it," Mace whispered raggedly. "I'm afraid what is between us has only just begun. You want to hate me for deceiving you, but you can't deny the fires we kindle when we touch. I can feel your body responding to mine." His fingertips drifted across the taut peak of her breast. "Especially here . . ." His bold caresses ventured down her belly to trace the gentle curve of her hip. The hint of a smile pursed his lips when he felt her tremble beneath his straying hand. "And here . . ." His fingertips glided across her thigh to rest familiarly against her abdomen. "You haven't forgotten one glorious moment of our lovemaking. Nor have I. The memories skip like shadows across my mind, interrupting thought, preying on my emotions. . . ."

His hand dipped beneath the band of her breeches to settle on her hip. Holding her unblinking gaze, Mace drew her to him, permitting her to feel the full extent of his own arousal. Although garments separated them, the imprint of his hand and his muscular body lying suggestively against hers seared Jacquelyn inside and out. She wanted to protest his seduction, to deny the sensations that sizzled through her, but no words formed on her lips.

Suddenly, his teasing smile evaporated and his caresses sought to please rather than tease. "I want you, Jake. And I've missed you this long week we have been apart." His hands and lips roved here and there, silently persuading her to surrender to the forbidden emotions that warred within her. "No matter what else is between us, there will always be this sweet ache that only our lovemaking can satisfy. Every thought of you feeds this flame within me. And when you consent to let the real Jon Mason kiss you, you'll know you are living a lie. You can't deny your desire for me or my insatiable passion for you. . . ."

Golden-brown eyes, surrounded with mud-caked lashes, bore down onto her smudged face. His hand fanned across her derriere, and then moved to caress her inner thigh. Wild, erotic sensations channeled through her blood as he lifted her aching body to his. Jacquelyn could feel the rapid beat of his heart against her breasts, feel the whipcord muscles of his thighs straining against her quivering flesh. All her senses were focused on this awesome mass of masculinity, and Jacquelyn couldn't think or see past the web of pleasure Mace wove about her. Monstrous cravings gnawed at her as his mouth made a slow, languid descent to take possession of her lips. Her body burned with desire as his practiced hands dived beneath her shirt to make stimulating contact with her bare skin. And despite all else, Jacquelyn kissed him back, hungry for another taste of him, aching to appease the torment of being so close and yet so maddeningly far away.

When her arm slid around his neck, Mace felt himself go up in flames. Lord, he had missed this feisty bundle of spirit, far more than he even realized. Each day they had been apart had blended into monotony. From the moment Mace had spied this daredevil minx galloping with the wind, his emotions and senses had come back to life. Mace had delayed his return to Galveston, reluctant to put more distance between them, even when he knew it would have been wise to avoid temptation. He had listed dozens of reasons why he should go, but he couldn't make himself leave when this dark-eyed enchantress was only a few miles away. And now that she was in his arms again, Mace knew why he had been unable to leave her. She had become his obsession. It was no longer enough that he had once wooed her into his bed. Now he needed her there, again and again, until his fascination for her faded and he could walk away without regret.

A muffled groan bubbled in Mace's throat when Jacquelyn arched against him. He could feel her impatient hands tripping over the buttons of his shirt, anxious to caress his hair-matted flesh. With devouring impatience, Mace kissed her deeply while his own roaming hands sought to make titillating contact with her silky flesh. He wanted to devour this delicious pixie, to relive those wild, passionate moments of splendor that tormented his thoughts and preyed on his soul. . . .

"Miss Reid? Yoo-hoo!" Jon Mason's voice sliced through the breathless silence, shattering the hypnotic spell.

Swearing vehemently at the interruption, Mace pushed away from temptation and assisted Jacquelyn to her feet. After planting one last devouring kiss to her soft lips, Mace disappeared in the underbrush.

For a moment, Jacquelyn stood there on wobbly legs, waiting for her heart to return to its normal beat. It annoyed her that Mace could come and go so quickly when it was his want. He moved with the silence and agility of a jungle cat. He had the uncanny knack of blending into his surroundings while she fumbled and faltered like a senseless giraffe, attempting to refasten herself into her gaping garments.

Inhaling a deep breath, Jacquelyn stuffed the hem of her shirt into her breeches and struggled to regain her composure. Lord-a-mercy, what spell had that raven-haired devil cast upon her? She actually resented Jon's interruption. Blast it, she should have been thanking her lucky stars Jon had come along when he did. But instead, she itched to pound Jonathan into the ground for disturbing what would have been her last passionate rendezvous with Mace.

That's crazy, Jacquelyn thought. Jon had saved her from herself. When Mace touched her, her mind went completely blank. She became putty in his hands. Mace was a magician who whispered incantations about her until her will suddenly became his own. He could make her want him in all the wild, wondrous ways she had discovered in his arms. It was obvious she had no fortitude when it came to Mace Gallagher. The only way to counter her irrational craving for him was to distract herself with another man.

"Ah, there you are at last," Jon enthused as he swung from his mount. He broke stride when he noticed the damp strands of hair that cascaded over her shoulders, the enticing way her wet clothes clung to her shapely figure. A curious frown clouded his brow when he spied the smears of mud that blemished her exquisite face. "Is something amiss?"

Finally, Jacquelyn assumed complete control of her senses. "Not a thing," she insisted as she knelt by the river to cleanse her face, hoping the cool water would erase the warm flush that claimed her cheeks.

"The Gen'ral thought it might be a good idea for you and me to become better acquainted." Jon was delighted with the possibility of courting this spirited beauty. When the General had hinted at a possible match between them, Jon's mind had teemed with possibilities and obvious advantages, not the least of which was the lady herself. With the General's blessing, Jon could acquire a lovely bride and a sizable inheritance.

When Jacquelyn rose to full stature, her eyes swam over Jon's flagpole frame and his hollowed cheeks. His features were too refined for her tastes. His clothes were much too formal, and they hung on his slight figure instead of stretching sensuously across his body the way Mace's . . .

Mace's words came back to haunt Jacquelyn and she impulsively burst out in request. "Kiss me, Jon."

His eyes popped from their sockets. He had been eager to woo this curvaceous sprite, but he hadn't expected to be offered such a bold invitation! The General had relayed Jake's antics in New Orleans to him, and he'd deemed it wise to proceed at a cautious pace.

"We have only met," Jon reminded her gently.

"Don't you find me attractive?" she demanded.

"Extremely, but . . ."

"Then kiss me," she insisted impatiently.

A muted growl rattled in Mace's chest when he saw Jacquelyn throw herself at the General's skinny-legged lackey. Damn her! Only moments before she had been lying in Mace's arms, responding to his ravishing kisses. And now she was seducing that milksop! What was she trying to prove, that Mace could easily be replaced? That any man could appease her fiery passions?

Mace couldn't tolerate another moment. Scowling, he backed away from his hiding place and headed toward his plantation. Confound it, Jacquelyn was playing right into the General's hands. And she would probably agree to marry that skinny galloot, just to spite Mace.

While Mace was galloping away, Jacquelyn was plastering herself against Jon's lean frame. She wanted to prove to herself that Mace held no strange powers over her, that she could forget what they had shared. But Jon's kiss lacked the spark that Mace's evoked. She could have stood there all day, kissing Jon for all she was worth, and she would have felt nothing but indifference. The depressing fact was Jon Mason kissed the way he looked—nothing extraordinary or exceptional. She received a plain, ordinary kiss from a plain, ordinary man! Damnit!

When Jacquelyn withdrew from his thin arms, Jon attempted to recapture her. But Jacquelyn flung him a disapproving frown.

"Unhand me, Jon," she demanded. "I requested one kiss. Don't expect to take more than I intended to give."

As Jacquelyn propelled herself toward Lancelot, Jon half collapsed. Lord, he felt as if he had been walking an emotional tightrope. His feelings had swung from curiosity about her odd behavior to instant desire . . . just before she'd plunged him headlong into frustration. Confronting this dark-eyed nymph was like facing the swirling winds of a hurricane, and Jon couldn't begin to guess what would happen next.

"Are you coming, Jon?" she questioned as she swung onto her powerful buckskin stallion.

Regaining his mental composure, Jon strode toward his mount. His mind was still spinning when Jacquelyn changed moods and challenged him to a race. He had barely gained his seat when Jacquelyn nudged her steed into his swiftest gait. Trailing two lengths behind her, Jon attempted to collect his scattered wits. He knew he wanted this rambunctious minx and the wealth she could offer, but he was at a total loss to determine how to handle Jacquelyn. The General had warned him that Jake was more than a handful. Completely unmanageable and unpredictable would have been nearer the mark, Jon decided.

Wearing a perplexed frown, Jon followed at Jacquelyn's heels, wondering how to approach her. Perhaps it would be best to speak of his intentions and determine how Jacquelyn felt about their possible match. Since an attempt had been made on her life, Jon wondered if she might be eager for the protection of a doting husband. Perhaps he should ask for her hand before the night was out.

Yes, that was exactly what he should do. The sooner

they were married the better. After supper, he would invite Jacquelyn to take a stroll. He would get down on bended knee and propose. Surely she wouldn't reject him after the eager kiss she had planted on his lips. That must have been her unique way of telling him she would be willing to become his wife.

While Jon was gloating over his magnetic charm, Jacquelyn was involved in a mental tug-of-war. Maybe she should seriously consider marrying harmless Jonathan Mason. The match would pacify her grandfather, and it might serve to dissuade Mace from taking unfair advantage of her. It was obvious she would never find a man who perfectly suited her. The only man who might have made her happy was not to be had. To save herself the humiliation and embarrassment of surrendering to Mace, she should marry Jon. He wouldn't inhibit her and she could remain on the family plantation until the end of her days.

Maybe it is better to wed a man I don't love (and probably never will) than to risk temptation in Mace's arms, she told herself as she raced the wind. It was far better than being hurt time and time again. Yes, a marriage to Jon would be her salvation—her protection against her own irrational desires.

Bitter laughter bubbled from her lips as she aimed herself toward the stables. Her reckless affair with Mace had distorted her dreams. There had been a time not so long ago that Jacquelyn ridiculed women who married for convenience. She had been harboring this childish whim that somewhere on this planet there was a man who could touch her heart and teach her soul to sing. Mace could have made her believe in lasting love if only he had wanted her in all the ways she wanted him.

Ah, such foolish dreams, Jacquelyn chided herself. There was no perfect match for her. She might as well wed Jon Mason and face the fact that she would never enjoy that special brand of love. Perhaps she was just woman enough to arouse Mace's desires, as he confessed, but she was not woman enough to hold onto him forever. Mace enjoyed short, shallow affairs, and Jacquelyn wanted no part of the pain she had already experienced. Let some other witless fool take her place in Mace's arms. That philanderer couldn't satisfy his lust in a hundred beds and she would be wise never to let herself forget that! Yes, she would marry Jon, and wedlock would be her protection against Mace Gallagher. It had to be, Jake reminded herself resentfully. She certainly didn't seem capable of resisting him without an excuse!

Chapter 13

Harlan beamed like a lantern blazing on a long wick while he watched Jacquelyn and Jon flirt with each other across the dinner table. To his amazement, Jacquelyn had accepted Jon's attentions and seemed satisfied with his companionship. Although she had quizzed Jon about several entries in the ledger, Jon fielded the questions with diplomatic ease. And when Jon invited Jacquelyn to accompany him on his evening rounds, she accepted without hesitation.

As the couple strolled into the foyer, Harlan slouched back in his chair and raised his glass in silent toast. Things were going splendidly. For once, Jacquelyn had bent to his wishes. If Jon didn't take advantage of Jake's gentler mood, Harlan intended to prod his overseer into a marriage proposal. Offering Jon part interest in the plantation should be incentive, Harlan speculated. Not only would Jon be entitled to Jacquelyn's dowry of land and trusts, but he would share in the cotton profits. Yes, that ought to do it, Harlan reassured himself. No man would refuse wealth and prestige when it was dumped in his lap.

While Harlan was bubbling with anticipation, Jon was casting pensive glances at his lovely companion. The full moonlight caught in her long hair, setting it to sparkling as if it were adorned with chips of diamonds. The soft shadows caressed her exquisite features, and Jon felt the stirring of desire. Fate had smiled on him when it had permitted this ravishing nymph to escape her assailants and return to the plantation. He would do his best to protect Jacquelyn from any harm that might befall her.

Encouraged by Jacquelyn's docile mood, Jon clasped her hand and fondly squeezed it. "I know we have just met, my dear, but I think you are aware of the Gen'ral's wishes where you and I are concerned."

With a flair for the dramatic, Jonathan performed a sweeping bow that landed him on one knee. Jacquelyn managed to contain her gurgle of laughter when she glanced down at her suitor. It wasn't the first time she found a beau kneeling before her. But Jonathan was more comical than most with his long, gangly legs sprawling in all directions. The tail of his green waistcoat dragged the ground, and he looked to all the world like a grasshopper poised on a blade of grass.

"My dearest Jacquelyn," Jon began as he unfolded the palm of his hand and uplifted it as if he were kneeling at heaven's gate, addressing the resident angel. "I would be greatly honored if you would accept me as your betrothed. I would strive to make you happy, to insure you wanted for nothing. Your wish will be my command and I will cherish you all of yours days." He paused for effect. "Will you do me the honor of marrying me, Jacquelyn?"

Her contemplative gaze wandered over Jon's folded form. He was a far cry from the man she envisioned as her husband, but she supposed she could have done worse. A troubled frown knitted her brow. Would it bother Jon that she had been with another man? Would he condemn her foolishness or accept her, tainted though she was?

"Will you take me as I am, Jon?" she inquired somberly.

"Without question," he hastily assured her. "Our life begins the moment we wed and the past has no place in our future."

"Then the answer is yes," she declared. "I will marry you."

Jacquelyn waited while Jon pressed a raft of enthusiastic kisses to her hand. Worming free, Jacquelyn stepped back, motioning for him to rise before his body froze in that ridiculous position. She opened her mouth to make a comment, but Jon's octopus arms enfolded her and his mouth swooped down to steal her breath. Again she found nothing offensive in his kiss, and nothing stirring either. The simple truth was that she tolerated his embrace without experiencing wild pleasure or repulsion. It was the mere touching of lips, the way it had always been before Mace taught her . . .

Perish the thought! Jacquelyn chided herself. Her vow to become Jon's wife symbolized her determination to forget Mace Gallagher existed.

When Jon released her, he clasped her hand in his and led her back to the mansion to formally ask Harlan's permission to marry. Harlan would have jumped for joy if he hadn't feared his gimpy leg would buckle beneath him. His wrinkled face radiated with pride and satisfaction as he uncorked a bottle of his finest wine and poured drinks to toast the occasion.

Jacquelyn listened with indifference while Harlan and Jon discussed the arrangements and set the wedding date. Odd, she mused as she sipped her wine. It was not at all like her to permit others to plan her future. But it didn't seem to matter to her anymore. Mace had stolen her zest for living. She only felt whole and alive when she was with him, as if he had become the flame that fueled her spirit and her emotions. No other man had made such a lasting impression on her, and certainly no one else had broken her spirit. But Mace had touched that special place deep down inside her, awakening her slumbering passions and stirring unexplainable needs. The world had been a different place after Mace came along.

Yes, she loved Mace Gallagher. And what a painful experience it was to know she could never have the man she truly wanted. Jacquelyn had vowed never to marry until she found the perfect man. Now that man had come and gone and she found herself bending to her grandfather's wishes without putting up a fuss. This was to be her just punishment for shunning so many suitors. She would marry a man who could not satisfy her in order to protect herself from a man who could. Besides, Jacquelyn reminded herself impassively, *I am following the General's wishes for once in my life. I owe my grandfather that much*, she supposed. To fight his wishes would only cause conflict, and there had been enough of that the past twenty years.

Harlan's brown eyes narrowed disconcertingly when Jon bid them good night and bent to press a kiss to Jacquelyn's upturned face. He knew his granddaughter far too well not to notice her reaction. There was no fiery sparkle in her eyes and her smile was a mite forced. And when she accepted Jonathan's kiss she offered little in return.

Wheeling away, Harlan scowled under his breath. Jake had consented to this marriage just to pacify him. This was all Mace Gallagher's fault. He had bedeviled Jacquelyn and she was still carrying a torch for him. Damn that miserable varmint. He had spoiled her chance at happiness with Jon. Would Jake ever recover from her fascination with that insolent rogue? She knew there could never be anything between them, but she couldn't seem to let go. She had agreed to marry Jon, but it wasn't

240

Jon she wanted. Harlan knew that as well as he knew his own name!

When Jon made his exit, Harlan pivoted to survey the drooping smile that slid off the corner of Jacquelyn's lips. "You know you can't do justice to Jon," he stated gruffly. "And I know you are doing this to please me, although *why* I cannot imagine."

Jacquelyn jerked up her head and tilted a proud chin. "Since when have I ever done your bidding unless it was my own as well?" she countered saucily.

Her attempt to appear her usual spirited self fell short of the mark. Harlan wasn't fooled for a minute. "Agreed, you never have until now, and that makes me a bit suspicious." His limping stride brought him directly in front of his granddaughter. "If Jon cannot make you happy, don't marry him," he insisted firmly. "I want this marriage, but not at the expense of your happiness. I will not have you destroying Jon's life and this family the way your mother did your father. This home has been broken apart once already."

Jacquelyn presented her back and stared at the portrait of her grandfather that occupied the wall above the marble mantel. "I am doing as I wish, Gen'ral," she said with more conviction than she actually felt. "I will make Jon a good wife."

A volcanic snort erupted from behind her. "You still fancy yourself in love with Mace Gallagher, and don't try to convince me otherwise. I may be old but I am not blind!"

Doing an about-face, Jake returned Harlan's scorching glare. "I cannot imagine why you are putting up such a fuss. This is what you wanted when you sent for me. And now you seem to be trying to talk me out of the notion!" Her voice rose steadily until she was all but shouting in his face.

"Lower your voice," Harlan roared back at her.

"You'll rouse the dead!"

"I will lower my voice the moment you lower yours," she barked loudly.

"Don't sass me, young lady," Harlan bellowed. His arm shot toward the door. "March yourself upstairs. This debate has ended. You are not marrying Jon until I believe you can be happy with him."

"I am going to marry him!" she boomed. "And my wedding day will be the happiest day of my life!"

When Jacquelyn squared her shoulders and flounced out of the room, Harlan collapsed in his chair. "Lord, what have I done?" he asked himself in exasperation. The one time Jacquelyn had consented to his wishes he was trying to dissuade her from carrying through with the commitment.

Harlan expelled a harsh breath and slammed his cane against the arm of his chair. Things were not going as he had anticipated. Jacquelyn had no deep affection for Jon Mason, and she never would until she got over Mason Gallagher. Blast it, this marriage wasn't going to work. He should never have tried his hand at matchmaking. All he had accomplished was making a tangled mess of things!

For three days Mace had prowled about his plantation like a caged predator, barking orders during the day and drinking himself insane at night. He no longer awoke in the morning, he simply *came to*. Even Raoul took a wide berth around Mace when he was in one of his irascible moods. Each day Mace had ventured to the river that marked the boundary between the Reid and Gallagher plantations, hoping to catch sight of the ornery minx who had turned him wrong side out. But never had he seen Jake without Jon following behind her like an obedient puppy.

Each time Jacquelyn's image flashed before his eyes,

Mace expelled several colorful expletives. Damnit, Jacquelyn intended to marry that two-legged mouse Jon Mason. He just knew it! That recurring thought cut Mace to the quick. If he hadn't thought the General would shoot him on sight, Mace would have barged in to point out the idiocy of marrying Jake off to a man who couldn't begin to match her spirit or her keen intelligence. (Something she seemed to have misplaced of late!) The fact that Jon Mason could never satisfy Jacquelyn was as plain as that dainty, upturned nose on her face, but she was purposely ignoring the obvious!

"What the hell should I care what she does?" Mace growled, causing Raoul to flinch at his sour tone. When Raoul rose from his chair in the spacious bedroom and attempted to make a discreet exit, Mace glared flaming arrows at him. "Sit down! Don't think you can slink out of here while I'm talking to you."

Resolutely, Raoul resettled himself in his chair and breathed a sigh. Angrily, Mace stuffed his belongings in his satchel. He had delayed his return to Galveston as long as he could. Although the hour was late, he fully intended to depart, riding through the night without stopping to rest. It was far better than tossing and turning and fighting the nausea caused from consuming too much whiskey. Maybe after he put some distance between himself and that contrary sprite she wouldn't monopolize his every thought.

When Mace completed his packing, he stomped downstairs to give final instructions to his overseer. As he strode across the veranda the click of his boot heels echoed in the darkness. With fiend-ridden haste, Mace galloped Diego across the moonlit pasture. Slowing the steed to a walk, Mace gazed toward the gracious plantation home that bordered his land. The flickering light in the upper-story window drew him like a moth to a flame. Even while he assured himself that he wanted nothing more to do with that exasperating female, he found himself aiming Diego toward the back of the mansion.

Why shouldn't he vent his irritation at its true source? He would tell that brown-eyed she-devil how foolish she was to marry Jon. He would wash his hands of her once and for all, and then point himself toward Galveston.

Satisfied with that course of action, Mace reined Diego to a halt beside the gallery. Standing on the saddle, Mace clamped his arms around the colonnade and shinnied upward to grasp the iron railing on the second-story balcony. With pantherlike grace he pulled himself up and swung over the rail. His legs threatened to fold up like an accordion when he spied the enchanting goddess garbed in her sheer gown as she restlessly paced the confines of her room. Her silky hair lay like a cape about her bare shoulders, rippling like waves on a dark sea. As she wore a path on her carpet, the lantern light shined through her gossamer white gown, outlining her shapely curves and swells.

Mace braced himself against the railing and gawked. He wasn't certain which picture aroused him most—the vision of the mermaid as she was gliding across sparkling blue water, or this angel now floating silently across her bourdoir in that luscious gown that revealed her arresting assets. The frustration that had driven him for days buckled beneath the overpowering urge to take this feisty nymph in his arms and lose himself to the heady sensations she could easily arouse in him.

Compelled forward, Mace moved toward the open door. While Jacquelyn's back was to him, Mace sidestepped behind the drapes. Craning his neck around the velvet fabric, he watched Jacquelyn, who, with head bowed, continued to pace from one side of the bedchamber to the other.

Jacquelyn heaved a frustrated sigh and unclenched the

fists that had knotted in the folds of her gown. She had vowed to follow through with this marriage, but her nerves were wearing thin. The past few days had found Jonathan sticking to her like glue. He was there to greet her at the breakfast table. He was beside her each time she saddled Lancelot. He was there every time she turned around. As a matter of fact, he hovered so close she was constantly bumping into him. And since Jonathan moved as awkwardly as a long-legged stork, he wasn't agile enough to avoid collision.

Jacquelyn had not counted on being smothered with attention. Her only relief came when Jon had pressing duties to attend. And when she'd interrogated him about the ledgers, he'd apologized for his sloppiness and promised never to spend a frivolous cent. Jon was always underfoot, apologizing for what he had done wrong and plying her with promises for a rosy future. Sweet mercy, she couldn't make a move without Jonathan scuttling along behind her. Indeed, he was the picture of devotion and made Jacquelyn nauseous with his overly sweet disposition.

And his kisses . . . An annoyed frown puckered Jacquelyn's brow when she contemplated the embraces she had been forced to endure of late. How could she sentence herself to a life of bungling embraces when she knew how potent lovemaking could be if she were in the right man's arms?

Pausing, Jacquelyn tapped her foot in restless rhythm while she mentally raced through her alternatives. "Separate bedrooms," she said with a thoughtful nod. That was the answer. Jonathan would agree. He agreed with everything she said. She couldn't even enjoy a good argument with the man, for heaven's sake! When she yearned to unleash her pent-up emotions she always found it necessary to seek out the General. He always relished a good fight. And thank God Harlan would be living under the same roof with—

A startled gasp resounded around the room when Jacquelyn noticed the toes of a pair of boots protruding from the hem of the drapes. For a moment she wondered if it were Jon, come to spy on her. Since he rarely allowed her out of his sight, it wouldn't have surprised Jake to find that long-legged giraffe tangled in the folds of her drapes.

"Separate bedrooms?" Mace's quiet laughter rumbled in his chest, causing the drapes to ripple. His tanned face emerged from the edge of the velvet and he flung Jacquelyn a mocking grin. "It sounds as if you are dreading your marriage to the Gen'ral's lackey."

Her betraying eyes ran the length of Mace's trim-fitting shirt and tight black breeches that clung to the muscular columns of his legs. His raven hair lay in disarray, and he looked to all the world like the reckless rogue he was. Willfully, Jacquelyn ignored the potent effect of his presence and the accelerated beat of her heart. Her chin elevated to a defiant angle as Mace swaggered toward her.

"I am not dreading the wedding," she informed him sharply. "Again you are trespassing into territory where you do not belong, not to mention the fact that you are not welcome here."

Mace bridged the space that separated them. His golden eyes beamed down on her like warm sunshine. He smelled like the whole outdoors, and Jacquelyn's senses sprang to life for the first time in days. She could feel her heart bounding off her ribs while her pulse hopped through her bloodstream like migrating frogs. The mere sight of this brawny rake was like setting a torch to dry kindling. Jacquelyn hated her spontaneous reaction to this raven-haired demon. She detested the manly scent that invaded her nostrils and fogged her mind. She scolded herself for wanting to reach and touch him when

246

she knew he was now and forevermore off limits.

When Mace's outstretched hand brushed her arm, Jacquelyn retreated a step. And knowing her lack of self-restraint where Mace was concerned, Jake located the farthest corner and stood in it. "If you have something pertinent to say to me, then out with it," she bit off. "If not, then leave the same way you came . . . posthaste."

Mace had something to say, all right, and he spat out the words without hesitation. "If you marry Jon you are a damned fool, Jake."

His words stung like a wasp. "You are wrong," she parried. "Marrying Jon is the smartest thing I ever decided to do. Becoming your temporary whore and permitting myself to become the brunt of your cruel jokes was the most foolish thing I have ever done!"

Her dark eyes blazed with irritation as Mace approached like an invading army that would permit no further retreat. His wry smile had transformed into an agitated frown that claimed every rugged line on his face. Jacquelyn felt a tingle of fear slither down her spine when she noticed his threatening expression. She was reminded of the intimidating look that had been stamped on Mace's craggy features the night he disarmed her male companion at the tavern. There was that same dangerous glint in his eyes, that same deadly aura that emanated from him. Although Mace usually appeared good-natured and nonchalant, there was a wild savagery beneath that calm, controlled facade. It was like confronting a coiled rattlesnake, knowing he could strike with swift efficiency if he were so inclined.

With more courage than she felt, Jacquelyn drew herself up. She was determined not to cower before this powerful creature. "You said what you came to say, now get out," she hissed, despising the fact that she was forced to look up to him. She would have given most anything if she were a foot taller so she could glare him straight in the eye.

"I'm not through talking," he snapped.

"What a pity," she flung at him. "I'm through listening."

"No you aren't, sweetheart." The endearment lacked sincerity. In fact, it sounded suspiciously like a curse, and that's exactly how he meant it. Mace braced his arms on either side of her and returned her fuming glower. "I have one or two other remarks I intend to make," he growled down at her. "In the first place, separate bedrooms won't solve your problem. No man is going to restrain himself once he obtains a legal license to have sex with you." Jacquelyn flinched at his blunt remark. "And that is what it would be—sex, not lovemaking. If you marry Jon you will quickly learn to distinguish the difference between the two. In the second place, you were never my whore."

His hot breath scorched her cheeks, giving rise to another splash of color. "From the beginning it was you who demanded that I kiss you when I had resigned myself to doing no more than sleeping beside you. And that morning during the thunderstorm it was you who requested that I teach you the ways of lovers in case we didn't survive our ordeal in the shack." His face was only inches away, his eyes glowing down on her like molten lava. "And that night at the inn you practically threw yourself at another man. When I intervened, you wound up seducing me." His body pressed familiarly against hers, mashing her further into her corner. "Now tell me, dear lady, who the hell was using whom?"

Jacquelyn couldn't have formulated a suitably nasty remark if her life depended on it. Her brain had malfunctioned when Mace filled up her world. She could hear the low timbre of his voice pounding on her eardrums. She could feel the vibrations of his words on her quaking flesh. Her thick lashes fluttered up to study the craggy features of his face. But when her eyes fell to the sensuous curve of his lips, all was lost. She ached to feel his mouth on hers, to reach out and touch the forbidden pleasure that would soon be beyond her grasp forever.

Mace was right, she suddenly realized. She was every kind of fool. But it was not because she'd decided to marry Jon. It was because this ill-founded love for Mace would bring her loneliness and misery in the years to come. She would die a little inside each time Jon touched her, knowing he could never win her heart when it belonged to this exasperating mountain lion of a man.

Mace had not intended to come this close. He knew better than to tempt himself. He'd wanted to air his griefs and begone. But he was like a senseless fly entrapped in a black widow's web. The scent of jasmine lured him ever closer. He could see the quiver of her heart-shaped lips—the characteristic signal that assured him Jacquelyn was as disturbed by their closeness as he was. He remembered, with vivid clarity, the sweet, intoxicating taste of her kisses—which Jon Mason had been enjoying while Mace was doing without. He recalled the splendor of touching this firebrand's silky flesh, the pleasure of her hands skimming over his skin. The memories lay just beneath the surface, waiting for release, waiting to become another set of stepping-stones that led him into the kind of passion that surpassed anything he had ever experienced.

The mere thought of what it had been like between them was enough to set his heart racing in triple time and unleash needs that had been denied for more days than Mace cared to count. "God, I can't seem to get enough of you, Jake," Mace breathed the split second before his lips slanted across hers.

Wild tingles of anticipation sailed down his backbone when he felt Jacquelyn involuntarily surrender to the erotic sensations they aroused in each other. Mace ached up to his eyebrows with wanting. Desire burned through him, unfolding and recoiling, over and over again. Instinctively, his arms slid around the trim indentation of her waist, clutching her to him as if he never meant to let her go. He could feel the thrusting peaks of her breasts against his heaving chest, feel the soft texture of her thighs against his. She was absorbing his strength into her, draining him of common sense, unchaining the riptide of emotions that churned inside him.

Her arms, as if they possessed a will of their own, glided across the massive expanse of his chest to settle on his broad shoulders. A soft sigh tripped from her lips when Mace's searing kisses tracked a path along the pulsating column of her neck. His hands began to wander on their own accord, locating each sensitive point and setting it to tingling. Skillful fingertips tunneled beneath the scooped-neck gown to make tantalizing contact with her soft flesh. Hands and lips that fluttered over her like a gentle draft of wind aroused and explored. Passion unfolded its mystical blossom, demanding fulfillment.

Emotions that had lain dormant burst forth like an erupting volcano, spreading a sea of fire over her skin. Jacquelyn felt her body surge helplessly against Mace's hard, muscular frame, wantonly begging for more. Her fingertips speared into his thick hair, holding his head to her while his lips flicked at the buds of her breasts. Breathlessly, she tilted his face to hers, seeing the flames of desire leaping in his tawny eyes. She longed to become a part of those golden flames, to feel the fire.

"Jake?" His voice was a pained plea. His eyes devoured her.

Jacquelyn died a thousand deaths in that tense moment. She knew what he wanted from her and she couldn't deny him, not when her body cried out for the pleasure he could offer, not when this might be the last time she found ecstasy in the magical circle of his arms.

A fleeting vision of Jon skitted across her mind. If she were to endure this loveless marriage she would carry one precious memory in her heart. It would be the cherished thought of this night and this irresistible rogue with eyes the color of the sun and hair as black as midnight.

A rueful smile rippled across Jacquelyn's lips as she unbuttoned his white linen shirt to slide her hands over his hair-matted chest. "Which one of us is the bigger fool, Mace? You for coming here? Or me for permitting you to stay when we both know you should go?"

His arm slipped beneath her knees to cradle her luscious body against his laboring chest, one bared by her adventurous caresses. "Perhaps we're two of a kind, minx, a perfectly matched pair of fools." He chuckled softly. "Maybe we deserve each other. . . ."

Mace carried her to her four-poster bed and gently laid her upon the satin sheets. Jacquelyn stared appreciatively at this giant of a man as he silently strided across the room to snuff the lantern. The moonlight streamed through the terrace door, spotlighting his powerful physique. Jacquelyn stared longingly as Mace shed his clothes and stretched out beside her. There had been a time when she blushed at the sight of his bare flesh. But no more. Now she marveled at the sinewy length of him. She was awed by the way he moved with such masculine grace. He was the picture of conrolled vitality, a mass of potential energy. And as much as Jacquelyn would have liked to regard Mace Gallagher as an ordinary man, she could not. His abilities seemed limitless and his effect on her bordered on spellbinding. . . .

Her thoughts took flight, accompanied by her careening senses, when Mace's knee guided her thighs apart. The spark of passion leaped between them, setting off a chain reaction. When his roaming hands rediscovered the feel of her pliant flesh she felt herself burning with a fever only one man could cure. Jacquelyn shamelessly returned the pleasures he offered, kiss for kiss, caress for caress. She wanted him, wildly, desperately. She yearned to escape the confines of her room and set sail among the stars, to touch each one as she soared past, to absorb their radiant warmth.

A tiny moan tumbled free when Mace's moist lips ventured down the slope of her shoulder to whisper over each dusky peak. His hot kisses trailed lower, sensitizing her skin. His practiced hands swam across her trembling flesh, touching her everywhere as he murmured his need for her. His skillful seduction took her from a dizzying plateau of rapture to an even loftier precipice of ecstasy.

Jacquelyn could feel herself letting go. She was experiencing the paradox of passion. Although she lay in the circle of Mace's brawny arms, she felt wild and free. It was as if she had sprouted wings to glide through time and space. Mace had introduced her to yet another dimension of pleasure, one she hadn't imagined existed. Turbulent sensations swamped and buffeted her, flinging her into a mindless whirl of passion. The feelings were fierce and intense. They could not be controlled until the storm of ecstasy had run its windswept course. Mace was doing delicious things to her body, numbing her to all except the exquisite feel of his hands and lips upon her skin. He left her throbbing all over, left her aching to satisfy this maddening craving he had instilled in her.

Although Jacquelyn desperately wanted Mace, she could not be content until he begged her to come to him, until he was consumed by the same fervent needs that engulfed her. Determined to leave her brand on him, Jacquelyn urged Mace to his back. Tenderly, she memorized every sinewy inch of him by touch and feel. Her lips feathered over his mouth in the slightest breath of a kiss and then migrated over his collar bone. While she tasted his aromatic skin, her hands glided to and fro, mapping his masculine contours and transforming them into melted butter. She teased and massaged, seduced and excited, until Mace groaned in bittersweet torment.

So quickly had she become a proficient seductress, Mace mused with a ragged sigh. She had incorporated the techniques he had taught her and turned them back upon him with such feminine finesse that he felt more the apprentice than the tutor of passion.

One day soon, Jon Mason would venture to this enchantress's bed. And when this sweet witch captured Jon in her spell, when she touched him as intimately as she touched Mace . . .

The thought haunted every corner of Mace's mind. It frustrated him to think this curvaceous nymph would soon belong to another man. It was not enough that Mace had been the first to discover Jacquelyn's boundless passions. And each time Jacquelyn subjected herself to her husband's touch, Mace would die a little inside.

It had never mattered so much where his lovers wound up after they left his arms, Mace realized with a start. He had never been so possessive with the other women in his life. But this ebony-eyed sprite was an altogether different matter because she refused to be classified as one of "the women in his life."

The tormenting vision of Jacquelyn sleeping in Jon's arms sprang at Mace, over and over again. He felt the irrational urge to possess this luscious nymph, to drive away his taunting thoughts. He wanted to leave his mark upon her when he made wild, sweet love to her, to insure that he had committed this magical moment to her memory. She may take Jon Mason as her husband, but Mace wanted Jacquelyn to see his face, to remember his caresses, to long for kisses that stole her breath away and left her aching for him and him alone.

Yes, it was a vain whim, Mace chided himself. But it

stung his male pride to think he would become a forgotten memory of Jacquelyn's past. And Mace knew damned well there could be no separate bedrooms when a man wed this saucy beauty. Jon would never permit her to deny him the pleasure she could provide. No man would. But time would not erase the memory of this night, Mace promised himself. He was going to love this feisty sprite the way she needed to be loved, thoroughly and completely, until there was not an ounce of strength left between them. If nothing else, he would become the quiet smile that hovered on her lips when no one was around. He would be the soft whisper that stirred her when his memory crept from the shadows of her mind.

Determined to make this a night to inflame her dreams, Mace twisted above Jacquelyn. Bending, he showered her with adoring kisses and worshipping caresses. He held himself at bay, tempting her with his nearness. And then, ever so slowly, he lowered himself to her. His hair-roughened body seduced hers as he murmured his need for her, as he assured her that she provided wondrous pleasure. Calling upon his crumbling self-control, Mace waited until Jacquelyn arched toward him. And when he came to her, his lips took possession of her sweet mouth. Yet, when she moved beneath him, setting the cadence of their lovemaking, Mace lost his battle of self-conquest. There was no holding back when he was engulfed by the holocaust of emotions that billowed within him. Primal needs took command of his mind and body, driving him, compelling him to surrender to desires that raged like wildfire.

Mace buried his head against the curve of Jacquelyn's neck, his cheek pillowed on the wild cascade of silky hair that streamed about her. The taste of her was on his lips. The feel of her delicious body was imprinted on his skin. The feminine scent of her enshrouded his senses. He thrust deeply into her, seeking ultimate depths of intimacy, aching to relieve the monstrous craving that had taken hold of him. He could feel Jacquelyn's nails digging into the tendons of his back, but he was oblivious to all except the sensual world of ecstasy that consumed them. There were of one body and soul, sharing the same frantic heartbeat, spiraling on the same outstretched wings that took them higher and higher.

Sometime during their ascent across the far horizon, Jacquelyn swore she had shed the prohibitive garments of the soul. It was as if she were standing apart from the physical pleasure of their lovemaking, as if she had transcended the realm of reality. She was drifting in paradise, clinging to the only man who had the power to stir and arouse her. It was love that had transported her into this world that defied description. And for that mystical moment that spanned eternity, Mace was hers alone. For this glorious instant she had become the pure essence of emotion.

And then it came, the wild tempest of converging sensations that sent her tumbling through time and space. Shock waves riveted through her and the dark world exploded in a kaleidoscope of brilliant colors. Jacquelyn clung to Mace, certain she had clawed at him until she left her mark upon his flesh. But she couldn't let go of him, not when these indescribable feelings of pleasure were assaulting her from all directions at once.

When Jacquelyn clutched at him, Mace felt the flood of passion spill forth, streaming from the very core of his being like a raging river pouring from its banks. He shuddered uncontrollably, mindless of all except the ineffable rapture that channeled through him. He was being tossed, helter-skelter, like water rushing over rapids. He was being sped along with the current of turbulent emotions and then dropped into a tranquil pool just beyond reality's shore. Mace wondered if he could summon the strength to move. He felt drained—

mentally, physically, and emotionally. Jacquelyn had left no part of him untouched by her splendorous love-making. She had stolen that essential part of him, leaving behind the shell of a man who didn't have the energy to stir a step.

A weary sigh rippled across Mace's lips while he waited for his strength to return. He had intended to leave this brand upon Jake's soul, but it seemed his intentions had worked in reverse. A man could not take from this wild, free-spirited witch without sacrificing a part of himself. Jacquelyn tugged at the strings of his heart, even when Mace would have preferred for her to leave his heart alone.

Repeatedly, Mace asked himself how this vivacious minx could settle for a marriage to Jon Mason after they had explored the intimate horizons beyond the sun. Didn't she realize what would happen in the months and years to come? Beneath that feisty, determined exterior was a woman who possessed explosive passions that ached for release. Jon would never satisfy her, not if she was already contemplating separate sleeping quarters. She would then search elsewhere, just like . . . Mace strangled the thought, along with the tormenting memories that threatened to unfold in his mind.

"Jake, you can't marry Jon. You'll make yourself miserable," he blurted out out of the blue. Mace cursed himself for making demands on this rebellious vixen. Barking orders at her was not the proper method of handling her. (If indeed there were a proper, effective method of handling Jacquelyn!) Jake was notorious for becoming proportionately more determined as resistance increased.

Jacquelyn glared at him. Blast it, why had he spoiled this beautiful moment with his abrupt command? Why couldn't Mace have said he loved her, even if it was only for the moment, even if he didn't care enough to want to marry her himself? Damnation, even a quiet, noncommittal goodbye would have been better than trying to boss her around!

"I will do what I feel I have to do," she insisted as she wormed away.

Growling at his own reckless remark and her defensive rejoinder, Mace flung his long legs over the edge of the bed and groped in the darkness for his clothes. "Hell, why can't it be the same with you as it was with the others? Why the devil do I care about your future happiness when you are determined to anchor yourself to a man like Jon?"

Jacquelyn sat up in bed, clutching the sheet around her. Her dark eyes bore holes in Mace's bare chest while he loomed over her bed. "Your only concern is for your monumental arrogance," she snapped back at him. "It rankles your pride to think a woman can lead a productive life after she's slept with you." Jacquelyn wasn't certain why she was so viciously attacking his character. Perhaps she was lashing out at him to protect her wounded heart. Or maybe she just didn't want to admit that Mace's prediction would come true. Confound it, she hated it when he was right. But it would kill her to admit it aloud!

"Let me tell you something, Mace Gallagher. There *is* life after sleeping with you," she assured him tartly. "I can and will function normally again. What we shared was passion for passion's sake. Jon Mason strives to make me happy. He dotes on me the way you never could."

"Dotes?" Mace pounced on her choice of words with a derisive snort. "Honey, you'll have that chicken-hearted galoot so henpecked that he'll molt twice a year."

Her chin tilted a notch higher. "I am not a demanding woman," she declared self-righteously.

Mace would have burst into incredulous laughter if he didn't fear waking the household. "Of course you aren't," he growled in sarcastic agreement.

Jake detested that caustic phrase, and hearing Mace utter it at that particular moment made her all the madder. "Get out of my room, damn you," she fumed at him.

"Gladly." Mace snatched up his shirt and stalked toward the terrace door. "Good night, Madam Attila."

Jacquelyn flounced back in bed, pulling the sheet over head and cursing a blue streak. "Good riddance, Casanova. May your adventures in bed-hopping land you in the den of a spiteful witch who turns you into a frog!"

Mace missed a step when Jake hit him with her vengeful curse. Angry though he was, he could not contain the amused smile that tugged at the corner of his mouth. Reversing direction, he swaggered back to the bed to tug the sheet from Jacquelyn's puckered face. Mace glanced down at he exquisite features bathed in moonlight and shadows and frozen in a mutinous frown.

"I fear I have already stumbled into the witch's lair and she has transformed me into a frog," he exclaimed, his voice rattling with laughter. Before Jacquelyn could protest (and she most certainly would have), Mace bent to plant a ravishing kiss to her lips. "Rivet." Mace helped himself to another tantalizing kiss. "Rivet." The third kiss was so tender and compelling that Jacquelyn melted into a sentimental puddle. "Croak." His index finger smoothed the frown from her flawless features. "Your curse worked, sweet witch," he assured her softly. "I have this insatiable craving to hop to the nearest pond and perch on my lily pad."

As Mace unfolded himself from her bed, Jacquelyn was stung by a gnawing emptiness. Mace was leaving her and she would never again share the magic of his lovemaking. He had kissed the irritation out of her and she had difficulty remembering what they were arguing about. But one thing was for certain, Jacquelyn would not allow him to leave on a sour note. This was to be their last

258

goodbye and she longed for the memory of their lovemaking to weigh heavily on his mind.

Determined of purpose, Jacquelyn leaped from bed in a single bound, dragging the sheet with her. Before Mace could swing his leg over the railing, Jake sailed into his arms, very nearly throwing him off balance.

"What the hell . . . ?"

Her arms flew around his neck, preventing him from taking a nasty fall, offering him a kiss that carried enough heat to melt the moon and leave it dripping on the stars. Mace swore lightning had struck the cast-iron railing, frying him to the metal. The potency of her embrace produced an electrical charge that burned bone and brain to a crisp.

When Jacquelyn finally withdrew to regather her drooping sheet, Mace struggled to inhale a breath. Streams of wild tangles sprayed about her enchanting face. Her attempt to cover herself only served to press her full breasts upward. Her bare shoulders glowed with moonbeams and an aureole of silver light encircled her head.

Lord, she looked positively breathtaking standing there, Mace mused with masculine appreciation. Jacquelyn was an unforgettable combination of fire-breathing witch and graceful angel. As always, Mace was pelted by contradicting emotions, none of which could master the others. He wanted her, and yet he wanted nothing more to do with her. He hated her for turning him inside out, and yet he adored what she did to him, what she had always done to him when he was nestled in her silky arms.

One dainty finger lifted to trace the sensuous curve of his lips, and then ventured to the cleft in his chin. "I never realized that kissing a frog could be so delightful," she purred provocatively. "I shall make a mental note of that and seek out frogs more often."

Mace's powerful body went boneless when she graced him with her impish grin. It was like viewing a magnificent sunrise at midnight. There was a special radiance about this dark-eyed hoyden that endeared her to him, even when Mace preferred to be unmoved by her, especially now. But he had the nagging feeling that "out of sight" would not necessarily imply "out of mind" where Jake was concerned. Why should it? Mace asked himself somberly. That theory had been shot all to hell the past week. He had resorted to drinking a gallon of whiskey to forget this spitfire. But nothing had washed away her memory or the taste of her addicting kisses.

Impulsively, Mace pulled her back into his arms, bending her shapely form into his muscular contours. His golden eyes held her hostage as he tipped her face to his. Jacquelyn had never been prone to tears, but his tender kiss misted her eyes. He held her as if she were fragile crystal. His lips moved expertly over hers, evoking warm, tingling sensations that she feared could never be laid to rest.

Without voicing a word to spoil their last kiss, Mace eased over the rail and vanished into the night. Jacquelyn dragged in a shuddering breath. She already missed Mace and he hadn't been gone a full minute. Lord, how could she have become so wishy-washy? She never had been before. One moment she had cursed Mace for infuriating her, and then she'd turned right around and sent him off with a sizzling kiss.

Mechanically, Jacquelyn wandered back to her empty room, knowing sleep wouldn't come without accompanying dreams. Her heart lay in her chest like an anchor, dragging her spirits to rock bottom. Who was the imbecile who said love was a splendorous thing? Jacquelyn sniffed in contradiction as she hugged the pillow on which Mace had laid his head. After inhaling the lingering scent of the man who had become an integral part of her, she expelled a melancholy sigh. Love was pure hell, she decided. It was like having one's heart ripped from one's chest and being expected to go on living. Mace had taken a part of her with him when he left, and she was never going to be the same again, even if she had valiantly assured him otherwise!

Chapter 14

Muffled noises roused Harlan Reid from his sleep. Drowsily, he hobbled from bed to view the shocking scene on the terrace, one that very nearly caused his heart to pop from his chest. Astonishment held Harlan paralyzed, and indecision prevented him from bursting onto the gallery to interrupt the clinging couple kissing in the moonlight.

The implication of what he saw weighed heavily on Harlan's mind. Awareness of Mace Gallagher's legendary reputation with women left Harlan to speculate on what had transpired, not only during the previous hours but also during the journey from Galveston to the plantation. Harlan had wondered about the sleeping arrangements during their trip, but he hadn't dared to ask such intimate questions of his granddaughter. But after what Harlan saw on the terrace, he had the frustrated feeling that Mace and Jake had been doing far more than conversing. A helluva lot more!

Muttering under his breath, Harlan limped across his bedroom and plopped down on his bed. Damnit all! What was he to do now that he knew? Harlan chewed vigorously on his bottom lip and mulled over the troubled thought until he worked up a throbbing headache.

Blast it, why couldn't Mace have left Jake alone? She might have convinced herself to be satisfied with Jon Mason if Mace had kept his distance. Why, Jake might even have come to love Jon, given half a chance. But she was never going to get over her fruitless infatuation for that ornery rapscallion if he kept creeping into her boudoir to stir her emotions and confuse her thoughts! The nerve of that man, sneaking into Harlan Reid's house!

Frustrated, Harlan punched his pillow until the feathers flew. This is all my fault, he suddenly realized. If he had ventured to Galveston to meet the schooner, Mace would have gotten nowhere near Jake. But no, Harlan had connived to throw Jon and Jake together.

Grappling with contrasting emotions, Harlan fell into a fitful sleep. He had interfered with fate and now he was left to face the consequences, ones that held far-reaching effects. If he permitted destiny to chart its own course, Jacquelyn could wind up the mother of Mace's child. And if he dared to interfere again, he could instigate another catastrophe.

Damnit, Jake had fended off dozens of suitors during her stay in New Orleans. Even Florence had made mention of Jacquelyn's skillful elusiveness. Why did this one man, this bold renegade who had been a constant thorn in Harlan's side, have to be the one who intrigued her? Because Jake and Mace were too much alike, Harlan reminded himself sourly. They both represented what Harlan had tried to control during his military career—the rebels who defied discipline and authority. He had molded respectable soldiers from the unruliest of men, but he'd had no luck at all with Mace Gallagher and his own granddaughter! They had held true to form while the others buckled to Harlan's domineering tactics.

Harlan expelled an exasperated sigh. Now the question was—what was he going to do about this tryst between

Mace and Jake? Jake knew how Harlan felt about Mace. And Harlan had witnessed the fierce fascination Jake and Mace had for each other. If Harlan thought Mace would be the one hurt by this frivolous affair, he wouldn't have cared a tittle. But he would be damned if he permitted Jake to carry a torch for a man while she was wed to another. Jon was pressing to move up the wedding date while Harlan held firm, silently monitoring Jake's responses to Jon's constant attentions.

Lord, what was he going to do? If Harlan could have puzzled out the answer to that question, he would have slept far better that night. But he couldn't, and he flopped on his feather bed like a fish out of water.

Mace froze in his tracks when he noticed the long shadow that drifted across his path. Squinting, he sought to determine the identity of the form that lingered beside Diego.

"Raoul, what the blazes are you doing here?" Mace growled when he realized who had been spying on him.

The moonlight glowed in Raoul's dark, brooding eyes as he glanced toward the Reid mansion. Slowly, Raoul focused his penetrating gaze on Mace.

"Is spying on me to become a hobby of yours?" Mace snorted as he stuffed a booted foot into the stirrup.

As usual, Raoul said nothing, but his mouth twitched in that unique way that spoke louder than words. Mace knew Raoul disapproved of sneaking into Jacquelyn's bedroom. It was written all over his homely face, and Raoul's mere stance—legs spread and neck bowed— indicated his annoyance with the situation.

Refusing to meet Raoul's potent stare, Mace settled himself comfortably in the saddle. "You intend to accompany me to Galveston, don't you?"

A muted sound rattled in Raoul's throat.

"Oh, very well, you can come along," Mace said, relenting. "But if you make one snide remark about tonight, I'll . . ." Mace rolled his eyes heavenward. "What the hell am I saying?"

Raoul wasn't going to voice a comment. He couldn't. He had been born mute and he would never utter a condemning remark. But that didn't stop Raoul from thinking them. Mace could *see* Raoul thinking condemning thoughts. And as they journeyed northeast, Mace was constantly aware of the cold disapproval Raoul felt.

"Well, I don't know what you expect me to do about that woman," Mace exploded twenty miles later. "You know how I feel about marriage. What if a situation were to arise that provoked me to react with the same violent—" He slammed his mouth shut before he disclosed information he wanted to share with no one. "If you knew Jake as well as I do, you wouldn't be so all-fired certain I should accept my obligations where she is concerned. She is as fickle as the wind, stubborn as a mule, and as feisty as a lion cub. Hell, she can drag me into an argument on any subject before I realize I'm there!"

Raoul's silence only made matters worse. It is like carrying on a conversation with my conscience, Mace mused resentfully. Indeed, Raoul had become the personification of Mace's conscience, his sounding board, these past few years.

Finally, Mace let his breath out in a rush. "If Jake is determined to marry that scrawny, spindly-legged Jon Mason, I'm not going to stop her," Mace declared with firm resolve. "Far be it from me to intervene in her life. Besides, what do I want with a woman who doesn't know what the devil she wants except free rein to do whatever suits her whim? I don't have time for marriage. And even

266

if I did, Jake is not wife material. She is one of those females who constantly gets herself into trouble. And to make matters worse, she attracts people who attract trouble!"

Mace stared at Raoul, who didn't look as if he had been swayed by the barrage of excuses. "She got herself shot, didn't she? She got herself betrothed to a man who will have her footprints all over his back, for Chrissake! I'd be a fool to attempt to halt that marriage. Harlan Reid would have a conniption if I did. He already delights in hating me."

By the time Mace and Raoul stopped to rest, Mace was hoarse from rattling off his many reasons for not becoming more involved with Jacquelyn. And Raoul's ear had been bent so far out of shape from listening that it seemed to hang on the side of his whiskered face like a limp flower.

Mace seriously doubted that anything he said would convince Raoul that Mace wasn't already in over his head. Why, Raoul was probably wondering why a usually sensible man would shinny up a colonnade and enter the boudoir of an engaged woman unless he wanted to purposely invite trouble. And maybe things were bound to get worse long before they got better, Mace mused. And perhaps he was fooling himself if he thought he could stand aside to watch that minx take wedding vows with Jon Milksop Mason. But Mace didn't want to get himself so entangled with Harlan's granddaughter that he could never worm free. Hell, he was already walking on a short leash. If he didn't guard his step, he would have himself wound so tightly he couldn't walk at all and certainly not *away* from the future Mrs. Jon Mason. The thought had Mace growling all over again!

*   *   *

Malcolm Reid ran a restless hand through his unruly shocks of chestnut brown hair. His green eyes blinked rapidly as he mulled over his alternatives. An annoyed frown covered his pinched face as he paced the confines of his Galveston office.

Things had been going splendidly until the previous month. And then suddenly his affairs had become a complicated tangle. The two bungling morons he had hired to dispose of his cousin the moment she returned to Texas had failed miserably. They'd thought the wound Jacquelyn had sustained would be the cause of her death, but obviously it hadn't been. Harlan had sent him a message, stating that Jacquelyn planned to examine the financial ledgers of the Reid Commission Company.

Wasn't it enough that Mace Gallagher's associate, Hub MacIntosh, had been pestering him, demanding to know why Malcolm was against the merger? And to frustrate Malcolm further, the General's feisty granddaughter would live to inherit the entire Reid fortune when he departed from this earth.

For three years Malcolm had been plotting and scheming to satisfy his avarice. He dreamed of building his own empire, and everything had fallen neatly into place when Florence had taken Jake under her wing in New Orleans while Harlan was waging war on the Mexicans. When Harlan had marched off to do what he did best—command soldiers on the battlefield—Malcolm had gained control of the commission company. He had skimmed profits from the company to increase his nest egg.

The land abandoned by the Spanish aristocrats in southern Texas during the war provided the perfect location and opportunity for Malcolm to construct his new empire. And to his good fortune, gold had been discovered in California. With the funds Malcolm had

268

swindled from the company, he had purchased man-power and weapons. His access to outgoing ships made it a simple matter to transport necessary firearms and supplies to the army of mercenaries he had employed to disguise themselves as Comanches and Mexican banditos.

The men who were raiding the area and stealing cattle from unsuspecting citizens worked for Malcolm. The stolen cattle were being driven to the vast acreages of Santa Gertrudis to be corraled and branded. Each time a sizable herd was gathered, the cattle were then driven to the California gold fields, where they could be sold for one hundred dollars a head rather than the thirty dollars a head Malcolm could receive for them in New Orleans.

With the huge profits he had made from the trail herds, Malcolm had begun the erection of his grand mansion in south Texas. But all his meticulous years of scheming would be spoiled if the Reid Commission Company merged with Mace Gallagher's. Malcolm would be exposed for fraud, and he was not prepared to sacrifice his dream of wealth and a vast empire. It would have simplified matters if his henchmen had disposed of Jacquelyn before she brewed trouble. Malcolm would have eventually inherited Harlan's property, and no one would have been the wiser about his fraudulent activities in the commission company.

"Would you mind telling me what all this pacing is about?" Gil Davis questioned after watching Malcolm wear a path on the carpet. "I assured you that no one suspects who is behind the border raids. I have sent several dependable vaqueros with the herd to the California gold fields. Before long we will be wading in wealth." Malcolm paused momentarily to shoot him an absent glance, and then went back to his annoying pacing. Gil snorted derisively. "What the hell are you so nervous about? Things couldn't be running smoother."

"Oh yes they could," Malcolm bit off testily. "And you are going to relieve me of my biggest worry before you return to Santa Gertrudis. I want you to kidnap someone for me."

Gil's blue eyes widened in surprise. "Who?"

Malcolm finally ceased his pensive pacing and eased a hip on the edge of his desk. "Jacquelyn Reid, my young cousin, has ideas about poking her nose into the finances of the commission company. My dreams of an empire will be just that—a crumbling vision—if I'm toted off to jail for embezzling money from Harlan."

"I'm beginning to see your problem," Gil murmured thoughtfully. If Malcolm were imprisoned he would squeal like a stuck pig, and Gil wouldn't be surprised to find himself convicted for cattle rustling and tossed in the cell beside his accomplice. Gil knew Malcolm well enough to realize the man cared only about himself. Malcolm would expose everyone involved in the intricate scandal if he thought it might grant him a pardon or a lighter prison sentence. Damn, if Malcolm's cousin learned what was going on, Gil would find himself beneath an avalanche of accusations.

Glittering green eyes bore down on Gil. "I can tell by your expression that you realize what you stand to lose if my cousin discovers fraud has been going on for three years. You are in this as deep as I am."

"Where is the girl?" Gil inquired grimly.

"She resides at General Reid's plantation southwest of Galveston. I don't give a damn what you do with her, but she is not to return to the area—ever again. When you have amused yourself with her, sell her to the Mexicans or Comanches. Those heathens are always eager for a white slave or mistress." Malcolm chuckled devilishly.

270

"As wild and unruly as Jacquelyn is, she should adapt nicely to living with those renegades. Or better yet, dispose of her when you have pleasured yourself with her."

"Your concern for your blood kin is touching." Gil smirked sarcastically.

"I'm more fond of my own hide than hers," Malcolm growled as he shoved the unmanageable shocks of chestnut hair out of his eyes. "And don't take that firebrand for granted either. She is handy with weapons and as agile as a cat. The two men I sent to dispose of her earlier had no luck apprehending her. She rides and shoots as well as any man. Even you, Davis," he added with a meaningful glance.

A dubious smile pursed Gil's lips as he brushed his serape aside to retrieve a cigarillo. "Surely you exaggerate."

"I most certainly do not!" Malcolm puffed up with irritation. "My two henchmen tried to drag Jacquelyn into an alley, and she nearly ran them through with a damned parasol! When they tried to ambush her, she slid off the side of her horse and used the animal as a shield. One shot couldn't stop her. Hell, it hardly slowed her down!" Malcolm wagged a bony finger in Gil's unconcerned face. "If you underestimate that little termagant, we will both be rotting in prison!"

After Malcolm laid out his plans for Jacquelyn's abduction from the plantation, Gil sank back in his chair to catch a much-needed nap while they awaited the arrival of the two other men Malcolm intended to send to the plantation with him.

Malcolm returned to his pacing. Damnation, he muttered irritably. He had schemed for weeks to have Jacquelyn meet her demise in Galveston, as if she had been the victim of robbery or molestation. The General would have been bereaved by his loss, and Mace Gallagher would be considerate enough not to press Harlan for the merger while he was grieving the death of his granddaughter.

No one would have suspected any connection between her death and Malcolm's dealings with the commission company. But the longer she was allowed to live and the closer she came to discovering the fraud, the more precarious was Malcolm's position. Gawd, he felt as if he were walking on eggs!

Inhaling a steadying breath, Malcolm tried to compose himself. All would be well when Gil abducted Jacquelyn. And within a few more months, after he had reaped all the profits from this season's cotton crop, he could leave the crumbling commission business and take up residence in his new home in Santa Gertrudis. The General would think Mace's business had crushed all competition. The General disliked Gallagher in the first place. This new twist would give Harlan one more reason to hate Mace Gallagher, and no one would suspect Malcolm of doing anything except abandoning a sinking ship.

Digesting that encouraging thought, Malcolm dropped into his chair to log the day's transactions into his ledger. He would hand over the financial statements Harlan had requested to divert any suspicion. It would never do to appear reluctant, Malcolm reminded himself. Jacquelyn wouldn't have time to study the ledgers before she dropped out of sight forever. She would never discover what was going on before Gil apprehended her. And Harlan would dump the ledgers back in Malcolm's lap while he mourned the loss of his granddaughter.

A wicked smile tugged at Malcolm's thin lips as his mind teemed with sinister thoughts. An ambitious, determined man always found his way around difficulty. If Malcolm didn't panic the General would be none the wiser. He would simply change a few entries in the ledger to make the earnings appear smaller than they truly were. Malcolm was not about to permit his carefully laid plans to backfire in his face. He had spent three years organizing this intricate scheme for skimming profits and shipping firearms to his mercenary army on the Texas border. By the beginning of the year he would be basking in the sun in south Texas, living like a king.

"Where the devil have you been so long?" Hub MacIntosh demanded when Mace's massive frame filled the office door. "I was beginning to wonder if the hurricane swallowed you up. . . ."

His disconcerted expression changed when he spied Raoul standing behind Mace. Hub, Raoul, and Mace had been inseparable during their crusades in the war. But these days Raoul spent most of his time at the plantation. Raoul had never been overly fond of crowds.

"Raoul!" Hub enthused. "It's good to see you again. Come sit down and rest your weary bones." Hub patted the empty chair beside him.

While Hub and Raoul were renewing their friendship, Mace was staring thoughtfully through the window that fronted his office. His eyes narrowed suspiciously when he spied the two men he had seen briefly the night Jake had snatched his Colt and opened fire. Since the moment Mace arrived in Galveston, he had been surveying the faces of those he passed on the dock, searching for the hooligans who had assaulted Jacquelyn. He would have bet his fortune the two men were the same ones who had bushwhacked Jacquelyn on the road north of the city.

"Come here, Raoul," Mace barked abruptly.

As Mace wheeled around to exit the office, Raoul rose from his chair, leaving Hub in midsentence. After asking Raoul to follow the two scraggly dressed men who were threading their way along the docks, Mace returned to his

273

office and plopped into his chair behind his desk.

"What was that all about?" Hub questioned curiously.

"Raoul is going to run an errand for me," Mace replied cryptically.

A wry smile dangled on the corner of Hub's mouth as his eyes slid over Mace's broad chest. "Did you insure that the Gen'ral's lovely granddaughter was safely delivered to his doorstep?"

Mace winced uncomfortably. How was he supposed to forget that minx if her name cropped into conversation? "She is under Harlan's roof, making preparations to marry Jon Mason," he managed to say without gritting out the words.

Hub's blond brows jackknifed. "She didn't look to be Jon's type at all!" he croaked.

"Jake doesn't have a type," Mace grumbled, his resentment getting the best of him. "That she-cat is in a class all by herself."

"So I noticed," Hub murmured suggestively.

Determined to change the topic of conversation, Mace cut to the heart of the matter that concerned him. "What have you learned about Malcolm Reid and his refusal to approve the merger?"

Hub had several prying questions he wanted to pose about what was going on between Mace and Jacquelyn, but he set them aside temporarily. "Malcolm wouldn't discuss the merger with me, even when I planted myself on his doorstep." A mischievous grin crinkled his sun-bronzed features. "So naturally I broke into his office after hours."

Mace returned the wry grin as he leaned forward to light his cigar. "Naturally," he chuckled. "And did your breaking and entering serve a useful purpose, my friend?"

Hub nodded, and then gestured toward the copies he had made from Malcolm's ledger. "One look at his books

274

should tell you why Malcolm Reid would reject the merger and any possibility of our company auditing his ledgers."

Mace frowned as he scooped up the papers. He bit into the end of his cheroot when his eyes looked over the statement Hub had hastily scribbled in evidence. "Well I'll be damned. . . ."

"No, Malcolm will be damned if Harlan finds out," Hub corrected with a snort. "The Reid Commission Company isn't faulty, only its financial administrator. Malcolm is robbing Harlan blind."

"So that's why Reid's company hasn't shown a respectable profit," Mace mused as his tawny eyes skimmed the revealing figures. "Malcolm has been buying top-quality cotton from his clients and paying them for second-grade produce. Then he turns around and sells it at premium prices to buyers on the East Coast. Lord, he's swindled Harlan out of thousands of dollars!"

"I thought I just said that," Hub sniffed. "After I saw those ledgers I spoke with a few of our clients who had once been associated with Malcolm. They were disgruntled with him for paying them for second-rate cotton when they knew damned good and well that their crops were prime quality."

"No doubt Malcolm has been plying the Gen'ral with lies, insisting that we stole their clients out from under them," Mace speculated. "Malcolm probably has Harlan believing that we are trying to undercut our competitors, just to force them out of business."

"You've been Malcolm's scapegoat," Hub insisted. "Since the Gen'ral wasn't fond of you, it was easy for Malcolm to convince him that you were a threat and that your reason for merging was to swallow Harlan alive and then cast him aside when you had control."

A muddled frown knitted Mace's brow. "If Malcolm has been skimming profits, where do you suppose he's stashing it? He isn't living beyond his supposed means."

Hub's bulky shoulders lifted in a shrug. "Damned if I know what he did with all that money. But you can bet there's a bundle of it buried somewhere."

"Buried or invested elsewhere," Mace predicted, thoughtfully puffing on his cigarillo. "Malcolm is making a killing at the Gen'ral's expense and I'm taking the blame. I doubt the old man even knows that his funds have dwindled to next to nothing."

"Harlan Reid made a grave mistake when he left his nephew in charge of the commission company. My guess is Malcolm planned to pick the old buzzard clean and then slither off," Hub sniffed disgustedly.

The prediction provoked Mace's agitated growl. Harlan would be humiliated beyond words if he were to face financial collapse. He had trusted Malcolm explicitly, never questioning his decisions. But knowing Jacquelyn as Mace did (and he was beginning to know her quite well), she would pry into the business and . . .

Mace's mind stalled when he recalled something Jacquelyn had said during their journey to the plantation. She claimed she had come home to take an active part in the family business. If Malcolm guessed her intentions, he would feel threatened by her intrusion. Good gawd! Surely Malcolm wouldn't try to dispose of his own cousin to save his greedy neck . . . would he? Hell, yes he would, Mace realized with a start.

Raoul's appearance at the office door interrupted Mace's troubled musings. "I thought I told you to follow those two scoundrels," Mace growled sourly.

Raoul stared straight at Mace and then glanced toward the street.

"Don't tell me," Mace muttered as he vaulted from his chair. "I think I know where they went."

"What the hell is going on?" Hub demanded impatiently.

"Someone tried to kill Jacquelyn when she first arrived in Galveston. Another attempt was made on her life during our journey to the plantation," Mace said hurriedly over his shoulder. "Who do you suppose will inherit Gen'ral Reid's fortune?"

"Jacquelyn Reid, of course," Hub answered, and then frowned. Hub quickened his step to keep up with Mace and Raoul, but he hadn't made the connection between Jake and Malcolm. "What has that got to do with—"

"Who do you suppose is next in line to inherit if Jake were to meet an untimely demise?" Mace fired the question as he stalked down the street.

"Malcolm," Hub muttered when understanding finally dawned on him. "Damn, that Malcolm certainly covered all the angles, didn't he? Without Jacquelyn around, the Gen'ral's personal property and remaining assets would fall into Malcolm's hands. Lordy, the man isn't greedy; he's downright ravenous for money!"

Mace expelled a wordless growl when Raoul paused beside the main office of the Reid Commission Company. Damn, he should have known Malcolm had had something to do with the attempt on Jake's life. And that was exactly what it had been, he thought furiously. Jake had insisted someone was trying to kill her when she first arrived, but Mace had declared that her imagination was running away with itself and that she had exaggerated the situation.

A puzzled frown clouded his brow as he mentally raced through the sequence of events that had transpired in the past few months. There were a few pieces of the puzzle missing. But, for the life of him, he couldn't figure out why he was plagued with this uneasy feeling that he had overlooked an important clue. It was there, just beyond his grasp—a fragment of thought that had yet to settle into its proper place. . . .

Another perplexed frown claimed Mace's craggy

features when the creak of the side door heralded the appearance of another of Malcolm's visitors. Hastily, Mace yanked Hub around the corner and out of view of the side exit. Craning his neck, Mace surveyed the swarthy stranger who was garbed in a sombrero and serape. It took a moment for Mace to place Gil Davis's partially veiled face. But when he remembered where they had met, Mace muttered several explicit obscenities.

"Would you mind telling me what has you growling like a rabid dog?" Hub whispered as he glanced back and forth between Mace and the man who had vanished into the alley.

"I would if I could," Mace grumbled crossly. "All I know is that something is very wrong."

"Amen to that!" Hub grunted sarcastically. "Your mind is decaying before my very eyes. You've got Raoul trailing only God knows who and you have us scampering around like a couple of criminals. And who the hell was that shaggy-haired hombre who sneaked out the side door?"

"Jake and I ran into him on the way to Reid's plantation," Mace explained. "But whoever he is, he rode into the wayside inn from the southwest. Where do you suppose he had been and what is his connection with Malcolm Reid?"

"You're asking me?" Hub hooted incredulously. "I don't even know who's in Malcolm's office at the moment!"

"I'll elaborate later," Mace promised.

When the main office door swung open, Mace yanked Hub back into the side alley and gestured for Raoul to join them. His narrowed golden eyes focused on the two men he had seen outside the restaurant the night Jake arrived in town.

Curiously, Mace watched Daniel Johnson count out several gold nuggets before depositing half the amount in Frank Norman's outstretched hand. What had Malcolm hired those two scoundrels to do now and where had he acquired nuggets?

Mulling over dozens of possibilities, Mace led the threesome back to his office and parked himself in his chair. For several minutes he stared unblinkingly at the wall, trying to anticipate Malcolm's next move. As near as Mace could tell, Jacquelyn still faced a life-threatening situation. Mace thought he knew *why*, but it was the *when* and *where* that had him miffed. Jake was miles away from Galveston, and Mace didn't have the faintest notion how the shaggy-haired stranger fit into the scheme of things. Was he a hired gunslinger perhaps? He certainly looked the part. Was Malcolm sending him off to accomplish what the first two hooligans had failed to do? And if the stranger had been hired to finish the deed, why was Malcolm paying the other two henchmen?

"Damnit, why don't you say something?" Hub exploded impatiently. "My curiosity is eating me alive and you're sitting there staring off into space!"

"I'm thinking," Mace mumbled absently.

"Then kindly do it aloud," Hub demanded. "Raoul and I would like to know what's going on, if it isn't too much trouble to tell us!"

Finally, Mace eased back in his chair and peered pensively at Hub. "As soon as we have finalized the last sales for shipment, the three of us are returning to the plantation."

"Is that your idea of an explanation?" Hub grumbled in question. "And what about Governor Wood's request to join the Rangers who are patrolling the southern border? You know he wants us to give 'Rip' Ford a helping hand. The outbreak of hostilities with Comanches and Mexicans is playing havoc with the frontier settlements. You have never turned down the request to lend our hands before."

"That will have to wait," Mace insisted. "We have unfinished business at the Reid plantation."

Hub's eyes bulged. "Now what are you suggesting? Surely not another conference about this business merger. You saw Malcolm's ledger. He would talk the Gen'ral out of the notion, even if you convinced Harlan to band together. And your chances of that are slim and none, I might add." Hub breathed in exasperation. He did not appreciate being left in the dark. Mace was making no sense at all. "And what about Jacquelyn? I thought you were certain her life was in danger. Have you already forgotten that possibility?"

An amused smile surfaced on Mace's lips. Hub was staring at him as if he had grapevines growing out his ears. And Raoul was silently condemning him for getting mixed up with that feisty minx in the first place.

"How many bales of cotton are left to be loaded on the schooners?" Mace questioned out of the blue.

Hub was contemplating pulling out his hair in frustration. "Too damned many," he growled. "It will take the shoremen three full days to load the exports, and another two days to transfer the imports from the schooner to the steamships that are headed upriver."

"We'll do it in three days," Mace announced as he rose to full stature. "That's all the time we can spare."

"Three days!" Hub chirped in astonishment.

"Three days," Mace confirmed as he discarded his waistcoat and rolled up his sleeves. "I want every man on our payroll on the dock in fifteen minutes. We're going to work around the clock."

Hub rolled his eyes in disbelief. "I thought the world was teeming with crazy people and we were the only sane ones. But now I'm beginning to wonder about you. We'll never complete all those tasks in that short amount of time."

A challenging smile hovered on Mace's lips as he

strode confidently through the warehouse to shout orders to his men. "The Good Lord made the world in six days, Hub. It doesn't seem unreasonable that we can squeeze five days' work into three if He could accomplish His feat in less than a week."

"Maybe we should request divine assistance," Hub said as he scampered to keep pace with Mace's long, swift strides. The job couldn't be done in three days, Hub assured himself. Mace was asking the impossible. Hub knew that as well as he knew the sun rose in the east!

Chapter 15

Listlessly, Jacquelyn wandered along the river bank while Jon rattled on in conversation. A look of utter boredom etched her exquisite features. It was beyond her how one man could talk for hours on end without saying anything pertinent. But Jon Mason had mastered the feat. Fortunately, Jacquelyn had learned the art of tuning Jon out. While he was babbling nonstop, she was lost to a forbidden fantasy. She could envision Mace lounging negligently on the river bank. His raven hair glowed blue-black in the midday sunshine. His tailored shirt had strained sensuously across the broad expanse of his chest. There had been an ornery smile twitching his lips and a mischievous twinkle in his golden eyes.

A warm tide of pleasure rippled down Jacquelyn's spine as she remembered the feel of Mace's skillful hands upon her flesh. She recalled the taste of his passionate kisses with such vivid clarity that she swore he was there beside her. She hadn't forgotten the way it was when they were lying in each other's arms that day beside the river or that night when Mace sneaked into—

Willfully, Jacquelyn squeezed back the tantalizing memories that still had the power to stir her emotions. It is over, she reminded herself sternly. Mace was gone, and her engagement to Jon Mason would be announced at the ball they were hosting in two days.

"Jacquelyn?" Jon frowned at the faraway expression that captured her lovely features. "I don't think you have heard a word I said," he complained.

"Of course I have," she assured him, mustering a reasonably pleasant smile.

"Oh?" Jon cocked a dubious brow. "You didn't look as if you were listening."

Her dark eyes flared with mischief. "Then you must have misinterpreted my expression," she countered saucily. "This is the way I look when I'm listening."

"Then what was I talking about?" he challenged her.

Maintaining her smile, Jacquelyn's mind sped back to the last comment she consciously remembered Jon stating and made a wild stab. "You declared that the South should secede from the Union if the North is going to continue fussing about Texas entering as a slave state and leaving the majority of power in Congress with the South."

Surprise registered on Jon's face. That was indeed the brief summation of what he had said. He could have sworn Jacquelyn wasn't paying the slightest bit of attention. When Jon took up where he left off, Jacquelyn breathed a sigh of relief. While he was babbling about Northern abolitionists she was free to pursue her own thoughts. Days ago Jacquelyn had relinquished all hope of trying to extract Mace's haunting image from her mind. It seemed she was destined to live with the forbidden memories, just as she had sentenced herself to a life with a man she didn't love.

Odd, Jacquelyn mused as they made the rounds of the plantation. It wasn't like her to do something she didn't want to do. In the past she would have loudly protested these circumstances. But that was before she'd learned the meaning of one-sided love. Now nothing mattered as much as it once had. She was going through the paces of living without feeling, without enjoying each precious moment. Even her arguments with Harlan had become the exception rather than the rule. No longer did she debate Harlan, just to get his dander up. Jacquelyn rather thought she resembled a puppet, moving mechanically from place to place, unaffected by that which transpired about her.

It's time you took yourself in hand, Jacquelyn lectured herself sensibly. Being deprived of Mace Gallagher's love was not the end of the world. If she wallowed in self-pity the rest of her life, Mace would enjoy the ultimate victory over her. He would see her from time to time, watching her pine away for a lost love, knowing he was the one who'd broken her spirit. Well, she wasn't going to give him that satisfaction! No man was worth this misery.

After delivering that encouraging sermon to herself, Jacquelyn straightened in the saddle and squared her shoulders. I do not have to marry Jon Mason for protection against Mace Gallagher, she realized. She was no simpering twit who lay down and gave up when life dealt her a punishing blow. As a matter of fact, she didn't have to marry at all! There was no rule that decreed a woman had to become a man's wife. Why had she wasted these weeks docilely accepting her fate? She could do as she damned well pleased and Mace Gallagher could go straight to hell—and he could take that dull, stuffy Jon Mason with him!

Her gaze swung to Jonathan, who had veered from the subject of politics to economics. Without waiting for Jon to cease his prattle, Jake interrupted him in midsentence. "I have thuoght it over and I have decided not to marry you, Jon," she announced abruptly.

Jon very nearly fell off his horse. "What? Why?" was all he could get out.

"You heard me. I don't want to marry you because I don't love you," she told him candidly. She would have handled the announcement more delicately, but Jon didn't respond to subtlety. When confronting Jon, one had to be blunt and to the point.

"But you will learn to care for me as deeply as I have come to care for you," Jon assured her frantically. "I'll make the model husband."

"For someone else perhaps," she contended. "But not for me. We have very little in common."

"I promise to love everything you like," Jon vowed desperately. Damn, he'd thought everything was falling neatly into place. And all of a sudden, his world had come tumbling down around him. If Jacquelyn refused his courtship he would never be more than a plantation overseer—the General's lackey. Jacquelyn was going to spoil everything!

"Perhaps you are just getting cold feet, my love," Jon cooed. "It's a perfectly natural reaction before marriage. When you have had ample time to reconsider, you will realize our marriage is practical."

Jacquelyn swung from the buckskin stallion, stepped around another of the bustling anthills that plagued the grounds, and propelled herself up the steps. "I won't change my mind again," she declared firmly. "It is nothing personal. I simply don't want to marry anyone."

As Jacquelyn breezed through the foyer, Jon clambered up the steps in fast pursuit. "My dear, you are being unreasonable. I have done nothing to warrant your refusal of marriage. I have catered to your every whim!"

The loud fracas in the hall brought the Gen'ral from his study. Bemusedly, Harlan watched Jon attempt to grasp Jacquelyn's arm. But she shook herself free and stalked up the staircase. Frantically, Jon turned to Harlan, beseeching assistance.

"Gen'ral, please talk some sense into your granddaughter. She has suddenly decided to cancel our engagement!"

Harlan's brow arched over his dark eyes. At last his granddaughter had displayed some of her notorious

286

spunk and self-assertion. The past two weeks Jake had been so lethargic and blasé that Harlan had sworn she would shrivel up and wither away. As much as Harlan would have preferred the match, he was having serious doubts. Jacquelyn would never be content with any man until she exorcised that raven-haired demon from her soul. Mace Gallagher still haunted her, but at least Jake was exhibiting a smidgen of her old spirit.

"Jake, is this true?" Harlan called after her.

Jacquelyn wheeled around on the landing and lifted a defiant chin. "Indeed it is, Gen'ral. I'm not marrying Jon or any other man," she told him matter-of-factly. "I'm going to become a spinster and haunt this mansion for the rest of my days. And no one is going to try to tell me what to do. I have been agreeable as long as I can stand!"

Harlan bit back an amused grin. Ah, it was good to see flames leaping from Jake's ebony eyes once again. She was her old self, and that was infinitely better than the meek, distracted shell of a woman who had been wandering around the plantation of late.

"There, you see?" Jon pointed an accusing finger at the rebellious hellion on the steps. "She is behaving like a madwoman. We have made all the arrangements. She can't back out now!"

"The hell I can't!" Jake yelled down at him. "If I've become a madwoman, it's because you have driven me crazy with your non-stop chattering. As near as I can tell you are nothing but a bag of wind!"

"But I love you," Jon declared to her and to anyone else who would listen.

"Love me?" Jake scoffed sarcastically. "You don't even know me, Jon. You've spent so much time talking you never bothered to listen to what I have to say. You don't have the foggiest notion what I think or how I feel because I can't squeeze a word in edgewise."

Jon's head swiveled toward Harlan. "Are you going to permit your granddaughter to speak so disrespectfully to me?" he snapped in annoyance.

Harlan finally took a good look at his overseer. The man showed no sign of possessing a backbone. When the going got tough, Jon turned elsewhere for support. He could take orders from others, but he would never truly be able to take efficient command of any situation without botching it up. And he certainly couldn't handle Jacquelyn. That was painfully obvious.

"This is between you and Jake," Harlan announced. "I will not force my own granddaughter to marry if it is not her wish. If she has changed her mind, then I must accept her decision."

Jon couldn't believe what he was hearing! He'd felt certain he could count upon the General to stand in his defense. Jon had spent three years catering to Harlan's wishes, obeying orders to the letter. The one time Jon requested a favor he was denied!

With his fists clenched by his sides, Jon stamped out the door without fighting his own battle against Jacquelyn. When the door slammed shut behind him, Jake expelled the breath she had been holding and stared down at Harlan.

"Forgive me for saying so, but the man is a bore," she declared.

A faint smile brimmed Harlan's lips as he hobbled over to prop himself against the balustrade. "I can't argue with that. But in his defense, I must add that Jon does what I need done around the estate."

A muddled frown settled on Jacquelyn's lively features. "You aren't upset with me then?"

Slowly, Harlan shook his gray head and smiled up at the hoyden, who was garbed in a colorful yellow shirt and trim-fitting breeches. "If you recall, I assured you I would not interfere in this matter. I would very much like to see you married to a respectable man, but your happiness is more important than my whims."

Jacquelyn flew down the steps to squeeze the stuffing

out of Harlan. "I'm sorry, Gen'ral, I tried to like Jon. But when it came right down to it, I coudn't subject myself to a life as his wife."

Fondly, Harlan hugged his granddaughter. "And I have mellowed in my old age. I have given up trying to order you about like a soldier, my dear. Despite my attempt, you are and you always will be a free spirit, a rebel in search of a cause. If you could withstand all the years of my badgering, you deserve to live your life the way you see fit."

Jacquelyn had never felt so close to her grandfather. During her childhood she had considered herself a thorn in his side. He had constantly complained about her willfulness, her contrary nature. But at long last Harlan had openly announced that he was accepting her for what she was, faults and all. Deep down inside, beneath that military brass and polish, was a sentimental old man who had her best interests at heart.

Harlan readjusted his spectacles and blessed Jacquelyn with a tender smile. "We will still host the grand ball in honor of your homecoming. But there will be no mention of a betrothal."

Jacquelyn stepped back to assess her grandfather. "Are you sure you aren't upset with me? I honestly expected us to clash over this matter."

"No, child," he softly assured her. "But I hope someday you can forget—" Harlan compressed his lips to stifle the remainder of his sentence. He was not going to bring Mace Gallagher's name into this conversation. "I hope you can forgive an old man for his attempt at matchmaking. I think those things are best left to Cupid."

"I can easily forgive you," she murmured. "Though I'm not sure Jon can forgive me for spoiling his plans."

"He'll survive," Harlan insisted. A meaningful frown wrinkled his weather-beaten features. "None of us can always have exactly what we want. The trick is learning to accept that."

Jacquelyn nodded mutely, wondering if Harlan was delivering general advice or hinting at her preoccupations with Mace. She had been so careful not to expose her inner feelings and her disappointment. No, she consoled herself. The Gen'ral didn't know she was still harboring a love for a man who didn't want her. Harlan was merely referring to the incident that had put Jon in a snit.

As if a heavy burden had been lifted from her shoulders, Jacquelyn bounded up the steps to her room. The charade with Jon was over and she was going to enjoy life once again. Even Mace's lingering memory wasn't going to depress her. Not a single guest at their party would know she had suffered a damaging blow to her heart. And more importantly, the General would never know she had been intimately involved with his competitor—Mace Gallagher.

Inspired by that positive thought, Jacquelyn sank into her waiting bath. But the vision of laughing golden eyes and a charismatic grin had her cursing. "Begone, Mace Gallagher," she commanded the apparition that flitted across her room. "You are no longer welcome here. Go practice your devilish charms on some unsuspecting female." In a symbolic gesture, Jake plucked the soap from its resting place. "I am washing my hands of you at last!"

And so she did, most rigorously. (As if that truly made a difference.) All she received for her efforts were clean hands. Mace's memory could not be rinsed away. It still remained in her mind. Put quite simply, she wasn't through loving Mace yet and there was nothing she could do about it!

Chapter 16

Malcolm Reid feigned a greeting smile when his lovely cousin floated gracefully down the front steps to mingle among the guests who had gathered for the Texas-style barbeque. Jacquelyn had blossomed into a bewitching beauty these past years, Malcolm mused. It was a pity she hadn't become domesticated during her stay in New Orleans. If she hadn't been so determined to meddle into the affairs of the Reid Commission Company, Malcolm might not have found it necessary to dispose of her. But Jake's independent nature had forced Malcolm to take drastic measures. He had come, bearing the ledgers as Harlan and Jacquelyn requested. Not that it would do them any good, Malcolm thought with a diabolical smirk. He had altered the books so no one would discover his unscrupulous activities. And before the night was out, it would make little difference. Gil Davis would spirit Jacquelyn away and she would never be seen or heard from again. Harlan would be so busy fretting over her disappearance that he wouldn't bother with the ledgers either. And even if Harlan did turn to the books for distraction, he wouldn't have a clue as to what was going on.

"Ah, dear cousin, you look absolutely radiant,"

Malcolm purred as he dropped into a bow. "Welcome home."

Jacquelyn's gaze flickered over Malcolm's chestnut brown hair and bland face. She had always contended that the Good Lord had gathered the plainest features and plastered them between Malcolm's ears. He had the type of face that could become lost in a crowd. And at age forty-two, even his wrinkles didn't add distinction. Besides his forgettable looks, Malcolm had the personality of a potted plant. Jacquelyn tolerated her grandfather's only nephew because he was family and because he had assumed responsibility of the company during Harlan's absence. In Jacquelyn's estimation, that was Malcolm's only saving grace. Had she known of his skullduggery and his desire to see her dead, she wouldn't have tried to like him at all!

"It's good to be home," Jacquelyn murmured, dragging herself from her contemplative musings. "I hope business is going well. I am most anxious to scan your ledgers and acquaint myself with the workings of the company."

She would never have the opportunity, Malcolm thought satanically. "Business is going as well as can be expected, considering Mace Gallagher is stealing our clients. We have become a shadow in comparison, and I've no doubt that Gallagher would swallow us alive if we were foolish enough to consent to a merger."

Fighting for composure, Jacquelyn displayed the semblance of a smile. "I doubt the Gen'ral will permit that to happen. He wouldn't bow to Mace for all the gold in California."

How odd that she would make that particular comparison, Malcolm thought with a wicked smile. "I should hope not!" he declared emphatically.

Jacquelyn enjoyed Malcolm's company for as long as she could tolerate it (which was only a few moments at a time). Excusing herself, she meandered through the crowd that milled on the front lawn, inhaling the tantalizing aroma of beef that was cooking over the barbecue pit. Malcolm was quickly forgotten when she was surrounded by several suitors who had courted her before she was whisked off to New Orleans.

It was a relief to be greeted by friendly faces after enduring Jon Mason's cold silence the past two days. How Jon had managed to keep his mouth closed for forty-eight hours was beyond Jacquelyn. Although she had no wish to place Harlan and Jon in conflict, she was thankful she was forced to do nothing more than nod a greeting when she chanced to cross paths with Jon.

Casting aside her rambling thoughts, Jacquelyn accepted the glass of spiked punch that was thrust into her hand. She fully intended to celebrate a new beginning, and she never allowed her glass to run dry during the evening. Like a carefree butterfly she drifted through the crowd, sipping and conversing with whoever paused beside her.

When the musicians struck up a lively dance, Jacquelyn found herself passed from one pair of arms to another. Ah, this was far better than moping about, feeling sorry for herself. Tonight she would live every moment to its fullest. And she did! Her mind was fogged with the giddy side effects of spiked punch, and her heart kept rhythm with the gay music that wafted its way across the sprawling lawn. At last I am free of Mace Gallagher's spell, she convinced herself. And no longer was she forced to pretend affection for the dull, stuffy Jon Mason.

While Jacquelyn was being tossed from one set of eager arms to the next, Mace and Hub clung to the shadows, watching from a safe distance. Although Mace was exhausted from his frantic attempt to tie up loose ends in Galveston, he felt the old familiar stirring of desire when he caught sight of Jacquelyn amidst her entourage of beaux. She reminded him of a pixie with her golden-brown hair piled atop her head. Wispy curls dangled about her exquisite face as she twirled to the beat of the lively music. The close-fitting blue satin gown accented her shapely curves and swells to such a degree that Mace's blood pressure soared at the sight of her. The decolleté dress left a generous display of bosom exposed to any man who cared to look, and Mace resented every pair of eyes that caressed Jacquelyn. Each time she moved, her breasts came dangerously close to spilling from the confines of satin and lace, and Mace was stung by the jealous urge to doff his waistcoat and drape it over her exposed shoulders.

Although Mace was relieved to see that no harm had yet befallen Jacquelyn, he was annoyed with her for looking so ravishing. This misplaced feeling of possessiveness frustrated Mace. After all, Jake was determined to marry that lily-livered Jon Mason . . . if she lived that long. And if Malcolm had his way, she wouldn't survive to speak those ridiculous vows.

An amused grin dangled on the side of Hub's mouth while he watched the emotions chase each other across Mace's craggy features. Mace had worked with fiend-ridden haste to transfer their cargo to its proper destination. Once Mace had performed the impossible, he had ridden toward his plantation as if Satan were following at his heels.

All that just to stand sentinel over a woman whose life might be in danger? Hub thought not, judging by Mace's silence and the odd way he was staring at Jake from afar.

"The lady appears to be thoroughly enjoying herself," Hub observed, and then glanced at Mace to gauge his reaction.

"Doesn't she, though," Mace snorted sarcastically. His glittering golden eyes scanned the crowd to see

Jon propped against a colonnade, guzzling his punch. "One would think Jake's fiance would be monopolizing her time instead of allowing her to flirt with everything in breeches."

"Maybe Jon isn't as possessive as some of us might be with Jake." Hub snickered, flinging Mace a meaningful smile.

Mace flinched as if he had been stung by a wasp. "Why should I care what she does? Jake is betrothed to Jon Mason. She's his concern, not mine."

One blond brow elevated to a taunting angle. "If you aren't worried about her, why did we work until we dropped and then drive our horses into the ground just to get here? It appears the only danger the lovely lady faces is having one of her overzealous dance partners squeeze her in two."

"We are here because Jake is the Gen'ral's grand-daughter," Mace growled defensively. "I can't very well stand by and watch Malcolm dispose of her, can I?"

"Of course you can't," Hub replied, teasing Mace and relishing every minute of it. He had never seen Mace work himself into such a stew over a woman. "Certainly not when you're in love with that feisty little beauty."

"I am *not* in love with her," Mace bit off.

For the sake of argument, Hub shrugged nonchalantly.

"I'm not, damnit!" Mace repeated with great conviction.

"Whatever you say," Hub answered, patronizing him. "Since you're so indifferent to her charms—and may I say she's overflowing with them," he added as his eyes devoured her obvious assets, "maybe the Gen'ral will permit you to give the bride away."

Muttering several disrespectful epithets, Mace stalked off to prop himself against his own tree. And there he stood brooding for the next few minutes. Watching Jacquelyn dazzle every man on the premises struck Mace like a physical blow. Finally he couldn't tolerate another moment. Drawing himself up, Mace straightened his cuffs and brushed off his jacket. With single-minded purpose he marched toward the enchanting goddess in blue satin and lace.

"What the hell is he doing here?" Malcolm hissed when he caught sight of Mace.

A troubled frown knitted Harlan's brow. Mace had barged in uninvited. The past two days Jacquelyn had begun to return to her old ways—playful, teasing, and vivacious. Harlan had thought, or least he had hoped, his granddaughter had put Mace out of her mind once and for all. Damn the man, he was going to reopen old wounds, ones that had only begun to heal.

The carefree smile that hovered on Jacquelyn's lips slid away when Mace weaved his way toward her. The arresting sight of him unfolded invisible tentacles that wrapped themselves around her mending heart. She unwillingly admired the raven-haired rogue who was garbed in a black velvet waistcoat that hugged his powerful physique like a glove. Jacquelyn couldn't imagine she could have forgotten how devastatingly attractive he was. But the image she carried around in her head was nowhere near as potent as Mace Gallagher in the flesh. He moved with lionlike grace, keenly aware of all that transpired around him. Those beguiling golden eyes peered through her to search out the secrets of her soul. His disarming smile held her immobilized while her heart flip-flopped in her chest. When he allowed his gaze to roam over her, Jacquelyn could feel the uncoiling of forbidden pleasure in every fiber of her being.

Oh, why did Mace always have to show up when she was just beginning to recover from her ill-fated infatuation for him? Damnit, he seemed hellbent on keeping his memory alive. Mace didn't want her, but he wouldn't permit her to forget him. Was he feeding his male pride again? Why else would he appear from out of nowhere to torment her?

Holding Jacquelyn's unblinking gaze, Mace took her hand and drew her trembling body against his. "As always, you look enchanting," he murmured against the swanlike column of her neck.

His softly spoken compliment rippled down each vertebra and set her nerves to tingling. His deep voice was a seductive caress that turned her knees to the exact consistency of grape jelly. His powerful arms brushed lightly against her, unleashing butterflies that began rioting in her stomach. The confident pressure of his fingertips on her waist burned brands on her flesh. Lord, if she didn't get hold of her emotions she would melt all over him! It wasn't fair that this golden-eyed devil could walk up and turn her world upside down.

When Jacquelyn refused to glance up at him, Mace curled his index finger beneath her chin and tilted her flushed face to his. His probing eyes focused on her quivering lips, assuring himself that his nearness still had the power to arouse her. Confound it! How could she marry Jon Chicken-hearted Mason when she knew damned good and well that sparks still leaped like crownfires each time their bodies made familiar contact?

"For God's sake, don't marry him, Jake," Mace commanded softly.

Stubborn pride refused to permit her to inform Mace that she had changed her mind about the marriage. If she told Mace the truth, he would arrogantly conclude she'd canceled the wedding because of her lingering affection for him. Jake would never give Mace the satisfaction of taunting her face to face. Let someone else tell him the marriage would not take place. She damned sure wasn't going to do it!

With her back as stiff as a ramrod, Jacquelyn stared up into Mace's ruggedly handsome features. "Why shouldn't I marry Jon? Just so you can creep into my bedroom when animal lust overcomes you?" she asked bitterly, and then winced in fearful anticipation. But to her relief, Mace didn't strike her, even though he looked as if he wanted to.

Jacquelyn would have flung herself away and stomped off if she could have escaped his steely arms. But the instant her muscles tensed in preparation for flight, Mace's lean fingers bit into her ribs and he crushed her tightly against him.

"Don't try to pick fights with me, minx. By now you should realize you can't battle against me and expect to win," Mace growled at her. The onlookers presumed Mace was whispering sweet nothings in this fiery imp's ear, but nothing could have been further from the truth. In fact, Mace was itching to clamp his fingers around her neck and strangle her for insulting him.

With her dark eyes snapping, Jacquelyn leaned back as far as his confining arms would allow. Spitefully, she ground her heel in the toe of his boot. Simultaneously, her nails dug into the bunched muscles of his shoulders like a feline sharpening her claws.

When Mace grimaced from her discreet attack, Jacquelyn displayed a smug smile. "I think perhaps you have underestimated me, sir," she purred in sticky sweetness. "I believe you'll find that I give as good as I get—" Her voice became an agonized gasp when Mace's fingers tunneled between her ribs, prying them apart.

"Can you, my sweet?" he cooed caustically. "I seriously doubt . . . ugh!" Mace's breath was forced from his chest when Jake's well-aimed knee caught him in the groin. But what infuriated him most was that no one else had viewed her painful attack. Her full skirts concealed her uplifted leg, which now came squarely down, sending her heel stabbing into his foot—the one which had not been previously mashed.

298

"Do you want to go another round?" Jacquelyn inquired as Mace spun her in a circle in rhythm with the music.

"There are several things I wish to do to you, she devil," Mace growled through a smile that was as brittle as an eggshell. "The least of them is dancing or sparring."

"I'm sure my fiance would disapprove of all else," she mocked lightly. Her eyes slid to Jon, who was glaring daggers at her. The visual gesture was enough to leave Mace with the misconception that Jake and Jon were still betrothed and that Jon did not approve of what he saw. For that Jacquelyn thanked Jon. His frown lent credence to her lie.

"I still fail to understand why a sane woman would deliberately make herself miserable by marrying a man she doesn't love." Mace snorted disgustedly. "If you wed that clumsy galoot, you will prove beyond a shadow of a doubt that you are a glutton for punishment."

One delicately arched brow lifted to a taunting angle. "I thought I had already established that truth," she countered all too sweetly. "The evidence lies in the fact that I'm dancing with a man who delights in proving his superior strength by trying to squeeze the stuffing out of me. Why don't you pick on someone your own size? Yonder tree perhaps?" Jacquelyn broke into an ornery smile as she gestured toward the towering pine. "Come to think of it, you and the tree have a great deal in common. You both are woodenheads with sap flowing through your veins."

While Mace and Jake were hurling biting rejoinders like poison arrows, Malcolm was swearing under his breath. He was sure Mace was attempting to sweet-talk his cousin into a merger. If Jacquelyn agreed to discuss the business transactions with her grandfather, things could get completely out of hand!

"Do something!" Malcolm grumbled to the General.

"Mace Gallagher is holding Jacquelyn so close he's practically drooling on her!"

Harlan was just as disconcerted by what looked to be an intimate conversation, but he had no intention of making a scene at Jacquelyn's homecoming party. He had promised not to interfere in her personal life and that was one vow he intended to keep, even if he didn't approve of the man who held Jake familiarly against him. Jacquelyn could handle Mace all by herself, Harlan reminded himself confidently. Whether she *wanted* to handle Mace was another matter entirely. But Harlan had tampered with fate twice before, and he had learned his lesson.

"What would you have me do, Malcolm?" Harlan replied as his nephew shifted uneasily from one foot to the other.

"Demand that Gallagher leave at once," Malcolm muttered, his burning green eyes fixed on the twirling couple. "Mace has gotten nowhere with us, but it looks as if he's decided to turn his charms on Jacquelyn. You know of his reputation with women."

A curious frown captured Harlan's weather-beaten features. Malcolm was acting a mite strange—almost frantic. "What has gotten into you?" he demanded to know. "I will make the ultimate decision about the merger. Even if Mace convinces Jake, he still has to contend with me. I will form my own conclusions about the benefits of a merger."

Malcolm's jaw dropped open and he stared aghast at his uncle. Harlan hadn't said he would agree, but neither had he said he wouldn't. Good God, was Harlan actually contemplating the merger? "If you dare reconsider, I'll—"

The General's stony gaze halted Malcolm in mid-threat. "You'll what?" he challenged in that authoritative voice he usually reserved for military commands. "It seems you have also forgotten who controls the Reid

Company. You are my financial advisor, no more, no less."

Harlan's no-nonsense tone warned Malcolm that he was treading on thin ice. The last thing he needed was to be at odds with the General. A falling out between uncle and nephew at this critical time could cause even more problems. Malcolm needed a few more months to conclude the last of his arrangements.

Masking his exasperation, Malcolm feigned a peace-treaty smile. "You are right, of course, Uncle. It's just difficult for me to stand idly by while the enemy is wooing my lovely cousin. I don't want to see Jacquelyn hurt by a man who goes through women the way most men go through their wardrobe of shirts."

A wry smile pursed Harlan's lips as he surveyed the striking couple in the dance area. Although it was true that Mace was followed by a reputation of being a lady-killer, he was testing his talents against a woman who was equally competent with men. Maybe Mace was playing Jacquelyn to his advantage, and then again, perhaps he had been caught in his own trap. Harlan had seen the way Mace stared at Jacquelyn that night on the balcony. And unless Harlan missed his guess, Mace was strongly attracted to Jake, whether he wanted to be or not.

Mace was not the marrying kind, it was true. But still, there was something very potent between these two renegades, Harlan surmised. It did Harlan's heart good to think Mace might also be suffering the same symptoms Jake had displayed of late. They were obviously infatuated with each other, but what would come of it was anybody's guess. Harlan had resolved not to meddle, and by God he wouldn't! That was one vow he wouldn't break, come hell or high water. And yet, wouldn't it be enjoyable for Mace Gallagher to find himself hopelessly enamored with the General's granddaughter after all the hell Mace had given Harlan over the years? The thought brought a devilish grin to Harlan's lips. If Mace actually fell in love with a hellion like Jake, the man would finally get exactly what he deserved.

While Harlan watched his granddaughter dance with Mace, Malcolm drew Jon aside. "Go ask Jacquelyn to dance," he ordered sharply. "Harlan may see no harm consorting with the enemy, but I don't like it a damned bit!"

Jon obeyed the command out of reflex. He had been ordered around for so long that he naturally did as he was told. Gulping one last drink of bottled courage, Jon set his glass aside and propelled himself toward Jacquelyn.

Jacquelyn was delighted to see Jon striding toward her. It would serve to convince Mace that nothing had changed between her and Jon. And come to think of it, this would be the first and only time Jacquelyn anticipated Jon's presence.

The moment Jon tapped Mace on the shoulder, Jacquelyn took advantage of the opportunity by eagerly flying into Jon's arms. A victorious smile lighted her features when Mace's face fell like a rockslide. His flaming golden eyes never wavered as Jon spun Jacquelyn in his arms and danced her a safe distance away. Scowling disgustedly, Mace elbowed his way through the crowd to resume his lookout position beside the tree. He was further annoyed to see that Hub had abandoned him. No doubt Hub had made a beeline for the plantation and a decent night's sleep. Hub must have been exhausted, Mace predicted. Why else would he bypass the opportunity to dance with some of the lovely young ladies who milled about the plantation? There was nothing Hub liked better than women.

Crossing his arms in front of him, Mace monitored Malcolm and Jacquelyn's every move. A wordless scowl burst from Mace's lips when he saw Jake polish off her fourth drink in less than an hour. Mace also took into

302

account the excessive amount of punch she had consumed earlier. Damn that minx, she would be so dazed with liquor she wouldn't be able to protect herself if Malcolm unfolded whatever fiendish scheme he had in mind.

Mace debated about going straight to the General and voicing his accusations about Malcolm. All that stopped him was his apprehension that Malcolm would twist the truth and use it as a weapon against Mace.

When Jacquelyn wandered from the crowd, Mace pushed away from the tree and circled the perimeters of the grounds. He was not about to allow that hoyden out of his sight with Malcolm looming like a vulture. Why had he dedicated himself to protecting Jake? Mace wasn't sure. That ornery minx infuriated him so often he wondered if he wouldn't be doing himself a favor if he let Malcolm have that troublesome bundle of spirit and beauty.

A silly smile dangled on the corners of Jacquelyn's mouth as she weaved through the row of oaks and stately pines that bordered the grounds. She was pleased with herself for fending off Mace's magnetic charms. A muffled giggle echoed in her throat when she recalled the stunned expression that claimed his bronzed features as she sailed off in Jon's arms. Feeling carefree and uninhibited, Jacquelyn tugged the pins from her hair and tossed her head, sending the dark waterfalls spilling over her shoulders. Pausing, she took another sip of the intoxicating brew, and then wandered wherever her footsteps took her.

A startled gasp bubbled in Jacquelyn's chest when a shadow leaped from behind a tree. Sluggishly, Jake coiled to strike, but her reflexes were too sluggish to prevent being captured in a pair of powerful arms.

"When did you become such a lush?" Mace growled down into her bewitching face.

Long, tangled lashes fluttered up to survey the disapproving frown that was stamped on Mace's face. Earlier, Jacquelyn had been rattled by Mace's nearness. But the liquor had taken the edge off her nerves, not to mention the drugging effect it had on the rest of her anatomy, especially her pickled brain.

"Who appointed you my personal guardian?" she slurred out.

"Someone needs to assume the task," Mace muttered, snatching the glass from her fingertips before she could gulp the remainder of her drink.

Jacquelyn attempted to glare at Mace when he tossed her glass on the ground, but her facial muscles refused to cooperate. She looked so comical that Mace grinned in spite of himself. And then a peal of laughter erupted from his lips when Jake stared cross-eyed at the tip of her own nose. Tentatively, she lifted a limp finger to inspect the unfamiliar object. It was her nose, all right, but it had been besieged by the strangest tingles.

"You're drunk," Mace accused, biting back another snicker.

A lopsided smile hung on her lips. "I thought so." Jake stared blurry-eyed across the lawn, seeing four-headed dancers swaying to the music that seemed to come at her from a long, echoing tunnel. Each time she turned her head she found it necessary to wait for her eyes to catch up with her. She felt oddly numb from the neck up. "I've never been intoxicated before," she confessed before an abrupt hiccup burst from her lips. "'Scuse me."

Mace had been put out with this unconventional minx, but her amusing expressions and sluggish movements melted his ire. All he really wanted to do was take this incorrigible spitfire in his arms and devour her soft, sweet lips. And without further ado, he did.

Jacquelyn's inhibitions had crumbled long ago. If she had been in command of her senses she would have protested his impulsive embrace, knowing this encounter would lead to more heartache. But there was no rejecting the feel of warm, persuasive lips on her mouth or the adventurous hands that knew where and how to touch to set her on fire. Jacquelyn's surrender was as reflexive as the batting of an eyelash. Her response to this exasperating man with the entrancing golden eyes had become as normal as breathing. He had become a habit that was impossible to unlearn. Her betraying body arched to make tantalizing contact with his muscular contours. Her hands slid upward to toy with the thick raven hair that curled at the nape of his neck.

Mmmm . . . it was so much easier to yield to the delicious sensations than to fight them, Jacquelyn thought with a sigh. She could defend her heart and pretend to detest Mace, but deep inside Jake knew what she felt for him would never go away. His taproot had channeled into every part of her being, as if he were an integral part of her, the living, breathing essence she required to function.

A shudder rippled through Mace's very core when Jacquelyn responded in wild abandon. Although it had been a mere two weeks since he had made love to this bewitching nymph, it seemed at least a century. Within an instant monstrous cravings were gnawing at him, compelling him to drink deeply from her honeyed kiss, to lose himself in passion's tempest.

His lips abandoned hers to drift along the pulsating column of her throat and the silky slope of her shoulder. Her quiet moan of pleasure aroused and encouraged Mace to continue his titillating investigations. Lord, how he loved tasting and touching this witch-angel. He delighted in stirring her emotions. He reveled in the rapturous feelings that recoiled upon him when he caressed her.

Yes, it was madness to dally with another man's fianceé. Mace had never been so unscrupulous in all his life. But this fairy princess with eyes of glistening ebony did not truly belong to Jon Mason, and she never would. Mace had been the first to introduce her to passion, and he resented the idea of permitting another man to touch what had first belonged to him. It was a selfish, possessive attitude and Mace knew it. But damned if he could leave Jacquelyn alone, even when he knew they could enjoy no future together. And yet, he could not bring himself to demand that she marry him instead of Jon. He could not risk having history repeat itself.

Mace wanted Jacquelyn on his terms. He wanted her to come to him because she cared for him, not because of a legal license that decreed she belonged to him, not because of what the General wanted or didn't want.

Blast it, why couldn't a woman take what he had to offer for as long as it lasted? Why must there be time limits and legal boundaries attached to affection? A piece of paper didn't insure lasting devotion. What difference did marriage make? And why the hell was he having this conversation with himself? His body was on fire, and his malfunctioning brain was posing questions Mace didn't even want to consider! Jacquelyn had never even suggested that she might want to marry him, for crying out loud! Other women had hinted at wedlock. Other women had attempted to tie him down, and Mace had polished his techniques as an escape artist. And suddenly he found himself imagining what it would be like to settle down with this hellion, of all people!

This is crazy, Mace yelled at himself. Jake had never once mentioned a lasting affair, nor had she said anything about forever. So why was he warring with himself? Because Jake had turned to another man, because she had voiced not even one demand on him.

That frustrated Mace because he would have expected as much from a female. . . . Was he making any sense at all . . . ? It was difficult to tell when Jacquelyn's lips melted like summer rain beneath his.

"Mmmm . . . I fear I will miss your brand of kisses," Jacquelyn murmured groggily. "Could you perhaps have them bottled, in case I find myself thirsting for them?"

Mace tensed. There it was again, that subtle suggestion that Jake didn't even consider him a part of her future. She wanted to bottle his kisses and toss the rest of him out with the garbage. Damnit, women were supposed to be sentimental creatures! Why couldn't she have said, "I need you, don't ever leave me"? Mace had pat responses for the typical female requests, but he was always at a loss with Jake. Usually, she stole his lines and left him floundering for a suitable reply. He hated it when she was the one who was being practical and sensible. Blast it, that was supposed to be his role!

"Do you intend to sample my kisses when Jon's don't satisfy you?" Mace growled resentfully. "Is that to be another of your solutions, along with separate bedrooms?"

"Let's not argue," Jacquelyn whispered as she guided his face back to hers. Gently, she smoothed away his angry frown. "Before long you will be gone, and I will let you go because it's the way of things. There is only the present, no past or future. I will be content with it. . . ."

Mace was set to spout off at the intoxicated beauty who was turning him wrong side out. But when her lips feathered over his and her supple body molded itself intimately to his, Mace forgot his indignation. For God's sake, why was she taking this so well when he wasn't?

"Take your hands off my cousin," Malcolm sneered contemptuously.

The loud interruption provoked Jacquelyn to glance sideways. With her head resting against Mace's heaving

307

chest and her silky hair tumbling over his supporting arm, she gave Malcolm a droopy glance. "Go 'way, Malcolm," she slurred. "I'm enjoying myself."

Malcolm's face turned the color of cooked liver. "You are making a fool of yourself," he corrected hotly. His blazing green eyes lifted to glare holes in Mace's wry smile. "You aren't welcome at this party, Gallagher. If Jacquelyn weren't so intoxicated, she would realize you are making a nuisance of yourself and she would be humiliated by her behavior."

"Your concern for your cousin is touching," Mace remarked in a tone that implied otherwise.

Malcolm jerked up his head. "What is that supposed to mean?"

Mace raked Malcolm with scornful mockery. "It means you could cause Jake far more harm than I ever could."

Malcolm struck an arrogant pose. "I don't have the faintest idea what you're babbling about. All I'm trying to do is save Jacquelyn from embarrassment. When she sobers up she will be thoroughly ashamed of herself."

Although Mace opened his mouth for a condemning remark, he swallowed his words when Harlan hobbled toward them. This was not the time or place to engage in a shouting match. Mace had no qualms about hurling accusations at Malcolm, but he was not about to allow the man to defend himself to Harlan.

"Jacquelyn," Harlan barked gruffly.

Her head rolled against Mace's encircling arm. A lazy smile tugged at her lips as she raised her arm to present the General with a lackadaisical salute. Harlan rolled his eyes and then glared at Mace.

"You have caused enough stir for one night, Gallagher. I don't wish to have this celebration ruined by fisticuffs. I would appreciate it if you would leave peacefully." His stern gaze dropped to his sleepy-eyed granddaughter. "Jake, come here this instant!"

Mace scooped Jacquelyn's limp body into his arms and strode toward the manor. "I'll put the lady to bed so I will be certain no harm befalls her." Mace's comment was aimed at Malcolm, whose answering glower consigned his adversary to the fiery pits of hell. Mace, of course, returned the glare, and prayed the Lord would call down His wrath on one of His most obvious sinners before he he armed this intoxicated pixie.

Harlan fell into step behind Mace. He wasn't the least bit surprised that Mace had disregarded the request. Malcolm, on the other hand, was hopping up and down in frustrated fury because Mace had refused to allow Jake to walk to the house under her own power. It further infuriated Malcolm to realize the General was mellowing in his old age. Indeed, Malcolm would have preferred to see Harlan draw his pearl-handled pistol and shoot Mace in the back. Harlan's silent acceptance of Mace's intentions left Malcolm wondering if his position was even more precarious than he suspected. After all, Harlan had allowed their competitor on the plantation. Might he be contemplating a merger just because Jacquelyn appeared to be enamored with this trouble-maker?

It was a good thing Gil Davis was to arrive after the ball, Malcolm thought with relief. From all appearances, time was of the essence.

When Mace paused at the foot of the steps to await directions to Jacquelyn's bedroom, Harlan almost laughed out loud. As if this rakehell didn't know the way to Jake's boudoir! Well, at least Mace had the decency not to flaunt his knowledge. If it had been his purpose to infuriate the Reids, Mace could have taken advantage of the ripe moment. That in itself left Harlan to wonder if perhaps Mace were far more involved with Jacquelyn than even he realized.

"There." Harlan indicated the proper room while Malcolm muttered and scowled in bitter protest over allowing Mace to set foot in the house, much less carry Jake to bed.

After Mace gently laid Jacquelyn on her bed, he rose to his full stature and smiled down at the drowsy beauty. "Good night, little princess. I hope the Gen'ral has a remedy for a hangover. I feel you're going to have a tender head come morning."

Malcolm peered around Harlan's bulky frame as if he were using his uncle for a shield. "My cousin's head is none of your concern, Gallagher. Now kindly take your leave!"

"Be still, Malcolm," Harlan snapped, gouging his elbow in the younger man's midsection. "Can't you see Mace's only interest is in Jake's comfort?"

Mace was astounded. Harlan had never before come to his defense. Had Jacquelyn's return mellowed the General? No, surely not, Mace decided, giving the matter a moment's consideration. Obviously the spiked punch had softened both Jacquelyn and her grandfather. Neither of them were behaving normally.

After Malcolm stomped off in a huff, Mace peered down at the sleepy smile that hovered on Jacquelyn's kiss-swollen lips. Lord, it was difficult to leave her lying there, knowing Malcolm was waiting for the opportune moment to strike. Impulsively, Mace reached out to brush away a renegade curl that tumbled over the side of Jacquelyn's face. An odd feeling of possessiveness stung him again. Mace had developed a sixth sense after his experiences riding with the Rangers. He had the nagging feeling Jake was on a collision course with danger. Damn, if only I could confide in Harlan, he thought. But the General would never believe his nephew wished to harm Jake, at least not until it was too late. Frustrated, Mace wheeled around, only to find Harlan staring specula-

310

tively at him.

There was a hint of confusion in Harlan's dark eyes. He wasn't quite sure what to make of Mace. For years Harlan had disliked Mace's reckless air, his disregard for authority. Harlan resented the fact that Mace had saved his life. It went against his grain to appreciate a man who was so unlike himself. And yet, seeing the tenderness and concern Mace displayed for Jacquelyn made Harlan wonder if there were far more to this man than he wanted to see. Harlan stood there, in a mental tug-of-war, wondering if he might have misjudged Captain Mace Gallagher.

"You really are fond of my granddaughter, aren't you?" Harlan questioned point-blank.

A wry smile rippled across Mace's lips as he swaggered toward the door. "She's a rare breed," he admitted.

Harlan's probing gaze halted Mace in his tracks. "That is not what I asked, Gallagher."

Amusement twinkled in Mace's amber eyes as he glanced sideways. "Would it please you to hear that I am hopelessly bewitched by an engaged woman, Gen'ral?"

"Engaged?" Harlan snorted. "Jake called off the wedding a week ago. She said Jon was dull and stuffy."

An annoyed frown clouded Mace's brow. His gaze circled back to the mischievous beauty who was sleeping off her bout with the spiked punch. Damn that little minx. She had purposely lied to him! The fickle chit had rejected Jon, and then used her engagement to taunt Mace. She delighted in toying with men, teasing them until they couldn't determine which direction was up. Mace would have dearly loved to shake that ornery vixen awake and tell her exactly what he thought of her. Hell, I should leave her to Malcolm, Mace thought spitefully. That woman was worth her weight in trouble!

"Good night, Gen'ral," Mace grumbled as he stalked toward the door.

311

A muddled frown settled on Harlan's face when Mace barreled out of the room. Just what the devil was going on? Why hadn't Jake told Mace she had canceled the wedding? And why had Mace appeared more agitated than relieved when he learned the truth?

Grumbling, Harlan threw up his hands and hobbled into the hall. Who could understand young people when they didn't understand themselves? Harlan thought sure there was a mutual attraction between these two willful people. But he was beginning to wonder if this was a private war they were waging against each other. Jake and Mace were trying to torment each other, out of pure orneriness.

Harlan wasn't sure what to make of the situation, but he was certain he was going to keep his nose out of it. These two strong-minded renegades were having enough difficulty sorting out their feelings for each other without outside interference. They didn't even know what they wanted or expected from each other. So how the hell could Harlan determine what was going on?

Exasperated, Harlan shook his head. Planning the strategy of battle was far easier than speculating on the outcome of this power struggle between Jake and Mace. In the beginning, Harlan had cringed at the possibility of having Mace as his grandson-in-law. But the more he thought of it . . . Good gad! What was he thinking!

Astonished by the changes that had come over him since Jake had returned home, Harlan hobbled outside to bid his guests good night. He was suddenly transforming into a sentimental old fool. He had begun to center his life around Jacquelyn. He had become aware of her needs, tolerant of her moods. After all these years he had become more than an authoritative figure who spouted orders at her. At last, Harlan had become more than family. He had become her friend and he cared about her future and her happiness. Harlan was no longer the self-centered general who expected the world to revolve at his command.

A wry smile pursed his lips when he pondered that fact. It seemed he wasn't too old to change his ways after all. That was an encouraging realization. And he rather liked fussing over his rambunctious granddaughter. As mischievous as she was, she could use all the help and guidance she could get!

Part III

Love is something different from delirium, but sometimes it's hard to tell the difference.

Chapter 17

The torchlights that illuminated Reid plantation had long ago faded into shafts of moonbeams and crisscrossed shadows. The music that had drifted in the wind had died into the familiar sounds of chirping crickets and croaking bullfrogs. Gone were the scores of guests who had danced and dined on the front lawn. The world had nestled down to a peaceful night's sleep while fireflies sprinkled their tiny golden lights across the meadow.

A muffled groan was the only noise that disrupted the serenity of the evening. Groggily, Jacquelyn propped up on her elbows and pried one eye open to stare at the silvery, moonlit path that sprayed across the carpet. The rustling of drapes beside the terrace door caught her attention. Levering herself onto one arm, she stared at the tips of the dusty boots that protruded from the hem of the curtains.

Mace has come to taunt me in my hour of misery, Jacquelyn decided. She had made a fool of herself at the party and Mace had returned to remind her how ridiculous she had looked while she was draped in his arms like his eager harlot.

"You can come out now. I know you're there, Mace," she said hoarsely. Lord, her mouth felt as if it had been stuffed with cotton.

When Mace made no move to reveal himself, Jacquelyn muttered irritably. After pushing herself into an upright position she braced herself against the furniture and weaved unsteadily toward the drapes. "Why do you insist upon sneaking into my room and tangling yourself in the drapes?" she grumbled. "I'm in no mood for your games. Don't you ever enter a room the normal way?"

Still Mace made no comment. He stood with his feet protruding from the curtains, just as he had the first time he'd crept into her room. Annoyed, Jacquelyn grasped the side of the drapes and flung them back. A shocked gasp erupted from her lips when a faceless specter peered back at her. The black hood that covered the intruder's face was shadowed by a huge sombrero. The man's torso was draped with a long, shapeless serape that disguised his physique. This wasn't Mace! Lord, how she wished it were!

Before Jake could scream at the top of her lungs, a gloved hand clamped over her mouth. Her brawny assailant whisked her around so quickly her head spun like a top. Panic speared through Jacquelyn's fogged brain and she cursed the lingering effects of the liquor she had consumed. Although she struggled to escape, she found herself chained in the man's unyielding arms.

With swift efficiency her abductor stuffed a gag in her mouth and then tied her hands behind her back. Jacquelyn flung herself forward, only to be yanked back by the hair on her head. Before she could regain her balance, a huge cotton sack was shoved over her face to envelop her entire body. A pained grunt died beneath the gag when she was abruptly flipped upside down and tossed over the man's shoulder.

Jacquelyn would have screamed for all she was worth when she felt herself rolled over the balcony railing to

318

dangle in midair, but the gag prevented her cry of alarm. Like a worm squirming inside its confining cocoon, Jacquelyn wiggled for escape, even while she was slowly lowered to the ground by a rope. (Or at least she supposed her abductor had employed a rope to remove his stolen baggage from the second-story bedroom. It was difficult to tell exactly what was going on when one was trapped inside a cotton sack.)

Another muffled groan rumbled from her lips when she was roughly dragged across the ground. The man's hands clamped around her buttocks to scoop her up and fling her over the back of a horse. Blind fury sizzled through Jacquelyn while she was strapped on the back of this four-legged creature. It left her wondering if this humiliating incident had any connection with her ambush or the assault by the two men she encountered in Galveston. But there weren't two men, she reminded herself. Her abductor was dressed suspiciously like the hombre she had met at the wayside inn. Could this be the same man? And if it were, what could he possibly want with her?

Damn, if only she had been in total command of her wits, she might have been able to prevent this disaster. But she had been too groggy and had erroneously assumed Mace had returned to pester her. God, she would have given most anything if Mace had been hiding in the drapes. She would much rather battle the turmoil of emotions he evoked from her than fight for her life . . . or what was left of it. From all indications, someone wanted her dead.

Jacquelyn couldn't fathom what she had done to invite this kidnapping. Who could possibly want her out of the way and for what reason? She hadn't been in Texas long enough to acquire such vicious enemies . . . had she?

There was plenty of time to consider all the possibilities while she was carted cross-country, upside

319

down in a cotton sack. She had lost all sense of direction and her head felt as if a bass drum had been implanted in her skull. With each jarring step the steed took, an accompanying echo plowed through her head. This was not the time to be battling a hangover, Jake thought sickly. She was in serious trouble and she felt horrible! Indeed, she was beginning to wonder if perhaps she had died during the night and this was the way sinful souls were transported to their private cells in hell.

She was reasonably certain she had hit upon the truth when a pair of unseen hands slid brazenly across her breasts and dragged her from the steed. Her outraged gasp vibrated inside the sack as she was rolled onto what she presumed to be a wooden raft. The River Stix, Jacquelyn concluded. She was being ferried to Hades to meet Satan and the other resident demons. Sweet mercy, she was about to pay penance for all her transgressions— as well as a few she didn't commit but might have if she had lived longer!

The sound of water sloshing against the raft interrupted her tormented thoughts. The scrape of boots and the clink of spurs on the rough wood invaded the tense silence. A shiver of dread slithered down Jacquelyn's spine when she felt her abductor's hands mapping her body. No doubt this devil was measuring her to determine how much space would be required to hang her carcass over hell's hearth.

When his hand brushed intimately over her breasts a second time, Jacquelyn attempted to vault to her feet. Her momentum surprised her assailant who expelled what Jacquelyn assumed to be curses. Satan spoke in Spanish! She never would have thought it. Indeed, she expected there to be a universal language spoken in hell.

Before Jacquelyn could pursue her musings, her foot became entangled in the cotton sack, throwing her off balance. Hands were clawing at her again and hissing curses echoed around her. And then suddenly, during her stumbling attempt to regain her equilibrium, she heard a splash—her own. In less than a heartbeat water poured into the sack. She was going to drown!

Icy fingers of dread clutched her heart as she sank in the dark depths. She was breathing her last breath. In a few more moments this nightmare would be over. . . .

Mace's ruggedly handsome features flashed before Jacquelyn's eyes. He was there, just beyond reality, smiling at her with that ornery smile of his. Never again would she feel his strong, capable arms encircling her. Never again would she experience the pleasure of his kisses and caresses. She was going to die and he was going to be her last thought!

Just when Jacquelyn had given up all hope, her abductor tugged at the rope, towing her back toward the surface. Jacquelyn's lungs were on the verge of bursting, and they would have if the hombre hadn't hoisted her back to the raft at the crucial moment. Jacquelyn lay there, gasping and sputtering to catch her breath while her assistant pronounced another vicious string of what she knew for certain to be curses. At that moment Jacquelyn was thankful she had never bothered to learn Spanish. Her situation was bad enough without being subjected to the man's colorful string of expletives.

Most of the fight drained out of Jacquelyn after her brush with death. She lay there like a wet corpse, wondering if she might have been happier if she had drowned and put an end to this terrifying nightmare.

After what seemed an eternity, she was slung over the man's shoulder and carried from the raft. Her soggy senses alerted her to the creak of a door. Footsteps scraped across a wooden floor of immeasurable distance, and the whine of yet another portal reached her ears. Jacquelyn was abruptly dumped on a cot and left to worm herself into an upright position while scraping boots and spurs reversed direction. When the door slammed shut, Jacquelyn fought the confining sack, attempting to locate its opening. But the cotton sack had been securely tied and she couldn't wiggle free.

The sound of muffled voices in the adjoining room caught Jacquelyn's attention. She strained her ears but she could make no sense of the Spanish that was being spoken. After several minutes the door banged against the wall and Jake tensely awaited her captor's approach.

With no forewarning, Jacquelyn was shoved backward. Wildly, she struggled against the man's rough handling, dreading what was to come. Growling at her resistance, her abductor grasped the bottom of the cotton sack, giving it a firm shake. With a thud, Jacquelyn tumbled onto the floor to stare at a pair of dusty boots.

Recoiling, she attempted to swing her feet upward, catching the hombre in the groin and bringing him to his knees. But Jacquelyn had just initiated her defensive maneuver when she heard a vicious growl that made her heart skip several vital beats. When the man sprang back to dodge her well-aimed foot, a gigantic black beast lunged forward to protect the hombre. Jacquelyn would have taken time out to laugh at the irony of this menacing-looking creature attempting to protect its wicked master, but she was too busy counting the sharp white fangs that were revealed when the animal curled its lips and snarled at her.

There before her, poised to pounce, was an oversized dog. Embedded in the creature's wide, offensive face were two coal-black eyes, and its powerful jaws could crush bone. The hair on the mongrel's back was stiff with threat. A guttural growl poured from its mouth as it breathed down on Jacquelyn's peaked face. The intimidating animal, one that reminded Jake of a wolf rather than a domesticated dog, held her paralyzed for an unnerving moment. Jacquelyn had the queasy feeling that one encouraging word from the Mexican bandito and the wolf-dog would gobble her alive.

A low rumble of laughter echoed in the region of what Jacquelyn presumed to be the scoundrel's chest. *"Pelar ajo, nina. Salir de Gualemala y entrar en Guatepeor,"* he snickered as he reached down to untie Jacquelyn's hands and remove her gag.

Jacquelyn dragged her wary gaze from the growling mutt. Her bloodshot eyes ascended up the towering mass of masculinity that loomed over her. Unblinkingly, she focused on the black hood that concealed the man's face. "Would you mind translating to English, hombre?" she managed to say in a reasonably civil voice. Her gaze darted back to the huge mongrel that stood like a posted lookout, wondering if the unfriendly beast could detect the underlying hostility in her voice. "I don't speak Spanish."

The bandito swaggered toward the chair and straddled it backwards. "Beware, my lady. You might find that you have jumped from the frying pan into the fire," he translated in a heavily accented voice. "If you attack me, the dog will make a meal of you."

After the hombre rattled off a command in Spanish, the vicious beast retreated to the door and sank down on all fours. Jacquelyn breathed a thankful sigh of relief and inched onto the cot. Her mutinous gaze swung to the bandito who had roughly dragged her from her bedroom and dumped her in this shabby hut. Perhaps she couldn't club him over the head as she itched to do, but she could most certainly glare flaming arrows at his multi-colored serape.

Another peal of laughter shattered the silence. "I think, senorita, if looks could kill, I would be a dead man," he declared in a low, husky voice that was so thick with a Spanish accent that Jake had to concentrate to decipher his remark.

To humor the dog, Jacquelyn flashed its demon master a pretentious smile. "Indeed, I would see you stabbed, poisoned, and hanged from the tallest tree in Texas," she assured him. "I wish you would go straight to hell and take that pitifully ugly beast with you."

"You are much too daring, *chiquita*," he taunted. "If you test my . . ." He paused, searching for the proper translation. ". . . my good disposition and my even temper, I will sic my dog on you."

"What do you want with me?" Jacquelyn burst out, only to hear another threatening growl from the powerful wolf-dragon which guarded the door.

"What do most men want from a beautiful senorita?" he questioned in a suggesive purr. "There is much about you that arouses a man."

Jacquelyn jerked her head up and showed him a glower that was meant to maim. Although she couldn't see his face, she could imagine the lusty expression that captured his homely features. "I would rather suffer the dog's bite than have your disgusting hands on me."

"*No me diga*," he chortled carelessly.

When the formidable bandito unfolded himself from the chair and sauntered toward her, Jacquelyn shrank back on the cot, wishing her tongue hadn't outdistanced her brain. She had challenged the hombre and invited more trouble, as if she didn't have enough of it already!

When Jake had backed herself as far away as the cot in the corner would allow, the bandito extended a gloved finger to trace the sagging bodice of her wet gown. "Later, *mujer*, we might discover if you truly detest my touch. You might learn that I'm not half the beast *el lobo* is. . . ." Brazenly, his hand brushed over the taut peaks of her breasts, causing Jacquelyn to flinch uncomfortably.

Jacquelyn murmured a silent prayer of thanks when the bandito withdrew without taking further privileges.

324

He had assured her she was safe from molesting for the moment, but had indicated that he would not rule out the possibility if lust got the better of him.

When the Mexican bandito sashayed toward the door, the dog stepped aside, and then quickly resumed its sentinel post. The beast's coal-black eyes never wavered from Jacquelyn during its master's absence and she refused to meet the wolf-dog's piercing gaze. It was unsettling to stare into that ugly, unpleasant face and count those deadly fangs.

Several minutes later, the hombre returned with a meager offering of food and some dry clothes. "You will be left alone to dress and eat, *chica*," he informed her in his thickly accented voice. "While I go to speak with my associate, the wolf-dog will watch over you." The hombre set the tray of food on the stand and rose to his full height. "Be warned, *nina*. The dog obeys each of my commands with relish. I have told him to attack if you take one step toward the door."

When she was left alone with the shaggy beast, Jacquelyn expelled several unladylike curses. Damnation, the hombre had refused to disclose why she had been kidnapped, and he had not allowed her to interrogate him. Was he seeking ransom from the General? Or had the hombre brought her here to become a between-meal appetizer for his oversized mutt?

Jacquelyn stared pensively at the pemmican that lay on the tin plate, and then shifted her attention to the black beast that stood between her and freedom. Perhaps if she attempted to befriend the mutt, he would permit her to leave without biting off one of her legs.

Grasping the dry cake, Jacquelyn waved it beneath the animal's nose. "Come here, Rover," she cooed sweetly. "Would you like something to eat?"

The dog came upon all fours and curled his lips to display his jagged teeth.

Jacquelyn was not to be discouraged. "*El lobo?* Is that your name?" she whispered softly. "Come here. . . ."

The oversized mongrel growled in response, and Jacquelyn's shoulders sagged. Either the mutt didn't understand English or he was so well-trained that he refused to waver from his master's commands, even when tempted with food.

Muttering at her perilous situation, Jacquelyn bit into the pemmican, hoping it would cure her sour stomach. Her head was still throbbing in rhythm with her heartbeat and she was chilled to the bone. When faced with adversity, Jacquelyn rarely responded with meek acceptance. But the hopelessness of her circumstances, compounded by her nauseating hangover, deflated Jacquelyn's spirits.

Mechanically, Jacquelyn struggled into the men's clothes the bandito had brought for her, and then stretched out on the cot. Unless she missed her guess (and she doubted that she had), she had been carried into the bayous and left without a means of escape, even if she miraculously found her way around the vicious dog which guarded the door. No doubt the bandito had secured the raft that had transported them to this secluded cabin in the marshes. She was still in Texas, but she may as well have been on the other side of the planet for all the good it would do her.

A cheerful smile lifted the corners of Emma's lips as she rapped on Jacquelyn's door. "Git up, chile," she called. "You've slept the entire mornin' away." Receiving no response, Emma tapped again. "Jac'lyn, the Gen'ral wants you to have lunch with him. Now you pry yerself outa bed dis minute!"

Again she was met with silence. Impatiently, Emma sailed into the room. "Git up outa dat . . ." Her eyes

326

landed on an empty bed that did not look as if it had been slept in for the better part of the night. Lord-a-mercy, where was that girl?

Wearing a worried frown, Emma waddled down the steps to consult with Harlan. Her announcement drew Harlan's immediate concern. He knew Jacquelyn had been well into her cups the previous night and had graciously allowed her to sleep until noon. Hell, he'd doubted she would rouse even then without Emma's coaxing. But to hear that Jake was nowhere to be found left Harlan dumbfounded. Limping alongside Emma, Harlan ascended the staircase to inspect his grand-daughter's room. The bed looked little different than it had when Mace had gently laid her upon it.

Keen brown eyes surveyed the bedchamber, searching for signs of a struggle. As if there would have been one in Jake's condition, he thought with a bitter snort. Jacquelyn would have been easy prey for anyone who might have crept into her room.

Harlan's curious gaze landed on the handgun Jacquelyn usually carried with her. If she had gone out of her own accord she wouldn't have left without her pistol.

Mace . . . Harlan frowned, disconcerted. He had seen Mace and Jake on the balcony on one occasion. Had they sneaked off together to continue where they'd left off after Malcolm caught them kissing in the shadows? Harlan immediately discarded that speculation. Mace was an ornery rapscallion, but he was smart enough to know he would be the first one suspected of wrongdoing if Jake turned up missing. And since Mace was too obvious, Harlan ruled him out. Perhaps Jon had attempted some foolish scheme. He had been upset since the day Jacquelyn canceled their wedding. . . .

"Gen'ral." Emma summoned him to the balcony. "Look here." She indicated the trail of cotton that was scattered across the gallery. "What do you s'pose dis is doin' outside Jac'lyn's door?"

Harlan hunkered down to inspect the strands of frayed rope and the puffs of cotton that led toward the railing. A feeling of dread overwhelmed him. From all indications, Jacquelyn had been unwillingly removed from her room and, it was apparent, had been toted off in a cotton sack. Why else would frayed rope and cotton be strewn from her door to the cast-iron rail?

"Damnation," Harlan roared. Who would dare to abduct his granddaughter? The list of possible suspects was endless. The plantation had been overrun with people the previous night. One more face in the crowd wouldn't draw suspicion. Someone had employed the party as a perfect opportunity to creep into Jacquelyn's room and spirit her away. There were too many people milling about to notice one unfamiliar face. But why? That baffling question buzzed through his mind without attaching itself to a logical answer.

Emma's expression bore evidence of her concern. "Gen'ral, what are we gonna do? Do you think somebody mighta kidnapped her?"

"I'm sure of it," Harlan muttered contemptuously.

With a stiff about-face, Harlan limped across the room and stalked down the hall to inform Malcolm of the shocking news. Malcolm, of course, accused Mace of being responsible and began listing all their competitor's faults, as he always had a habit of doing.

Scowling, Harlan descended the steps. Malcolm was no help at all, not when he insisted on blaming Mace for every disaster that befell them. The fact that no ransom note had been left in Jake's room puzzled Harlan. What the blazes was he supposed to do? Sit and twiddle his thumbs until a note arrived with instructions or until Jake wandered back all by herself? That was a remote possibility, Harlan thought disconsolately. Jake was a resourceful young woman, but she could well be dealing with a malicious madman or an entire passel of them. At this very moment she could be . . . Harlan flung the deplorable speculations from his mind. He had to concentrate on his plan of action instead of dwelling on dispiriting predictions.

Harlan's first order of business was to interrogate Jon, who was horrifed his employer would suggest such a thing of him. Jon's eagerness to offer assistance discouraged Harlan from making further accusations. If Mace was smart enough not to whisk Jacquelyn off into the night, and Jon didn't have the intelligence to think of the scheme on his own, who the devil had kidnapped Jake and why!

While the plantation buzzed like a bees' nest in search of its queen, Malcolm was grinning with malicious glee. He was delighted to hear that Gil Davis had accomplished his mission. Harlan would be so distraught by Jacquelyn's disappearance that Malcolm could collect the ledgers and return to Galveston within a few days.

Ah, things were going splendidly, Malcolm mused as he watched Harlan wear a path on the grass. Harlan may have been a brilliant military strategist, but Malcolm had taken him and that pesky female cousin of his for the ride of their lives. And in two months Malcolm would be living in the lap of luxury in Santa Gertrudis.

Under the pretense of trying to make himself useful, Malcolm strode off to search for his missing cousin, leaving Harlan to stare helplessly around him. This waiting game was agonizing torment and Harlan was on the verge of tearing out his hair, strand by strand. He kept visualizing Jacquelyn in the hands of a fiendish gang of outlaws. Damnit, why hadn't the bastards left a ransom note? Harlan would gladly pay whatever was asked of him if it would guarantee Jacquelyn's safe return.

An idea suddenly hatched in Harlan's mind. Lord, I

should have thought of it immediately, he chided himself. Hastily, Harlan walked back to the barn to have his mount saddled. Mace Gallagher could track Comanches and Mexican guerrilla bands better than any scout Harlan had ever encountered. If it were possible for anyone to locate Jake, Mace could do it. After all, the man did have a fond attachment for Jake, whether he would admit it or not.

As Harlan galloped toward the Gallagher plantation that lay to the northeast, Malcolm and his search party came trotting from the grove of trees that lined the river. A curious frown knitted Malcolm's brow when he noticed the direction Harlan had aimed himself.

"Do you intend to strike off on this hunt all by yourself?" Malcolm scoffed sarcastically.

"I'm going to inform Mace Gallagher and request his help," Harlan announced. "The man's tracking abilities are legendary."

The last person Malcolm wanted sniffing around was that wily, raven-haired devil. Mace had muttered several snide remarks the previous night that worried Malcolm. The man knew something, Malcolm predicted. And before Mace could point an accusing finger, Malcolm repeated the arguments he had voiced earlier that afternoon.

"Gallagher is probably the one who whisked Jacquelyn off in the first place," Malcolm growled. "You won't find him at home because he has Jacquelyn stashed somewhere out of sight while the rest of us are frantically trying to locate her."

"I told you before that is ridiculous," Harlan muttered in contradiction. "You saw Mace and Jake together. He wouldn't harm her. If that was his intention he would have attempted to kidnap her when he first met her in Galveston."

With his eyelids batting characteristically, Malcolm

floundered for a convincing comment to counter Harlan's logic. But he couldn't formulate a reasonable argument. While he groped for another excuse not to involve Mace Gallagher, Harlan gouged his roan gelding and thundered away. Muttering under his breath, Malcolm ordered his cavalry of servants to comb the clump of oak and pine trees in their futile search.

A Machiavellian smile settled on Malcolm's freckled features as he weaved through the underbrush. Even if Mace Bloodhound Gallagher went in search of Jacquelyn, he would never find her. Gil Davis was no man's fool. He knew better than to leave tracks. The man had dealt with Comanches, Mexicans, and Comancheros long enough to incorporate their cunning tactics. Mace had met his match this time, Malcolm mused confidently. There was no way in hell Mace would bring Jacquelyn back alive. Gil would see to that or he would find someone who could! Gil knew he had as much to lose as Malcolm, and the hombre would insure that there were no mistakes.

Chapter 18

Moaning miserably, Jacquelyn lifted one heavily lidded eye to see the sun glaring at her through the window of the shack. Wistfully, she wondered if she could crash through the glass pane before the vicious beast which guarded the door could clamp his powerful jaws around her throat. Discreetly, Jake cast the ugly mutt a contemplative glance. The dog lifted his head from its resting place on his huge paws and expelled a venomous growl. His dark eyes glistened in the sunlight, warning Jacquelyn that his attitude toward her hadn't softened one iota. The beast still looked as if he would just as soon tear her into bite-sized pieces as look at her.

Fighting the wave of nausea that rolled over her stomach, Jacquelyn mustered a pleasant smile and sat up. "Come here, puppy . . . nice dog . . ." Her purring voice must have reminded the beast of a cat because he bolted to his feet and bared his teeth. "Dumb dog," Jacquelyn growled back at him. "Your loyalties are misplaced. You should be protecting me from that Mexican bandito, not the other way around."

Her hateful tone only antagonized the shaggy creature. With a single bound the animal gobbled up the distance between them, sending Jacquelyn beneath the quilts for protection. Satisfied that Jake had been properly reprimanded, the creature lumbered back to the door and parked himself in front of it.

And then suddenly the animal's mood changed. His tail began wagging, a gesture that affected the back half of his stout body. He emitted a whine as he glanced back at the door.

Curiously, Jacquelyn poked her head from the quilts to see the animal staring expectantly at the portal. Within a moment Jacquelyn heard approaching footsteps. The door eased open to reveal the same faceless bandito who had snatched her from her home. Bitterly, Jake watched dog and master greet each other. The man's voice was soft and husky as he murmured Spanish to his obedient mutt. And the dog, who had posed such an ominous threat to Jake, melted into sentimental mush when his master patted his broad head.

A bowl of scraps was shoved beneath the mutt's snout, and he swallowed his food like a starved python. Chuckling, the bandito stroked the beast's back, and then rose to focus his attention on the wild-haired female who was glaring murderously at him.

"Am I also to enjoy a decent meal or am I to be fed what your devoted beast leaves behind?" Jacquelyn queried flippantly.

"*Que raro!* Senorita Reid has the tongue of a venomous viper!" he taunted as he sashayed toward her. "Are you always such pleasant company, *nina?* No wonder *el lobo* doesn't like you. What is there to like besides that luscious body of yours?"

If nothing else, Jacquelyn was learning the art of self-control. In the past, she had yielded to fits of temper and had gone at her nemeses with her claws bared. But in this instance she was forced to control her fury instead of going for the bandito's throat, if indeed he had one. It was difficult to tell with that concealing hood and oversized serape draped over him.

Jacquelyn clamped down on her tongue, even when it was her wish to fire a barrage of curses. With wary trepidation, she eyed the hooded outlaw as he bridged the distance between them. Oh, how she detested her predicament. It left her feeling frustrated, angry, and (God forbid!) helpless!

Carefully, the hombre tucked his gloved hand beneath her chin, lifting her furious gaze to his. "I will be more lenient and compassionate with you if you humor me during your captivity, *chiquita.*"

Humor him? I'll just bet a comedian is what he wants, she thought cynically. More likely, the rascal was suggesting sexual favors. Jacquelyn would die before she yielded to this bastard! He would have to take what he wanted from her. She would never give into him without a fight.

Quiet laughter split the brittle silence. "You are foolish, *querida.* I'm giving you the chance to offer, without a futile battle, what I can easily take from you." His wandering hand smoothed away her contemptuous glare. "Surely you are not denying me because of some silly notion that you must keep yourself pure for another man."

Brown eyes flashed as Jacquelyn jerked away from his touch. "At least he leaves the choice to me," she bit off without thinking. "A man like you cannot have a woman without forcing yourself on her."

A deep skirl of laughter bubbled beneath the concealing mask. "So there is an hombre in your life, *si?* And does he care enough to pay to have you returned in the same condition you left?"

The question hit a sensitive nerve, and Jacquelyn ducked her head to ponder her clenched fists. Damn, all this nervous energy and nowhere to release it, she mused in exasperation. She hated being intimidated. And more

335

than that, she detested the fact that the man she loved probably wouldn't give a fig when he learned she had been kidnapped. Why, when Mace heard the news, he would probably be saying good riddance to the late Jacquelyn Reid.

Her grudging silence provoked the bandito's unseen smile. "Perhaps the truth is that you are not woman enough to please your man, eh? Indeed, maybe I will have to pay a ransom to your man to get him to take you back!" he teased unmercifully.

Jacquelyn responded without thinking. The palm of her hand cracked against the black hood. Her furious attack provoked both man and beast. Shrieking in horror, Jacquelyn recoiled as one hundred and five pounds of sharp fangs and taut muscle lunged across the room. Her breath came out in a pained grunt when the hombre sprawled on top of her, mashing her into the cot. The bandito barked an abrupt command in Spanish, halting the snarling beast before he clamped his teeth on Jacquelyn's throat.

Still growling, the shaggy black mongrel sank down on his haunches. The ominous creature was quickly forgotten when Jacquelyn became all too aware of the man who held her pinned to the cot. His muscled body was meshed familiarly against hers. The pistol he carried beneath his serape jabbed into her hip, causing her to grimace uncomfortably.

"You very nearly invited your own death," the bandito muttered into her blanched face. "The dog will defend me with his life and with no regard for yours. I voice no idle threat, *mujer*. If you harm me the dog will kill you without batting an eye."

Jacquelyn heard and she believed. But the frustration of her situation got the best of her. Although Jake rarely succumbed to tears, this seemed the most appropriate moment to cry, if ever there was one. The dam of barely controlled emotions burst, unleashing a flood that trickled down the sides of her face. The hombre appeared shocked by her teary outburst. It seemed out of character for this wild, daring female to be choking on sobs. She had displayed very little fear during her captivity. She had faced her adversary with bitter defiance.

Slowly the bandito pushed into an upright position, straddling her hips. Mutely, he watched her breasts heave as the tears streamed down her cheeks. "I will bring you something to eat, Senorita Reid," he offered.

"I don't want to eat. I want to go home!" Jacquelyn wailed hysterically. It was the first time Jacquelyn could remember refusing to feed her frustrations.

"*¡Ni en suenos!* That is not possible," he told her.

"Then go away and leave me alone!" Jake railed as she rerouted the river of tears with the back of her hand.

"For now," he consented. "But I will be back. . . ."

When the door swung shut behind him, Jacquelyn buried her head in her pillow and cried for all she was worth. She was thoroughly embarrassed to be blubbering like a defenseless female, but she couldn't seem to get herself in hand, no matter how hard she tried.

If Jacquelyn had been paying attention, she would have realized her tears affected the beast who guarded the door. A snarl no longer tightened the mongrel's lips. His ears were cocked, listening to Jacquelyn wail like an abandoned child. If his master had not ordered him to stand watch, the beast would have consoled his captive . . . at least until she made a threatening move toward the door.

Heaving a troubled sigh, the bandito stepped outside the shack to locate his waiting companion. After tugging the wide-brimmed sombrero from his head, he removed the black hood. Golden eyes scanned the bog to see Hub

337

MacIntosh waiting beside the raft.

Muttering under his breath, Mace Gallagher shrugged off his serape and stashed his disguise in the small shed that sat adjacent to the shack. He had not expected Jacquelyn to strike him in a fit of temper. And when she did, Mace had been forced to straddle her before Raoul came to his immediate defense, just as he always did. If Mace had delayed a split-second, Raoul would have been at Jacquelyn's throat.

Lord, that was close, Mace thought as he ambled toward the raft. Since their years together in the war, Raoul had become overly protective of Mace. Although the oversized dog was complacent most of the time, he took Mace and his commands seriously. There had been two memorable instances in battle when Mace's assailants in hand-to-hand combat had found themselves viciously attacked by the ugly beast (as Jacquelyn had so cruelly referred to Raoul). It was a good thing Raoul didn't understand English, or his feelings would have been hurt by her insult.

Mace had learned to employ the dog's devotion, and never once had Raoul disobeyed a Spanish command. Indeed, Mace trusted the shaggy creature explicitly. If he ordered Raoul to guard the door and not let Jake leave, she wouldn't get within five feet of the portal.

An ornery smile tugged at Mace's lips as he strided toward Hub. Mace had been fully convinced that Jake was getting exactly what she deserved after she lied to him about her *dis*engagement to Jon. Mace had relied upon a disguise, similar to the clothes Gil Davis had worn, when he abducted Jake from her room. The nagging fear that Malcolm's henchman was lying in wait had spurred Mace into action the previous night, especially after Jake had overindulged in liquor.

Mace had ridden all of a mile from the Reid plantation before he'd decided an ounce of prevention was worth a pound of cure. It was at that moment that he'd decided to kidnap Jake before the kidnapper could kidnap her. Although Hub had protested the scheme, Mace was certain the incident could be played to their advantage. With Raoul to guard the captive, Mace and Hub were free to come and go without inviting suspicion. And, before the day was out, the wheels would be set in motion to expose Malcolm Reid for what he was—a would-be murderer and a swindler.

Mace had convinced himself that everyone involved in this situation was getting what they deserved. But he hadn't counted on this feeling of guilt that plagued him after his last encounter with Jacquelyn. It startled him to see that fiery minx reduced to tears. For a moment he had contemplated removing his mask and explaining his intentions. But that would have made her all the madder. Mace wanted to teach Jacquelyn a lesson she would not soon forget and expose Malcolm's skullduggery all at the same time. But seeing that wild-haired hellion lying there so temptingly had aroused Mace to the point of making lurid demands on her.

How had he expected her to react to his suggestions of bargaining for her freedom and her life? Knowing Jake as he did, Mace should have guessed she would fight back, no matter what the consequences. The situation had very nearly gotten out of hand when Jake struck out at him in anger and frustration. Raoul had gone for her throat! In most instances, Raoul behaved better than most humans, but he hadn't forgotten his fighting tactics. Jake's outburst simply brought out the beast in Raoul.

Mace heaved a heavy sigh. Hell, he should have explained his suspicions about Malcolm and his reasons for kidnapping her the moment they arrived at the shack. By the time he got around to revealing himself, Jake was going to be absolutely furious. Mace dreaded the moment of reckoning. It wasn't going to be a pleasant scene. Jake would finally learn the truth and she would give Mace hell for frightening her.

"Well, did you tell her what's going on?" Hub questioned, jolting Mace from his pensive deliberations.

"No."

"Why not?" Hub croaked in disbelief. "I think you've kept her in suspense long enough."

Mace unwrapped the rope that anchored the raft and hopped on board. "I'll tell her tonight."

Hub's breath came out in a rush. "That's what you said last night! If you ask me, this whole idiotic scheme is going to blow up in your face."

"Malcolm's face," Mace contradicted. "If the Gen'ral reacts the way I think he will, he should be paying us a visit this afternoon."

"You think you've got this all figured out, don't you?" Hub smirked sarcastically. "Well, I don't think you do! I think this is a hair-brained idea that will have the Gen'ral disliking you more than he already does."

A wry smile hovered on Mace's lips as his gaze drifted back to the hut that sat among the thick clump of trees. "By the time this all blows over Harlan Reid will thank me for kidnapping his granddaughter and stashing her in a safe place."

Hub grumbled under his breath and shoved the other oar into Mace's hand. "Maybe so and maybe not." His blue eyes followed Mace's gaze to the shack that disappeared in the distance. "You're fortunate Raoul is being such a good sport about this. I doubt he enjoys being confined to that shack. He's had the run of the plantation for almost a year."

"Raoul is a trained dog," Mace reminded Hub.

"Dog?" Hub scoffed. "We have never treated him like one. If Raoul could hear what you said about him, he would be insulted. And if he didn't worship the ground you walked on, he'd wander off and leave Jacquelyn to her own devices. Then you would be in bigger trouble than you're already in."

"If you can think of nothing positive to say, keep your opinions to yourself," Mace grumbled.

"Well, it seems strange to me that you would keep the woman you love in the dark and on such a short leash if you have any hopes of—"

"I am not in love with that feisty female," Mace exploded. "I'm simply saving Jake's neck. Not that she will thank me when she discovers who kidnapped her. But she could have awakened to find herself dead if Malcolm's henchmen had gotten hold of her first!"

A smug grin replaced Hub's disapproving frown. "All this scheming and plotting for the Gen'ral's grand-daughter?" he teased unmercifully. "Next I suppose you'll be proclaiming that you have also devised a way to obtain the merger you wanted."

"I have," Mace insisted matter-of-factly.

Hub gave Mace a withering glance. "Now that we know the foundation of the Reid Commission Company is crumbling, a merger might not be as profitable as you anticipated. What do you expect to gain from it?"

A somber expression captured Mace's craggy features. "The Gen'ral deserves better than being hornswaggled and bankrupted by his nephew. Harlan has spent his life defending this country. He deserves a few considerations. I gave him fits while we served with him during the war. I owe him."

"As if that was all there was to it," Hub scoffed. He wasn't fooled a bit!

"That is all there is to it!" Mace glared holes in Hub's mischievous smile.

"For the sake of argument, we will say you are laboring under a purely noble purpose," Hub said with a patronizing air. "So what happens next?"

"Tonight you are going to deliver a ransom note to the Gen'ral," he announced.

"What?" Hub tapped the side of his head, certain his ears had malfunctioned. "Surely I didn't hear you correctly."

"You did," Mace assured him with a cryptic smile. "And when the Gen'ral rushes to Malcolm, demanding that he gather the money, Malcolm will be squirming in his seat. In order to protect his hide, Malcolm will be forced to hand over the cash he has been stealing from the Gen'ral all these years."

So that was Mace's ultimate goal—to expose Malcolm and insure the return of the money stolen from the company. Damn, it was a brilliant scheme. All except for the part about holding Jacquelyn hostage, Hub amended. He wasn't certain that saucy lass or her grandfather was going to appreciate having her played as a pawn in this dangerous game of wits. Hub hoped Mace hadn't underestimated Malcolm. The man hadn't gotten where he was by being a blundering fool. Malcolm was not about to lie down and let Mace tromp all over him—not by a long shot!

Although Hub had had serious reservations about this complicated tactic of kidnapping Jake before Malcolm's henchman could abduct her, he'd kept his doubts to himself. Mace was a stubborn, determined man. Once he made up his mind to something, there was no deterring him from his purpose. In fact, Hub wasn't sure who was more bull-headed, Mace or that shapely firebrand Raoul was guarding in the shack. But one thing was for certain. Jake was going to give Mace hell when she learned who had taken her captive. She would hold this incident over him for the rest of his natural life! Mace should have told Jake the truth at the onset, Hub thought to himself. By the time Mace finally got around to explaining himself, Jake was going to be madder than a wet hen. Not that

Hub blamed her. Her experience had been harrowing, and Raoul could appear the snarling beast when he needed to. And as much as Hub liked Raoul, he had to admit the dog would scare the socks off anyone who didn't know him personally.

Mace could never redeem himself after he fell from Jake's good graces, Hub mused thoughtfully. That was going to make a great deal of difference to Mace whether he would admit it or not. No man went to such drastic extremes to protect a woman and save her granddaughter from financial ruin if he didn't care a great deal about her. By the time Mace realized he wanted more than Jake's gratitude and Harlan's respect, the lady in question would have resolved to hate Mace forevermore. Mace might manage to save the day but he damned sure wasn't going to endear himself to Jacquelyn by allowing her to think some ruthless Mexican bandito had snatched her from home and stashed her in that secluded shack!

Chapter 19

Harlan slid from the saddle, careful not to put excessive strain on his crippled leg. Proudly drawing himself up, Harlan straightened his jacket and pointed himself toward the monstrous plantation home that dwarfed his own spacious manor.

The moment the door opened to him, Harlan demanded to see Mace Gallagher. After the servant ushered Harlan into the study, he trotted off to inform the master of the house that a distinguished guest awaited him. Within a few minutes, Mace ambled into the study, followed by Hub—who had no intention of missing out on any part of Mace's tangled scheme. After nodding a greeting to Harlan, Mace lit his cheroot and sank down behind his desk.

"To what do I owe this monumental visit, Gen'ral?" Mace innocently inquired. "I am honored, but I must admit, I am baffled. Have you suddenly decided to accept my offer to merge?"

Hub silently snickered. Mace sounded so innocent that Hub expected to see him sprout wings and a halo. The General didn't have a clue that Mace knew exactly what had prompted this first visit to the Gallagher plantation.

Harlan clutched his cane until his knuckles turned

white. "The merger is the least of my concerns," he muttered, unable to contain his frustration. "Someone has kidnapped Jacquelyn and I am desperately in need of your help."

Feigned shock registered on Mace's bronzed features. "What? When?"

"Last night, early this morning . . ." Harlan gushed. "How the hell do I know! The maid went to check on Jake at noon and she wasn't in her room. She left without a weapon for protection—something she has never done since I taught her to shoot like an infantryman!"

"Have you searched the grounds?" Mace interrogated between puffs on his cigarillo. "As much as Jake had to drink last night, she might have wandered off and found some place to sleep off her overindulgence of whiskey."

"Of course I've torn the area upside down to locate her!" Harlan exploded in exasperation. "Don't you think I considered every possibility, even the fact that you might have been responsible?"

Mace's golden eyes narrowed. "Is that an accusation, Gen'ral? If it is, you have my permission to search the house. . . ."

Harlan waved Mace to silence. "I have already scratched you off the list of possible suspects, but Malcolm hasn't." His breath came out in a rush. "I don't think this is a prank. Someone is up to no good. I've got all available manpower combing the countryside. Thus far we haven't found a clue, other than a few balls of cotton strewn across the balcony."

"Cotton?" Hub interjected in surprise.

"Someone carted Jake off in a damned cotton sack," Harlan elaborated. "I tell you, someone purposely and maliciously planned to abduct my granddaughter. I need your help!"

Mace waited until the General's booming voice completed its orbit around the room. "I'll do whatever I can to find her," Mace assured him solemnly. "Have you nothing else to go on? No clue as to who might have taken her or why?"

"I don't have the faintest notion," Harlan said with defeat. His frantic gaze swung around the room. "I was hoping you could use that dog of yours to track Jacquelyn. Where the hell is that ugly mutt?"

Mace shrugged nonchalantly, although he was annoyed that the General referred to one of his dearest friends in such a degrading manner. "He's probably wandering around the grounds, doing what dogs usually do. But it won't take me long to locate Raoul."

"I wish I could say the same for Jake," Harlan muttered sourly.

Probing amber eyes regarded Harlan's worried frown. "I will do as you ask, Gen'ral, provided you agree to the merger."

Harlan came out of his chair as if he were sitting on live coals. "Damn you, Gallagher. I thought there was a heart beneath that calloused exterior! My granddaughter's life is in imminent danger and you are maneuvering to play this disaster to your advantage!"

Mace didn't even bat an eye. "You have denied my request for three months, for no other reason than your apparent dislike for me. I do not mix sentiment with business, as you are prone to do, Gen'ral," he said bluntly. "If I do track your granddaughter's abductors and safely deliver her to you, I expect payment in the form of a merger which will benefit your company and mine."

Harlan ground his cane into the floor and gnashed his teeth. "I was almost beginning to like you," he sneered disdainfully. "But you haven't changed from those days when we clashed on the subject of military strategy. I swear your greatest aspiration in life is to aggravate me!"

The insult bounced off Mace's thick skin without

347

leaving a mark. "I have stated the terms that will buy my talents as a scout and bloodhound," Mace declared. "The last time I did you a favor by escorting Jake home from Galveston you shouted me out of your house. And when Hub and I saved your life, you reciprocated by demanding that both of us be court-martialed for disobeying orders. I've been burned twice, Gen'ral. You'll have to make this mission worthwhile."

A resentful growl erupted from Harlan's lips as he wilted back into his chair. He well remembered how he had reacted on the two occasions Mace cited. Harlan had done nothing to endear Mace to him. And now that he needed a favor, he shouldn't be surprised that Mace wouldn't leap to assistance without a promise of compensation. But Harlan, desperate though he was, had too much pride to buckle without assurance that Mace wouldn't gain control of the commission company and then boot out his new partner, as Malcolm had predicted.

Malcolm had sabotaged Harlan's thinking. Although Harlan carried grudging respect for Mace, he couldn't quite bring himself to put blind faith in the man. The General hesitated in giving his consent to the merger without a guarantee that the Reids would not be used and discarded by this self-made cotton entrepreneur.

Frantically, Harlan's mind raced, grasping at fragments of thoughts, hoping to secure his position and permanently bind Mace to any financial agreement they might make.

The seconds stretched into minutes and Mace fidgeted in his chair. He had predicted that Harlan would come to him with a plea for assistance, grudging though it would be. But Mace was beginning to wonder if he had pushed Harlan further than his stubbornness would permit. Mace didn't know what he would do if the General rejected the compromise. If the General refused, he would drive another wedge between them, one that could not be easily removed. And if Mace relented and agreed to help without compensation, Harlan would know he had gained the advantageous edge.

While Harlan silently pondered his ticklish situation, Mace gave Hub a discreet glance. Hub was delighting in watching this battle of wills. Amusement was dancing in Hub's blue eyes as he glanced first at the overinflated general and then at Mace.

"Well?" Mace prodded impatiently. "Time is wasting. Each moment you delay could place even more distance between us and your granddaughter."

Still, Harlan refused to speak. He wasn't accepting Mace's proposal without a counterproposal. . . . An idea flickered into Harlan's mind, and a wry smile replaced his pensive frown. Perhaps there was a way to insure the Reids would never be swindled out of their commission business. Although Harlan had resolved not to interfere in Jacquelyn's private life, he could see no other alternative in this situation. Mace would fall through his chair when he heard what stipulation Harlan placed on the merger. Let him fall, Harlan decided. Turn about was fair play.

"Very well," Harlan proclaimed with an affirmative nod. "The Reid and Gallagher Commission Companies will merge."

A victorious smile pursed Mace's lips as he blew a lopsided smoke ring into the air. "I thought you would see it my way, Gen'ral." He chuckled.

"I have only one small provision to attach to our contract," Harlan added calmly.

"Name it," Mace generously offered as he took a long draw on his cigar. What could it hurt to pacify the old man with a small request? After all, Mace had considered all the angles. Whatever Harlan was about to suggest was undoubtedly a possibility Mace had previously contemplated.

Harlan looked Mace squarely in the eye. "To insure our merger is permanent and beneficial to both families, I insist that you marry Jacquelyn."

Mace sucked in his breath and choked on his cigar. Coughing and sputtering, Mace stared frog-eyed at Harlan, who remained as sober as a judge. Hub, on the other hand, was practically rolling on the floor, cackling like a hen.

"Oh, that's ripe!" Hub said between guffaws. "The legendary lady-killer of Texas married to Gen'ral Reid's granddaughter?" The prospect had him snickering all over again. "Mace Gallagher married?" Hub exploded in hysterical laughter.

Harlan surveyed Hub for a few sober moments before concentrating on Mace, who had yet to recover. "Well? Do we have a bargain?" he demanded impatiently. "Every moment we delay could mean another minute of terror for Jake. Her life is at stake."

Marriage? The word roared through Mace's mind like a train echoing in a tunnel. Marry a woman who was going to despise him when she discovered who had kidnapped her? Hell, it wasn't going to matter that he had saved Jake's gorgeous hide by stashing her in the shack for safekeeping. It wasn't going to make a whit of difference that he would expose Malcolm and save Harlan from the embarrassment of financial ruin. Jake wouldn't give a hoot about his noble purpose because she would be too busy breathing the fire of dragons when he finally found the right words to explain why he did what he did. Or maybe I can find a way around telling her the truth, he mused thoughtfully.

"Damnation, man, have you swallowed your tongue?" Harlan growled. "Contrary to your opinion, there is life after wedlock! You could do worse than my grand-daughter. There are scores of men who are standing in line to marry her! Now do we have an agreement or not?"

Muffling his laughter, Hub crawled back into his chair to massage his aching sides. He couldn't wait to hear how Mace was going to weasel out of this new twist in his scheme. The clever rascal thought he had neatly backed Harlan into a corner and wrapped up all the loose ends where Malcolm was concerned. But Mace had been so busy patting himself on the back that he'd failed to notice he had wedged himself into that same corner, right smack dab beside Harlan. Yes siree, Harlan and Mace were two peas in a pod, Hub thought with wicked glee.

"Well, my friend?" Hub snickered, flashing Mace a grin as wide as the Gulf of Mexico. "What's it going to be? A merger and marriage? Or are you going to let Harlan's granddaughter's death weigh on your conscience the rest of your life? If anyone can find her, you can." Of course he could, Hub silently chuckled. After all, Mace was the one who'd put Jake where she was and left dependable Raoul to guard the door.

Mace's glittering golden glare sliced Hub in two equal pieces. The subtle jibe had flown over Harlan's head, but it had slapped Mace in the face. Hub was relishing the predicament in which Mace suddenly found himself.

For another long moment Mace wrestled with the tormenting memories from his past, memories that had made such a grave impression on his childhood. He had vowed never to take a wife. He had refused to force himself into any situation that might provoke him to behave the way . . . Hurriedly, Mace strangled the thought, and puffed on his cheroot until he was engulfed in a cloud of smoke.

And what about Jake? Mace asked himself grimly. She didn't seem crazy about the idea of marriage either. She had rejected Jon's proposal, along with only God knew how many others. Why would he expect that spitfire to accept this marriage Harlan had planned for her a second time? Hell's bells, that contrary woman had gone out of her way to keep Mace at arm's length by lying about her broken engagement. Jake didn't want him. Her actions suggested that. Now what in heaven's name would become of two staunchly independent individuals who were joined in wedlock? As near as Mace could tell, all they would gain from the arrangement was a license to fight, and they were managing quite nicely without one the way it was!

Before Mace had finished wrestling with his dilemma, voices in the hall interrupted his contemplations. Without awaiting permission, Jon Mason barged into the study, waving a letter over his head.

"Gen'ral, this ransom note arrived after you left," Jon announced breathlessly, and then placed the parchment in Harlan's outstretched hand.

Mace's jaw fell off its hinges. His head swiveled around to peer incredulously at Hub, who was staring back at him in wide-eyed astonishment. Sweet Jesus! Who was sending a ransom note to barter for a woman they could not possibly have in their custody? Yes, Mace fully intended to send a ransom note in hopes of exposing Malcolm for the swindler he was, but Hub had yet to deliver the letter to Reid plantation. As a matter of fact, Mace's ransom note was still folded and tucked in his vest pocket, and it did not resemble the one Jon claimed to have found tied to the rock that came crashing through the parlor window.

"Let me see that note," Mace growled as he bolted from his seat. Without ado, he snatched the parchment from Harlan's fingertips. "Fifteen thousand dollars!" he hooted in disbelief. Hell, Mace had only planned to ask for ten thousand. That was more than a cotton-plantation owner could turn in profit after three years of laboring over his crops!

Swearing a blue streak, Harlan struggled out of his chair and clutched his cane. "It looks as if I won't require your services after all, Gallagher," he grumbled. "I'll have Malcolm collect the cash and exchange it for Jacquelyn's life."

Mace glared at the instructions for delivering the ransom, and then stared in bewilderment at Harlan. The General was so distraught by Jake's disappearance that he had failed to consider the idiocy of his intentions. "You can't be serious." Mace scowled. "The extortionists demand that you, and you alone, put the pouch of cash on a raft and set it adrift downstream. They will have your money, but the note says nothing about when and where Jacquelyn will be returned to you."

Harlan's misty brown eyes lanced off Mace's agitated frown. "I don't see that I have much choice. You have yet to agree to search for my granddaughter. I must have hope that Jake's abductors will release her when they lay their hands on the ransom money."

"What is to keep these scoundrels from retaining Jacquelyn and demanding a second ransom?" Mace argued. "And worse, how do you know they won't kill her and be done with it? You can't pay for something you might not have returned to you!"

"Something?" Harlan grimly shook his head. "Not something, Mace, but rather someone. That someone is my granddaughter, my flesh and blood." His potent gaze nailed Mace to the wall. "I happen to love that girl, even more than I thought I did before I shipped her off to New Orleans. And from what I have seen and heard of late, I don't think I'm the only one who loves Jake."

On the wings of that subtle remark, Harlan drew himself up and limped out the door, leaving Mace to spew a string of colorful curses. Infuriated by the tangled chain of events, Mace crushed the ransom note in his fist and hurled it at the wall.

Hub negligently braced himself against the door jamb and crossed his arms over his chest. When the

General had made his exit with Jon one step behind him, Hub's mocking gaze landed on Mace. "So you had this all figured out, did you?" he scoffed. "The Gen'ral and Malcolm were going to play right into your hands, were they? It sounds to me as if you might have been outmaneuvered by the very man you sought to outmaneuver. You have Jacquelyn in your custody and someone else is trying to ransom her. That is the craziest thing I ever heard!"

"I need your assistance, not your ridicule," Mace snapped as he rammed his hands in his pockets and paced the floor.

Hub watched Mace prowl the study like a caged tiger. "Who do you suppose sent that ransom note?" he mused aloud. "Surely it couldn't have been Malcolm. If he did, he would be cutting his own throat. When Harlan demands that he gather cash, Malcolm will have to sacrifice the money he's been swindling from the company."

A pensive frown knitted Mace's brow as he paced in deliberate strides. "Maybe Malcolm is trying to redeem himself by assuring all of us that he has the cash and that my accusations are vicious lies. Or maybe one of Malcolm's henchmen is trying to cheat *him*," Mace speculated. "Perhaps Malcolm doesn't even know his men weren't able to abduct Jake."

"Or maybe Malcolm hadn't intended to have Jake kidnapped and he figures it was you all along," Hub interjected.

Spinning about, Mace snatched up his hat and strode toward the door. "I don't know what to make of this note, but I intend to be there to see the look on Malcolm's face when Harlan demands the money to pay the ransom."

Hub snorted disgustedly. "How is Malcolm's facial expression going to help you determine who did what?" he asked skeptically.

When Mace stopped in his tracks, Hub slammed into his back. Annoyed, Mace glanced over his shoulder. "I don't know if it will make any difference," he muttered in frustration. "I know what I did, what I had to do to protect that feisty female. Now someone is trying to take credit for the kidnapping, and I damned well intend to find out who that someone is!"

"Malcolm may be more clever than you think," Hub commented as they trotted to the stable to retrieve their horses. "He'll be scrambling to maneuver this situation to his advantage. You can bank on that! The only way you will truly be able to entrap him is to agree to the merger and the marriage and bring Jake back before the ransom is to be delivered. If Malcolm pays the ransom and then retrieves it from the raft, he will have lost nothing. The merger is the only certain tactic that will expose his fraudulent activities in the commission company."

Hub was right and Mace knew it. If Malcolm was responsible for the ransom note, he would emerge from this predicament smelling like the proverbial rose. But blast it, if Mace agreed to marry Jacquelyn—who probably wouldn't even have him, they would kill each other in two months time! She would sorely resent being manipulated, and would spite Mace every chance she got. Doggone it, Mace should never have gotten mixed up with that high-spirited hellion. He had allowed his obsessive desire for her to drag him into a situation that had been completely blown out of proportion. He had attempted to second-guess Malcolm's tactics, and now someone had employed the same technique on Mace. God, now he wasn't sure who he could trust!

Shock claimed Harlan's strained features when he arrived home to see the carriage that rolled to a halt beside the front steps. Swinging from his mount, Harlan hobbled around the coach to find his sister in conversation with their nephew.

"Flo, what in God's name are you doing in Texas?" Harlan croaked in astonishment.

The thin dowager, who was twelve years Harlan's junior, turned to greet her brother with a condescending frown. "I was lonesome," she declared tartly. "After having Jackie underfoot for three years, the house was empty without her. I have yet to set foot in your manor and Malcolm tells me someone has kidnapped the poor girl." Florence inhaled an agitated breath, twirled the parasol she always carried with her, and glowered at her older brother. "It is beyond me how I could ride herd over that high-strung granddaughter of yours all this time and you can't keep her from harm's way for less than two months after she returned to you! How could you possibly have commanded an entire army when you can't even keep track of your own granddaughter?"

Isn't it just like Florence to rub me the wrong way the moment she opens her mouth? Harlan thought resentfully. He was worried sick about Jake, and along came Florence to lecture him on his incompetency. Florence hadn't changed a tittle. She still ridiculed him in order to inflate her own self-esteem.

"I should have known better than to permit Jackie to return to this half-civilized state. Wild Indians are still harassing the settlers on the frontier, politicians are playing tug-of-war with Texas, and outlaws like the ones who abducted Jackie run rampant! This is no place for a young woman," she fumed indignantly. "If you manage to get that poor child back alive, Harlan, I'm taking her back to New Orleans with me. . . ." Her shrill voice trailed off when the clatter of hooves heralded the arrival of Mace and Hub.

Malcolm immediately scowled at their unwelcomed guests. "We are up to our necks in trouble and here comes another armload of it. Texas Rangers are supposed to arrive to save the day, not spoil it." He glared accusingly at Mace. "I'm not sure which side of the law you are truly on, Gallagher."

Florence frowned bemusedly at her nephew's sour remark. Before Malcolm could fire another barrage of insults, Harlan made the hasty introductions and then heralded the entourage into the parlor. When everyone was planted in a chair, Harlan hobbled over to collapse on the sofa beside his sister. Why? Harlan wasn't sure. He would rather be sitting on the opposite side of the room from his sister. Florence had been home for only ten minutes and already he preferred to place great spaces between them.

Directing Malcolm's attention to the shattered window pane, Harlan blurted out, "We have received a ransom note demanding that fifteen thousand dollars be paid tomorrow night for Jacquelyn's return. I want you to gather all available cash from the commission company so I can pay the ransom."

Mace's golden eyes were glued to Malcolm's freckled face. Although Hub had scoffed at the theory of reading Malcolm's expression, Mace discovered what he wanted to know. Malcolm's bland features whitewashed and he stared bug-eyed at the General. For a full ten seconds the astonished man sat there with his mouth opening and closing like the flapping of bed linens on a clothesline.

"Ransom?" Malcolm chirped like a sick parrot. "We don't have that kind of money lying around the office."

A muddled frown creased Harlan's graying brows. "We should have all the profits from this year's commission on Texas cotton," Harlan reminded him gruffly. "I want you to gather the cash immediately."

"We don't have any ready cash," Malcolm squeaked, his eyelids batting furiously.

"Why the hell don't we?" Harlan roared. "We are not

357

running a charity. We have to have ready cash lying around."

"I've a . . . It's already been invested in a . . ." Malcolm stuttered over his paralyzed tongue. His eyelids were batting so furiously Mace swore they were about to fly off Malcolm's face.

"Invested in what, for God's sake?" Harlan boomed in frustration. "Spit it out, man!"

"In . . . in real estate . . . in new equipment . . . and other necessary expenses . . . Even if we had that kind of money, how could I possibly ride to Galveston and collect it in time to pay the ransom? I'm not a bird, you know. I can't fly from here to there in less than a day!"

Ah, but he was a bird, Mace thought sourly. Malcolm was a vulture, even if he weren't equipped with the customary wings.

Malcolm tugged at the collar of his shirt to relieve the pressure on his throat. The entire roomful of family and guests stared at him as if he were on the witness stand and they doubted his testimony.

Damnation, Gil Davis had probably decided to make extra cash for himself by sending that ransom note, Malcolm thought murderously. Gil intended to cheat him, but Malcolm couldn't get his hands on that kind of money at the drop of a hat. The cash had been stashed for safekeeping in a place that even Malcolm couldn't touch without making proper arrangements.

Harlan's face flushed with fury as he glared at his nephew. "What the Hades is going on, Malcolm?" he gritted out between clenched teeth. "You're trying to hide something from me. I can sense it."

"Nothing!" Malcolm declared all too quickly. "We are turning a profit in the commission company, but Mace Gallagher has cut wide gashes in our business. I've told you that a dozen times before." Mutinously, Malcolm glared at Mace, whose bland expression disguised the turmoil of emotions that were churning within him. "We are barely staying afloat because Gallagher is stealing our clients!"

After giving Mace a hesitant glance, Harlan focused his attention on his sister. "Florence, I need a loan to save Jacquelyn's life."

Florence blinked in bewilderment. "I don't have that kind of money and you know it. If I did, you surely don't think I would carry it around with me! I wish I did. I would hand it over to you in a minute to save my poor grand-niece. But I don't. I live comfortably, but I can hardly afford fifteen thousand dollars!"

Dismally, Harlan's eyes swung back to Mace, who had refused to commit himself to a compromise earlier that afternoon. Harlan saw no reason why his competitor would consent to a loan. And yet, Harlan was desperate enough to ask. He was prepared to sacrifice his soul if it would insure Jacquelyn's safe return.

"Mace, you are my only salvation," Harlan acknowledged, his voice crackling with rarely expressed emotion. "I have nowhere else to turn."

Mace saw no reason to donate money to ransom a woman he had in his custody. Yet the broken, defeated expression that claimed the Gen'ral's aging features tugged at Mace's conscience. Fifteen thousand dollars was a helluva lot of money. Suppose he was unable to catch the culprit who sent that fake ransom note? How could he finance Reid's crumbling commission company without that ready cash?

Frantically, Mace deliberated his alternatives. Perhaps he could offer the cash and then return Jake before the ransom had to be paid. In that case no money would need to exchange hands. By damn, that's exactly what he would do. Harlan would be eternally grateful. Malcolm would still be exposed, especially since the General was beginning to harbor a few suspicions about his nephew's integrity. And Jake would finally be back where she belonged.

"The money is yours, Gen'ral," Mace said quietly.

Relief washed over Harlan's face and he slumped against the sofa to breathe a heavy sigh. "And the merger is yours . . . without any stipulations," he promised. "All I want is my granddaughter back. I care about nothing else."

"Merger!" Malcolm vaulted out of his chair and tripped over Jon's long legs. Yanking himself up, Malcolm glowered at Harlan. "Uncle, you can't do that! Gallagher will gobble you alive. There will be nothing left of our floundering company."

A menacing smile tightened Mace's lips as he studied Malcolm's unruly shocks of chestnut brown hair and chinless face. One day soon that weasel was going to get what he deserved and Mace was going to relish watching him get it. "The best thing that can happen to the Reid Commission Company is to extract the business from your incompetent hands, Malcolm," Mace growled down at the bundle of twitching nerves. "No ready cash?" His tone conveyed his skepticism. "When the truth comes out, I wonder how much sympathy Harlan will have for you. My guess is he'll be passing out wanted posters that request your carcass be returned dead or alive. And I intend to be the man who comes after you."

"I fully intend to investigate the ledgers you brought with you," Harlan muttered accusingly. "It seems I have left you in control of my finances longer than I should have."

"Do you see what he's doing?" Malcolm screeched like a disturbed owl. "He's trying to cause dissension between us. And if you agree to this merger, there will be nothing left of our company."

Mace's temper had been stretched until it snapped.

360

Like an angered lion he pounced on the scrawny little man who was spewing lies. Before Mace could satisfy his irritation by rearranging the features on Malcolm's plain face, Hub grabbed his arm.

"Malcolm will receive his just desserts in due time," Hub murmured confidentially to Mace. "The Gen'ral has begun to soften toward you. Don't go hurling obstacles between the two of you all over again."

A deadly smile pursed Mace's lips as he watched Malcolm slither away to seek protection behind Harlan. "When this is all over, Malcolm, I have a personal score to settle with you. And when the Gen'ral realizes what you've done, he won't let you use him as your shield of defense. You may try to run for your life, but there will be no place you can hide that I can't find you."

The threatening remark and rumbling purr with which Mace conveyed it provoked Harlan and Florence to stare speculatively at their nephew.

"Jon, fetch those ledgers from my desk," Harlan demanded abruptly.

As was his custom, Jon snapped to attention and scuttled off to obey the order. When Mace and Hub pivoted to leave, Harlan pushed off the sofa and limped after them. Once they were out of earshot of the others, Harlan stared bemusedly at Mace.

"What is it you expect me to find when I study those ledgers?" he questioned point-blank.

Mace peered up at the old man, who lingered at the top of the marble steps. "According to some of my clients who were once associated with your company, they were paid second-rate prices for top-quality cotton. That's the real reason for your reduction in clients," Mace told him candidly. "No doubt Malcolm listed payment for below-standard crops in the ledger, but he has been turning around and selling crops as top-quality cotton to Eastern buyers. He must be stashing the margin of profit in a private account, depriving you of money you rightly deserve."

Harlan steadied himself on his cane and sought to compose himself after hearing the damning accusations. For a long moment he simply stood there digesting Mace's words. God, he didn't know who to believe. If the ledgers indicated that Malcolm had paid top price for prime-quality cotton, it would be Mace's word against Malcolm's.

A muted growl erupted from Mace's lips. He knew exactly what the General was thinking. The poor old man didn't know who to trust. "I will have Hub deliver the ransom money to you tomorrow night," Mace promised. "But with any luck at all, I'll find Jake before you float my cash down the river without a guarantee."

Indecision clung to Harlan's brow. "You might endanger her life if you're seen snooping around," Harlan warned. "Her kidnappers may dispose of her if they feel threatened."

"Whoever sent that ransom note made no promises about returning your granddaughter to you," Mace parried, and then offered the frustrated old man a consoling smile. "You sent me on dozens of reconnaissance missions during the war, Gen'ral. I haven't forgotten how to vanish into thin air when need be."

Harlan grinned in spite of himself. If nothing else, he knew Mace was a competent scout. The man had the knack of smelling trouble before it pounced on him. The Comanches were known for their uncanny ability to appear out of nowhere and evaporate into nothing, and Mace could also perform the same miraculous disappearing act. But it hadn't mattered quite so much to Harlan until Jacquelyn's life hung in the balance.

"Very well, do what you can. But for God's sake, be

careful," Harlan grunted. "Just keep in mind that if you upset the applecart, those bastards might make applesauce out of my granddaughter! I want her back in one piece."

Mace did something he had never done before in his life. With perfect military precision, he snapped his heels together and bestowed an honorary salute on the General. "Yes, sir. I will do my best."

Harlan very nearly fell through the porch. He'd never thought he would live to see the day that ornery renegade offered anything that remotely resembled a salute. Indeed, he doubted Mace's arm would bend into such a position without paining him. The gesture of respect was enough to solidify his confidence in Mace and confirm his nagging suspicions about Malcolm. Although Mace was a great many things, many of which Harlan had never approved, the man was a dynamic individual who got things done when no one else could.

When all was said and done, Harlan had the feeling his nephew was going to wish he hadn't made such a formidable enemy. Malcolm was flustered and intimidated by Mace Gallagher. Although all of Mace's accusations might not have been warranted, Malcolm had indeed defaced his competitor's character every chance he'd gotten. If Malcolm knew what was good for him, he would retract every derogatory remark about Mace and issue a public apology.

Reversing direction, Harlan went in search of Jon and the ledgers. Just in case Mace's speculations were correct, Harlan intended to mentally tabulate the margin of cash between top-quality and second-quality cotton. If Malcolm had indeed been skimming profits, Harlan wanted to know how much money they were discussing. But surely Mace was wrong, Harlan convinced himself. Malcolm wasn't living like a king. If he had been swindling money he would have something to show for it, wouldn't he? And where was the profit from the company being stashed? Harlan was anxious to find answers to his befuddled questions. Without wasting a minute he planted himself in his chair and thrust his nose into Malcolm's ledgers.

Chapter 20

Hub tolerated the uninterrupted silence for as long as he could stand. Mace hadn't uttered a word since they left the Reid plantation. "Well? What are you going to do now? Retrieve Jake tonight, hand her over to the Gen'ral, and scribble out a contract for a merger before Malcolm can slither off to only God knows where?" he pried.

"Something like that," Mace murmured absently. He was still stuck on the part about retrieving Jake and explaining himself to her. Lord, he dreaded that particular confrontation. He would prefer to take on a Comanche war party single-handed! Mace hated to hazard a guess at Jacquelyn's reaction. But he had the sinking feeling there would be no fury like the woman deceived.

Maybe he wouldn't have to tell her. The inspiration provoked Mace to sit a little taller in the saddle. Perhaps he could devise a way to retrieve Jake without explaining what had really happened. Jacquelyn would never have to know what had become of the Mexican bandito. She would be thankful to be returned home and Mace could bypass the—

"What am I suppose to do?" Hub queried, yanking

Mace from his contemplations. "Do you want me to keep an eye on Malcolm while you fetch Jake?"

Mace nodded agreeably. "Just make certain you give Malcolm enough rope to hang himself," he warned. "If you stick to him too closely, he might conclude that you know more than you should. Malcolm is getting desperate. He'll do anything to save his neck, and that includes accusing you of whatever he thinks will aid in his own defense."

"Dealing with that wily fox will still be easier than your task," Hub smirked. "I'd love to be a mouse in the corner when you try to explain to that feisty lady that you kidnapped her for her own good. I'm not so sure your confession will be well received."

"Neither am I," Mace grumbled grumpily.

A curious frown creased Hub's brow as he scrutinized Mace's chiseled features and rigid profile. "What exactly are you going to tell her?"

"I haven't puzzled that out yet." He sighed, deflated.

"If Jacquelyn strangles you, I'll read some kind words over you at the funeral," Hub offered with a teasing grin.

"You jest, my friend," Mace snorted bitterly. "But in case your prophesy comes true, make sure I'm buried facing east. If that spiteful termagant has her way I'll be eternally staring west, deprived of watching the rising sun until the end of time."

Hub heaved a melodramatic sigh. "After you are dead and gone, I'll tell her you loved her all along and that you did what you did to protect her. I'm sure she'll relent and let you face the sunrise."

"I am *not*—I repeat, *not*—in love with that minx!" Mace shouted as if Hub were deaf.

"The hell you aren't," Hub growled in contradiction. "Never in your life have you gone so far out on a limb for a woman. In case you've forgotten, kidnapping is a criminal offense. And if this crazed scheme of yours runs

366

amuck, you stand to lose the foundations of a friendship with the Gen'ral, as well as fifteen thousand dollars to only God knows who! A man doesn't behave the way you have been unless he's in love." Hub nodded philosophically. "I always said love deteriorates a man's brain. You've shown all the symptoms since you pretended to be Jon Mason so you could escort that saucy beauty home."

"If I want a sermon I'll consult a preacher," Mace bit off sarcastically.

"I disguised myself as a priest on that reconnaissance mission into Monterrey," Hub reminded him with a taunting chuckle. "You said yourself that I portrayed a padre most convincingly."

"Don't you ever grow tired of hearing yourself rattle?" Mace scowled sourly. "I'm trying to decide how to solve my problems with that brown-eyed she-cat and you're giving me hell!"

"And that is exactly where you're going to wind up for lying," Hub needled unmercifully. "You're a damned liar if you won't admit you're in love. You may not want to love Jake, but you do. I saw you and Jake together at that barbecue. It was killing you to think she was going to marry that skinny-legged milksop. And you were furious when you discovered it was all a ruse. But what really got your goat was that Jake didn't fall at your feet the way most women do." Hub's grin became proportionately wider as Mace's scowl turned a darker shade of black. "You have finally met your match, Mace. If you ask me, you should tell Jake you're in love with her and then unveil yourself and explain your actions."

"I didn't ask your opinion," Mace snapped irritably. "I never have the chance because you're always spouting like a geyser!"

With a wordless growl, Mace gouged Diego in the flanks and thundered off, drowning Hub's goading laughter in the clatter of hooves. Damnit, he wasn't in love with that sassy hoyden. He desired her because she was a beautiful woman who could arouse a man without even trying. But that was the beginning and end of it, Mace assured himself sensibly. He was not the kind of man a woman could use to satisfy her fickle whims. Jake didn't need him, not the way a woman ought to need a man. That dark-haired vixen was an entity unto herself. Hell, when he walked out of her life once and for all, she wouldn't even care if he left. The night she'd declared she loved him hadn't meant a thing to her. By dawn she'd shrugged off that magical moment the way a man tosses aside a worn shirt. And Mace was not about to become Jacquelyn's dirty laundry!

As soon as he resolved this situation and reinstated the General to his respected position, Mace was going to avoid all contact with Jacquelyn. They would rarely see each other, and Mace would never again remember those mystical nights of passion, the unique sparkle that danced in those expressive brown eyes when she smiled, the tantalizing way her heart-shaped lips melted like thirst-quenching rain upon his . . .

Mace cursed the betraying sensations that leaped through his blood when Jacquelyn's enchanting vision materialized before him. It was frustrating to realize her mere memory was enough to ignite fires within him. Jake doesn't want me, he reminded himself harshly. Her actions and her words exemplified that fact. She had always made it clear that she did not consider him a part of her future.

Lord, that woman was hard on a man's pride, Mace mused resentfully. And as soon as this ordeal was over he was going to put Jake out of his mind . . . permanently . . .

Attempting to maintain a purely objective attitude toward Jacquelyn, Mace concentrated on his upcoming encounter. He would confront Jacquelyn with the truth and they would debate his course of action like two reasonable, sensible individuals. She would state her dislike of his methods and he would defend himself. . . .

Who do you think you're kidding, Gallagher? Mace scoffed at himself. That woman would test the patience of St. Peter, and she lost her temper at the slightest provocation. Jake would probably express her displeasure by snatching up his pistol and blowing him to kingdom come. Maybe it would be safer to lie to her. He had never been honest with her, even in the beginning. Hell, Hub was getting such a kick out of this predicament that he should be the one to explain, Mace thought to himself.

Although Mace hadn't decided exactly how to handle Jacquelyn, he had plenty of time to weigh his alternatives during his two-hour ride to the cabin that sat on the small island in the marsh. And by the time he arrived he damned well better have thought of something!

His eyes lifted beseechingly toward the heavens. He could use a little divine assistance. After murmuring a hasty prayer, Mace waited a long moment, chagrined that the solution to his problem had not been immediately printed on the sky.

"I was afraid Your answer would be—no help forthcoming. And sure enough it was," Mace grumbled deflatedly. "Since I got myself into this, I suppose You think it only fitting that I get myself out of it without Your assistance." Mace couldn't be sure, but he thought the sun winked at him from behind a fleeting cloud.

A gnawing hunger rumbled in Jacquelyn's stomach. The lingering affects of whiskey had finally dissolved and she was feeling her old self again. The fact that she was being held hostage by a monstrous black dog that closely resembled a wolf annoyed her to no end. Determined not to accept her fate lying down, Jake sat up. After a token glance at the guard dog, she nibbled on the stale food that sat on the night stand.

It was time to assert herself. Although the bandito had absolute confidence in the ability of his shaggy beast, Jacquelyn resolved to make a valiant attempt to escape. Her grudging respect for the animal assured her that she could die if her attempt failed. But she was not going to sit and wait for the bandito's return. That varmint was not going to control her life and her future . . . if indeed he intended her to have one.

Pensively, Jake scanned the meagerly furnished room. Her eyes focused on the exposed rafters, wondering if she could walk the beams to the window, kick out the pane, and leap to freedom before the snarling beast could take a bite out of her. Hesitantly, she shot a glance at the dog. As if he had read her thoughts, Raoul came upon all fours and issued a warning growl.

Giving the idea a second consideration, Jacquelyn doubted she could fly through the window before the animal clamped onto her leg and dragged her back into the room. Tossing aside that possibility, Jacquelyn stared thoughtfully at the small closet on the far side of the room. Although she was desperate enough to leave an arm or leg behind, she preferred to flee with all her appendages in tact. Her mind strained to concoct a workable solution that would insure she could escape without becoming the ugly beast's next meal. But no matter what, Jacquelyn wanted to be long gone before the Mexican bandito returned.

When a practical scheme hatched in her head, Jacquelyn grasped the sleeves of her oversized shirt and rolled them up so they wouldn't hinder her when she ran for her life. Then she tied the hem of the threadbare garment in a knot beneath her breasts. Likewise, she tied a knot in the band of the breeches that surely must have been tailored to fit a man with a waist size twice her own. After rolling up the long breeches, she surveyed her appearance and actually managed a smile. The garments now concealed very little of her midriff, but Jake had no concern for modesty. Indeed, she would have stripped naked if it would have helped.

Grabbing her discarded gown, Jacquelyn taunted the beast. If she could lure the mongrel into a game of tug-of-war with the dress, she might be able to maneuver him into the closet. The dog wouldn't allow her close to the bedroom door, but he might just let her near the closet. Clinging to that encouraging thought, Jake shook the gown and growled back at the mutt, who had lunged toward her with a toothy snarl.

"Come on, you ugly brute," Jacquelyn taunted, flinging the garment at him.

Raoul pounced, clamping his sharp teeth in the hem of the dress. Bracing himself, he tugged back, growling all the while. For a full minute Jacquelyn pulled in the opposite direction, slowly but surely maneuvering the beast toward the closet. Her heart stopped when the mongrel's sharp fangs ripped the satin skirt to shreds. But to her relief, the beast took another bite of the fabric to regain his grasp.

As if he were shaking the life from his prey, Raoul tugged and yanked, very nearly toppling Jacquelyn off balance. Hurriedly, she darted a glance over her shoulder toward the closet. Reaching behind her, she eased open the closet door without distracting the mutt, who was jerking with such force he threatened to dislocate her right arm from its socket.

With the closet door opened, Jacquelyn sidled sideways to maneuver the beast's backside toward the niche. A panicked shriek burst from Jake's lips when the animal's razor-sharp teeth shredded another portion of the gown. Instinct urged her to loosen her clenched fist when the ominous beast's jaws came dangerously close to her hand. But Jake gulped down the lump that leaped to her throat and held on to her end of the improvised rope.

As the growling dog braced his huge paws and pulled backward, Jacquelyn kept the tension steady, forcing the creature to tug with every ounce of his strength. Her eyes darted to the closet, insuring the animal was in its direct line. Jacquelyn's body was taut with apprehension. If she didn't perform this next tactic with accurate precision, the beast would have the opportunity to pounce on her and she would find herself in his bone-crushing grasp.

Mustering her courage, Jacquelyn abruptly released the garment. Raoul stumbled back with the gown still clamped in his mouth. Like an exploding cannonball, Jake shot toward the closet door. A frantic squeal burst from her lips when Raoul regained his balance and leaped toward her. With her heart pounding as if it meant to beat her to death before the mongrel could make mincemeat of her, Jake slammed the door in Raoul's whiskered face.

Shoving her shoulder against the portal, Jacquelyn mashed the paw that was wedged against the door jamb. Never in her life had she heard such a combination of snarling, barking, and growling! The beast was infuriated to find himself confined to the closet. Not only did Raoul detest crowds, but he also had a strong aversion to cramped spaces. Like a wild creature caught in captivity, Raoul pounced at the door, jarring both the hinges and the terrified young woman, who was as determined to keep him in as he was determined to get out.

Setting both feet, Jacquelyn braced her back against the rattling door. A string of expletives erupted from her lips when she realized the door would not remain shut unless an object was securely lodged against it. The flimsy latch couldn't contain the snarling mutt.

Damnation, how was she to retrieve a stick of furniture to blockade the door? If she removed herself for even an instant, the furious creature would be free to devour her. And he most certainly would, Jacquelyn reminded herself shakily. Raoul did not take kindly to being shoved into the closet. He wanted out as badly as he wanted to tear Jacquelyn to pieces, bit by excruciating bit.

"Get a grip on yourself," Jacquelyn lectured sternly. She had come this far, and by damn she could devise a way to secure the door! Wide eyes flew around the room, calculating the distance to the chair. Inching around, Jacquelyn pressed her hands to the door and stretched out a leg. While the growling beast hammered at the portal, Jake extended herself until she hooked her foot around the back of the chair. Taking particular care not to ease the pressure on the door, Jacquelyn dragged the chair toward her. Only when she had braced the back of the chair beneath the latch did she dare step away. A long sigh of relief gushed from her lips when the mongrel slammed against the barred door and failed to gain his freedom.

Wheeling about, Jacquelyn charged toward the bedroom door, and then cursed a blue streak when she found it locked. The bandito obviously trusted his devoted beast. But as a precautionary measure, he'd locked both her and the mutt inside. Casting an apprehensive glance toward the closet, Jake darted to the window. When it wouldn't budge, she snatched up the nightstand and hurled it through the glass. She would have preferred to close the window behind her in case the frothing beast burst free from the closet, but she decided to take her chances rather than risk having the mutt attack her before she slipped outside.

Self-satisfaction swelled up inside her as she strode around the dilapidated shack. She had relied upon her wits to escape the dragon-dog. Now all she had to do was . . . Her spirits tumbled down around her like a rockslide when she scrutinized her surroundings. Jacquelyn had escaped her prison, but she was still nowhere near safe. Dismally, she peered across the grassy slopes that disappeared into the murky marsh. The wide expanse of the bayou, choked with weeds and God only knew what else, seemed to stretch out for miles in all directions.

Disgruntled, Jacquelyn searched the area for an object that might ferry her through the treacherous murk, but there was nothing. Damn it all, she muttered bitterly. How she wished she could sprout wings to fly across this weed- and insect-infested marsh!

The sight of a man standing upon a distant raft caught her attention. She squatted down beside the cabin and squinted into the blinding sun. It was difficult to tell much about the rapscallion when the sun was directly behind him, glistening off the water.

Cautiously, Jake inched along the side of the shack and shrank around the corner to await the opportunity to escape. With precise timing, she could make a dash for the vacated raft as soon as the bandito stepped through the front door. Before he and his vicious dog could locate her she would be drifting down the bayou. Then that ruthless varmint would be stranded with his man-eating mutt. The two of them could stay there and rot for all she cared!

Golden eyes focused on the hut that sat among the thick clump of trees on the tiny island that was nestled on the bayou. For two hours Mace had devised and discarded a dozen ingenious schemes. He knew he should be honest with Jake. Lord, he had never been so deceitful with any other woman in all his life! But the plain truth of the matter was Mace had turned coward. Yes, for crying out loud, he had become a lily-livered, faint-hearted coward! When Jake learned the truth she was going to hate him with a vengeance. And damnit, all he really wanted to do was scoop her up in his arms and grant himself one last taste of those addicting lips before he walked out of her life forever.

Well, there was only one way to save face, one way to grant himself the pleasure he knew awaited beneath that fiery exterior of strong will and stubborn independence, Mace convinced himself. He was going to do what had to be done to insure that he would enjoy a few moments of pleasure instead of catching hell.

After securing the raft, Mace squared his shoulders and marched toward the shack. He was going to stage a rescue, have a knock-down-drag-out brawl with the imaginary Mexican bandit, and then pretend to save the lovely damsel in distress. Jake would be none the wiser and she would be so grateful she would shower him with adoring kisses.

Determined in his wily scheme, Mace retrieved his bandit disguise, snatched up a few stray logs, and stormed the cabin. As the door sagged on its hinges, a booming roar erupted from his lips. To add credence to his charade, Mace switched from one role to the other, bellowing curses in English and then in Spanish. From behind the closed door, Raoul yelped and barked at the top of his lungs when Mace fired his pistol at the wall and then heaved a log against the bedroom door.

This will be my finest performance, Mace mused as he bounced off the wall and growled like a wounded lion. Jacquelyn would certainly believe two avenging warriors were battling in the adjoining room. And if he pulled off this hare-brained stunt he would seriously contemplate a career in the theater!

With a menacing snarl, Mace grabbed himself by the

front of the shirt and threw himself against the opposite wall. Lord, he was a genius, he thought smugly as he kicked over a chair and spouted a few Spanish curses. It was a pity no one was around to witness his acting debut. He deserved an award for portraying both the hero and the villain, all in the same moment!

While furniture and logs were crashing against the walls, Jacquelyn rose from her crouched position and scampered along the side of the shack. What in heaven's name was going on? she wondered, bemused. There was no one in the outer room. She knew that for a fact. If there had been, she would have spotted him while she was investigating her surroundings.

Demons of curiosity danced in her head as she ducked beneath the front window. Indecision etched her brows when her eyes darted toward the waiting raft. This might well be her one and only opportunity to escape the tiny island and her formidable captor! And yet, she couldn't leave until she knew who was tearing whom to pieces inside the shack.

Cautiously, Jacquelyn poked her head toward the window without drawing the attention of whoever was battling like two clashing armies. Serenaded by the howling mongrel that was locked in the closet (or at least she hoped that was where he still was) and, listening to the accompaniment of roaring voices that spouted Spanish and English, Jacquelyn peered through the sooty window pane.

Her eyes bulged from their sockets when she recognized Mace. She watched in mute amazement as Mace placed a stranglehold on his own neck with his left hand and slammed his head against the wall. Choked fragments of Spanish flowed from his lips as he fought against his invincible foe. After feigning punches against himself, Mace clamped his right hand around his left hand to tear it away from his throat. Emitting a few explicit curse words, Mace propelled himself across the room and crashed into the opposite wall. He snatched up the garments that had been worn by the Mexican bandito and whipped them around his head like a lariat. And then, to Jacquelyn's outraged astonishment, Mace snapped the garments against the lantern, sending it toppling from the table, shattering it in a thousand pieces.

Like a sinking rock, Jacquelyn dropped to her knees to stare at the outer wall that was only inches in front of her face. Mace was the Mexican bandito? Her mind reeled in disbelief. Mace had kidnapped her, terrorized her, and left her to that flesh-eating monster? Curse the man! That low-down, miserable, good-for-nothing sidewinder! Oh! Jacquelyn was seeing the world through a furious red haze. How she itched to repay that scoundrel for scaring the wits out of her. When she got her hands on him she was going to tear him limb from limb. . . .

The clatter of flying furniture jostled Jake from her murderous musings. Slowly, she reared her head to watch Mace make a complete ass of himself. And, furious though she was, Jake could not contain the faint smile that tugged at her lips when Mace grabbed his own arm, swung himself in a dizzying circle, and hurled himself across the room. To emphasize the crash, Mace clanked a log against the rough timbers of the shack and groaned in agony.

Growling like a disturbed panther, Mace kicked over the table and then staged his climactic scuffle with his invisible enemy. Diving forward, he collapsed on the floor. Grasping the leg of a nearby chair, Mace slammed it against the wall and spouted another string of fluent Spanish curses.

That should put the finishing touches on my magnificent performance, Mace mused as he retrieved his pistol to blow several more holes in the floor.

Moaning as if he were dying of multiple gunshot wounds, Mace collapsed against the wall and slid to the floor. Gathering the scattered clothes, he pretended to drag the carcass toward the door.

Now, all that was left to do was heave the bandito's clothes into the marsh, thereby destroying the evidence and the body that had never been there to begin with. As soon as he had discarded the garments, Mace intended to return to the cabin to save Jacquelyn from a fate she presumed to be worse than death. Lord, what a clever man he was! Jacquelyn would never know he and the Mexican bandito were one and the same. She would thank him for saving her instead of hating him all the days of her life. Ah, things are going even better than I had anticipated, he thought with a smug smile. He had devised an ingenious way to prevent telling Jacquelyn the truth. Mace was so proud of himself he mentally patted himself on the back . . . until he opened the door . . .

Chapter 21

Mace stumbled to a halt when he spied Jacquelyn standing on the stoop. Her arms were crossed beneath her breasts and one delicately carved brow arched high over her glittering brown eyes. Her heart-shaped mouth was compressed in annoyance and one dainty foot tapped irritably against the planked porch. Her measuring gaze flooded over Mace's deliberately torn shirt and the ruffled shocks of raven hair that shot out in all directions from his flushed face. Finally, she focused on the Spanish-styled garments that were clutched in his right hand.

"My, my, you certainly whipped the pants off that vicious Mexican bandito, didn't you?" she purred sarcastically.

Mace turned all the colors of the rainbow. It was the first time in two decades that he could remember blushing. And in that moment he compensated for all the times he might have reddened with embarrassment in previous years. "I . . . I . . . can explain . . ." he croaked like a waterlogged bullfrog.

"Of course you can," Jake scoffed caustically. "And, no doubt, your explanation will be as unbelievable as the fierce battle you just waged against yourself. I have heard

379

it said that a man's worst enemy is himself. You just proved that theory." Her tone dripped with scornful mockery. "I would have expected such antics from a raving lunatic who was bent on self-destruction." Her brow arched even higher. "Tell me, Mace, do you fall prey to these delirious fits often?"

Not only had Mace behaved like a long-eared ass, but he felt like one. Lord, what she must be thinking of him!

When Jacquelyn suddenly lunged to snatch away his Colt, Mace grabbed her wrist. He knew full well she intended to blow him to smithereens for trying to deceive her again. And she might have shot a hole through his heart if Mace hadn't stopped her. Twisting her arm behind her back, Mace herded his hissing captive into the ransacked cabin.

"I hate you!" Jacquelyn fumed contemptuously.

"Fine, hate me if you like, but you are going to listen to my explanation!" Mace growled at the back of her head. "I did what I did to save your lovely neck."

"By nearly drowning me? By scaring ten years off my life?" she spat as Mace shoved her into the chair he had uprighted.

"That wasn't my fault," Mace defended tersely. "You leaped to your feet on the raft and knocked me sideways. Before I could get a firm grip on you, you plunged into the water."

"And you took your Texas time retrieving me." Flaming brown eyes burned him to a charred crisp.

"I might have been more compassionate if you hadn't lied about your broken engagement to Jon," Mace retaliated as he returned her scathing glare.

Jacquelyn turned up her dainty nose and tossed her head, sending a waterfall of golden-brown curls cascading about her. "My broken engagement was none of your concern," she reminded him flippantly. "I have made no demands on you and we have no commitment to each other. It isn't your place to tell me what I should do or shouldn't do and with whom!" When Raoul struck up another round of barking and growling in the closet, Jake flung Mace a venomous glower. "And that's another thing! How dare you leave me with that man-eating monster. He could have killed me!"

A muddled frown clouded Mace's brow. How the devil had this minx eluded Raoul anyway? Curiously, he strode over to unlock the bedroom door. Hearing the ruckus in the closet, Mace removed the blockade and released Raoul. Pitifully, the beast tucked his tail between his legs and slinked out of the niche to resume his position as sentinel.

"A helluva lot of good that will do now," Mace growled in Spanish. "I asked a small favor of you, Raoul. All you had to do was keep that mere wisp of a woman captive for a couple of days. And here you are, locked in the confounded closet! You just lost your rank as an honorary Ranger."

Raoul whined dejectedly as he raised his big black eyes to Mace's condescending frown. But when he picked up Jacquelyn's scent he bolted to his feet and skidded around the corner to locate the escaped hostage, hoping to redeem himself in Mace's eyes.

Terror glazed Jacquelyn's eyes when the shaggy creature reappeared—all fangs and flying fur. With a shriek, Jacquelyn hopped from her chair and raised it as if she were fending off an attacking lion.

"Raoul!" Mace barked harshly. "¡Sientete!"

Reluctantly, Raoul sank down on his haunches. But his whiskers twitched threateningly as he bared his teeth for Jake's inspection.

"Where did you find this brutish beast?" Jacquelyn queried, still eyeing the mutt with wary trepidation. Raoul looked as if he were itching to tear her to shreds.

"We met during our march into the heart of Mexico,"

381

Mace explained as he rubbed his hand across the bristled hair on Raoul's back. "The Spanish aristocrats who retained land grants in south Texas abandoned their homes when our army approached. I suppose Raoul was separated from his Spanish family." A fond smile grazed his lips when Raoul leaned affectionately against Mace's leg. "Raoul adopted me and we became best friends. Even though he hasn't learned to master the English language, he understands a great deal of Spanish. Mostly I converse with him in his own language, and sometimes I forget he isn't human."

Jacquelyn was stung by the most peculiar brand of jealousy imaginable. If only Mace could look at her with the same affectionate respect, the same caring smile. Raoul was Mace's friend, his devoted companion, while she was a plaything to be toyed with when Mace longed for physical pleasure. Bitterly, Jacquelyn wondered which of them Mace would save if they both faced life-threatening predicaments. No doubt Raoul would be Mace's first consideration, she speculated with resentment.

After flouncing into her chair, Jake presented man and beast with a cold shoulder, one that dripped with icicles. "I am still waiting to hear why you tossed me in a cotton sack and carted me off to this Godforsaken shack in the middle of nowhere and then left me stranded with that ugly mutt."

"Raoul isn't ugly," Mace protested since the dog couldn't defend himself.

"Well, he certainly isn't a handsome specimen," Jacquelyn bit off. "And he almost ate me alive!"

Mace glanced speculatively at the huge black dog. Raoul had not approved of this stormy affair with Jake. In fact, Raoul had followed him to the Reid plantation the night Mace sneaked into Jacquelyn's room. Obviously, Raoul had intimidated Jacquelyn with relish.

"Better to face a snarling beast than to be murdered by one of your own relatives," Mace burst out.

A dubious frown knitted Jacquelyn's exquisite features. "Which relative?"

"Malcolm," Mace clarified.

"What makes you think my cousin wants me dead?" Was this another of Mace's deceitful ploys? A prevarication to save face? She wouldn't put it past this scoundrel. He never told her the truth about anything, damn him!

Mace heaved a heavy sigh as he set the table in its normal resting place. Uprighting another chair, Mace plopped down to stare pointedly at the shapely bundle of curiosity. "I think you were right when you claimed those two hooligans in Galveston were trying to kill you," he declared. "And I also think the ambush was linked to that attack. I saw those same men in Malcolm's office when I returned to Galveston. I have reason to believe your cousin has been skimming the profits from the Gen'ral's commission company. When you proclaimed you wished to take an active part in the business, Malcolm feared he would be exposed." Mace set aside his personal frustrations with Jake and met her startled stare. "That is why Malcolm adamantly protested the merger and why he's been spreading lies about my purpose for wanting your family's company."

Jacquelyn listened, open-mouthed. When the implication soaked in she peered skeptically at Mace. "You may refer to that nonsense as logic, but I call it jumping to ridiculous conclusions. And even if what you say is true, that was no reason for you tote me here without telling me why or who you really were. That was a rotten trick, Mace!"

"I was trying to save you from impending doom," Mace scowled. "When I was in Galveston, Raoul trailed your two assailants to Malcolm's office. The man you threw yourself at in the wayside inn was also there with them. It was my opinion that Malcolm was planning to send his henchmen after you again. With you out of the way, your cousin would have covered all the angles. He would not only have the profits he's been stealing for three years, but he could also lay claim to your inheritance."

Mace raked his fingers through his raven hair and then let his hand drop loosely to his side. "My intentions were honorable, but somehow things got tangled up when I whisked you away before Malcolm's men could perform their dastardly deed. Now someone has sent a ransom note demanding money for your return."

"What?" Jacquelyn's expression displayed the extent of her confusion.

"I haven't the foggiest notion who is responsible for the ransom note, but Malcolm seemed as surprised as I was when he heard the news. The Gen'ral ordered Malcolm to gather money, but Malcolm claims he can't put his hands on the cash." Mace heaved an exasperated sigh. "Damned if I know who is trying to cheat whom. But whatever is going on, Malcolm has to have that money stashed somewhere for safekeeping. Since Malcolm couldn't come up with the funds, the Gen'ral begged a loan from me. I agreed to give him the fifteen thousand dollars demanded in ransom."

"You?" Jacquelyn squawked in disbelief. None of this was making sense. "But you're the one who kidnapped me. Why would you agree to pay a ransom when you knew exactly where I was?"

Mace glared at her as if she were daft. "What the hell did you expect me to do? Tell the Gen'ral I was the one who stuffed you in a cotton sack? If I had, he wouldn't have listened when I announced my suspicions about Malcolm. I had to whisk you away from disaster and attempt to corner Malcolm. If I had waited, Harlan would have realized too late that his nephew was a swindler and a murderer. He would have been sorry, but you would have been *dead!*"

Jacquelyn supposed she should be grateful for Mace's intervention . . . if what he said was true. But she would never forgive him for scaring the wits out of her more times than she cared to count. And she could strangle him for leaving her with that vicious mongrel of his! As far as she could tell, Mace had put her through cruel and unnecessary torture just for spite.

Impulsively, Jacquelyn vaulted to her feet and aimed herself toward the door. Before she reached the stoop, Mace snagged her arm and spun her around.

"That's it?" he growled sarcastically. "Don't I even deserve a thank you for saving your stubborn hide? Don't you appreciate all the trouble I've endured to protect you from your own cousin?"

Jacquelyn's back was as stiff as a flagpole. Her eyes narrowed on his heaving chest, trying desperately to ignore the aura of masculinity that naturally oozed from this exasperating man. She was infuriated to no end and she was not going to permit her vulnerability to Mace to soften her. "Consider yourself thanked for all your trouble," she said tersely. "After I witnessed that fiasco you staged for my benefit, I realized you were trying to trick me into being grateful for the rescue." An icy smile glazed her lips. "Were you expecting me to fall into your arms and appease your lust because you saved me from that imaginary bandito?" Her gaze flew over his muscular torso in disdainful mockery. "I don't know what I saw in you that aroused me in the slightest, Mace Gallagher. You are underhanded and conniving and as much an animal as that vicious mutt of yours."

Jacquelyn would have made a dramatic exit if Mace's arm hadn't stolen around her waist, mashing her against him. "You know damned well what attracts you to me," he breathed onto her already flushed face. "We're just alike, you and I. You see in me all the saintly qualities as well as the sinful flaws you possess. And to be honest, I'm not sure I could live with you without one of us killing the other, but neither could I imagine life without you, minx. The thought of Malcolm disposing of you turned me inside out. I couldn't imagine the world without you in it."

His dark head came deliberately toward hers. His amber eyes flamed with awakened desire. He could feel her scantily clad body meshed familiarly against his and it was doing impossible things to his self-control—something he had very little of when he was within five feet of this tempting sprite.

"I want you, Jake," he told her hoarsely. "I've wanted you since the first time I laid eyes on you. I can't explain why and I don't really care why. I only know what I feel when I touch you . . . when you touch me . . ." His lips hovered over hers like a bee courting nectar, draining her will to resist. "Is it so wrong for a man to be drawn to a beautiful woman, to want the pleasure we can give each other without spouting promises that neither of us can keep?"

His tone could have charmed a charging buffalo, and Jake was too vulnerable not to be affected by his husky voice. Her resistance drooped another dangerous notch. The feel of his virile body brushing suggestively against hers and the compelling aroma that warped her senses were Jacquelyn's undoing. She could feel his masculine warmth enveloping her. She could see the rough sensuality in his craggy features. She was entranced by the sparks in his golden eyes, sparks that triggered the memory of forbidden dreams.

As much as she disliked his deceitful ploys, she could not resist the man himself. It was impossible to combat the erotic sensations that overwhelmed her body when his mouth took sweet possession of hers. His kiss was slow and incredibly tender—a mystifying contrast to this powerfully built man. It was this gentle side of this lion of a man that had always fascinated Jake. When he held her as if she were a delicate treasure, she forgot the obstacles that stood between them.

Mace was offering no promises and he never would. She was every kind of fool if she surrendered to the wild, physical attraction between them. But, God, rejecting him was nine kinds of hell. Maybe they couldn't enjoy forever together. Maybe what they shared was like the life cycle of a butterfly—beautiful and yet so brief. But it was all she had, all she would ever have.

Oh, why deny it, Jake thought as she melted beneath his persuasive kiss. Mace aroused her to the very core of her being. He always had. And for these few precious moments the world was theirs.

A rueful smile touched her quivering lips as she peered up into those hypnotic golden eyes that were fringed with black velvet lashes. "Do you ever lose a battle or a debate, Mace?" she questioned as her hand involuntarily lifted to trace his commanding features.

His fingertips drifted across her bare waist to unfasten her shirt. "If it's any consolation, Jake, I never feel as if I win with you, not in the ways that truly matter."

Reverently, his lips whispered over hers. Mace felt like a man who had been deprived of food and drink for weeks on end. He was starved for the taste of her. He ached to caress her. A muffled groan erupted from beneath their kiss when her straying hand dived beneath his shirt to make titillating contact with his hair-roughened chest. She could release monstrous cravings with one caress. She could blow the stars around and brew storms with one kiss. She could make him glad he was a man, and Mace felt every inch of one when this curvaceous sprite responded to his embrace.

Gently, Mace scooped Jacquelyn off the floor and

strode into the bedroom. When he set her on her feet to unveil her naked beauty, Raoul's whine destroyed the mood of the moment. Grumbling, Mace dragged his ravishing gaze from Jake and focused on the oversized mongrel which stood at the foot of the cot.

"*Guarde la puerta,*" Mace snapped. When Raoul made no move to obey, Mace glowered at his suddenly disobedient dog. "*Guarde la puerta . . . por afuera . . . ahorrita!*"

Dropping his broad head, Raoul lumbered across the room and plopped down outside the door, his back to the cot, just as Mace had demanded of him. Although the shaggy mongrel couldn't speak, his behavior conveyed his displeasure with the situation.

"Now, where were we?" Mace questioned with a rakish grin that melted Jacquelyn into a sentimental puddle.

"Here, I believe," she murmured throatily. After she loosened his tattered shirt, her palms splayed across his broad chest. Her tongue flicked at each male nipple until Mace groaned in unholy torment. "Or perhaps we were here. . . ." Her adventurous hand slid down the lean muscles of his belly and then dipped beneath the band of his breeches.

Mace sucked in his breath when her bold caress wandered even lower. His knees threatened to fold up like an accordion when Jacquelyn pushed his breeches from his hips, permitting herself the freedom to explore and further arouse. As her warm lips and gentle hands flowed over his body like a tide ebbing and flooding the seashore, Mace lost track of time. She was doing delicious things to his mind and body. And as always, Jake was the victor in this gentle battle. Her tenderness was far more devastating than strength, and he wilted beneath her worshipping caresses, adoring the feel of her hands on his flesh.

When Jacquelyn urged him to the cot, Mace went without protest. He found himself sinking into the canvas bed as if it were a puffy white cloud and he was being attended by an angel. Her touch was as light as the flutter of a cherub's wings. Her kisses were like the warm draft of a heavenly breeze.

Ah, this was paradise, Mace thought with a contented sigh. He was drifting just beyond reality, chasing rainbows, gliding across the arc of tantalizing sensations. The momentum of his emotional journey sped him along until he was flying at a breathless pace. Jacquelyn had instigated the cadence of this sensuous assault and the sweet, tormenting pleasure magnified until Mace wasn't certain he could endure the rapture of it all.

Pastel colors shattered before his mind's eye as Jacquelyn stroked and aroused his passions to a fevered pitch. Like a master harpist, she plucked at his nerves and strummed on the deeply embedded emotions until they echoed in chorded harmony. Mace could feel himself losing control. There was no self-restraint left when Jacquelyn transformed his body into an instrument of passion. Her fingertips played upon his skin as if he were equipped with musical strings and keys. His soul sang as she teased and aroused him. His heart beat like a bass drum when she crouched above him.

Mace stared up into those dark, expressive eyes and into that seductive smile. In this vibrant beauty Mace saw the personification of all he wanted and needed in life. Although Jacquelyn was the essence of loveliness with her flawless features, olive complexion, and shapely body, there was a depth to this woman that remained unparalleled. Mace could touch her, possess her for a time, but he could never master her lively spirit and undaunted will. It had been his intent to seduce her and yet she had become the skillful seductress.

A moan of tormented pleasure bubbled from his chest

when her soft body caressed his. Mace could feel the taut peaks of her breasts brushing his flesh, feel her hips gliding provocatively against his thighs. He could feel her breath against his parted lips, offering the essence of ecstasy. She was so close, like a hovering angel, and yet she was agonizing inches away.

Finally, Mace could endure no more of this seductive torture. His body arched toward hers, aching to appease the incredible craving she had evoked from him. He moved upon command, lost to primal instincts that could not be satisfied until he was one in body, mind, and spirit with this ebony-eyed sorceress.

Jacquelyn gasped at the holocaust of fiery pleasure that exploded within her when Mace twisted above her. Her body caught fire and burned when he engulfed her in his sinewy arms. She welcomed his hard thrusts, the savagery of emotions that poured forth to consume him and her as well. He had become the living flame that ignited a thousand internal fires. He drove into her, feeding the blaze of passion that already raged out of control. Her body was now his to command and she moved in perfect rhythm with him. Together they forged a path of fire across the late afternoon sky, reveling in the rapture of lovemaking.

Jacquelyn knew it was love that held her suspended above the wildfire of sensations that consumed her body. It was love that created the mystical melody that played on her soul. And even if she could not spend eternity with Mace, she had found forever in his arms each time they made wild, passionate love. In the years to come she would pause to remember the way they were, the sweet magic they shared. She would reach back through time to grasp these glorious moments and she would recall each forever they had created. And in her heart, she knew she had found a love that could have outlasted eternity if only Mace believed in everlasting emotions. . . .

Her drifting thoughts scattered in a hundred different directions when each soul-quaking sensation that had assaulted her earlier began to converge simultaneously. Uncontrollable shudders rocked her as Mace's powerful body surged into hers. The magical combination of each splendid emotion and each rapturous sensation she had previously experienced uncoiled in the core of her being. Jacquelyn cried out as ecstasy drenched her body and soul. She clung to Mace as if the world were about to end, as if he were the only stable force in a careening universe. For several moments the indescribable feelings continued to channel through her body like the remnants of a devastating tidal wave. She thought she knew all there was to know of passion. But nothing she had learned of passion compared to what she was feeling now. It consumed and lingered to consume all over again. It was as if she were living and dying, all in the same maddening moment.

While Jacquelyn was contending with the epitome of emotion, Mace was struggling to regather the shattered remnants of body and soul. Ecstasy numbed his mind, leaving him dangling in time and space. Fragments of jumbled thoughts skitted through his head, but he was too delirious with the fever of passion to understand the simplest of thoughts. His arms and legs had been reduced to the consistency of melted butter—matching the composition of his mind. If the shack caught fire, Mace doubted he could muster enough strength to move, much less save himself. The irony would come in knowing he had been burned to the same degree, inside and out. It was for damned sure that Jacquelyn's brand of love-making had cooked his insides as thoroughly as if he had been left boiling in a witch's caldron for the better part of a day.

Mace contemplated rising from the cot long before his reluctant body got around to responding to the thought.

By the time he pushed himself into an upright position, he had expended his regenerated strength. Defeated, he collapsed beside Jacquelyn, whose twinkling brown eyes mocked his lack of self-mobility.

"It appears that fierce battle you waged against that Goliath of a Mexican bandito cost you your energy," she teased unmercifully. "It's a wonder you found the strength to seduce me at all."

"Me seduce you?" Mace crowed like a plucked rooster. "It was the other way around and you damned well know it!"

"Was it?" Jacquelyn queried in mock innocence. Gracefully, she levered up on one elbow. Her unruly hair tumbled over Mace's shoulder as she bent close. Her admiring gaze drifted across his broad chest and then journeyed down to survey the whipcord muscles and tendons, missing not one minute detail of his arresting physique. Impulsively, her fingertips moved to investigate the scar on his ribs, the flatness of his belly, the manly curve of his hips.

"Perhaps you could refresh my memory," she murmured suggestively. "What did I do to overwhelm you when I haven't the strength to match a victorious warrior like yourself . . . ?"

"Don't do that. . . ." Mace removed her wandering hand. "Even invincible knights have their limitations," he grudgingly confessed. Lord, his body was spent. If he couldn't rise from bed on his own accord, it was certain he couldn't repeat the same performance that mentally, physically, and emotionally exhausted him.

"They do?" Jacquelyn inquired with an impish smile.

"I am only a man," he grumbled as he removed her adventurous hand a second time. "A man needs ample time to rise to the occasion you are suggesting."

Her sensuous lips feathered over his mouth. "I think you underestimate your abilities, Sir Knight," she whispered provocatively. "Shall I show you how marvelously capable you are . . . ?"

It was on the tip of his tongue to protest, but Jacquelyn skillfully kissed away his excuse. And when her persistent caresses skimmed his flesh, Mace was startled to realize she had created strength where there was none moments before. Her touch rekindled fires Mace swore had completely burned themselves out. And yet, in every fiber of his being, a myriad of tiny flames began to burn. Mace knew the incredible pleasure that awaited him, and he felt desire unfolding like flower petals opening to greet the warmth of the sun. His body roused to her light, teasing caresses, to kisses that breathed life back into him.

Mace returned each caress, eager to touch and explore, to tantalize and excite. Bracing himself on one arm, he allowed his searching hands to wander across the silky terrain of her flesh, to rediscover each sensitive point on her exquisite body. In wonderment, he watched the deliberate flight of his fingers across her shapely form. He saw the flicker of desire in her eyes when he made contact with the rose-tipped buds of her breasts. His raven head lowered to taste what his index finger had touched. And while his moist lips flitted over each throbbing peak, his hands migrated over her abdomen. Lower still, his hands meandered to arouse every inch of her perfectly sculptured body, to instill the same breathless need of passion she had aroused in him.

Jacquelyn felt as if she were flying into the sun. Each place Mace touched became an instant flame and each fire burned back atop the others. Pleasure streamed through her like a molten river. Bone and flesh became hot lava. His practiced hands scaled each crest and valley. His kisses fueled the wildfires, and her need for him became so intense she ached in places she didn't recall she had. When his lips trailed lower to retrace the erotic path of his hands, Jacquelyn feared her stampeding heart would trample her ribs as it thundered around her chest. Goose bumps sailed down her quivering body, meeting themselves coming and going. She felt giddy, lightheaded, unsure she could survive this ineffable pleasure Mace was weaving upon her skin. She was entrapped in the silken maze of sensations that tangled her thoughts and her senses. The musky scent of him invaded her nostrils. His soft words vibrated on her flesh. His hands (and he must have sprouted an extra dozen of them) were delving and massaging, kneading and stroking, until she swore she would go mad before he satisfied the wanting.

"Mace . . . please," Jacquelyn pleaded shamelessly.

"Not yet, sweet nymph," he murmured against her trembling flesh. "I want to teach you things about pleasure that we have yet to explore. You have only begun to learn what loving is all about. . . ."

Jacquelyn doubted there was anything this skillful lover had yet to teach her. But she soon realized how naive she had been. Mace revealed a new dimension in the dark world of splendor. What she had enjoyed earlier became another plateau on the pyramid of splendorous sensations, each one more devastating than the one before. Each kiss and caress led her onto a higher pinnacle of pleasure. Jacquelyn had come so far she wasn't sure she could navigate her way back to the secluded hut on the bayou. And when she was certain she would die from aching for him, Mace guided her thighs apart with his muscular hips. Wild and breathless, Jacquelyn surrendered her body, her soul, and her sanity. This was the ultimate rapture of love. She was prepared to sacrifice her last breath to remain in this splendorous universe that was bounded by the unending circle of Mace's arms. His embrace, tight and unyielding though it was, encircled the pure essence of existence. It encompassed the star-spangled sky and surrounded the windswept seas. The pleasure stretched onward and upward, sparkling like a distant beam of pure white light that somehow reversed direction to race back to its source.

Jacquelyn could not contain the astonished cry that burst from her lips. She couldn't imagine how she could survive such an incredible ecstasy. She was like a disembodied spirit watching from afar and yet cognizant of the emotions that seized her body. And although she was crushed beneath Mace's massive weight, she felt as if she were soaring on weightless wings. . . .

Raoul's loud bark resembled a rock crashing through a glass window. Jacquelyn was not permitted to make a graceful descent from her orbit around star worlds. She landed with a thud in reality. Turning her head from Mace's shoulder, she found two glowing black eyes glaring at her while Mace fluently cursed in Spanish and English.

"Go take a swim in the bayou," Mace growled back at Raoul. Muttering, Mace realized he had barked the command in the wrong language. When the order was repeated in Raoul's native tongue, the mutt flung his master a disgruntled glance and trotted out the door with his snout in the air.

When Mace rolled away, Jacquelyn giggled at the infuriated scowl that was plastered on Mace's craggy features. "I'm beginning to understand why you never married," she chortled as she scooped up her discarded shirt and shrugged into it. "You can't keep a wife and your overprotective dragon in the same house. Raoul is jealous of anyone who demands more of your time than he does."

Although the remark was spoken in jest, it struck a sensitive nerve. Mace's handsome face clouded with undecipherable emotion. "It isn't Raoul's jealousy that concerns me, Jake," he mumbled as he gathered his scattered garments. "The strongest of bonds between two people are the most dangerous kind. I couldn't bear to have history repeat itself."

Jacquelyn blinked in bewilderment as Mace uttered his remark and then exited the room posthaste. She didn't have the faintest notion what Mace implied or why he'd walked out, dressing as he went. Why was he so terrified of wives and wedlock? What ghost haunted his mysterious past? Jacquelyn had learned to read a few of Mace's complex moods, but this one had her baffled.

Well, I understand him as clearly as he allows any woman to understand him, she consoled herself. Mace was elusive when it came to discussing his past. If one didn't know better one would think Mason Gallagher had been born at the age of twenty. He'd mentioned his service with the Rangers and cited a few of his experiences during the Mexican war, but that was the extent of his revelations. The man truly could have hatched from an egg or just awakened one morning and crawled out from under a rock for all Jake knew about his ancestry. Never once had he mentioned his parents, brothers, sisters, grandparents, or cousins.

Determined to learn the truth, Jacquelyn fastened herself into her clothes and marched outside. Mace and Raoul were already waiting on the raft, and Mace's mood had swung from secretive to sulking and then to rakishly observant. As Jacquelyn weaved through the tangled brush, Mace's hawkish gaze penetrated the thin garments to visualize how she had appeared to him minutes before. Although Jacquelyn was garbed in uncomplimentary clothes and her hair looked like a bird's nest, her natural beauty mesmerized Mace. The fleeting rays of the sunset caught in her hair, creating a golden halo around her head. The pastel lights speared through her ragtag garments, molding itself to her voluptuous form.

Even when this dazzling minx was at her worst, every other woman he had ever known ran a distant second to Jacquelyn. There was an aura of femininity and unrivaled spirit radiating from this feisty sprite that perpetually intrigued Mace. Even when she was ruffled and ragged, she was positively breathtaking. And those dark, compelling eyes seemed to reach out to ensnare him. Even at what he had assumed to be a safe distance, those spellbinding eyes tugged on the strings of his heart.

When Jacquelyn hopped onto the raft, Mace hooked his arm around her waist and planted an unexpected kiss on her lips, red and swollen from the score of kisses he had bestowed on her earlier.

"What brought that on?" Jacquelyn inquired when Mace allowed her to breathe.

"Your mere presence, vixen," he replied as he reluctantly released her and grabbed the pole to steer the raft.

Following his lead, Jacquelyn grasped the other pole and took her position on the opposite side of the vessel. "There are a few questions I want answered," she began. "You may delight in evading your past, but I would like to know—"

"We have important matters to discuss," Mace cut in before she encroached on topics that left him uneasy. "I have yet to determine who sent that ransom note. If I immediately return you to the Gen'ral, we may never learn who is responsible. And there is also Malcolm to consider." The thought thoroughly soured Mace's mood. "I have no intention of allowing that weasel to scurry off, only to organize another attempt on your life. And by the way, your great-aunt is visiting the Gen'ral."

The abrupt announcement provoked Jake's muddled frown. "Whatever is Florence doing here? I thought she would have been relieved to have me out from underfoot. She swore time and time again that I was personally responsible for the new crop of gray hair she acquired these past three years."

Mace shrugged his broad shoulders and then stabbed the pole into the muddy bayou. "She claims she grew accustomed to your coming and going and that she was lonesome without you. She was in a snit when she learned the Gen'ral had lost you after you had been home for less than two months."

Jacquelyn tittered at the image that rose in her mind. "Knowing Florence, she probably gave my grandfather hell for misplacing me. She is notorious for poking holes in the Gen'ral's pride. Indeed, she thrives on it."

"Florence didn't permit opportunity to pass her by," Mace assured her. "She needled Harlan until he looked as if he wanted to strangle her."

A curious frown knitted Jacquelyn's brow when she recalled Mace's previous comment. "Do you suppose Malcolm's henchmen truly tried to cheat him by sending that ransom note? Surely they would realize he would come after them with fiendish vengeance. My cousin has such high esteem for himself that he couldn't tolerate being played for the fool."

"Greed provokes men to behave strangely," Mace reminded her. "Fifteen thousand dollars can launch a man into a life in a remote region of the country where Malcolm wouldn't think to search, especially while the Gen'ral is breathing down his neck. And Harlan *will* be when he realizes Malcolm has indeed been bleeding him dry." Mace breathed a heavy sigh and strained against the poles.

"Does the Gen'ral believe your accusations?" Jacquelyn queried.

"Not entirely," Mace grumbled resentfully. "But he is becoming suspicious. When Malcolm couldn't produce the ready cash to pay the ransom, he gave the Gen'ral a dozen flimsy excuses. When I left, Harlan was scanning the ledgers with a fine-toothed comb. No doubt Malcolm covered his tracks, but I intend to prove my accusations . . . all of them."

"How?" she wanted to know.

"By assuming control of the Reid Commission Company," Mace responded. "When I audit the books, Malcolm will be exposed for what he is. But you won't be safe until Malcolm and his greedy henchmen are behind bars."

Jacquelyn's eyes drifted to the awesome mass of masculinity and she fell in love all over again. My, what a hopeless romantic she had turned out to be! Someone was trying to kill her and all she could think of was this ruggedly handsome rogue. It was certain she was losing her mind!

Chapter 22

Riding in the cloak of darkness, Malcolm weaved through the thick underbrush to arrive at the designated location where he was to meet Gil Davis. Although Malcolm was relieved to have his cousin out of the way, he was furious about the ransom note. Malcolm had come armed and ready to retaliate against Gil for cheating him. Gil couldn't have known what repercussions Malcolm would face when he was ordered to collect cash for a ransom. But the back-stabbing bastard was about to find out, Malcolm vowed viciously. With Gil out of the way, Malcolm could collect the fifteen thousand dollars and declare it to be the profit from the company that he had managed to convert to cash. Harlan wouldn't doubt Malcolm's integrity if he could produce the money on his own.

The rustle of bushes so close behind him very nearly caused Malcolm to leap out of his skin. Twisting in the saddle, he aimed his pistol at the silhouette that was framed in moonlight. "Gil, is that you?" he growled.

Gil cautiously eased into the light, his own pistol trained on Malcolm. "Step down, Malcolm. We have a problem to discuss."

"We most certainly do," Malcolm sneered as he swung

to the ground. "How dare you send a ransom note without consulting me! Did you think I would tolerate your attempt to make extra money at my expense?"

A frown furrowed Gil's brow. "What are you raving about? I sent no one a note demanding money."

Malcolm didn't believe him. "Don't lie to me, Gil. The Gen'ral told me exactly what was in that note. You wanted fifteen thousand dollars in return for my meddling cousin!"

Gil's mouth narrowed into a threatening snarl. "The last man who insulted me wound up dead. It was one of those worthless hoodlums you sent along to help me. The other one lit out for parts unknown, and you lost every penny you paid them to help me," he growled. "And I don't know a damned thing about a ransom note!"

The fury drained from Malcolm's puckered features. "If you didn't send the note, who did?" he mused aloud.

"Maybe the same person who kidnapped your cousin," Gil snorted. "When I sneaked into the mansion to abduct the chit, she wasn't where you said she'd be."

"What?" Malcolm squeaked in astonishment. "You don't have Jacquelyn in custody?" Suspicion captured his plain face. Gil had to be lying through his teeth. He had apprehended Jacquelyn and sent the note. Now he was trying to bamboozle Malcolm. "How stupid do you think I am?"

For a long, tense moment both men stared each other down. Their pistols never wavered from each other's chest. Finally, Gil expelled a harsh sigh. "I'm telling you the truth," he proclaimed. "There was no one in the girl's room, so I returned the following night. I waited until well after midnight, but the wench never came in. Why the devil would I send a ransom note if I didn't have the woman under lock and key?"

Baffled, Malcolm replaced his pistol in its holster. Damnit all! Who had kidnapped Jake? Or had that mischievous chit staged her own abduction to throw Harlan into a turmoil? Malcolm wouldn't put such a shenanigan past his rambunctious cousin. Even as a child she had delighted in playing pranks, just to ruffle her grandfather.

Malcolm jerked up his head when he found Gil Davis looming over him. The menacing smile that stretched Gil's lips sent a shiver of apprehension down Malcolm's spine.

"I do not appreciate being accused of lying," Gil hissed. "I followed your orders because you can afford to pay a hired gun to do your dirty work for you. And don't ever point a pistol at me again unless you plan to use it." The warning crackled like a log tossed on a blazing fire. "You seem to forget your new empire in Santa Gertrudis could easily become my domain if you were to meet with your untimely demise."

The threat hung heavily in the air and Malcolm shifted uneasily from one foot to the other, as if he expected to be simultaneously attacked from all directions. He had made a grave mistake by accusing Gil of scheming. The man was not to be taken for granted. He was potentially dangerous when he was angered. Gil could easily assume the throne Malcolm had designed for himself in south Texas. After all, Gil had made the necessary arrangements with the army of vaqueros. Gil was in the perfect position to enjoy the dream that had taken Malcolm three years to organize. Malcolm's only alternative was to hold a counterthreat over Gil's head, which Malcolm proceeded to do.

"And you seem to forget that a message sent to the Rangers could expose you as the infamous leader of the banditos who have been terrorizing the border." His narrowed green eyes pinned Gil to the tree. "Together we can benefit each other. And separately, we can destroy each other, Gil."

403

A low rumble echoed in Gil's chest. "What's to keep me from blowing a hole in your expensive waistcoat and returning to Santa Gertrudis to reap the rewards?"

Malcolm managed a courageous smile. "You can't be certain if I have already taken the precaution of writing a message which will be opened in the event of my death."

Gil shoved his Colt into its holster and cautiously backed away. "Meet me here tomorrow night," he demanded. "If the girl hasn't turned up by then, I'm heading back to the border. I've wasted enough time with this wild-goose chase."

When Gil disappeared into the shadows, Malcolm half collapsed in relief. Damnation, he had enough trouble without inviting Gil's ire. To compound Malcolm's frustration, he hadn't a clue as to where Jacquelyn was and who was attempting to ransom her.

Scowling at his predicament, Malcolm stomped back to his horse and aimed himself toward the plantation. Blast it, things had been going well, and then suddenly Malcolm's position had become precarious. What he needed to do was intercept the ransom money and hightail it to Santa Gertrudis before the entire scheme exploded in his face.

That is exactly what I am going to do, Malcolm decided. He would have enough cash to sustain him, and the Gen'ral wouldn't know where to begin looking for him. And if, by some remote chance, the Gen'ral did locate him, the old man would face an army of outlaws that rivaled nothing he had ever seen.

A sardonic grin swallowed Malcolm's bland features as he thundered toward the mansion. If he didn't panic, he could still make the most of opportunity. And what would please him most was scampering off with Mace Gallagher's fifteen thousand dollars. It was what Gallagher deserved for attempting to poke his nose into the Reid family's business. That cocky varmint needed to be taught a lesson!

An appreciative smile hovered on Hub's lips when the lantern light caressed Jacquelyn's bewitching features. His blue eyes made a slow descent to scrutinize the unusual attire of a cropped shirt and low-riding breeches. There was something irresistibly fascinating about Jake. She continued to draw Hub's gaze like a magnet. She naturally provoked lusty thoughts and left a man feeling warm and giddy inside. Perhaps it was that lively sparkle in her eyes or the intriguing way that golden-brown mane rippled about her when she moved. Or perhaps it was that arresting figure that could halt a stampede. Hub couldn't pinpoint the exact cause of his reaction to Jacquelyn, but he was definitely disturbed by her presence. He had felt it the first time they met. He had experienced it again at the barbecue, and he was feeling the effects now.

It was little wonder Mace was mesmerized, Hub mused as Jake and Mace plopped down at the dining table to enjoy a late night meal. The only problem was that Mace was a dedicated bachelor who harbored irrational fears. And for a man of Mace's abilities it seemed unnatural to Hub that his longtime friend could be such a captive of his own past. Those bitter memories had been something Mace had never outgrown or forgotten. They hung like an iron shield on his heart, preventing him from committing himself to the one woman who could rival his dynamic personality and persuasive charm. Their two renegade hearts were a matched pair. Jake and Mace belonged together.

While he sipped his coffee, he asked himself how long Mace could pretend to play this ridiculous game of rejecting a legal claim on this feisty female. Mace never allowed Jake to forget him, and couldn't seem to let her go completely. Well, he couldn't continue on this course forever, Hub predicted. He would have to admit the truth.

Damnit, it wasn't right for Mace to treat the General's granddaughter this way! She deserved better. And if Mace wasn't going to do right by her. Hub would. It wouldn't hurt Hub to settle down either, and Jacquelyn was the kind of woman who could make life an adventure. . . .

"Well, what has Malcolm been doing while I was away?" Mace questioned, drawing Hub from his contemplative deliberations.

Hub extended an arm to retrieve a biscuit for Raoul, whose big black eyes were focused on the tray of food the servants had placed before them.

"Raoul prefers his biscuits with marmalade," Mace reminded Hub.

The comment brought a faint smile to Hub's lips. How could he have forgotten Raoul's preference? Raoul had a sweet tooth and would do most anything to satisfy his craving. Hub reached for the marmalade and apologized to Raoul for being so inconsiderate.

While he spread the marmalade on the warm biscuit, Jacquelyn rolled her eyes in disbelief. Mace took particular care to insure Raoul received his heart's desire. But she was the one he treated like a confounded dog!

Hub offered Raoul the treat, and he wolfed it down in one bite. "Our friend Malcolm was doing a little nocturnal prowling this evening," he informed Mace as he smeared marmalade on Raoul's second biscuit. "Malcolm slithered out the back of the mansion and met someone beside the river."

"Did you get a look at the man?" Mace quizzed him before munching on his ham and biscuits.

"I still don't have a name to attach to the face, but I

406

think Malcolm's companion was the same man we saw sneaking out the side door of his office in Galveston." Hub sighed with disappointment. "I couldn't get within earshot to discover what they were discussing before they each went their own way."

Mace frowned, upset. "He was hoping Hub would have been more informative.

"I suppose you also believe my cousin is stealing from the Gen'ral and that he's out to get me," Jacquelyn remarked as she tossed Hub a speculative glance.

Hub nodded affirmatively. "I'm the one who broke into Malcolm's office to examine the ledgers before he tampered with them. Malcolm is sure enough buying top-grade cotton from clients and paying them for second-rate crops." His blue eyes darted to Mace momentarily, and then swung back to the shapely beauty who had the uncanny knack of sending his thoughts off in the most arousing direction. "As far as this business of Malcolm wanting you dead is concerned, that's Mace's speculation."

"It is my opinion that we should confront my cousin with the evidence and accusations," Jacquelyn declared.

"And I say we should catch the criminal committing his crime," Mace growled in contradiction.

"What do you plan to do?" Jake smirked sarcastically. "Lead me home and wait for Malcolm to make an attempt on my life?"

"No, damnit! If that was my intention, I wouldn't have abducted you before he had the chance," Mace bellowed in irritation. "You need to take the matter more seriously. It is your future . . . or lack of it . . . that we are discussing here!"

"You needn't shout," Jacquelyn blared.

Hub bolted to his feet and leaned across the table. "I think we have all endured a long day," he exclaimed before Mace jumped down Jake's throat and she reciprocated in a like manner. "I will accompany Jacquelyn to the guest room." His gaze drilled into Mace, assuring him there would be no dallying with this desirable minx under this roof. Indeed, Hub did not want the woman he was considering courting to be sleeping in the master bedroom while Master Gallagher was in it!

When Hub shuffled Jacquelyn out the door and up the steps, Mace expelled his breath in a rush. "What do you suppose he's up to?" he questioned Raoul.

Raoul trotted around the table to lay his head in Mace's lap. Reflexively, Mace stroked the mongrel's shaggy head.

"Did you see the way Hub was assessing Jake?" Mace grunted disgustedly. "His intentions were printed on his face in bold letters." An annoyed frown puckered Mace's handsome features. "You know how Hub is. He never met a woman he didn't love at first sight."

Mace grumbled under his breath when the vision of Hub and Jacquelyn sharing a romantic embrace shot across his mind. "Go fetch me a bottle of brandy, Raoul, and you can polish off the last two biscuits."

Wagging his tail, Raoul loped out of the room to obey the command.

"Hub and Jake," Mace sniffed. "Now wouldn't they make a fine pair!" The thought of that dark-eyed nymph paired with anyone turned Mace's disposition pitch black.

When Raoul reentered the dining room with the brandy flask clamped in his powerful jaws, Mace retrieved it and poured himself a tall drink. He was far too distracted by Jake's frustrating image to note that Raoul was awaiting his promised treat. Impatiently, Raoul sank a huge paw into Mace's lap, causing him to groan uncomfortably.

"Have a care where you stuff your foot," Mace snapped grouchily. "You'll render me useless to all women." His accusing gaze dropped to Raoul's whiskered face. "Or is that your intention? Between you and Hub, I'll never get within ten feet of that frustrating female again."

"That's the general idea," Hub chuckled as he swaggered up behind Mace. "I've decided to turn my charms on the lady. She needs a husband who can keep a watchful eye on her, a man with my kind of experience. She's far too attractive to be running around loose. Men naturally flock to her."

Mace swallowed his brandy in one gulp and poured himself another. "You? Married?" he scoffed cynically. "You have fallen in love with every woman you ever met, my friend."

Hub's broad chest swelled with indignation. "I happen to like women of all shapes and sizes. There's nothing wrong with that!"

"And I have never known you to be between women," Mace countered. "Giving up all women and remaining true to only one would be an impossible feat for you. It is my opinion that you would make a terrible husband."

Hub's chin tilted in offended dignity. Huffily, he grabbed the bottle of brandy and slopped it into a glass. With a flair for the dramatic, he flounced into his chair and glared at Mace. "I'm thirty-four years old and it's time I put down roots," he said tartly. "I'm not exactly ugly, and I would treat Jake a helluva lot better than you have." His damning glower sliced across Mace's countering frown. "You maneuvered her into your hotel suite the first day you met her and—"

Mace's mouth fell off its hinges. "How do you know that?" he croaked in amazement.

"Because I followed you and eavesdropped outside your door," Hub told him calmly. "And I'm not stupid enough to think you didn't take advantage of the poor girl while you had her cooped up in that musty shack on the bayou."

Mace stared at the opposite wall, as if something there had suddenly demanded his attention. He sat brooding, refusing to utter a word in his own defense. Hell, he had no defense and he knew it.

"I'm willing to overlook Jacquelyn's indiscretion with a man who probably offered her little say in the matter. After all, I've had my share of women," Hub honestly admitted.

"Your share and that of at least a dozen other men," Mace added scornfully.

"Look who's talking!" Hub hooted. "But I'm willing to put the past behind us and make a new beginning with Jacquelyn." He guzzled a sip of brandy and continued philosophically. "Jake and I would be good for each other. We could have a family of two or three children, and I would take Jake's vivacious spirit and independent nature into consideration. I think we understand each other. We could enjoy a satisfactory marriage." A wry smile pursed his lips as he contemplated his glass. "I know she's woman enough to keep me happy for the next century. I won't want to be flitting around all over town with that seductive hellion waiting at home."

The suggestive remark aroused the green-eyed monster who lurked in the dark dungeon of Mace's mind. Hub was painting a vivid picture of life after wedlock. "You call that a sensible life?" he growled sarcastically. "I call that insanity! One month after supposedly wedded bliss your roving eye would lead you astray. And Jake is the sort of woman who would turn to another man just to spite you."

"I would have no reason to be unfaithful," Hub loudly protested. "What's not to love about Jake? She is quick-witted, high-spirited, and stunningly beautiful. She is totally uninhibited . . . and I intend to begin courting her first thing in the morning."

"You most certainly will not!" Mace roared. "I won't permit it!"

Hub broke into a goading grin as he unfolded himself from his chair. "I don't need your permission or your blessing," he reminded his scowling friend. "The Gen'ral's approval is all I require. The old man is a tender-hearted softy where his granddaughter is concerned. After the nightmare Harlan has endured the last few days, he will be grateful to have Jake back. And I'm willing to bet the Gen'ral wouldn't protest if Jake decided to marry me. Why, I wouldn't be surprised if he welcomed me into the family with open arms. Hell, I might even become the financial advisor for the Reid's side of our business merger."

On that taunting comment, Hub sashayed toward the door. "And don't bother to check on Jacquelyn before you retire, I'll tuck her in bed and insure she has all she needs to make her stay as comfortable and pleasurable as possible."

Leaving Mace snarling like an injured grizzly bear, Hub snickered his way up the staircase. After he tapped on Jacquelyn's door and was granted entrance, he stepped into the room. All thoughts of Mace evaporated when Hub found Jacquelyn draped in nothing but a towel.

A becoming blush stained Jake's cheeks when Hub's devouring gaze feasted on every inch of bare flesh. She had assumed it was Mace who had knocked on her door and, without demanding to know the identity of her visitor, invited him in.

Clutching the towel closely about her bosom, Jacquelyn mustered an embarrassed smile. "This is not the way I usually greet a man," she assured her owl-eyed guest. "It was not until after I stepped from my bath that I realized I had nothing to wear."

"You look marvelous in everything, especially a towel," Hub murmured honestly. "I'm not the least bit

411

offended. . . ." His attractive blond features wore a rakish smile. "Or disappointed."

Jacquelyn liked Hub. He was straightforward without being obnoxious. He was handsome, good-natured, sharp-witted, and capable. In no way did he resemble the dandies she had met in New Orleans. Hub was a man's man who had also learned to survive by his wits. Jacquelyn was neither offended nor threatened by his presence in her room. Hub's approving glances did not hold a disgusting leer that put her on immediate defense. His smile assured her that he liked what he saw and his appreciative stare was meant as a compliment rather than an insult.

"Would one of my shirts suffice as a nightgown?" he inquired as he looked her over again.

An impish smile twitched her lips. "I have no aversion to sleeping in the buff."

A low rumble of laughter gurgled in his throat. Boldly, Hub swaggered close. "A lady after my own heart." His dancing blue eyes tracked a deliberate path down the shapely terrain of her body. "Perhaps my shirt would be of more benefit tomorrow while I take you on a tour of Mace's plantation. I'm afraid it would disturb Mace's plans if you return home before we discover who is trying to ransom you." His index finger grazed her creamy cheek to remove a lingering soap bubble. "I'm sure the two of us can find something to while away the hours. I have been told on several occasions that I can be stimulating company. . . ."

"Have you put that to a vote before all the females you've encountered this past decade?" Mace's question rolled across the room like a thunderclap.

Two pairs of wide eyes swung to the looming figure that blocked the doorway. Mace was smoldering and he didn't give a damn who knew it. Finding Jacquelyn entertaining Hub while she was draped in nothing but a

412

towel had turned his mood a darker shade of pitch. Apparently Hub had decided not to procrastinate until morning. The varmint was practicing his courting rituals at midnight!

Mace glared flaming arrows at Jacquelyn. "Do you always make it a habit of greeting guests in such scanty attire?" he inquired with an intimidating smile. "No wonder Anna Marie was passing sordid rumors about you in New Orleans. You were probably guilty of doing everything your rival accused you of doing."

Jacquelyn tilted a proud chin, refusing to buckle beneath Mace's sarcastic insinuation. It aggravated her that Mace had revealed part of a confession that he'd sworn he would take with him to his grave. The lout! "I only traipse around in a towel when I have no clean clothes to wear," she informed him with an accusing glare. "My abductor failed to provide me with any other garments besides oversized rags."

To further infuriate Mace (and it took very little provocation in his present frame of mind), Hub offered Jake the chambray shirt off his back. As Hub helped her into the garment he sent her a conspiratorial wink. There was something satisfying about seeing this muscular giant reduce himself to a pile of smoldering coals, and Hub played the situation for all it was worth.

"If you're through ranting, why don't you run along to bed." Pivoting, Hub gestured toward the mongrel who stood at Mace's heels. "And take Raoul with you. I'm sure he will be relieved to return to a soft feather bed after roughing it in the shack for the past two days."

Jacquelyn's delicately arched brows jackknifed. "You allow that flea-infested mutt to share your bed?" she questioned in astonishment. "How disgusting!"

Mace didn't dignify the question with an answer, nor did he fling a suitably nasty rejoinder at Hub. The two of them deserved each other, Mace mused sourly. By damned, Raoul was more faithful than either of these two so-called friends!

Hub was welcomed to that troublesome witch, Mace grumbled as he tore off his clothes in his room and plopped into the tub. Before long Hub would realize he wasn't man enough to handle Jake either. No man was. The only way to get along with that contrary woman was to give in to her. And once a man made such humbling concessions, that flightly minx would trample all over him. If Hub thought he could live his life with footprints on his spine, that was fine with Mace. As a matter of fact, Mace wasn't going to waste another thought on either of them!

Mace's muted growl shattered the dark silence when Raoul hopped upon the foot of the bed and turned in a tight circle. Once he had pounded down his nest, the mutt plopped down.

"The rug is yours and the bed is mine," Mace snapped harshly.

Raoul twitched his ears and stared at Mace's thunderous scowl. Graciously, Raoul granted his master a moment to reconsider his rash decision. Raoul was as fond of feather beds as the next man. He had no inclination to curl up on the cold floor when there was half a bed to utilize.

"¡Bajate, perro sucio!" Mace barked.

Offended by the fact that Mace had just referred to him as a mangy mutt, Raoul crawled off the bed and skulked to the rug. With a disappointed sigh, he sank down and closed his eyes.

Determined to sleep, Mace wormed beneath the quilts, searching for a comfortable position. But there was none. No matter which way he turned he landed on his bruised pride. Jacquelyn was flitting from one man to the next, the way she always had. Hub was actively pursuing Jake, even when he knew Mace was . . .

Mace was what? Emotionally involved? Physically attracted? Just exactly what was he when it came to that brown-eyed spitfire? He was in over his head, that's what he was! Mace had a strong aversion to marriage, but he couldn't release Jake to another man, not even his best friend.

"Women!" Mace muttered as he punched his pillow. "The whole lot of them are nothing but trouble."

Heaving a frustrated sigh, Mace attempted to clear his mind of cluttered thoughts. He was going to sleep instead of sulking the night away.

Two hours later he was still brooding, unable to extract thoughts of that sable-haired hellion from his head. Jacquelyn kept emerging from the shadows of his mind, tormenting him, refusing to grant him a moment's peace.

Rather than counting the customary sheep to fall asleep, Jacquelyn chose to list Mace's annoying faults (and the man was full of them!). She had been furious with him for insulting her in front of Hub, and she sorely resented his misplaced possessiveness. Jacquelyn was sick to death of being manipulated and ordered about by that billy goat of a man. Mace was attempting to run her life as if she were one of his servants. He tried to tell her where to go and when, who to see and what to do. Well, she had rebelled against the General when he resorted to that tactic during her childhood, and she would not tolerate it now.

Mace was putting her grandfather through undue stress by refusing to tell him Jake was safe from harm. He had even meddled into the Reids' affairs without anyone asking for his assistance. Who did Mace Gallagher think he was anyway? God himself?

Aggravated by her train of thought, Jake flung back the quilts and swung her legs over the edge of the bed. She was going home whether Mace thought she should or not! The General had a right to know where she was instead of worrying himself sick.

After tugging on her tattered garments, Jake aimed herself toward the terrace door. As she veered around the corner she collided with Mace's solid frame.

"Nocturnal prowling must be characteristic of your family," Mace said sarcastically. "You and Malcolm enjoy slinking around like creatures of the night."

"Why are you lurking outside my room? Did your dog hog the bed?" Jacquelyn sniped just as caustically.

Two dark brows formed a single line over Mace's glittering golden eyes. "Are you stealing off to Hub's room?" he hissed in question.

"That is none of your business," she answered.

"I'm making it my business. Hub is a decent man who believes all women are angels. But when you get through with him he'll be as cynical as I am." Mace stuck his face in hers to rap out his stern command. "Keep your distance from Hub. I don't want to see him hurt."

It took incredible willpower not to plant her fist in his scowling face. Jake didn't know why she restrained herself. Mace certainly had a punch coming. The domineering, overbearing tyrant!

"I happen to hold Hub in high regard," she growled between clenched teeth. "He seems infinitely more the gentleman than you are."

A roguish grin carved deep lines around his eyes and bracketed his sensuous mouth. Mace reached out to lower Jacquelyn's defiant chin a notch. "He is," he agreed softly. "And you, little nymph, are no lady and you never will be, even if Florence hauls you back to New Orleans to enroll you in another finishing school."

Jacquelyn hated it when Mace blessed her with that disarming smile and made her forget why she was annoyed with him. Oh, why couldn't she look upon Mace with the same harmless affection she felt for Hub? If only she could enjoy that warmth of companionship with Mace. Why did Mace have to be the one to stir these forbidden feelings that had no future? Why couldn't she accept Mace as the lost cause he was and bury these foolish notions of love?

"Jake . . ." Mace's velvety voice dragged her from her private conversation with herself. "If you want to tear a man to pieces on the inside, let it be me, not Hub."

Jake made the critical mistake of peering into those hypnotic amber eyes. She could feel the compelling attraction tugging at her heart. The luring aroma of Mace's cologne compelled her closer to his muscular frame, even when common sense advised her to retreat. A defeated sigh skipped from her lips when his sinewy arm stole around her waist. Her body caught fire and burned when he bent her into his hard contours. As if they belonged there, her arms migrated around his shoulders to toy with the thick raven hair at the nape of his neck. She could feel the accelerated thud of his heart pounding in rhythm with hers, and her defenses came tumbling down.

Just one more night, Jacquelyn whispered to herself. Ah, how many times had she told herself that? Since she found herself hopelessly in love with this cynical man, she had lived for each stolen moment of splendor. She had tried not to let her feelings show, tried to project a carefree image so Mace wouldn't know how much it hurt to be just another of his many conquests. But when Mace encircled her in those strong capable arms, the deeply embedded emotions gushed out and her foolish heart ruled her head.

It was as if she were plagued with a split personality. The strong side of her nature dominated her actions until she encountered this exasperating man who was the devil's own temptation. No matter how wrong it was to submit to her desires, it felt so right when she was with Mace. Their contrasting differences and their conflicting similarities fell away. Their petty arguments were forgotten when the old familiar spark leaped between them.

"I must be bewitched," Mace mused aloud. "I can never seen to get enough of you, Jake."

He could feel her sweet body beneath the threadbare garments, and his passion burned like a bonfire. Mace had only to close his eyes and he was transported to that mystical dimension of time he had enjoyed with this witch-angel. Yes, Mace knew he was courting trouble, that he was strengthening the fragile bond between them, but he couldn't help himself. He wanted her—wildly, passionately. Yet it frustrated him to admit it to himself. Jacquelyn had burrowed into his soul. She had become a part of him that time and determination couldn't erase.

Each time another man stood between him and this beguiling sorceress, Mace thrust himself in harm's way to protect his obsessive possession. And there was the rub, Mace mused as he took Jake's soft, responsive lips beneath his. He couldn't tolerate the thought of another man enjoying this sprite's unique brand of passion. She could thoroughly devastate a man, and Mace was too selfish to share the indescribable pleasure she offered.

"Mace, love me. . . ." Jacquelyn murmured as she pressed herself into his muscled flesh, absorbing his strength, his manly scent.

A deep skirl of laughter rumbled in his heaving chest as he led her into her dark room. Cupping her face in his hands, Mace displayed a rueful smile. "I doubt I could do anything besides make love to you, even if I tried," he admitted. "If I settled for simply tucking you in bed, I would reduce myself to a frustrated pile of ashes before I reached my own room." His smile evaporated as he stared straight into those fathomless brown eyes that

418

sparkled with moonbeams. "Raoul interrupted us this afternoon, but nothing is going to disturb us to-night. . . ."

The resonance of his quiet voice vibrated on Jac-quelyn's spine and she felt her bones turn limp. Oh, how she loved this man! Yes, she loved in vain, but there was no getting over Mace, no matter how many inspiring sermons she delivered to herself. She feared her emotions would reveal themselves in her adoring gaze, that Mace would know how she felt and become threatened by what he feared would be a clinging vine of a woman. But I won't make demands on him, she vowed faithfully. She would take what Mace could offer and accept the limitations of her love for him.

So you have finally reduced yourself to that shameless state, have you? her pride questioned indignantly. *Are you going to sacrifice your self-esteem to spend an uninterrupted night in this devil's arms? You know you'll only get hurt, just as you always have.*

Pride be damned, Jacquelyn thought as Mace's practiced hands swam over each sensitive inch of her body and set each nerve to quivering. She had responded shamelessly each time Mace touched her. When it came to this persuasive rogue she possessed not one iota of willpower. He had crumbled the barriers of her defenses long ago, and there was nothing left as a buffer between this charismatic man and her vulnerable emotions.

The last sediment of logic was swept away in the flood of sensations that tumbled over her. Moist kisses flitted over her eyelids and cheeks while his roaming hands reclaimed her as his possession. Pleasure trickled over her as his hands cruised across the sea of bare flesh. Jacquelyn was drifting with the current of desire, sailing toward that magical paradise that only lovers shared.

Torrents of pleasure crashed down upon her as Mace proved his power of her. Passion raged like a cloudburst.

Jacquelyn could endure no more of his sweet, maddening caresses. The feel of his sensuous lips and roving hands were no longer enough to satisfy the craving that had swelled out of proportion. Mace had created a monstrous need that he alone could appease. The pleasure was empty without the feel of his sinewy flesh molded tightly to hers. Only when they were one did Jacquelyn feel whole and alive.

Breathlessly, she reached out to bring his lips back to hers. Hungrily, she devoured the taste of him. Her body instinctively arched to ease the longing he had aroused. And when Mace held himself away from her, Jacquelyn swore she would die with aching. Her long lashes swept up to see his handsome face among the shadows. He was staring down at her as if he had never seen her before in his life.

Mace had taken great pains to insure Jacquelyn wanted him as fiercely and desperately as he wanted her. He had denied himself to insure that she experienced each wondrous sensation of lovemaking. He had given of himself to please her, to prove that he was and always would be a tender, caring lover. His unselfish consideration left him wondering if he hadn't allowed this sweet witch to tunnel too deeply into his heart. And when he paused to analyze the reason for his action, he made the mistake of staring into that lovely face.

Mace had contemplated similar thoughts before. But they had never been as vivid as they were now. He had allowed this sprite to get too close, to touch something deep inside him. And when he peered down at Jacquelyn just then, he swore her vision would haunt him all eternity. Her spellbinding eyes were misty with barely restrained passion. Her lips were moist from the kisses they had shared. Her cheeks flushed from the abrasiveness of his whiskers, ones he had failed to shave during his hasty bath. He had left his brand on her body, and yet the imprint she left on him went much deeper than the telltale signs of lovemaking. She had monopolized his thoughts for so long he couldn't remember what life was like before Jake came along. She had taken a part of him with her each time they made love. And bit by bit, he had become a part of her and she a part of him. They had become like two pieces of a puzzle that made no sense until they were one living, breathing essence.

The seconds ticked by and Jacquelyn longed to smooth away the frown that shaded Mace's bronzed face. Why was he staring at her with that indecipherable expression? Sweet mercy, if he turned away from her now, she feared her overworked heart would collapse in her chest.

"I want you," she whispered as her wandering hand glided down the taut tendons of his neck and chest. "I've never wanted another man the way I want you." Her voice was like the soft song of a siren. "Make the ache go away, Mace. . . ."

When she touched him Mace knew he was fighting a hopeless battle. And when her lips melted on his like rose petals he knew he could never refuse anything she requested of him.

His muscled body settled exactly over hers and the dam of self-restraint burst. Passion burned like a shooting star that blazed a fiery path across the heavens. His thoughts, his fears, fled the holocaust that raged out of control. Primal instinct drove him to her, but he could not seem to get close enough to ease the wild, intense craving, the insane hunger that gnawed at him, inside and out.

Mace feared he would crush Jacquelyn with the savagery of his embrace. He held her so tightly she couldn't possibly breathe. He took possession of her body, only to find he had become a prisoner of his own heart's desire. But before Mace could pursue that peculiar enigma, he felt the ineffable sensations of

421

pleasure crashing down on him like an avalanche of fire.

Sweet, satisfying pleasure engulfed him. The turmoil that hounded his emotions became a tranquil sea that carried him into tantalizing dreams. And again he surrendered to this bewitching beauty who had cast her spell upon him. Or at least he thought he had dreamed it all. . . . Mace couldn't swear to it. He had the lingering feeling that he had been awakened several times during the night to find Jacquelyn's gentle hands lifting him from the arms of sleep and setting him adrift in another arousing fantasy.

Part IV

Of all human passions love is the strongest, for it attacks simultaneously the head, the heart, the senses.

Chapter 23

The rattle of the door knob brought Mace awake with a start. His sleep-drugged gaze swung to Jacquelyn, who lay peacefully on her side. The drooping sheet exposed a generous amount of bare flesh. The split second before the door swung open, Mace whipped the quilt over Jake's shoulder, and then glared daggers at the intruder who had the audacity to come barging into Jacquelyn's room without announcing him or herself.

"You could have . . ." Mace growled when he saw Hub's brawny frame fill the entrance, ". . . knocked."

The sound of Mace's harsh voice brought Jacquelyn awake. Shoving the tangled tresses from her face, she glanced lethargically at Mace. Frowning bemusedly, she followed Mace's mutinous stare to see Hub swaggering toward her side of the bed.

With a humiliated shriek, Jake yanked the sheet over her head, and then mumbled several of the colorful curses she had heard pour from Mace's lips on occasion.

"What the sweet loving hell do you think you're doing?" Mace scowled at his friend. (Or at least he thought Hub was his friend. It was difficult to tell of late.) If Mace had had possession of his pistol, he would have seriously considered emptying it at the swarthy blond.

"Good morning, princess," Hub said cheerfully as he tugged the sheet from Jacquelyn's scarlet red face. Purposely, Hub ignored Mace's venomous growl. In fact, Hub refused to acknowledge Mace's presence in the guest room or in the bed at all!

With her face flushed from the base of her throat to her eyebrows, Jake mumbled a sheepish good morning. A shocked gasp exploded from her lips when Hub plopped down on her side of the bed as if he belonged there.

Mace would have shouted in furious protest if he could have located his swallowed tongue. Hub's outrageous behavior left Mace thunderstruck.

"I rounded up some suitable clothes to replace the disgusting rags Mace had you wearing," he informed her as he set the garments at the foot of the bed. With his nonchalant smile intact, Hub reached down to rearrange the renegade strands of hair that camouflaged Jake's beet-red cheeks. "After breakfast, I would like to escort you around the plantation. I have planned a picnic for the two of us this afternoon." His grin became even broader as he traced Jacquelyn's heart-shaped lips. "And later I intend to ask you to marry me. I thought perhaps you would appreciate the courtesy of being forewarned so you can give the proposal careful consideration."

Jacquelyn blinked like a disturbed owl. Her mouth kept opening and closing at irregular intervals. Had she heard Hub say what she thought he said? "You . . . you would propose . . . knowing . . . I . . ." Her astounded gaze swung to Mace and then circled back to Hub. "With him?" she questioned in a stuttering croak.

"I consider myself a reasonable man," Hub proclaimed proudly. "I will not come to you pure and inexperienced. Nor do I hold with double standards. If we were to marry—and I could list a dozen reasons why the match would benefit both of us," he added offhandedly.

"I would let bygones be bygones. Our past mistakes would be inconsequential. It is our future together that interests me most, Jacquelyn."

Hub straightened himself on the edge of the bed and looked her squarely in the eyes, now as wide as dinner plates. "I know we have just begun to get acquainted, but already I admire your spirit and keen wit. I also think I love you."

Jacquelyn stared at Hub as if he had tree limbs sprouting from his ears.

Mace grumbled several disrespectful epithets half-aloud before expelling his snide rejoinder. "You think you love every female of the species . . . and a few of that gender which should have been categorized with the canines!"

Again Mace was treated as though he weren't there at all. Hub's gaze never wavered from Jacquelyn's astonished face. She had imagined herself being proposed to in her whimsical dreams. And she had heard a variety of propositions from men—some on bended knee, a few from beneath her window as well as other appropriate locations. But never in her worst nightmare had she envisioned a suitor proposing to her while she lay abed with another man! Hub was too good to be true. He was willing to overlook her indiscretions, even when he had walked in on one!

"I'll have to think it over, Hub," she murmured, still blushing up to the roots of her hair.

"Think it over?" Mace parroted in disbelief. "You can't be serious!"

Jacquelyn's head swiveled around to glare at Mace's outraged expression. "I have never been more serious in my life," she assured him tartly.

"That's what you said when you decided to marry Jon Mason," Mace snorted sarcastically.

"Hub is more understanding and forgiving than any

427

man I have ever met," she argued. "He is also delightful company, and we have yet to disagree on anything. I happen to think Hub and I would be very compatible. He has graciously consented to accept me as I am. No woman could ask for more."

"This is absurd!" Mace hooted.

Jake puffed up with so much indignation she would have popped the buttons off her oversized shirt had she been wearing it. "What is absurd is that you are trying to dictate to me again," she fumed at him, eyes blazing. "For your information, I am perfectly capable of making my own decisions. I decided to marry Jon, and I would have if he hadn't had the personality of a wet blanket. And if I decide to marry Hub, then I shall!" Her voice was becoming higher and louder by the second. "Hub is the kind of man who would make a woman a fine husband. He is considerate and caring and he doesn't compare marriage to a prison sentence, like some people I know!"

Mace opened his mouth to unleash the half-dozen remarks that stampeded to the tip of his tongue, but Hub spoke before he could say one word.

"I appreciate the compliments, Jacquelyn," Hub murmured affectionately. "I will be the luckiest man in Texas if you decide to accept my proposal." Rising, Hub graced her with an adoring smile. "Join me downstairs for breakfast and later we will enjoy a morning ride." His eyelid dropped into a wink. "I might even challenge you to a horse race. Mace has a stable brimming with swift steeds that are chomping at the bit to stretch their legs."

Jacquelyn returned his charming smile. "I'd like that."

"I rather thought you would," Hub purred as he folded himself at the waist and pressed a parting kiss to her tempting lips.

As Hub strolled out the door, Mace rattled off every curse word in his vocabulary and then coined a few new phrases that were colorful combinations of Spanish and English. "Damnit, Jake, you can't marry Hub. The man has a perpetual roving eye. He has fallen in love with every woman he's ever met and that is a fact!"

Hastily, Jacquelyn snatched up the garments Hub brought for her and wrestled into them. "I have often heard it said that reformed rakes make the best husbands," she parried in a rapier-sharp voice. "Hub sounds as if he is ready for a change in his life, and maybe I am too!"

"And what is that supposed to mean?" Mace fired the words like a volley of bullets.

Jacquelyn fastened the last button on her tight-fitting blouse, one that exposed what lay so temptingly beneath it. "It means I have played your harlot for the last time," she all but shouted at him. "The idea of marriage is not as distasteful as it once was to me. I am tired of courtship rituals and pretended pleasantries. I am sick of coquettish games, of fending off unwanted suitors who leave me cold and unmoved."

Jacquelyn inhaled a sharp breath and plunged on before Mace could squeeze a word in edgewise. "And most of all I'm tired of feeling something for a man who has no respect or regard for what I want and need. You wanted my body but you had no interest in the problems and feelings attached to it." Her chin tilted to that indignant angle Mace had come to recognize at a glance. "You can have your shallow affairs, but I want something permanent and lasting. I'm ready for a change, and if I do decide to love and honor Hub MacIntosh, then that is exactly what I'm going to do!"

After delivering her booming soliloquy, Jacquelyn stomped over to the bureau to run a brush through her wild hair. Flinging Mace a frosty glare that could have caused the onset of another Ice Age, she stamped out the door. When the arctic winds that followed in her wake settled to the floor, Mace showed a wordless scowl. Why was he putting up such a fuss? He wanted Jake out of his life, didn't he? So what if Hub couldn't make Jake happy? That wasn't Mace's problem. In two months, her stubborn defiance would wear away and she would realize she had made a drastic mistake. She would come crying to Mace, asking him to gently break the news to Hub so she wouldn't hurt him worse than she already had.

Growling, Mace paced the confines of the room, cursing Jacquelyn with every step he took. What was that rubbish about her being his harlot? Mace exploded in a thunderous snort. Jake had made Mace her whore. She flitted from one engagement to another, employing Mace as a spring board. Damnit, for a woman who notoriously refused the attentions of men, Jake certainly had changed since she returned to Texas. While she was in New Orleans, her suitors couldn't have coerced her into marriage without a shotgun. But in the last month she had accepted two proposals. That female was unstable, that was what she was! How could any man satisfy her when she didn't even know what she wanted or needed?

"To hell with the both of them," Mace muttered as he stormed into the hall and down the steps. His irascible mood blackened when he veered into the dining room to hear Jake's lighthearted laughter mingling with Hub's throaty chuckle.

Just look at the two of them, Mace thought resentfully. There were serious arrangements to be made and a mystery to be solved, and they were behaving as if they didn't have a care in the world. Neither of them seemed to recall that Jake's life was still in danger while Malcolm was running around loose. And what were they doing? Planning a confounded picnic!

When Jake and Hub strode outside, hand in hand, Mace aimed himself toward the study to drink his breakfast. Between sips, he monitored the chummy couple's progress to the stables, incensed that Hub had looped his arm over Jacquelyn's shoulder, the very one Mace had stitched back together! Jacquelyn didn't remove Hub's arm, damn her. No, double damn her, Mace amended. That fickle woman! Lord, he itched to strangle the life out of her.

While Jacquelyn was fastening the girth of the saddle, Hub strode up behind her. Patting the belly of the palomino mare she had selected to ride, Jacquelyn glanced back at her companion. The solemn expression on Hub's blond features drew her curious frown.

"Is something amiss?"

"With me?" Hub chuckled ruefully. "No, but I wonder if something might be amiss with you." Tenderly he cupped her chin in his callused hand, forcing her to meet his probing gaze. "I intend to stand by my commitment to you. I believe we could be good together and good for each other." Hub released a quiet sigh. "But first I have to know if you honestly love Mace. I don't want to have my best friend's image standing between us each time I touch you."

Jacquelyn's eyes dropped like a kite plunging to the ground without a breath of wind to sustain it.

"Jake," Hub persisted. "Look me in the eye and tell me you aren't in love with that billy goat of a man who wouldn't recognize love if it marched up and sat down on top of him."

"I can't," Jacquelyn choked out. It suddenly struck her that she had run to Jon Mason in desperation and that she was now considering Hub as her salvation. But she hadn't truly run to either man, but rather had tried to run *away* from the one man who had taken a firm hold on her heart. She could never make any man a decent wife while her heart was being held hostage by that golden-eyed devil.

Hub forced her face upward and smiled compassionately at the mist of tears that clouded her eyes. "I didn't really think you could, not if you were honest with both of us." Grasping her hand, Hub led her to the cotton storeroom in the back of the barn. The fluffy, improvised mattress made a soft lounge chair, she stared at the small niche that was carpeted in white—remnants of Mace's bumper cotton crop.

"Hub, I appreciate what you did and I—"

Jacquelyn was cut off by Hub's firm, but gentle voice. "Don't talk, honey. Just listen," he insisted. "I have known Mace for over a decade. He is one of the most competent and dependable men I've ever met. The policy of the Texas Rangers is to travel in pairs. Mace and I were introduced when we were assigned to ride together on scores of dangerous missions. Through the years we've tracked Comanche war parties, trailed a raft of outlaws, and run down a sheriff who was as crooked as a winding mountain pass in Big Bend Country."

Hub scooped up several bolls of cotton and squeezed them in his fist. "For over two years Mace, Raoul, and I traveled on reconnaissance missions for the Gen'ral's troops." A low chuckle echoed around the storage room. "The old man didn't appreciate our lack of military discipline, but when he wanted a job done, he went straight to Mace. Oftentimes, the Gen'ral asked the impossible. Sometimes I think he made the requests expecting us to fail, so he could bring us down a notch or two."

The wry smile faded from Hub's bronzed features. "After one of our daredevil missions that nearly cost all three of us our lives, we stopped in a dusty little Mexican town to ease our nerves in a bottle of whiskey. Even Raoul indulged in a little brew to calm his nerves. Mace got drunk and started pouring out his life story. To

432

this day, I'm not sure he remembers telling me about his past. But that night he unfolded the bone-chilling tale from his childhood."

Hub glanced at Jake, who would have been on the edge of her seat if she had been sitting on one. "I think you will better understand Mace after I convey the story to you. Then you'll know why he is so elusive when it comes to commitments and marriage. The fact is, Mace cares very deeply for you, Jake."

"Perhaps you should be having this conversation with Mace. I don't think he knows it," she grumbled resentfully. "If he gives a whit about me he has an odd way of showing it."

"The more Mace cares for you the harder he fights the feelings," Hub told her frankly. "Mace is as capable as two good men, but he is deathly afraid of falling in love. I think he's afraid he'll care too much. And in his estimation, that would be disastrous."

Hub tossed the clump of cotton across the room and twisted to peer directly at Jacquelyn. "Mace came from a well-to-do family in Louisiana. His grandparents contracted the marriage between his mother and father to insure a proper match. Mace's mother was only sixteen years old when she was given to a man more than twice her age. Lawrence Gallagher doted on his bride, but she had been infatuated with a young man of less wealth before she was forced to wed. Mace's father tried to win the girl's love. In fact, he became obsessed with making her forget the young upstart. When Mace was born, his mother set aside her heart's longing to raise her son. Lawrence believed he had finally succeeded in winning his wife's love. But when Mace was only twelve years old, he and his father were hunting in the woods near their estate. They interrupted his mother and her lover—the same man who had never been cured of wanting Lawrence's wife and had been secretly seeing her

433

for years."

Jacquelyn's gaze dropped to study the fluffy cotton beneath her hand. She could understand that Mace was upset by what he had seen. When she learned the truth about her mother and lover, it had hurt to imagine the agony her father endured. But Jake had not become cynical of love and marriage because of it. Obviously, Mace used the incident as an excuse to avoid marriage.

"Granted, the incident might have left scars, but I don't see why—"

"You'll see why when I'm finished," Hub interjected, flashing her a silencing frown. "Lawrence Gallagher fell into a mad fit when he found his wife in the arms of another man. He began spouting accusations and curses at them. The younger man reacted by declaring that Mace was his son and that he wanted to claim his child and the only woman he had ever loved.

"Lawrence went wild with jealous fury and humiliation. He raved like a maniac as he yanked his rifle from its sling and opened fire. Not only was Mace forced to watch his mother and her lover shot down in cold blood, but he found himself a victim of Lawrence's insane jealousy and bloody vengeance. Mace tried to flee when his father turned on him. The scar on his ribs was caused by the rifle shot and the subsequent fall that laid him open. When Lawrence came back to his senses and realized what he had done, he grabbed his pistol and put it to his head. Within a few terrifying minutes three people lay dead or dying and Mace was seriously wounded."

Hub heaved a sigh and glanced at Jacquelyn, who had turned as white as the cotton. "Mace is afraid he inherited his father's streak of insane jealousy. He fears he might react the same way if he found himself betrayed by the woman he loved more than life."

A muddled frown clung to Jacquelyn's brow. "I thought you said Lawrence wasn't his real father. How

434

could Mace possibly inherit such violent tendencies?"

"Before Mace's mother died she assured her son that he was a Gallagher and that her lover had only made that declaration to force Lawrence to let her go. She died begging Mace's forgiveness without hearing his answer." Hub offered Jake a tender smile. "Mace will never commit himself to love unless he is sure beyond all doubt that the woman he wants would forsake all others to be true to him. He lives with a nightmare that fate might repeat itself. It will take some coaxing to get that cynical man to take that first difficult step toward marriage."

Jacquelyn stared skeptically at Hub. "It seems the die is cast. Mace Gallagher wouldn't marry for love or money, not if his family's tragedy made such a lasting impression on him."

Hub checked his timepiece and then shoved it back into his pocket. An ornery smile pursed his lips. "If I know Mace, he is wondering what is keeping us so long in the barn. And if he loves you as much as I think he does, he'll be coming to investigate very soon."

"I don't think you know Mace as well as you think you do," Jacquelyn scoffed cynically.

"Wanna bet?" Hub asked with a challenging smile. "I'll wager a ten-dollar gold piece that Mace would pop his cork if he came looking for us and found us entwined in each other's arms."

"I'll take that bet. Mace doesn't care enough to come investigate," she declared with great conviction.

Wearing a rakish grin, Hub slipped his arm around Jacquelyn's trim waist and drew her curvaceous body against his. "I've maneuvered myself into a no-lose situation, princess," he assured her huskily.

His blue eyes dipped to the luscious curve of her lips, fully understanding why Mace had been unable to resist this woman's mystical lure. His body sizzled from its close contact with hers. And even though Jacquelyn timidly returned his kiss, Hub was sure he was going to enjoy this tête-à-tête before he paid the price for dallying with the lively firebrand Mace couldn't put from his mind.

A gutteral growl burst from Mace's lips as he stood sentinel watch at the study window. How long did it take to saddle two horses, for Chrissake? Frustrated, Mace threw down another drink and swore under his breath. That woman had reduced him to this lowly state of drinking and cursing. It was barely ten o'clock in the morning and he had already guzzled three drinks and sworn two blue streaks.

Blast it, if it took twenty minutes to fetch their horses, Mace hated to hazard a guess as to how long their picnic would last. They hadn't even made it out of the barn yet! What could be taking them so long? That question was quick to attach itself to a conjecture, and Mace expelled a few more choice words.

Glancing down at Raoul who had treated himself to a luxurious night's sleep on the master bed, Mace gruffly ordered the mutt to accompany him to the barn. When Mace spotted the two half-saddled horses that had been abandoned, he cursed all over again.

"Go find Hub," Mace demanded brusquely.

Raoul sniffed the straw beneath his feet and then trotted toward the back of the barn. Mace was one step behind the shaggy mongrel. When Raoul paused in front of the storeroom, Mace heard the quiet giggles form behind the door. His barely restrained temper exploded like a keg of gunpowder. As the door yielded to Mace's furious kick, Hub glanced over his shoulder to note the fuming glower that was stamped on Mace's features. He looked positively dangerous standing there with his mouth curled in a malicious sneer, his eyes flaming like hot lava.

The sight of Hub and Jake sprawled in the cotton, arms and legs entangled, was too much. Mace came apart at the seams.

Before Hub could utter the witty remark he had formulated for this occasion, Mace jerked him up by the front of the shirt and delivered a brain-scrambling blow that very nearly knocked Hub's head from his shoulders and set Raoul to barking in confusion. In all the years Raoul had scouted with Mace and Hub they had always been on the same side of the battle. Raoul didn't know who he should attack. And so he just stood there yelping while Jacquelyn screeched in outrage.

"Have you lost what little sense you were born with?" she growled at Mace. When Mace's victim slid down the wall and collapsed on the mattress of cotton, Jacquelyn carefully inspected the swollen side of Hub's face, the one that was pulsating with color. "If this is the way you treat your friends I shudder to think what you would do to your mortal enemies. . . ."

The thought of what Jacquelyn had learned about Lawrence Gallagher's violent temper caused her to stare dumbfoundedly at Hub, who cast her a now-you-are-beginning-to-understand-what-I-meant glance.

"You are not marrying that human octopus!" Mace roared, his chest heaving with every angry breath he took. "And you are not employing my barn for your love nest!"

Jacquelyn bounded to her feet to face Mace's venomous sneer. Although Mace had enough air in his lungs to bellow over Raoul's incessant howling, Jacquelyn did not. Her annoyed gaze dropped to the wolf-dog. "Sit down and shut up, Raoul."

When the dog countered by displaying his fangs, Hub repeated Jacquelyn's command in Spanish. But he did so with great care, fearing his loosened teeth would fall out if he dared open his mouth too wide. Damn, Mace's fist was as potent as a mule's kick. That's an appropriate comparison, Hub decided as he propped his arm over Raoul's bristled back. Mace had most certainly been behaving like an ass of late.

After flicking the clinging cotton from her shirt, Jake squared her shoulders. Her flashing brown eyes clashed with flaming gold. "Now, what is it you want that warranted this rude interruption?"

Mace's breath came out in a rush. "I want to hear you say you love me and not that blond-haired octopus!" he burst out without thinking.

"I said I loved you once and you didn't want to hear it. I'm not about to repeat that confession now," she hissed at him.

A wry grin dangled from the corner of Hub's mouth, the side Mace hadn't severely bruised with his fist. "Will you get this over with, Mace? Quit dragging your damned feet. Tell Jake you love her so she can tell you she loves you back."

"Stop trying to put words in my mouth," Mace grumbled without taking his eyes off Jacquelyn's animated features.

"The words are already there," Hub contended. "All I'm asking you to do is spit them out. This is your last chance, friend." Hub was pushing Mace to the very limits of his self-restraint, and he wasn't letting up until Mace came to terms with his emotions. "If you don't tell her how you feel about her now, I'm going to marry her, even if she can never love me the way she loves you." The smile evaporated from his swollen lips. "You know what can happen if a woman marries the wrong man. The only way to prevent disaster is by insuring she weds the right man the first time around."

The subtle comment caused Mace to swivel his head toward Hub, who was using Raoul as a prop. "You know?" he asked, bewildered. "How?"

438

"You told me one night over three bottles of whiskey," Hub informed him somberly. "And I told Jacquelyn."

Jacquelyn watched the conflicting emotions chase each other across Mace's stony features. He looked angry, frustrated, tormented, and even a little relieved.

"I'm sorry you were forced to endure such a horrible tragedy," she murmured compassionately. "I know you don't wish to embroil yourself in anything remotely close to marriage."

Her thick lashes fluttered down to caress her cheeks. Willfully, Jacquelyn drew a steadying breath. She well remembered the advice Hub had offered her and this was the moment of reckoning. Only when Mace was absolutely sure she loved him beyond all else would he dare confess his true feelings for her—if indeed there were any. She was taking a terrible risk by baring her heart a second time. But it was now or never, Jacquelyn realized.

"I do love you, Mace," she told him, her voice quivering with genuine emotion. "Perhaps it takes some women a great deal of time to sort out their feelings. I have always known what I wanted in a man, but I could never find the perfect combination in one individual . . . until you came along." Her gaze lifted to survey his face, allowing him to decipher the sentiment in her eyes. "The first time I said I loved you it hurt to know you didn't feel the same way about me. And to protect my wounded pride, I pretended it didn't matter that you said nothing in return."

Still Mace voiced no comment. He simply stood there gaping at her as if there were two heads resting on her shoulders. Nervously, Jacquelyn wrung her hands and plunged on. "I agreed to marry Jon, hoping I would get over wanting you when I was another man's wife. But I realized I couldn't settle for Jon and still live with my conscience. It wouldn't have been fair to either of us."

Her misty brown eyes swung to Hub and she graced him with a remorseful smile. "Hub was willing to wed me if I could convince him you wouldn't always stand between us, that I could allow my fondness for him to blossom and grow into love. But I couldn't lie to Hub any more than I could lie to myself." Hesitantly, Jake returned her attention to Mace. "The simple truth is I don't think I'll ever truly get over loving you, Mace Gallagher, but neither will I make demands that you cannot freely accept."

Jacquelyn rather thought she deserved a medal of valor for holding her chin high for as long as she did. But her self-control began to crumble when Mace refused to speak. He just continued to stand there like a stick of furniture.

Ducking her head, Jacquelyn sidestepped and dashed out the door. She had to find a place to fall apart, some place where Mace couldn't see her reduce herself to heart-wretching sobs.

"Jake . . ." Mace's husky voice caused her to break stride, but she refused to stop or look back for fear she would burst into humiliated tears.

"Jake, I . . ." Mace wrestled with the words he had never uttered to a woman before in his life. He swore he would strangle on them before he could choke them out. "Jake . . . *Te Quiero.*"

Hub rolled his eyes in disgust. "You'll have to do better than that. You know she doesn't understand Spanish," he snorted. "How can it be so hard to utter three words in plain English!"

"Because I haven't said them to every female I've met, the way you have," Mace exploded in exasperation as Jacquelyn disappeared from sight. "In fact I've never said them at all. Damnit, it's like speaking a foreign tongue!"

A heavy sigh tumbled from Hub's bruised lips. "Well,

she's gone now, you damned fool," he scowled. "I hope you're proud of yourself. How would you like to be standing in her boots? She poured out her heart and you had the sensitivity of a tree stump."

"I'm no good at this sort of thing," Mace muttered sourly.

Grumbling, Hub struggled to his feet and stomped out the door. "Well, at least I can provide a shoulder for Jake to cry on and she's going to need it. Right now she's probably wishing Malcolm had disposed of her."

When Hub strode into the stable, Jake and her horse were nowhere to be seen. Emitting a curse, Hub hurriedly stuffed the bridle in his mount's mouth. Before he could swing into the saddle, Mace grabbed him by the shoulder and moved him bodily out of the way.

"Now what do you intend to do?" Hub sniffed as he watched Mace hop onto the steed's back. "Track her down to see if you can possibly make her feel worse than she already does?"

"No, damnit, I'm going to tell her I love her!" Mace snapped, and then blinked in surprise when his own words rebounded off the walls and came at him from all directions.

A triumphant smile stretched across the uninjured side of Hub's mouth. "Do you want me to come along and interpret in case you lose your nerve?" he teased unmercifully.

Finally, Mace managed a smile and his shoulders slumped. "No thanks, *amigo*. I think I can handle it from here."

Hub wagged a lean finger in Mace's face. "You better not botch it up this time or I'll return that punch you delivered," he threatened.

As Mace thundered off, Hub reached down to pat Raoul's broad head. For Mace to openly admit his affection for that lively sprite was going to be worse than tearing off an arm, Hub predicted. Well, at least Jacquelyn would be assured this was Mace's first time. If Mace managed to force out the words that were locked in his heart, it would most definitely be the first time his vocal chords had put those deeply embedded emotions into speech!

Chapter 24

As if the Evil One himself were in hot pursuit,
Jacquelyn thundered across the sprawling meadow and
plunged into the thicket of trees. Tears flooded her eyes,
forcing her to give the steed his head, hoping he would
guard his steps. Jacquelyn couldn't see where she was
going and she really didn't care where she wound up. She
knew it was difficult for Mace to overlook the tormenting
nightmare that stained his every thought. He had lived
with his secretive fears for two decades. Did she expect
her soft confession to work miracles? And maybe it
wasn't even love that inspired Mace's possessiveness.
Maybe Hub's speculations were wrong. Maybe Mace
really didn't care for her at all. And if he didn't, she had
made a fool of herself again.

The thought provoked Jacquelyn to cry even harder.
The tears kept pouring out like a cloudburst. Yanking on
the reins, Jacquelyn vaulted to the ground to cry without
the horse's jerky canter to jostle the sobs out of her.
Covering her face with her hands, Jacquelyn permitted
the frustrated emotion to fall into her hands.

Damnit, she wanted to go home and lock herself in her
room, to put a safe distance between herself and that
raven-haired devil. But she was in no condition to

confront Malcolm, if he did indeed have evil designs on her. Neither could she face the General or Florence without falling apart before their eyes.

While Jacquelyn was treating herself to a good cry, Mace was following the sounds that wafted their way from the underbrush. Quietly, he swung from his mount and trailed the sobs to their source. There, amid the trees, stood Jacquelyn. Her tangled hair sprayed wildly about her face. Her shapely body shuddered as if it had been besieged by an earthquake.

Lord, Mace had no idea a mere wisp of a woman had so much water in her! The sight of this spirited sprite crying convulsively tore Mace's heart in two. He had never seen Jake fall completely apart. That night at the shack she had come close to hysterics, but it was nothing compared to this!

With the silence of a stalking cat, Mace stepped into the narrow clearing. "Jake, I'm sorry," he murmured apologetically.

Her back stiffened in humiliation. "Go away," she railed as she sought a tree to lean against.

"I can't," Mace declared. "I've tried to leave you alone since I found myself attracted to you. But the strings to my heart won't stretch very far. I keep rolling back to you like a damned yo-yo!" He raked his fingers through his hair and then dropped his hand in frustration.

When Jacquelyn darted toward another tree, Mace pounced. His arms slid around her hips and he braced her struggling body against his unyielding frame. With his free hand, Mace tilted her puffy face to his. "The very fact that I hit Hub convinces me that I am just like my father," he insisted. "He was fiercely protective of that which he held dear. And when my father realized he had lost his precious treasure, it drove him over the brink to insanity." Mace heaved a ragged sigh. "I almost hated you when I watched you flit from one man to another.

And jealous though I was, I couldn't turn to another woman to nurse my wounded pride."

Mace met her teary gaze, frustrated that he couldn't put his exact thoughts into words. "I know how strong-willed and independent you are, how defiant you become when a man attempts to set down rules for you to follow. But I couldn't tolerate watching you flirt with another man if you were my wife. A marriage between us would have to be on my terms. You would have to conform to the boundaries of wedlock. I would be jealous, possessive, and unforgiving." Mace expelled a harsh breath. "Damnit, Jake, it would have to be all or nothing!"

Jacquelyn muffled a sniff, wiped her eyes, and stared into the ruggedly handsome face of the man who formed the boundaries of her world. "Are you proposing or reading me the riot act?" she wanted to know, mustering the semblance of a smile.

"Both," Mace grumbled. "I want to be all you ever need. I want you to be satisfied with what I can give you. I want to be the most important thing in your life."

My, but he was demanding and domineering, Jacquelyn reminded herself. Well, if he was laying down the law, she had a few regulations of her own that must be observed. "And if I were ever to consent to become your wife, I would not wish to wonder if you were being faithful to me while you were flitting between here and Galveston or when I grow round with your child. I would want to be assured that you loved me above all others, that you respected my opinions, that you regarded me as your equal, not your obedient slave." Her smile grew more impish as she looped her arms around his neck to toy with his wavy black hair. "And most importantly, I would expect you to find Raoul a bed of his own, because the one we would share each night of each year of our life together would not leave room for an extra body. I would be very demanding of you, and I would not wish an audience when I was expressing my love for you in all the arousing ways you've taught me."

The strained lines that bracketed Mace's mouth relaxed into a rakish smile. "Raoul is as good as gone," he murmured as his lips whispered over hers. "I vow to honor your demands if you promise to respect mine. . . . Will you marry me, Jake?"

Slowly, Jacquelyn withdrew from what had every indication of becoming a passionate embrace. "As much as I would love to become your wife, as eager as I am to honor my commitment to love and cherish you until the end of my days, I cannot accept your proposal."

Mace felt as if he had been punched in the midsection. He had never even considered marriage to another woman. He had never even discussed such a permanent relationship with another female. The one time in his life he had dared to step so far out on a limb, he found it sawed off behind him. It was damned frustrating to be rejected!

"Why the hell not?" he snapped irritably. "You know I can provide for you in the manner to which you have grown accustomed. I demanded your fidelity, but I made no stipulations about restricting your wild spirit. Damnation, Jake, I have no intention of stifling you. Indeed, your freedom would be limited only when it pertains to observing a respectable distance between yourself and other men! Is that asking so much?"

Jacquelyn displayed a rueful smile. "Living in the lap of luxury is the least of my concerns. Shunning other men would not be difficult when my heart belongs to you. . . ."

"Then what the blazes is keeping you from saying yes?" Mace demanded impatiently.

Her dark eyes locked with those rippling pools of gold. "I can't marry you unless I know you love me in all the soul-consuming ways I love you. You must not only display your affection every day of our life together, but I have to hear you say you care . . . and with a great deal of conviction." Her chin tilted to that stubborn angle Mace had come to know all too well. "I want to hear the words, Mace."

Mace inhaled a deep breath and stared straight into those big brown eyes that could melt his heart and leave it dripping on his ribs. "I love you, Jake."

A frown knitted Jacquelyn's brow. She was absolutely certain Mace had never linked those three words together in a phrase before this particular moment. They sounded stilted, as if he were speaking a foreign tongue that was unfamiliar to him.

Her arms glided up his muscled chest and her body pressed familiarly to his. A mischievous sparkle danced in her eyes as she peered up into his bronzed features. "Say it again," she encouraged. "And this time . . . with feeling . . ."

Mace felt his knees buckle beneath him when he stared into Jacquelyn's lovely face, memorizing each enchanting feature. This time he repeated the words in a soft whisper that was sweet music to her ears. "I do love you, *nina* . . . with all my heart . . ."

There, he had said the words—twice as a matter of fact. But to Mace's amazement, his private thoughts and emotions poured out as if the door that had been locked for decades had been thrown open to release the flood of feelings deep inside him.

"The moment you burst into my suite in Galveston, looking like a wild, ruffled bird, I was bewitched. The night you snatched my pistol to satisfy your vengeance on your assailants, I was intrigued by your undaunted spirit." His voice dropped to a husky caress as his hands molded themselves to her curvaceous contours. "And that morning during the storm, I discovered the incredibly passionate woman beneath that fiery ex-

447

terior." Soft laughter tickled her senses as Mace traced the delicate line of her jaw. "Do you know, I first realized I was falling in love with you when I watched you take that sniper's bullet in the shoulder."

Jacquelyn blinked, bewildered, and Mace chuckled. "I know it sounds crazy and not the least bit romantic," he admitted. "You shrugged it off so carelessly, but I felt as if I were the one who had been wounded. Seeing you injured left my soul to bleed. It scared the hell out of me, knowing I had never experienced such a sensation before, even in battle. I would have sooner taken the bullet than watch that living fire dwindle in your eyes. I didn't want to care so deeply. I didn't want to risk the agony my father experienced. I couldn't bear to love a woman who couldn't devote herself to me."

Mace's index finger lifted to reverently track each flawless feature of her face. "Men are naturally attracted to your beauty and your dynamic spirit. I've watched them swarm around you for almost two months. You are accustomed to their attention, but I love you too much to share you with another man. I couldn't bear to lose you."

Jacquelyn could have sworn she saw his mouth quiver before he drew her possessively against him.

"I will dare to love only once in my life, Jake. I'm entrusting my heart to you until the end of time. It's a fragile, precious gift that I have offered to no other woman. It is yours . . . because I can't help loving you . . ." His lips slanted over hers and Mace felt the waves of emotions splashing over him, carrying him away from his fears and concerns.

When his mouth worshipped hers in the tenderest of kisses, Jacquelyn was certain she would burst with sheer happiness. Mace Gallagher had finally said he loved her! He had put those difficult words into speech and she knew he meant it with all his heart. Her arms tightened around him as if she meant to squeeze the stuffing out of him. Eagerly, she returned his kiss, transforming gentle love into blazing passion. She ached to convey her emotions in whispered words as well as offering the physical expression of her love for him.

Jacquelyn didn't care that their bed would be a nest of fallen leaves. It didn't matter where they were, only that they were of one heart and soul. This sometimes exasperating, this bold and yet cautious man loved her as thoroughly and completely as she loved him. They needed no mansion, no abundant wealth, not when Mace satisfied the one emptiness in her life, not when he became her answer to her quest for everlasting love. Mace was the personification of her hopes and dreams. She looked into his golden eyes and saw the mystical combination of the sun, moon, and stars. She touched him and life blossomed into boundless dimensions. Here was the essence of her being, her source of inspiration, her heart's desire. When she was in Mace's sinewy arms, the sun shone twice as bright. Jacquelyn was whole and alive and hopelessly in love!

A soft sigh tripped from her lips as she returned Mace's adoring caresses, touch for touch. He weaved a tapestry of pleasure around her, and she around him. And from within that silken cocoon, a majestic monarch of love unfolded its petal-soft wings to take flight. Uplifted by a breath of wind, it fluttered and glided to light upon each of their emotions. Ineffable sensations unfurled when touched by love's treasured kiss. And as each tender emotion unveiled itself, Mace and Jacquelyn murmured soft confessions of love. It was a wild and yet precious joining of body and soul, a perfect union of masculine strength and feminine tenderness, the unique combination of passion embroidered with love.

Jacquelyn reveled in the splendor that sprinkled over her. It was as if a pitcher of twinkling stars poured forth to bathe her flesh with warmth, as if a rainbow of sunshine caressed her skin and touched her soul. Passion had never been so fulfilling until it was offered with the whispered utterances of love.

When the delicious spell that had cost Mace most of his strength began to ebb, he braced his arms on either side of Jacquelyn and glanced down into her flushed face, watching her dark eyes shimmer up at him with all the wondrous emotions that swirled inside him. Confessing his affection had been the most difficult task he had ever undertaken. But once he bared his heart and overcame his reluctance, the words wouldn't stop. He seemed to be compensating for the scores of times he'd felt his love for this saucy minx engulfing him and had refused to admit his feelings to her and to himself.

"Lord, how I love you, my wild, sweet nymph," he breathed in awe. His hands splayed across the lustrous cape of golden-brown hair that cascaded across the grass. "Earlier I thought it would kill me to speak those words, and now they tumble from my tongue in limitless supply."

A radiant smile to rival the sun blossomed on her enchanting features. Her long nails raked across the whipcord muscles of his back, playfully stroking this lion of a man. "I'll never grow tired of hearing the words, Mace," she softly assured him. "I want loving me to come easy for you. I want it to be as natural as breathing."

A deep skirl of laughter echoed in his chest and vibrated across Jacquelyn's flesh. "Loving you was always easy. Saying so was the agonizing part. When a man has been as cautious and cynical as I have been, words don't come without a struggle. But now they fall like rain, and I'm left to wonder if I'll ever be able to contain them, even amid a crowd."

Mischief flared up in her eyes and tugged at the corners of her mouth. "I won't complain if you shout

450

them in a crowd, so long as you aim the words in my direction. I should hate for some other female to intercept them."

"The words will always find their intended mark." Mace laughed as he helped himself to another honeyed kiss. Reluctantly, Mace hoisted himself to his feet and drew Jacquelyn up beside him. "It's time we relieved the Gen'ral's worst fears and asked his permission to marry." Mace tossed Jacquelyn her clothes and hurriedly stepped into his breeches. "I hope you won't fuss over a lengthy engagement and a gigantic wedding. I haven't the patience. I will resent every day you are forced to remain under the Gen'ral's roof instead of mine."

"I think you will find me to be very sensible," Jacquelyn proclaimed as she shrugged on her shirt. "Tonight wouldn't be soon enough to please me, and I would consider a handful of friends at the ceremony to be a crowd."

Golden eyes glistened in rakish anticipation as he mapped Jacquelyn's tantalizing figure. "No lengthy reception either. I will be eager to share . . . er . . . a long, interrupted conversation with you in the privacy of our room . . ."

His provocative smile and his suggestive tone of his voice sent a raft of goose bumps sailing across her skin. "I will be counting the moments. . . ."

Tonight! The words seared across Mace's brain. Hell's bells, he had almost forgotten about the ransom note. They couldn't wed until they had learned who sent the letter, until Malcolm was brought to justice. Jacquelyn would never truly be safe until they knew exactly what the note had to do with Malcolm's scheme. Mace had critical decisions to make in the next few hours. The wedding would have to wait a few days. Blast it, now that he'd finally found the woman with whom he wanted to share the rest of his life, there were dozens of loose ends

451

to tie up before he could tie the matrimonial knot!

Determined of purpose, Mace escorted Jacquelyn back to the plantation, only to find Hub grinning like a Cheshire cat. Hub surveyed Mace's carelessly buttoned shirt and dangling hem that flapped in the breeze. Hub then appraised Jacquelyn's kiss-swollen lips and the assortment of leaves that had snagged in her tangled tresses.

"It must have been a grueling battle to the end, judging by your ragged appearance." Hub snicked. "Who won?"

Mace flung his friend a silencing glare, but it bounced off Hub's broad grin. When Mace refused to explain what had occurred during their two-hour absence (two hours and ten minutes, to be exact—Hub knew that for certain since he had been checking his timepiece), Hub demanded details.

"Well, are you going to get married?" he questioned, striding behind the couple who walked arm in arm to the mansion. "Am I to be the best man or not?" Still no answer. "Doggone it, Mace, you did tell her you loved her, didn't you?"

Mace grinned down into Jake's bewitching features. "The lady knows exactly how much I love her. I believe I thoroughly conveyed my feelings and she realizes I meant what I said."

Hub let loose with an elated whoop that resembled a Comanche war cry, and then he bounded through the house to announce the good news to the servants. Although Mace had plans to make, he buckled beneath Jacquelyn's suggestive smile. What would a few extra moments alone with Jake hurt? Mace asked himself as his male body warmed to her light caress. Detouring past the study, Mace took the opportunity to repeat his affection for Jake in the privacy of her room. Graciously, he honored her request to lock Raoul on the outside of the door.

Raoul stared at the portal, impatiently waiting for Mace's return. His ears twitched as he listened to the quiet giggles and soft murmurings that seeped beneath the door. He was not at all pleased to find Jake occupying his space, and what irked Raoul most was that Mace was treating him (God forbid!) just like a dog!

Shafts of sunlight cut a path of gold across the meadow. In the distance, the warble of birds orchestrated the spectacular sunset. Although the scenery was meant to soothe the most troubled souls, Harlan Reid could think of nothing but his missing granddaughter. His apprehension had led him into an argument with Florence, who'd proved herself to be more harassment than compassionate support during this nerve-racking crisis.

To make an impossible situation worse, Harlan had calculated the sum of money Malcolm could have been stealing from the company if Mace's accusations proved correct. Harlan had confronted Malcolm, only to be presented with dozens of excuses and counteraccusations against Mace. The General's temper, sorely tried already that day, had exploded. He had demanded that Malcolm account for every penny of profit and list each business into which he had invested without Harlan's consent. When Malcolm had voiced several more stuttering excuses, Harlan had lost the last remnants of his temper. By the time he'd finished railing at his nephew, he'd fired Malcolm as his financial advisor and ordered the weasel out of his house.

And now to contribute to an already disastrous day, Mace arrived, requesting that Harlan follow him to only God knew where! Harlan was assaulted by the nagging fear that Mace had come bearing bad news that he wished to convey in private. Harlan could no longer tolerate the unnerving silence. If catastrophe had befallen Jacquelyn, Harlan wanted confirmation now, not two miles down the cussed road!

"Damnit man, if you have something to tell me, say it now!" Harlan demanded crossly. "This not knowing is killing me."

Mace grimaced when he noticed Harlan's strained features and the dark half-circles that were draped beneath his eyes. Mace regretted forcing the General to endure this anguish, but he would have gained nothing if Jacquelyn's whereabouts was public knowledge.

"Rest your fears, Gen'ral," Mace murmured as he drew Diego to a halt. After he released a sharp whistle, Raoul and Jacquelyn appeared from the underbrush.

The tension drained from Harlan's weather-beaten features and he slumped in relief. "Thank God . . ." Before Jacquelyn reached him, Harlan was off his mount, waiting with outstretched arms. When she hugged him close, Harlan glanced up at Mace with misty brown eyes. "How can I ever repay you for returning Jake to me?" he questioned brokenly.

"By giving us your blessing," Mace replied, his eyes sketching Jake's shapely figure. "We plan to marry as soon as possible."

Assured that Jake was safe and sound, Harlan stepped back to compose himself. "As well you should be," he sniffed. "I do not intend to have you shinnying up the colonnades to pay her any more late night visits at my home. You will be confined to the front door, young man!"

Harlan wasn't certain whose face turned a brighter shade of pink, but it did his heart good to have the edge over Mace Gallagher for once in his life. Yet, the satisfaction of getting Mace's goat wasn't half as rewarding as seeing the tender expression that claimed the rapscallion's face when he peered at Jacquelyn. From all appearances Mace cared as deeply for Jake as she did for him. There was a time when Harlan would have claimed Mace to be the last man on earth that he wanted for a grandson-in-law. But, considering his feisty granddaughter, Harlan had come to realize Mace was the perfect match. The ornery renegades deserved each other.

"Yes, er . . . well." Mace shifted in the saddle as if he were sitting on a cactus. "Now that we have that settled . . ." Lord, Mace knew Harlan was going to come unglued when he learned the truth about Jake's kidnapping. "There . . . a . . . is . . . the . . . a . . ."

Jacquelyn grinned mischievously as Mace stumbled and stuttered. "What Mace is trying to tell you is that he was the one who kidnapped me to protect me from Malcolm," she informed Harlan without batting an eye.

"What!" Harlan would have hit the ceiling if he had been standing under one. His mutinous glower riveted on Mace. "Damnit, you should have told me what you were planning. I've endured nine kinds of hell the past few days, and all for naught!"

"I had to do what I did so you would react the way you did. If I had told you, I couldn't have backed Malcolm into the corner he now finds himself in," Mace hastily reminded Harlan. "And I cared too much about Jacquelyn to risk Malcolm's henchmen getting their hands on her first. I knew I would be damned if I intervened and damned if I didn't." Mace heaved an exasperated sigh. "I'm sorry I had to put you through hell, Gen'ral. But I love your granddaughter and I couldn't live with myself if I permitted something to happen to her."

Hearing Mace's confession took away the sting. Harlan would endure the same frustrating torment all over again if it would insure his granddaughter's safety and her happiness. And she was definitely happy, Harlan assured himself. Jacquelyn looked radiant standing there staring at Mace with so much love shining in her eyes that she could have lit up the evening sky. Lord, Harlan never thought he would live to see the day Jake found a man to match her undaunted spirit and her rebellious nature. But she most certainly had.

"I'm glad this nightmare is over," Harlan breathed in relief.

"I'm afraid it isn't," Mace grumbled. "I didn't send you that ransom note. The only way to expose the guilty party or parties is to pretend to deliver the money as requested. . . ." Mace eyed the General for a pensive moment. "Well, almost as they requested," he amended. "I intend to borrow your clothes and take your place when the money is to be set adrift on the raft."

Harlan puffed up with indignation. "You will do no such thing. I will take—"

"I advise you not to cross him, Gen'ral," Jacquelyn insisted. "You might find yourself kidnapped, stashed in a dilapidated hut on the bayou, and left under the watchful eye of this man-eating mongrel."

Harlan stared at Raoul and recalled the vicious attacks the mutt had made on numerous enemies. "Oh, very well," he grumbled. "But don't try to push me aside just because I'm an old man. If you catch Malcolm red-handed I intend to be the one to extract a few pounds of his flesh! I will be the one to decide if he is to be shot, stabbed, or hanged! Indeed, I contemplated all three this afternoon. And even then I wasn't sure any or all of them would have satisfied my vengeance!"

After Harlan promised to pretend to be on his way to deliver the ransom so that no one at the plantation would be aware of the change of plans, Mace and Jake lingered in the woods until darkness settled over the countryside. Harlan had agreed to make the switch of clothing in the barn after Hub arrived with the satchel of ransom money.

But it was difficult for Harlan to contain his elation over Jake's safety and her upcoming wedding. He wanted to shout the announcement to the world. But the moment he hobbled into the foyer, Florence emerged from the cracks in the woodwork to harass him yet again.

"Has it occurred to you that delivering that staggering amount of money to those hooligans may not insure Jackie's safety?" Florence nipped at Harlan as she followed in his wake. "You should be delivering an answering note stating no money will exchange hands until we are assured Jackie is alive and well! Honestly, Harlan, it's a wonder to me the army placed you in a position of authority when you have bungled this ordeal with my grand-niece!"

Harlan counted to ten twice. He could endure this nagging sister of his much better when she was residing in the neighboring state rather than under the same roof. And the moment Jake spoke her vows to Mace, that meddling old woman was going to be shuffled out from underfoot and carted back to New Orleans where she belonged!

"I have faith that this will all work out," Harlan tried to be civil but his voice carried a biting edge. "And when this nightmare is over Jake is going to marry Mace Gallagher."

Florence sniffed at her brother's ill-founded confidence. "I have my doubts the girl will survive to enjoy wedding anyone. But if she does, I can only hope Mr. Gallagher can take better care of Jackie than you have!" she sniped.

Harlan had enough. His cane cracked against the wall and his narrowed gaze sliced Florence into bite-sized pieces. "Silence, old woman! You may be family, but you are one of the bitterest, most unpleasant individuals I've ever had the misfortune of knowing. I never should have sent Jake to stay with you. The fact that my dear granddaughter tolerated your spiteful moods is commendable. Indeed, it must have been an incredible test of endurance for her!"

A shocked gasp erupted from Florence's lips. "How dare you speak to me like that, Harlan. I took that misfit into my home and attempted to make a respectable lady out of her. Test of endurance?" Her nasal voice hit such a high pitch that Harlan swore his eardrums had burst. "I am the one who deserves extra compensation for putting up with her embarrassing shenanigans."

Harlan burst into mocking laughter. "I still contend that Jake got the worst end of the arrangement. I paid you a handsome sum for room and board, far more than you inherited from that worthless husband you married against my wishes."

Florence's lips curled in a venomous sneer. "You delight in flaunting my mistakes in my face, don't you, Harlan? Well, I cannot see that you have made great strides in your life. Your own son wasn't man enough to hold onto his wife when temptation crossed her path, and you did a miserable job of raising Jackie. She is wild and unruly, and if you never get that child back alive the blame falls squarely on your shoulders!"

"Get out!" Harlan screeched in outrage. He had been in good humor until his sister had started picking him clean like a scavenger vulture. "If you wish to remain in Texas until Jake's wedding, you can reside at a nearby inn. I'm not spending another penny on your room and board. Pack your belongings and be gone by morning, Florence." Harlan limped toward his fuming sister. "In a crisis, when I could have used compassion and support, you have done nothing but criticize and insult me. It has taken me years to realize you got exactly what you deserved when you married Geoffrey."

Florence raised her wrinkled face and returned her

brother's disdainful glare. "Fine, Harlan, just don't come crying to me when your plans run amuck and you never lay eyes on Jackie again. You won't receive one iota of pity from me! Your rude manner has severed our family ties."

As Florence flounced through the hall, Harlan muttered a heart-felt good riddance and stamped into the study to pour himself a drink. He wasn't wasting another thought on that resentful old woman. He had been surprised to see her in Texas in the first place. Harlan had the sneaking suspicion Florence had come to request extra compensation for acting as Jacquelyn's guardian during the war. And if Florence hadn't arrived in the middle of a crisis, she probably would have been nagging Harlan to supplement her monthly income, as if he hadn't sent her enough these past three years! Damnation, if Malcolm truly had been robbing him blind, there would be no extra cash to donate to Flo, even if I wanted to, Harlan thought sourly.

Malcolm . . . The name echoed through Harlan's brain. If Mace's speculations proved correct, Harlan would grant his nephew no mercy. He had betrayed Harlan's trust, and for that he would pay dearly.

A muddled frown creased Harlan's graying brows. Where was that weasel anyway? Although Malcolm had not planned to leave until the following morning, he had made himself scarce after their last trenchant argument. But after what Harlan had learned from Jake and Mace, he wasn't about to let his nephew prance off to Galveston. And when Harlan got his hands on that varmint, Malcolm would be sorry he ever crossed his uncle.

Mulling over a dozen vengeful thoughts, Harlan downed another drink and counted the minutes until Hub arrived with the satchel that was to be floated down the river as ransom. Once Harlan took the fake ransom and marched off to the barn, the exchange of roles would be made and the scheme would be set in motion. By dawn his house would be free of the pests that had infested it of late. Malcolm would be exposed for what he was and Florence would be turned out like the snapping, growling bulldog she was!

Chapter 25

"I'm going with you," Jacquelyn declared as Mace struggled into Harlan's waistcoat, one that fit far too snugly to be comfortable.

"We have been over this twice already," Mace growled. Huffily, he pulled Harlan's narrow-brimmed hat down around his ears. "You are going to stay outside the barn and keep a watchful eye out for anyone who comes and goes from the plantation. Hub and Raoul are standing lookout downstream . . . ouch!" Mace shook his leg to ward off a nasty bite. Furiously, he glared at the anthill he had unknowingly stepped on.

"And what if you confront a band of thieves instead of only one or two men?" Jake muttered as she watched Mace dance a jig to free himself of the stinging ants. "I am competent with a pistol and knife and I could—"

"I said no!" Mace interrupted in a tone that brooked no argument. He wasted his breath.

"You can't stop me," Jake snapped back at him. "I may love you, but I will not be dictated to as if I were a helpless child!"

Mace pulled her away from the bustling anthill and stared down into her moonlit features. The anger and frustration seeped out of him. A faint smile pursed his

461

lips as he bent to kiss away the exaggerated pout that claimed her mouth. "You can't go with me because I love you."

Curse the man. First Mace refused to admit he cared for her. And when he finally learned to speak the words, he employed them as an excuse to have his way. Well, two could play that game, she reminded herself before Mace could melt her into a senseless puddle with his persuasive kiss.

"And I'm going with you because I love you," she insisted.

"You may not be around to love me back if you get yourself killed. And that is why I want you to stay here," Mace countered. "If you wind up dead I'll never forgive you for depriving me of all the years we might have spent together."

When Jake opened her mouth to parry his remark, Mace enveloped her in his arms. "I've gone to considerable effort to keep you safe. For once, do as I ask," he requested before his lips slanted over hers.

It was useless to argue with him, Jacquelyn realized. If she refused to conform to his wishes, he might resort to tying her to a tree and leaving her there until he returned . . . if he returned alive.

In frustration, Jacquelyn watched Mace grasp the improvised tree limb he employed as a cane and the satchel that was supposed to be heaping with ransom money. As Mace swung onto Harlan's horse and rode along the path to the waiting raft, Jake heaved a tremulous sigh. Did Mace truly expect her to remain here, twiddling her thumbs, wondering what trouble awaited him? He knew she could conform just so far before she was inclined to let conformity go to blazes. A wry smile rippled across her lips. Of course, Mace knew she wouldn't obey his commands. She never had before and she wasn't about to start now, not when Mace might face an armload of trouble.

Digesting that thought, Jacquelyn inconspicuously led Lancelot from the rear of the barn and threaded her way toward the river. Mace probably didn't think he needed her assistance, but even a Texas Ranger could use an extra hand in case the going got rough. Besides, if Mace got himself killed, her life wasn't worth much to her. Mace wasn't going anywhere without her, even if he were soon to be removed to another sphere. They would go together, Jake decided. That was the way it should be.

For the benefit of anyone who might have been interested in his departure, Mace made himself conspicuous as he rode past the Reid plantation in Harlan's clothes. But he was discreet as he made alterations on the raft. According to the ransom note, the satchel of cash was to be strapped to the raft and set adrift. But Mace was determined to accompany the empty satchel to the would-be extortionists' hands.

After chopping a notch in the timbers, large enough for his arm to slide between the lashed logs, Mace secured the bottomless satchel over the hole on the raft. Once he had shoved the floating vessel into the current, Mace dived beneath the surface and situated himself beneath it. The raft floated above its supporting beams, leaving an air pocket that would sustain Mace as he drifted downriver. A wicked smile caught the corner of his mouth as he ferried himself beneath the raft. Wouldn't whoever awaited at the bend of the river be surprised when they opened the satchel to find a disembodied arm clutching at them! The element of surprise would provide Mace with ample time to swim to the side of the raft and apprehend his challengers.

Biding his time, Mace inhaled a breath and arched backward to keep his head above water. Very soon,

Jacquelyn's nemeses would be rounded up and marched off to jail. If Malcolm wasn't somehow connected with this ransom scheme, Mace would be surprised. The man was too greedy to bypass the chance to retrieve another fortune after he had tried to swindle the General out of his—

A startled yelp burst from Mace's lips when he felt something latch onto his leg. Impulsively, he jerked upward, slamming his head against the underside of the raft. A wordless growl erupted from his throat when a pair of bold hands moved familiarly up his anatomy to clamp around his shoulders. When Jacquelyn surfaced to inhale a breath and giggle mischievously, Mace expelled several unprintable curses.

"Damnit, woman, can't you obey the simplest order?" he muttered bitterly.

"What order?" she questioned in mock innocence before planting a wet kiss on his lips.

Mace rolled his eyes and mumbled something about strangling her when his hands were free, but Jake shrugged off the threat and held onto his shoulders as they drifted beneath the raft.

After Mace had left the barn, Jake had ridden downstream to await the appearance of the raft. Sliding from her steed, she had crept into the water to join Mace beneath the raft. Now it was too late for him to send her away. They were nearing the bend in the river. Once the raft slammed into the steep bank on the far side of the river, the ransom would be easy to retrieve. And if Mace thought to shout her back to shore he would spoil his chances of learning who had delivered the ransom note. In short, Mace was stuck with her, whether he wanted her there or not (which of course he didn't).

"If we survive I'm never going to forgive you for disobeying orders," Mace promised vindictively.

Jake presented him with another dripping kiss. "Just

the same, I'm going to go on loving you. . . ."

Mace grumbled under his breath. "I'm beginning to wonder if that is to be a curse rather than a compliment. . . ." His voice subsided when he heard the whinny of a horse somewhere above them on the river bank. "Hold on, Jake," he whispered urgently. "I have a feeling we're about to collide with the shore."

Inhaling a deep breath, Jacquelyn clamped herself around Mace and submerged before the raft rammed into the steep incline that overlooked the bend of the river. When the raft came to a shuddering halt, dirt and pebbles clanked upon it, heralding the arrival of the unidentified extortionist. Footsteps echoed across the raft and Jacquelyn tensely waited for the man to attempt to snatch up the satchel and make a mad dash for the underbrush. But the satchel had been nailed down and the scoundrel was forced to reach inside to retrieve the contents.

Mace was poised to pounce, and Jake could feel his taut muscles against her as she held onto him. The grumbling voice above them was Mace's signal. The moment he heard the latch sprung on the bottomless satchel, he shot his arm through the hole he had cut in the logs.

The extortionist emitted a surprised squawk when a doubled fist emerged from the satchel to crack against his jaw. He was knocked backward from his crouched position and sprawled on the raft. Dazed by the blow, he floundered to draw his legs beneath him and run for his life. Before he could gain his feet, Jacquelyn pulled herself onto the raft. The moonlight reflected the glittering steel blade that was clamped in her hand. He yelped at the top of his lungs when the dripping wet apparition appeared before him.

His frantic screech was overshadowed by Mace's angry snarl. Mace's arm had stuck between the timbers and he had very nearly ripped off the appendange in his haste to

465

climb aboard the raft and attack his victim.

When Mace finally bounded onto the raft with his Bowie knife clutched in his fist, his eyes bulged from their sockets. Jacquelyn was sitting on Jon Mason's belly, holding her blade against his skinny neck.

"You?" Mace hooted in disbelief. "How did you get mixed up in this?"

"What are you doing alive?" Jon chirped at Jacquelyn as if he had confronted a ghost.

His astonished remark provoked Jacquelyn and Mace to stare curiously at each other. Obviously, Jon had not come to intercept the ransom before the extortionist could retrieve it. Mace was prepared to bet his right arm that Jon knew what was going on or he wouldn't have been there.

After removing Jacquelyn from Jon's sprawled body, Mace yanked him to his feet. "Why would you think Jacquelyn had been put to death?" he snarled into Jon's peaked face.

"I . . . I . . . was . . . only assuming," Jon stammered as Mace twisted the shirt around his neck and left him dangling in midair.

Mace wasn't satisfied. His clenched fist dragged Jon close enough to breathe down his neck. "You're lying," Mace growled ferociously. "And if you don't start talking, you're going to be part of the drift wood that floats down this river. . . ."

"I don't know anything!" Jon squealed when the vise-like grip on his throat restricted his breathing. "I only thought to intercept the money."

Mace was running short of patience. His doubled fist rammed into Jon's midsection. When Jon's knees buckled beneath him, Mace held him up by the nape of the neck. "Don't test my temper, Jon," he snarled maliciously. "I've dragged information from better men than you . . . and you don't want to know what methods

466

of torture I employed on some of those poor departed souls." To emphasize the threat he backhanded Jon across the cheek, sending his head snapping backward.

"Knock his teeth out. Maybe that will convince him to talk," Jacquelyn encouraged, hoping to scare the wits out of Jon. She wanted the scoundrel to know she wasn't giving him any sympathy either.

Jon's gaze darted frantically toward Jake, and then circled back to Mace's chiseled features. Golden eyes glittered in the moonlight and the coldest smile Jon had ever viewed on a human face lay like a block of ice on Mace's lips. It was apparent Mace's sophisticated veneer had cracked and the ruthless part of his personality, the one he had displayed during battle, was about to spill forth. A chill slithered down Jon's spine. He knew he was staring death in the face. Mace looked as if he were prepared to kill and would delight in doing so. To make matters worse, Jacquelyn had not one ounce of compassion for him.

"I swear I don't know anything," Jon declared in the most convincing voice he could muster. His charade didn't fool his captors.

"Just kill him and be done with it," Jacquelyn insisted after an impatient moment. She bit back an ornery smile when Jon blinked like a startled owl. "I don't have much use for him anyway. We'll tell the Gen'ral his clumsy lackey fell in the river and drowned."

When Jon's composure cracked, Mace tried his hand at using Jacquelyn's scare tactics. "Perhaps we should begin by chopping off a finger or two," he taunted.

"I agree that he deserves to die a slow, agonizing death," Jake concurred. "But I'm chilled to the bone. Let's just slit his lying throat and get this over with."

When Mace raised his Bowie knife to Jon's Adam's apple, he decided to save his own hide and let Malcolm fret over his own set of skin. "This was all Malcolm's doing," Jon blurted out as the dagger drew blood. "He has been skimming the profits from the commission company for years. He's also been paying me to purchase extra supplies for the plantation, and then he ships them to his new ranch on the Texas border where he plans to set up his new operations."

Jon dragged in a hasty breath and plunged on. "When Malcolm learned Jacquelyn was interested in taking a hand in running the business, he decided to dispose of her the moment she set foot in Galveston, and make her murder look as if it were the result of a robbery and molestation."

"And you pretended to be the victim of a robbery yourself, didn't you?" Jacquelyn hissed furiously.

Jon nodded reluctantly. "Malcolm told me to feign the assault. But when I saw you I decided to go along with the Gen'ral's attempt to match us as husband and wife. I would have had nothing to lose and everything to gain."

Mace muttered under his breath, and then glared murderously at Jon. "When Malcolm finally disposed of Jake you were going to act the grieving widower and accept her inheritance, living like a leech off Harlan," he speculated.

"When Jacquelyn refused my proposal and turned up missing after the barbecue, I assumed Malcolm's henchmen had abducted her. I thought to collect payment for my time and trouble by sending the ransom," Jon admitted as the blade pressed ever closer to his jugular vein. "I was after the money, but I had no hand in trying to kill Jacquelyn!" he railed. "I swear, I was only taking orders from Malcolm until I tried to make money on the side!"

"Obviously Malcolm doesn't know you tried to cheat him." Mace smirked. "You put him in a dangerous situation because he couldn't come up with the money when the Gen'ral demanded the funds for the ransom."

Mace hauled Jon's sagging body closer, spilling another drop of blood. "Where is Malcolm stashing all the profit for his new endeavor on the Texas border?"

"I don't know. Maybe Gil Davis, his hired gun, is holding it for him. Gil is the one who has been organizing the cattle raids and arranging the cattle drives to the California gold fields."

Mace gave Jon a sound shaking. "You're lying again. You know damned well where all Harlan's money has been stashed."

"I swear to God, I don't know!" Jon shrieked as he stared cross-eyed at the deadly blade. "If Malcolm doesn't have it, Gil must be keeping it. If I knew where it was I wouldn't have tried to take my share by sending a ransom note and disappearing into parts unknown before Malcolm could catch up with me."

Now Mace knew who was behind the cattle thefts that had sent the Rangers to Corpus Christi to investigate. But he still didn't know where the profits from the Reid Commission Company were stashed. Apparently Jon didn't either. Mace had become adept at reading people's faces. He felt certain Jon had confessed all he knew. Jon had been secretly working for Malcolm, and had only thought to take advantage of opportunity by extracting what he felt was his share of the profits. Jon wasn't a killer, only a crook who followed orders better than he schemed on his own.

Roughly, Mace spun Jon around, twisting his arm up behind his back to prevent him from escaping. "You're going to repeat your story to Harlan, and then you're going to inspect our prison system," Mace sneered. "Be sure to let us know the conditions of the cells while you're rotting away in one of them."

When Jon squirmed for release, Jacquelyn scoffed cynically. "I still think we ought to dispose of him permanently," she declared. Her comment had a quieting effect on Jon, just as she had hoped. Jon trudged obediently up the riverbank without causing any more trouble.

As they trekked back toward the plantation, Jake laid her hand in the crook of Mace's free arm. "It seems I owe you my life," she murmured appreciatively. "How can I ever repay you?"

A rakish grin settled on his ruggedly handsome features. "I'll let you know, love. . . ."

The suggestive gleam in his amber eyes assured Jacquelyn that the payment Mace had in mind would place no pressure on her purse strings.

"I cannot wait to hear what sort of compensation you desire," she murmured provocatively. "I am most anxious to express my gratitude. . . ."

Mace glanced down into her sparkling brown eyes and caught his breath when he noticed the living fire flickering there. From all indications, this lovely minx was thinking the same thing he was thinking. For a whimsical moment, Mace contemplated tying Jon to a nearby tree. Lord, if only I could, Mace thought as he squelched the wave of desire that rippled through him. Unfortunately, there was Malcolm to contend with, and Mace couldn't have Jake all to himself until her conniving cousin was occupying the cell beside Jon.

Later, Mace promised himself. Later he would appease this insatiable craving for this daring nymph. Then he would compensate for all those lonely nights he had spent wanting Jake the way a starving man craves a feast. . . .

Chapter 26

As the threesome approached the distant lights of the plantation, Jacquelyn sighed contentedly. She felt safe and protected while she strode alongside Mace and their silent captive. Although they had yet to apprehend Malcolm, the worst was over, she assured herself. With two Texas Rangers in their midst, Malcolm would soon be carted off to jail with his accomplices. They deserved no better for trying to hornswoggle the General and attempting to dispose of her.

The approach of a rider interrupted her musings. Jacquelyn stared toward the sound of thundering hooves to see Hub's bulky torso on horseback and Raoul's shaggy frame appear from the crisscrossed shadows.

Hub had come prepared, leading extra horses in case they found it necessary to pursue the extortionists. But from the look of things, there would be no high-speed chase on horseback.

"Jon Mason?" Hub choked in disbelief when he recognized Mace's captive. "Don't tell me he was behind all this!"

"He had a hand in Malcolm's scheme," Mace explained. "Jon was kind enough to unfold the details for us."

Hub studied the swollen side of Jon's face momentarily and then smiled to himself. He and Mace had often been forced to persuade reluctant Mexican guerrillas to disclose their battle plans. Judging from Jon's tattered appearance, Mace had resorted to a few of the old, familiar techniques necessitated by war and desperation. Jon was fortunate. Mace had obviously been lenient with him. The man could have found himself beaten to a pulp. With Mace's strength and ability to fight with any and all weapons, including his feet and his fists, Jon could have looked a great deal worse than he did after he had roused this sleeping giant.

"Keep an eye on the hombre, Raoul," Mace instructed his devoted dog as he and Mace swung onto the horses Hub had brought along with him. "If he tries to escape, bite off his legs at the knees." After barking the order in Spanish, Mace had translated into English for Jon's benefit.

To prove he could do as Mace requested if he were so inclined, Raoul bared his fangs for Jon's inspection. Jon flinched as the wolf-dog trotted over to walk at his heels.

"I promised not to attempt escape," Jon grumbled at Mace.

Fondly, Mace stared down at Raoul. "And Raoul will insure you keep your word. Hub and I occasionally fed this mongrel Mexican guerrillas for between-meal snacks. Be warned, Jon, Raoul is very fond of raw meat. . . ."

Mace's teasing taunt was interrupted by a bark—one that exploded from a distant pistol, not from the intimidating wolf-dog. All eyes swung toward the silhouette of the barn that lay two hundred yards in front of them.

"Damn, what now?" Mace scowled as he peered into the distance.

Gouging their steeds, the three of them flew toward the

472

stables. Jacquelyn's heart flip-flopped in her chest as she thundered after Mace. Fear shot through her as she wondered if, in desperation, Malcolm had opened fire on the General. Her grandfather had been so trusting of those around him, expecting his family and acquaintances to respond as obediently as the soldiers under his command. But Malcolm and Jon had betrayed that generous trust. And if Malcolm had harmed a hair on the General's head, Jacquelyn vowed to do much more than send her murdering cousin to jail. By damn, she would shoot him herself!

Harboring that vindictive thought and the nagging guilt that she should have stayed at the barn as Mace ordered her to do, Jacquelyn raced along the path that led to the stables. An astonished gasp burst from her lips when the moonlight revealed the form of a man who held a pistol in his hand. Wide-eyed, Jacquelyn glanced down to see a body sprawled in the dirt.

Grimly, Mace stared at Harlan Reid, who was, in turn, staring dazedly at Malcolm's lifeless body. Harlan's left hand was clenched around his cane. His right hand was clamped around the pearl-handled revolver he had carried in battle.

As Jacquelyn darted toward Malcolm to determine if he were dead or alive, Mace caught her hand to detain her. A muddled frown creased his brows as he peered at the trail of blood that covered the ground. It looked as if Malcolm had dragged himself across the loose dirt. That fact did not disturb Mace. But what baffled him was that Malcolm had collapsed near an anthill. The inhabitants of the underground den were crawling all over him. If Jake had attempted to roll Malcolm onto his back she would have suffered several painful bites.

The sight of hundreds of red ants parading over Malcolm's still form caused Jacquelyn to reverse direction. Malcolm may have received his just desserts by collapsing on an anthill, but it was a most unpleasant sight.

Her anguished gaze flew back to Harlan, who remained frozen to his spot. "Gen'ral, are you all right?" Jacquelyn questioned anxiously.

Harlan never had the opportunity to respond. The rustle of skirts heralded the appearance of Florence, who let out a shriek that pierced several eardrums, including Raoul's. The mutt howled in unison with Florence's bloodcurdling scream as Jon walked up with Raoul at his heels.

"My God, Harlan, what have you done?" Florence wailed as she stared at Malcolm's lifeless body. "You've murdered our nephew! Have you gone mad?"

Harlan's tormented gaze swung first to Jacquelyn and then to Mace. "I didn't kill Malcolm," he insisted shakily.

"No?" Florence sniffed in contradiction. "Then why are you holding that pistol? No one else around here seems to have a weapon in hand!"

"I found my pistol lying in the dirt," Harlan explained.

"Oh, for heaven's sake," Florence snorted in that grating tone of hers that would shatter nerves. "We all know you murdered him, so you may as well own up to it. I overheard the two of you squabbling earlier this afternoon. I knew you would kill someone. It was only a matter of time. Military men always perceive themselves as demigods who have the right to take law into their own hands." She raked her brother with a scornful glare. "You've been overwhelmed by your medals of honor and lofty rank for decades." Flinging her nose in the air, she eyed her brother with blatant disgust. "You may be family, but I will not lie for you, Harlan. I heard you tell poor Malcolm you would kill him for swindling you out of your fortune. If you were man enough to take his life, you should be man enough to admit it."

474

"I tell you I didn't kill him!" Harlan loudly protested.

Florence flung her guilty brother a withering glance, and then focused her eyes on the two Rangers. "Mr. Gallagher, you and your friend Mr. MacTavish—"

"MacIntosh," Hub corrected.

"Whatever." Florence waved Hub off with an impatient flick of her wrist. "Harlan informed me that you were members of the Texas Rangers. You have the authority to arrest Harlan for Malcolm's murder. I refuse to permit my brother to go free just because of the influence of his name and military rank. Justice is for the mighty as well as the meek, and you must do your duty."

Mace swore he detected smug satisfaction in Florence's wrinkled face when she glanced at him. Damn, with a sister like this one, Harlan didn't need enemies!

"The Gen'ral swears he didn't fire the pistol," Mace reminded Florence.

"Of course, he does." Florence smirked. "Our jails are brimming with criminals, all of whom proclaim themselves innocent of wrongdoing."

Pensively, Jacquelyn stared at Malcolm's outstretched hand, and then cringed at the swarm of insects that trailed over his arm. Her gaze shifted back and forth between her cousin and her grandfather, who had a haunted look about him.

"Do your duty, Ranger," Florence demanded impatiently. "A crime has been committed and the criminal stands with weapon in hand."

"How can you be so certain the Gen'ral fired the shot?" Jake questioned her great-aunt. "Did you see him shoot Malcolm?" Lord, she didn't want to believe her grandfather was guilty, although he had every right to dispose of Malcolm, scoundrel that he was.

"Well, no but—"

"Then perhaps Harlan announced to you that he was going outside to dispose of Malcolm." Mace smirked.

Florence puffed up like an offended toad. "No, but he was furious with Malcolm. Harlan has been shouting accusations and threats all afternoon!"

"Jon has recently informed us that Malcolm has another partner in crime," Mace informed her tartly. "A man named Gil Davis has been ramrodding a gang of thieves who have been stealing cattle on the Texas border and driving them to the California gold fields. It seems to me that Davis would have far more to gain from your nephew's death—"

The thunder of hooves interrupted Mace, and all eyes swung toward the sound of a departing horse that carried an unidentified rider.

"That must be Gil Davis," Hub speculated as he stuffed a boot into the stirrup. "When he heard his name mentioned, he must have decided to get the hell out of here."

Mace was in the saddle in a single bound. As Hub and Mace and Raoul galloped away, Florence stood sputtering in outrage. "I am not about to stay here with a murderer while those idiotic Rangers go racing off to find a scapegoat for you, Harlan. I am going home where I belong," she muttered, casting Harlan and Jacquelyn a condemning glance. "And if you have any sense, Jackie, you will come back to New Orleans before Harlan loses his temper with you and guns you down the way he did Malcolm."

"I . . . did . . . not . . . kill . . . Malcolm." Harlan's booming voice was punctuation in itself.

"And I believe the Gen'ral," Jacquelyn chimed in.

Florence made a melodramatic pirouette and stamped toward the house. "Goodbye and good riddance to the both of you," she hissed furiously. "And don't attempt to correspond with me the next few decades. As far as I'm concerned, I no longer have relatives in Texas!"

When Jacquelyn nudged Jon toward one of the outbuildings, where he was to remain under lock and key until his trial, Harlan fell into step behind his granddaughter.

"I swear I didn't kill that bastard," Harlan grumbled in exasperation. "I wanted to, but someone got to him before I did."

"Everyone who ever knew Malcolm could be a suspect," Jacquelyn assured Harlan. "No one who had any connection with Malcolm liked him. Great-Uncle Jesse was a good man, but Malcolm inherited none of his father's saintly qualities."

After Jon had been stashed for safekeeping, Jacquelyn tucked her arm around Harlan's elbow and aimed herself toward the house. "I feel partially responsible for what happened," she confessed soulfully. "If I'd remained behind as Mace ordered, you would have had a witness to your innocence and Malcolm might not have wound up dead."

Harlan squeezed Jake's hand and blessed her with a faint smile. "At least someone believes me." His eyes shifted to the front door and he frowned, disconcerted. "I suppose I should have a horse and buggy readied for Flo. It appears she is determined to leave posthaste."

"As well she should," Jake sniffed disdainfully. "I have nothing to say to her after the way she verbally attacked you."

While Jacquelyn trotted back to the barn to have the buggy brought to the front door, Harlan went toward the study for a drink to calm his frayed nerves. He could only hope Mace and Hub located the rider who had made a speedy exit after overhearing the conversation. It would be humiliating to stand trial for his nephew's murder, even if Malcolm deserved to die for all the crimes he committed—along with the dastardly crime Mace had prevented him from committing against Jacquelyn.

And Jon! Harlan poured himself another drink. How

could Harlan have been such a trusting fool? After what Jacquelyn had told him, it appeared Jon had betrayed Harlan's trust as well. Damn the man! And to think Harlan had considered matching Jake with that weasel— Jon Mason. That most certainly would have been the catastrophe of the century! Harlan cursed himself for being so blind. Like a fool, he'd expected his authority to be respected without question.

Hastily, Jacquelyn shrugged off her wet clothes and quickly bathed. After donning a bright emerald-green gown, she glanced into the mirror to rearrange the wild sable tangles that hung about her. As she combed her hair, an unsettling thought flitted across her mind and the color waned from her cheeks. Something Jon had said earlier that evening had struck her odd. But so much had happened so quickly that she had had no time to analyze it.

Jon had insisted that Malcolm had arranged to have Jake put to death the moment she arrived in Texas. But Jacquelyn had told no one but Aunt Florence of her intention to take an active part in the family business. How could Malcolm have known of her plans unless he had been in personal contact with Florence? And if Florence had relayed the news of Jake's intentions to Malcolm, why wouldn't she have conveyed the same information to Harlan? Florence had certainly tattled all else to the General. And yet, Harlan had been surprised when Jake broached the subject of taking a hand in business after she'd arrived at the plantation. So why would Florence withhold that particular piece of information from her brother, unless she knew about Malcolm's scheme to steal the profits?

The fact that Florence was all too quick to accuse Harlan of Malcolm's murder disturbed Jacquelyn. She knew there was no love lost between brother and sister, but Florence had been adamant about having Harlan arrested on the spot. Just why was that? She seemed infinitely more upset that Harlan wouldn't admit to the crime than she was about seeing Malcolm lying dead atop a hill of ants. . . .

A repulsive shiver skitted down Jacquelyn's backbone when the vision of Malcolm's ant-infested body speared through her troubled thoughts. She cringed, remembering how Malcolm had dragged himself through the dirt. His outstretched hand lay upon the bustling anthill. Why would a man purposely crawl forward, knowing what lay ahead of him? Why would he chose to die beside an anthill . . . ?

Jacquelyn's heart skipped several vital beats. Oh God! It wasn't the anthill that Malcolm wanted to call to everyone's attention, but rather his *aunt!* Malcolm hadn't wanted his murder to go unsolved. He was too vengeful and spiteful not to make an attempt to name his murderer. No one would drag himself into a colony of ants unless he was trying to convey his last message before he departed from the earth!

A perplexed frown knitted Jacquelyn's brow. Was Malcolm hinting that Aunt Florence was the one who killed him? Or was he suggesting that Florence knew where he had stashed the profits he had swindled from the General . . . or was he suggesting both?

Jacquelyn swallowed the lump that constricted her throat. She would have bet her life Aunt Florence had an ulterior motive for coming to Texas when she had. If Malcolm had planned to set up his new empire in south Texas, he would need the money that Florence had probably been holding for him while she was residing in New Orleans. Malcolm could have shuffled money to Florence each time he sent the monthly compensation Harlan paid for Jake's room and board.

Well, there is only one way to determine if I have leaped to the right conclusion, Jacquelyn convinced herself. She had to inspect Florence's belongings before the conniving old woman scuttled off in the buggy. If the money was in Florence's room, the incriminating evidence would speak for itself.

Determined of purpose, Jacquelyn marched down the hall to Florence's room. The murmur of voices that wafted their way up from the lower floor assured Jake that Florence was still flinging orders to every servant in the house before her departure. Hurriedly, Jake dashed to the trunk that sat in the corner of the room. If her hunch proved correct, Florence had stashed the cash in with her belongings. If Jake could find proof of her speculations, she wouldn't have to confront Florence without evidence. Mace did not approve of the direct approach, Jake reminded herself as she rifled through the trunk. And, considering how ruthless her aunt was, Jake decided that caution might be advisable.

A muttered growl erupted from Jake's lips when she came up empty-handed. She had been so certain Florence would have kept the money with her.

The sound of footsteps echoing in the hall provoked Jacquelyn to chew indecisively on her bottom lip. Her eyes swung to the closet, and she immediately tucked herself into it. Since Florence was buzzing around the house like a disturbed hornet, Jacquelyn predicted her aunt would sail in and out of her room several times before she finally made her melodramatic exit. And while Jake was waiting for her aunt to stamp out again, she decided to inspect the closet—from the inside.

Groping in the dark, Jacquelyn fumbled through the hat boxes Florence had stashed in the closet while she listened to the old woman spout commands. This is ridiculous, Jacquelyn chided herself as she waited to determine if Florence were coming or going. She should have simply invented some reason to detain Florence. When Mace and Hub returned they could interrogate her aunt. Florence might be willing to spill the truth after Mace used some of his powers of persuasion on her.

Finally, Florence stamped out the door to bark an order to Emma. When the room was quiet again, Jake grasped the door knob. But the creak of the terrace door halted her. A muddled frown furrowed her brow as she strained to detect other sounds to alert her to the entrance of another person in the room. My, Florence's room was a hub of activity this evening. And damnit, this was no time to be shut in a closet and without a weapon of defense! Who could have possibly sneaked into the room from the gallery, for heaven's sake?

"Have my lunch basket ready in ten minutes," Florence insisted, nudging Emma on her way. "I have no wish to faint from hunger before I find a wayside inn to spend the night."

As Emma waddled down the hall to obey the brusque command, Florence breezed back into her room. Heaving an agitated sigh, Florence folded the gowns that lay at the foot of her bed and carefully laid them in her trunk. Time was of the essence. Things had gone from bad to worse and she was anxious to depart Texas. . . .

The rustle of the drapes caught her attention. Florence clutched her chest when she spied the oversized bulge in the gold brocade drapes. The color seeped from her wrinkled features when the hombre who was garbed in a sombrero and serape emerged from the curtain.

"You seem to be in a rush to leave your brother's home," Gil Davis said sarcastically.

"Who are you and what are you doing in my boudoir?" Florence snapped indignantly. "Leave at once or I shall scream these walls down and you will be carted off to jail."

Gil swaggered across the room, sending Florence stumbling back. "By all means, summon your brother," he taunted with a threatening smile. "I'm sure he would like to hear what really happened to Malcolm."

Florence clutched the bedpost before she collapsed at the intruder's feet. Jacquelyn grinned in spiteful anticipation. The voice sounded familiar and Jacquelyn was quick to link Gil Davis's name to the man she had met at the wayside inn. Gil had obviously returned to blackmail Florence. And by the time their conversation ended, Jake was sure she would have all the evidence she needed to point an accusing finger at her conniving great-aunt.

"I don't have the faintest notion what you're babbling about," Florence declared with bravado.

Gil elevated a mocking brow and tipped back his sombrero. "Don't you?" Laughter bubbled in his chest. "The name is Gil Davis. I was to meet your nephew this evening. When he didn't arrive at the appointed time I came looking for him." His penetrating gaze clashed with Florence's mutinous glower. "I overheard your conversation with him, my dear Florence," he drawled in taunt. "Malcolm wanted to intercept the ransom money, split the cash you swindled from the commission company, and hightail it to Santa Gertrudis before the General had him carted off to prison. When you refused to tell him where you had stashed the money, he threatened to expose your scheme to General Reid."

So my suspicions were correct, Jacquelyn mused as she pressed her ear against the closet door. Florence was as guilty as Malcolm, maybe even more so.

When Florence wilted onto the gowns she had laid on the edge of the bed for packing, Gil chuckled victoriously. "I waited around to see who was going to take the blame for disposing of Malcolm. After my name came into the conversation I decided to lead those two Rangers on a wild-goose chase."

His mouth widened to display a jeering smile. "I don't appreciate being accused of a murder I haven't committed. Nor do I intend to return to Santa Gertrudis now that our cattle rustling operations have been exposed to the Rangers." His intimidating grin became a spiteful sneer. "I want half the money you've been holding for Malcolm. If you make the split with me, I won't tell what I know about you."

"I don't have the money," Florence hissed in seething irritation. "I was planning to retrieve it before I booked passage to Europe. . . ."

"Where your family would never think to look for you if and when they finally realized who was responsible for Malcolm's death and the missing funds," Gil added with a snort.

Gil regarded Florence's hateful glare for a thoughtful moment. "You are the one who devised this swindling scheme, aren't you? Malcolm said he had another associate in New Orleans who was handling his financial interests. But after hearing your argument with Malcolm, it sounded as if this whole scheme was your idea."

"Of course, it was," Florence muttered as her eyes darted around the room, frantically wondering how she could catch this oversized hombre off guard. "Malcolm was greedy enough to agree to my plans. As soon as I had Jackie under my roof, Malcolm began sending the extra money to be stashed in savings. I had intended to meet him in Galveston and take up residence in Santa Gertrudis. But when I arrived in Texas, Malcolm's message informed me there was trouble brewing at the plantation. He was to have disposed of my meddling grand-niece long before now."

"And now I'm the one who poses a threat to your scheme," Gil declared, eyeing her warily. "But I know

483

what kind of woman I'm dealing with, and I won't be as lenient with you as your family might have been." Roughly, Gil yanked Florence to her feet and pulled her close. "Unless you hand over half the money, you'll be rotting in jail with that skinny idiot, Jon Mason."

Florence sputtered to catch her breath. "I told you I don't have the money on my person. If you want it you will have to escort me to Galveston. And if anything happens to me between here and Galveston, you will never lay your hands on a penny!"

Gil swore under his breath as he unhanded the wily old dowager. "Then be quick about your packing," he growled. "I have no wish to be here when those Rangers realize I backtracked to the house. If I'm apprehended I'll be screaming your name."

Muttering at the disastrous turn of events, Florence scooped up the rest of her gowns and haphazardly piled them in the trunk. "Fetch my hats from the closet," she ordered Gil. "I'll have the servants load the buggy and I'll meet you on the north road in fifteen minutes."

Jacquelyn froze like an icicle. The closet? Damn, she should have crawled under the bed! With her heart beating furiously, she inched as far back in the closet as the small niche would allow. She had no qualms about confronting Florence, but Gil Davis was another matter entirely. Surprising a hired gunman by clubbing him over the head with a hat box wouldn't stop him. Damn, it wouldn't even startle him enough to allow her to dash out of the room.

Plastering herself against the wall, Jacquelyn held her breath and waited. When Gil flung open the door Jake prayed for all she was worth. After he snatched the boxes from the upper shelf, he wheeled to toss them on the bed. A wicked smile caught the corner of his mouth as he spun about. Gil had noticed the dangling hem of Jacquelyn's green gown just before he turned back toward the bed.

484

Pretending to reach for the last two hat boxes, Gil drew his Bowie knife from beneath his serape.

A mute gasp lay on Jacquelyn's lips when Gil's hand snaked out to yank her from her hiding place in the dark corner of the closet. Before she could scream at the top of her lungs, the dagger pressed against her throat.

A smug smile twitched Florence's lips when Gil pivoted with his captive. "I think perhaps a hostage will insure our safe passage to Galveston," she said, smirking as she raked Jacquelyn with scornful mockery. "You always were too inquisitive for your own good, Jackie. I'm sure you remember the adage about curiosity killing the cat. . . ."

It only took a moment for Gil to recognize the face of the woman he had met the previous month. Gil's hawk-ish gaze drifted down Jacquelyn's luscious figure, remembering the night he had been deprived of the pleasures this tempting bundle could offer.

"The little lady will provide far more services than that of a hostage." Gil laughed sardonically. When Jacquelyn looked as if she meant to expel a cry of alarm, even if it cost her life, Gil struck out a doubled fist. "Damned daredevil," he grumbled.

The world turned pitch black. Faintly, Jacquelyn recalled the jarring blow to her cheek, but the painful memory faded as her knees folded up beneath her.

As Jacquelyn wilted, Gil scooped her into his arms and strided toward the terrace doors. Flinging his uncon-scious hostage over his shoulder like a feed sack, Gil eased over the railing and clamped himself around the colonnade.

Muttering under her breath, Florence stomped back into the hall to summon servants to collect her belongings and carry them outside. Damn, if Malcolm hadn't panicked and tried to change their plans, she wouldn't have found herself facing a mountain of difficulties. Well, at least Jacquelyn would insure their safe journey to Galveston, Florence consoled herself. No one would dare attempt to intercept them, even if they realized what had occurred. No doubt those blundering Rangers were halfway to Santa Gertrudis. By the time they realized they had been duped, Florence would be bound for Europe . . . just as soon as she devised a way to rid herself of Jacquelyn and that pesky hombre Gil Davis.

Inhaling a determined breath, Florence breezed down the steps without bothering to tell her brother farewell. It irked her that she had been unable to lay the blame on Harlan. It would have been the ultimate triumph in her ingenious scheme to steal her arrogant brother blind. And if Jacquelyn hadn't returned from the dead, Florence would have gained complete control of Harlan's property while he was pacing his prison cell for the murder of Malcolm. Well, Jackie wasn't going to return from her intended grave this time, Florence vowed to herself. She was the only one who knew the truth, and she wasn't going to live long enough to tell anyone!

A muddled frown clouded Mace's brow. Even though the clatter of hooves still echoed in front of them, Raoul had skidded to a halt and reversed direction.

"You're losing your touch, mutt," Mace growled at Raoul.

Raoul faced the direction they had come from and let loose with several gruff barks and snarling growls.

Mace and Hub peered curiously at each other, and then surveyed the shaggy mongrel, who refused to stir another step. The thunder of hooves provoked Mace to squirm impatiently in his saddle. He was eager to pursue the unidentified rider, but neither could he ignore Raoul's odd behavior. They had always relied upon Raoul's keen senses when tracking renegade Comanches nd Mexican guerrillas. Seldom had Raoul miscalculated he flight of their enemies.

"Do you suppose it was Davis and he backtracked to he plantation afoot?" Hub asked as Raoul struck up nother round of protests and pointed himself in the pposite direction.

"A desperate man might attempt to take a hostage," Mace speculated.

"Well, he can have Florence," Hub snorted disdainfully. "That spiteful old woman would have had us drag Harlan to the gallows for a hanging without a trial!"

Mace stared somberly at Hub. "If Malcolm sent you to kill Jake and you were unable to accomplish the deed, who do you suppose you would be inclined to take as a hostage?"

Mace hated himself for putting his logical deductions into words. The thought sent a snake of dread slithering down his spine. He well remembered the way Gil Davis had leered at Jacquelyn that night at the wayside tavern. No doubt Gil would be anxious to settle the score with Mace, as well as pleasure himself with Jacquelyn. Damn, they had been fools to give chase. They had played into Gil's hands and had left Jacquelyn vulnerable to abduction.

Scowling, Mace wheeled his steed around and thundered back to the plantation at breakneck speed, while Hub and Raoul followed a length behind him. Again Mace cursed himself for racing off half-cocked. He had desperately wanted to prove Florence wrong and clear the General's name. Damn that viper-tongued shrew. Florence had clouded his thinking during a crisis. And if it cost Jacquelyn her life, Mace was going to drag that troublesome old bat to Galveston and toss her onto the first outgoing schooner himself!

Chapter 27

The jingle of the harness and the methodic thud of horses' hooves greeted Jacquelyn when she roused with a throbbing headache. Flinching at the tenderness of her jaw, Jake pried one eye open to find herself propped on the buggy seat beside Florence. Jake muttered under her breath when she realized her hands had been tied behind her back and her legs had been bound at the ankles. Even if she threw herself off the buggy, she couldn't escape her aunt and Gil Davis, who rode beside them on a horse he had stolen from the stables.

Moonlight sprayed across Florence's wrinkled features, and Jacquelyn silently cursed the woman who was the mastermind behind the intricate scheme to extricate money from the commission company. Damn, if only Jake had pieced the puzzle of events together earlier, she could have alerted Mace. But now he was hunting a man who had led them on a wild-goose chase.

"So you finally roused, did you?" Florence smirked as she spared her grand-niece a glance. "I had hoped you would remain unconscious for a few more hours. It has been peaceful thus far."

Jacquelyn didn't dignity the comment with the equally nasty reply that flocked to the tip of her tongue. She simply sat there staring at her surroundings, wondering how many miles they had come while she was sleeping off the effects of Gil's painful blow to the jaw. It was difficult to get her bearings in the darkness, but Jacquelyn suspected they were miles from the plantation and even farther from Mace and Hub.

Deflated, she let her shoulders slump. Her predicament seemed hopeless. Even after Mace and Hub realized they had been sent off in the wrong direction, they would be hours behind Gil and Florence. And when Mace finally caught up with them, Jacquelyn knew she would become the shield of protection. Jacquelyn didn't appreciate being used as a gambit, and she was smart enough to know her captors wouldn't bat an eye at killing her when she had served her purpose for them. She knew far too much. So why should she meekly accept her fate when she was going to wind up dead? If she was checking out of this world, she was going in a blaze of glory, defying her captors!

With that valiant thought, Jacquelyn flung herself at Florence, using her feet to rip the reins from her aunt's hands. Florence's furious squawk startled the horses. Although Gil managed to regain control of his mount, the horse that was pulling the buggy bounded off in a burst of fright, serenaded by Florence's outraged screeching, which was notorious for shattering eardrums.

"You stupid bitch!" Florence railed as she fiercely clung to the bouncing buggy seat.

Using her head and shoulders as battering rams, Jacquelyn butted against her aunt, forcing her to hang on for dear life instead of attempting to retrieve the reins. The speeding buggy wobbled on its wheels as the steed thundered blindly through the darkness.

Gil raced along behind them, spouting curses that would have burned the ears off a priest. Texas's terrible roads kept the carriage jostling over bumps and ruts, tossing Jake and Florence from one side of the seat to the other. The excessive strain on the buggy at such high speeds on treacherous roads caused the axle to snap. With a bone-jarring thud, one side of the coach skidded in the dirt while a back wheel went rolling off in the opposite direction—minus a few spokes and a hub.

By the time Gil grabbed hold of the horse's harness the damage had been done. Florence's hat boxes and luggage had been scattered hither and yon, leaving a trail that was infinitely easy to follow.

Jacquelyn had accomplished her purpose. Florence was spewing with fury, and her coiffure looked as if it had been styled during a cyclone. Gil was cursing and swearing in unison with Florence, and Jake pushed onto the lopsided seat to smile in smug satisfaction.

"Now what are we going to do?" Florence hissed as she clambered out of the buggy on wobbly legs. "Those Rangers will know exactly which direction we've taken after we left a trail of baggage behind us." Her fuming glower landed on the broken axle. "I don't ride horses!"

Gil swung to the ground and stamped toward the buggy to assess the damage. Muttering, he glanced toward the river that lay like a silver thread in the moonlight. "It looks like we'll have to wait for the Rangers to catch up with us." His eyes swung to Florence, whose face was the color of boiled shrimp and who was still sputtering in outrage. "And between now and then, you better change your opinion of riding horseback or you'll be the one sharing Jon Mason's prison cell."

"Let the Rangers catch up with us?" Florence parroted in disbelief. "Are you mad?"

Gil ambled over to pluck Jacquelyn from her perch on the lopsided seat. "I've got a plan. . . ." His menacing gaze wandered over the defiant tilt of Jacquelyn's chin. It galled him that there was no fear in her eyes, only rebellious sparkles. "And this little lady is going to be the bait. . . ."

"Well, it had damned well better be a good plan,"
Florence snorted derisively. "I intend to live long
enough to enjoy Harlan's money."

"*Half* of Harlan's money," Gil corrected as he carried
Jacquelyn toward the steep bank of the river and dropped
her in an unceremonious heap.

While Gil stomped off to retrieve his mount and
unhitch the flighty steed from the buggy, Jacquelyn
grumbled under her breath. She had the dispirited feeling
this ordeal was far from over. Gil wasn't through with her
yet. And that was a crying shame because Jake would
certainly like to be through with her avaricious aunt and
her ruthless sidekick. But Jacquelyn promised herself,
then and there, she was going to live long enough to
expose Florence for what she was. No doubt Mace would
assume Florence was also being held hostage. And if Jake
died before she was permitted to explain, she was never
going to forgive herself!

Seeing the world and everything in it through a furious
red haze, Mace bounded from his steed and took the steps
to the Reid mansion two at a time. With a pistol poised in
each hand, Mace kicked open the door, prepared for
anything. He didn't know whether to be disappointed or
relieved when Harlan limped from the parlor to stare
bewilderedly at him.

"What the hell's going on?" Harlan gasped when Hub
entered, packing another pair of loaded Colts.

"I was afraid Davis had doubled back to the house to
take a hostage," Mace growled as he aimed himself
toward the spiral staircase. "Where's Jake?"

"She was going upstairs to bathe and change after her
swim in the river," Harlan answered as he limped along
behind Mace.

"Hub, search the ground floor," Mace commanded as he leaped up the steps.

Mace's heart galloped around his chest like a racing thoroughbred as he strode down the hall to Jacquelyn's room. It was too quiet. The sixth sense he had developed in battle warned him that trouble still awaited him. Where? He wasn't exactly sure, but something was very wrong!

"Florence left two hours ago, thank God," Harlan said breathlessly. Keeping up with Mace on the steps took tremendous effort. "At least . . ." His voice trailed off when Mace opened the door to find Jacquelyn's room unoccupied. Wide, anguished eyes swung to Mace's murderous scowl. "God, do you suppose Davis took her hostage?"

Mace rammed his pistols into their holsters and reversed direction. "I'd bet my life on it . . . damn," he swore vehemently as he stalked down the hall. "Raoul!" His voice thundered through the quiet house.

Within an instant Raoul trotted through the front door that sagged on its hinges. The booming voice also brought Hub from the rear of the house. The look on Mace's face spoke volumes. Hub didn't bother posing questions when Jacquelyn didn't appear on the landing beside her pale-faced grandfather.

Without uttering another word Mace sailed out the door. Murderous thoughts whipped through his head as he leaped onto his steed. Gruffly, he ground out the order for Raoul to trail Jacquelyn's scent. With his snout to the ground, the mongrel trotted around the mansion and then loped off to the northeast.

A curious frown knitted Hub's brow as he trotted alongside Mace. "Do you suppose Davis took both women captive?"

Mace didn't respond. He only glared resentfully at the darkness, knowing how his father must have felt when he

493

learned another man had taken possession of the woman he treasured more than life. Mace thirsted for blood. The killer instinct took command of his thoughts. He wanted Gil Davis's head on a silver platter. He wanted the man drawn and quartered!

Nothing had ever stirred Mace's fury or hatred as much as the thought of losing Jacquelyn. He had wasted two months fighting his obsessive attraction for that vivacious pixie. He had withheld his emotions, trying not to fall prey to the powers of love. Now Mace resented each precious moment he had wasted when he could have been loving Jake with every beat of his heart. And if he were deprived of a lifetime with that spirited vixen, Gil Davis would rue the day he tangled with Mace. He would employ every Comanche torture ritual he had ever witnessed. Gil Davis would be begging to die.

Harboring that vengeful thought, Mace followed Raoul along the road that led toward Galveston. Hub rode beside Mace in stony silence. He knew what Mace was going through because he was entertaining his own vindictive thoughts. Hub shuddered to think what would become of Mace if he lost Jacquelyn now that he had come to terms with his emotions. There would be no one more bitter and spiteful than Mace Gallagher. Lord, Mace would be impossible to live with!

Hub had never considered himself a religious man, but he indulged in some serious praying as they tracked Gil Davis and his captives. Jesus! He was even feeling sorry for Florence, crotchety old woman that she was. She was probably beside herself with fear. And to make matters worse, Mace would find some excuse to blame Florence for his woes. Hub would bet on it!

As the first rays of dawn spilled from the horizon, Mace stood in the stirrups to work the kinks from his

494

back. His eyes narrowed when he noticed the trail of hat boxes and clothes that littered the road. His breath froze in his chest when he spied the broken buggy that had been dragged onto the steep bank that overlooked the river.

"Damnit." Mace scowled when his glittering golden eyes fastened on the silhouette that was poised on the buggy seat. Attached to Jacquelyn's neck was a rope that stretched across the river channel. Mace didn't have to be a genius to guess who was holding the other end of that rope. Curse that vicious bastard!

"It's a trap," Hub muttered as he surveyed the clump of trees that crowded the opposite side of the river. "If we try to free Jake before Davis drags her into the river, we'll be sitting ducks!"

"And if we don't try, Davis will yank her into the channel to drown," Mace predicted grimly. "He's got her tied up tight! She couldn't swim, even if she wanted to." Reining his steed to a halt, Mace wrestled with the few choices Davis had granted them. Heaving an agitated sigh, he gestured his raven head to the east. "Take Raoul and cross the river," Mace ordered abruptly.

"While you're doing what? Letting Davis cut you to pieces as you ride toward Jake?" Hub scoffed disgustedly. "You know damned well he's lying in wait. Even if you manage to cut the rope before he sends her plunging into the channel, he'll still fill you with bullets."

Mace's stony gaze swung to Hub. "If you've got a better idea, now's the time to unveil it, my friend."

Hub expelled an exasperated snort. "Damn, I wish this were only a wild-eyed nightmare and you could shake me awake and tell me everything's going to be all right." His blue eyes focused intently on Mace. "If things don't work out . . ."

"Get the hell out of here. This isn't the time to turn sentimental on me," Mace grumbled before he clamped the reins between his teeth. With one fist clenched around a colt and the other hand clamped on his Bowie knife, Mace nudged his mount in the flanks.

Frowning grimly, Hub retrieved both of his pistols and gouged his steed. Firing toward the end of the rope that disappeared into the clump of trees, Hub tried to provide cover for Mace, who had aimed himself straight at the buggy.

It was as if a keg of blasting powder had suddenly exploded to spoil the serenity of sunrise. Pistols and rifles shattered the silence, sending a cloud of birds from their nesting place in the trees.

Jacquelyn died a thousand deaths when she heard Mace's steed galloping toward her. A choked sob bubbled from her lips when she felt the noose tighten around her neck. Although she resisted, the painful yank on the rope knocked her off balance and sent her toppling from the buggy that was perched on the edge of the steep bank.

In horror, she watched the river come at her with incredible speed. Mace's name flew from her lips as she awaited the murky water below, knowing she could never fight her way to the surface with her hands and feet bound and the noose on her neck dragging her further into the cold depths.

As the volley of bullets whistled past him, Mace heard Jacquelyn's bloodcurdling scream and watched helplessly as she plunged headlong into the river. But Mace refused to allow his steed to break stride as he flattened himself in the saddle. The horse's shrill whinny intermingled with the whine of bullets as they flew through the air with no solid ground beneath them. With his eyes fixed on the spot where Jake had gone down, Mace dived from the saddle before his horse plunged into the water.

A wordless growl tripped from Gil's lips when Mace charged over the cliff. Gil had expected Mace to pull up short and dismount when Jake was dragged into the river. And while Mace was swinging to the ground, Gil had intended to pellet him with bullets.

Gil's frustration was compounded by the barrage of gunfire that ricocheted through the trees, keeping him pinned down, making it impossible for him to rush to the river to finish Mace off while he floundered to save Jacquelyn. And Florence was no help at all. The whining bitch was ridiculing his scheme. If he didn't need her to lead him to the money, he would have shot the old bat where she sat!

Determined to save her own hide, Florence slithered through the underbrush while Gil was trying to fire in several directions at once. It infuriated Florence that Gil's scheme hadn't unfolded as effectively as he assured her it would. Gil had been certain he could drop Mace in his tracks and then unleash a barrage of bullets on Hub. But from the look of things, Gil wouldn't live long enough to name her as his accomplice and Jacquelyn would drown, if she hadn't already. If Florence could sneak away, she could proclaim Gil had taken her hostage along with Jacquelyn and no one would be the wiser. No one would have known Florence had instigated the whole scheme. Why, she could even insist that Gil had killed Malcolm and there would be no one to dispute her word.

While Florence was crawling to safety, Jacquelyn was fighting for her life and losing. The confining ropes and the tight noose on her neck kept her submerged in the murky depths. Her lungs threatened to collapse and there was naught else to do but pray. . . . And then, even praying proved to be fruitless. Jacquelyn felt the arms of eternal darkness engulfing her, luring her into a peaceful silence. The last ounce of precious breath slipped away and her struggling ceased. . . .

Frantically, Mace pulled, hand over hand, along the rope. It incensed him that he couldn't tug on the rope to bring Jacquelyn to the surface without choking what life might be left in her. She had remained underwater far too long. Only a fish could have submerged for such a length of time without facing disaster. Desperately, Mace felt his way through the cloudy depths until his hand collided with Jacquelyn's neck. Clamping his arm around her lifeless form, he thrashed upward to gasp for air.

Sickening dread gnawed at Mace's insides as Jacquelyn's head rolled lifelessly against his heaving chest. The instant Mace found solid footing he scampered toward the protection of the underbrush that lined the creek bank. His murderous gaze swung toward the trees that concealed Gil Davis. Tearing his mutinous gaze away from Gil's hiding place, he glanced down to cut the rope that was tied around Jacquelyn's neck.

The sight of Hub scuttling through the bushes toward Gil brought the only satisfaction Mace was to enjoy in those tense moments. Mace was torn between the need to remain with Jake, in hopes that she would rouse to consciousness, and the maddening urge to appease his vengeance.

Frustrated, Mace rolled Jacquelyn to her stomach and forced the water from her lungs. (Mace was sure she had swallowed several gallons during her ordeal.) When he felt her shallow breath beneath his trembling hands, relief washed over him. Jake might not have been at the peak of health but she was alive, thank God!

Clamping his knife in his fist, Mace crept toward Gil's hiding place in the bushes. While Gil and Hub exchanged rapid fire, Mace crawled toward Gil's blind side.

Groggily, Jacquelyn reared her head and choked to catch a breath. Her anguished gaze flew to Mace, who was slithering through the brush like a snake waiting to strike. She marveled at this man's abilities. How he had managed to rescue her from drowning was beyond her. But then she reminded herself that Mace Gallagher did

498

not know the meaning of impossible. The word served only to challenge him, to encourage him to test himself to the limits of his abilities, to perform death-defying maneuvers.

Mace Gallagher in action was poetry in motion. He moved with masculine grace as he drew his legs beneath him to crouch twenty feet from Gil Davis. With the quickness of a pouncing cat, Mace sprang from the underbrush, bellowing Gil's name like a deadly curse. Gil spun around to fire at his enemy, but while in midair Mace hurled his dagger and completed his graceful movement by somersaulting into the underbrush. As Gil's trigger finger contracted, a shuddering groan tumbled from his curled lips.

And then there was silence—the eerie kind that follows death. . . .

Cautiously, Hub poked his head from behind the tree he had employed as a shield. His shoulders sagged in relief as the rifle toppled from Gil's hand and he fell face down on the ground—the victim of a mortal knife wound.

"Mace!" Jacquelyn choked out in gasping breaths. Struggling, she pulled herself into an upright position and tossed the wet tangles from her peaked face.

Mace unfolded himself from the bushes and stood up. Jacquelyn almost managed a smile when she realized he had escaped unscathed. Pulling herself together, she peered into the distance to see Florence scampering toward the horses that had been tethered a hundred yards away.

"Florence is the one who schemed to cheat the Gen'ral. She killed Malcolm," she informed him hoarsely.

Wheeling around, Mace caught sight of the old woman. "Raoul!" He gestured toward the escaping old woman.

The mongrel tore off through the underbrush in fast pursuit while Mace dashed back to untie Jacquelyn. The furious squawks in the distance caught Jacquelyn's attention. In wicked glee she watched Raoul leap at Florence just as she struggled to pull herself into the saddle. Another round of piercing shrieks erupted when Raoul clamped his sharp teeth into the hem of Florence's dangling skirts and yanked her backward. The rending of cloth was proceeded by Florence's unladylike dismounting—or rather the fall provoked by Raoul's fierce tugs. From her sprawled position on the grass, Florence stared up into Raoul's menacing snarl. When she tried to regain her feet, the mongrel pounced. He was all teeth and bristled hair, and Florence froze before Raoul went for her throat.

When the threesome arrived upon the scene, surprise registered on every face. The money that had been carefully stitched to Florence's petticoat lay scattered around her (thanks to the gashes Raoul had torn in the garment).

A triumphant smile twitched Jacquelyn's lips as she peered down at her great-aunt. "Ah, the irony of it all," she taunted mercilessly. "Gil didn't live to discover just how close he was to his share of the money, and you won't be able to spend your half of it since you'll be cooped up with the other inmates in prison. I'm sure the Gen'ral will be pleased to know you have been saving his money for him these past three years. But I doubt your brother will be lenient with you. Indeed, he will be as eager to see you behind bars as you were to see him hanged for the murder you committed."

While Hub tied their prisoner in the discarded ropes, Mace led Jacquelyn back to the river to retrieve his horse. All the frustrated emotion that had hounded him the past twelve hours exploded like a volcano. To Jacquelyn's astonishment, she found herself swallowed in Mace's sinewy arms and crushed against his muscled torso. In all their time together, she couldn't recollect Mace being so rough with her. The kiss he bestowed on her was ravishing, suffocating, and frantically desperate. My, one would have thought he had just learned the world was about to disintegrate and intended to devour her before it did!

When Mace finally raised his ruffled raven head to grant her a breath of air, Jacquelyn stared incredulously at him. "What is the matter with you?" she croaked as he squeezed the stuffing out of her.

"What's the matter with me?" Mace growled. "I almost lost you, for Chrissake! You could have been hit by a stray bullet, hanged by the neck, and drowned, all at the same time! What's the matter with me? Damnit, I was scared to death!"

Lovingly, Jacquelyn reached up to caress away the rankled frown that was stamped on his craggy features. "Would you have minded so much? Being rid of me, once and for all?" she questioned with an impish smile that turned his knees to mush.

The frustration finally ebbed, and Mace relaxed enough to return her grin. "I'm not so sure I can function without you anymore, little minx," he confessed as he traced the exquisite lines of her face. "You have become every breath I take, Jake, my sun and moon. I would never get used to losing you. . . ."

"We're ready to ride," Hub announced as he halted his horse and his prisoner's horse beside the loving couple.

Florence said nothing. She couldn't. Hub had heard enough out of her while he was tying her to her mount. He had stuffed a gag in her mouth to spare himself from suffering through her nerve-shattering screeching.

"Jake and I will be along in a minute," Mace murmured without taking his eyes off Jacquelyn's bewitching face.

Biting back a wry smile, Hub nudged his steed, and Florence's, toward the road, heading toward the Reid plantation. "Whatever you say, Captain. . . ."

Mace was too distracted by the shapely bundle in his arms to rise to Hub's taunt. He didn't give a fig if Hub knew why Mace wanted a few moments alone with Jake. He had waded through the fiery pits of hell to retrieve Jacquelyn, and nothing was going to prevent him from holding her until he had recovered from the shock of learning Gil had taken her hostage.

"*Te amo.* . . ." Mace whispered as his lips slanted across hers. "God, you'll never know how much. . . ."

"Is that Spanish for 'I love you'?" Jacquelyn breathed raggedly. The feel of Mace's powerful arms encompassing her triggered all the wild yearnings she had always experienced when her body came into intimate contact with his.

With a rakish smile, Mace unfastened the lacings of her gown and tugged it to her waist. His golden eyes roved over her olive skin. His gaze was so potent she could have sworn he had reached out to touch her. "*Sí*, Senorita Reid," he replied in the heavily accented voice he had employed while he masqueraded as the Mexican bandito. "And this is Mace Gallagher for 'I love you.'"

Deftly, he removed her damp gown and draped it over a low-hanging branch. "Allow me to translate. . . ."

Jacquelyn needed no translation when Mace set his gentle hands upon her bare flesh. Love was embroidered in each worshipping caress, each adoring kiss. He tasted and touched every inch of her trembling flesh, leaving her to wrestle with gigantic cravings that mushroomed into monstrous yearnings. Her body ached with tormented pleasure as he weaved his tapestry of passion about her.

Her near-brush with death made his skillful lovemaking more precious than it had ever been. Jacquelyn reveled in the rapture of being loved by this awesome man. Theirs had been a rough and rocky courtship, each one of them afraid of the vulnerability that came with loving someone too much. But there was no such thing as too much, Jacquelyn thought as she looked up into the strikingly handsome face that was poised above her. There weren't enough years in a lifetime to express all the wondrous emotions she felt for this man. Mace was all she had ever hoped for, all she would ever need to make her life complete.

And when he came to her, whispering his love in a language that required no words, Jacquelyn knew she was living her dream. She gave herself up to the wild pleasures of passion, assuring Mace that he could never want for more than Jacquelyn could give.

As they navigated their intimate journey through the fluffy clouds that paraded across the far horizon, Mace knew what he had been searching for, and yet afraid to find, all his life. This was the sweet magic of love, the giving and sharing, the total commitment of caring so much that the mere thought of Jacquelyn was enough to leave him quivering in awe. He was possessed, bewitched, and he didn't care if he ever woke from this splendorous spell. His renegade heart had met its match and he was eager to make a place in his hectic life for love. Besides, if he had this lively nymph by his side, he would need nothing else. Her love was enough to sustain him through all eternity.

Much later, Mace reminded himself that Harlan was probably walking on pins and needles, wondering what had become of his granddaughter. Reluctantly, Mace shrugged on his dried clothes and fastened Jacquelyn into her garments.

When he had set Jacquelyn atop his steed, he glanced up to issue his order, knowing full well he would meet with resistance. After all, that was this contrary sprite's middle name. "To insure nothing else goes amiss before our wedding, I'm sending Raoul home with you to act as your bodyguard. He is going to become your shadow while I'm wrapping up some loose ends with Jon Mason, Florence, and the banditos who are giving the Rangers fits on the border."

Her chin tilted defiantly, as he knew it would. "I don't need—"

"Yes, you do," Mace interrupted in a stern voice. Hastily, he hopped up behind her and took control of the reins. "You and Raoul can use the time to get to know each other. You'll find that he really isn't a bad sort, once you become acquainted with him. Why, the two of you might even come to like each other, given half a chance."

Skeptical though she was about being followed, day and night, by a mongrel who seemed more inclined to take a bite out of her than befriend her, Jacquelyn remained silent. She was weary from her ordeal—stiff and sore from being tied at the wrists and ankles for hours on end, not to mention the exhausting aftereffects of loving a man like Mace.

As they charted a course cross-country to catch up with Hub, Jacquelyn leaned contentedly against Mace's sturdy frame. She hadn't expected to live to enjoy the luxury of a catnap in his protective arms. Odd, she mused as she settled more comfortably in the saddle. Even the simplest pleasures provoked a warm sense of satisfaction. . . . And loving Mace had been the easiest thing she had ever done. It just came naturally. . . .

Chapter 28

It was a small wedding, just as Mace had requested. Only immediate family and close friends were there to hear Jacquelyn and Mace speak their vows. Although Mace had hoped to return from the Ranger headquarters at Corpus Christi within a week, it had taken a full three weeks to round up the gang of cattle rustlers who had worked for Malcolm and Gil. After that length of time, Mace and Hub had been forced to make a hasty trip to Galveston to insure the Reid and Gallagher Commission Companies were in proper working order.

And of course, when Mace finally had returned, Harlan had been there to insure his granddaughter had no late-night visitors creeping into her boudoir from the balcony. The General had demanded that Mace observe propriety since the rake had failed to do so while he was wooing Jacquelyn.

In short, Mace had become a man deprived of that which he cherished above all else. He'd not been allowed a moment alone with Jacquelyn before their wedding, and he'd felt like a man who had been strung out on a medieval torture rack. The deprivation of Jacquelyn's affection had played havoc with his disposition—a fact that had Hub snickering in wicked delight.

Even Hub's prank of placing a ribbon around Raoul's neck and having him march in the wedding procession had failed to bring a smile to Mace's strained features. And to further annoy Mace, Hub and Harlan had planned a huge reception, which was attended by scores of friends and neighbors. It began in the early afternoon and dragged into the night.

Mace knew damned well Hub was purposely antagonizing him and relishing every moment of it. And by ten o'clock that evening Mace had enjoyed all the celebrating and congratulating he could tolerate. If he didn't get Jacquelyn alone, he swore he would burst a seam!

With more candor than tact, Mace grasped Jacquelyn's hand and announced that he and his lovely bride were leaving the grand affair and that the guests could do what they pleased, especially the snickering Hub MacIntosh. Squaring his shoulders, Mace shepherded Jacquelyn through the crowd of faces beaming with knowing smiles and whisked her into the waiting carriage.

By the time they arrived at the Gallagher plantation, Mace's imagination had run rampant, knowing full well what he was going to do when he finally got Jake all to himself. He intended to compensate for the month of celibacy he had been forced to endure.

Although Mace thought he had removed all obstacles that stood between him and his eagerness for his new wife, he discovered one more stumbling block when he strolled into the master bedroom.

Jacquelyn had donned a sheer blue negligee that had Mace's blood boiling. The gossamer fabric left just enough to the imagination to leave Mace tingling with anticipation. She lay on the fluffy feather bed, looking absolutely ravishing. The golden lantern light sprayed across the room to form a halo around the unbound tendrils of dark hair. The light glowed like honey on her olive skin and twinkled like living fire in her ebony eyes.

Like a reckless fool, Mace dived toward the bed to playfully wrestle Jacquelyn to her back. But what a mistake that turned out to be! Before he could envelop Jacquelyn in his arms, Raoul, who had followed them home, bounded onto the bed to bare his teeth—at Mace of all people!

"What the devil has gotten into you?" Mace croaked when Raoul growled at him.

"Raoul has become very possessive of me this past month," Jacquelyn remarked, peering up at Mace's astounded expression. Her eyes traveled lovingly over his chiseled features, aching to touch him, to lose herself in the ecstasy that she knew awaited her. But unfortunately, the growling mongrel stood between her and the man she longed to love. "You told Raoul to guard me like a dragon and he is but obeying your command. To compound his confusion, he probably thinks you abandoned him after your long absence."

"You don't have to protect Jake from me!" Mace growled back at the snarling dog. When he tried to reach for Jake a second time, the hair on Raoul's back bristled in threat and he assumed his pouncing stance—right smack dab in the middle of the bed! Frustrated, Mace glared into Raoul's black eyes. "Is this the thanks I get for taking you in when you had nowhere to go? Is this how you repay me for nursing you back to health after your scrap with a pack of coyotes? And need I remind you that you have had the run of this house and the surrounding grounds since the war?"

Glancing sideways, Jacquelyn smiled reassuringly at her overprotective bodyguard. She didn't know what Mace had told Raoul, since he had rattled off his comments in fluent Spanish, but she could tell the soliloquy hadn't fazed the snarling mutt. "Raoul, fetch the basket I packed for you," she requested softly. The mongrel spared her a quick glance, and then curled his lips at Mace. "Go on now, Raoul. I can handle this handsome hombre."

To Mace's mute astonishment, Raoul gave him a keep-your-distance-until-I-get-back glare and leaped off the bed. But what really floored Mace was that Raoul was responding to English commands as if he understood every word Jacquelyn had said. With mouth gaping, Mace watched the shaggy beast trot over to Jacquelyn's luggage to retrieve the basket. With his head held high, Raoul pranced back to place his huge front paws on the edge of the bed. Jacquelyn extracted two biscuits that were seeping with strawberry jelly and offered them to Raoul with a fond smile.

"Take your treats out on the terrace. I'll call for you if I need you, Raoul," she assured him.

Dumbfounded, Mace watched Raoul worm his snout under Jacquelyn's hand, encouraging her to stroke his broad head. Laughing softly, Jacquelyn murmured silly nonsense to the oversized mongrel and bestowed several affectionate pats on him.

"Be a good boy and tell Mace good night," she commanded.

After sniffing Mace's clenched fist, Raoul offered his paw, and his tail finally began to wag. Nonplussed, Mace shook Raoul's paw, and then watched the mongrel clamp his powerful jaws around both of his biscuits and prance out the terrace door.

"I thought peach marmalade was his favorite," Mace mused aloud.

"Raoul has acquired a taste for strawberries," she declared as she watched Raoul and his wagging tail disappear from sight.

"I think I lost my dog," Mace grumbled, still staring in the direction Raoul had taken.

Jacquelyn's gentle hands slid across Mace's broad

chest to loosen his shirt. "You may have lost your dog, but you have gained a wife. . . ." she murmured provocatively. Her body arched to make arousing contact with his bare chest. "I hope you won't mind too much." Her lips feathered over his mouth in the lightest breath of a touch, and Mace's muscular body became the exact consistency of Raoul's strawberry jam. "I can accomplish all the tasks Raoul has undertaken at your command . . . plus so much more." Her straying hand skimmed across his ribs to unfasten the buttons on his trousers. "Shall I show you all the tantalizing ways I can accommodate you that Raoul cannot?"

He was going to go up in flames, burn himself to a crisp, and scatter like ashes in the wind. He just knew it! Jacquelyn's seductive techniques had already fried him, inside and out.

"Raoul who?" Mace squeaked, his voice two octaves higher than usual. Her adventurous hands were doing impossible things to his male body and his self-control. It made Mace wonder whom this vixen had been practicing on during his lengthy absence. She certainly had the ability to fully arouse him in a matter of seconds. Of course, this vivacious minx had always had it, but Mace was too full of frustrated passion to remember that fact.

The suspicious thought found its way into words. "Who have you been practicing your provocative techniques on during my lengthy absence?" he demanded to know.

Her soft lips parted in an impish smile as she came upon her knees to shed her gown. Mace swallowed a roomful of air when he was granted an unhindered view of her exquisite body. But it wasn't only the view that titillated him. It was the seductive way Jacquelyn removed the garment that caused him to gasp in masculine appreciation.

"I've been loving you from afar, every night while you

509

were away," she insisted as she stretched like a cat and then curled up on his heaving chest. "Didn't you feel my hands gliding over your skin each night . . . like this . . . ? Didn't you feel my kisses exploring every inch of your magnificent body . . . like this . . . ?"

Yes, he had felt her loving touch for four long, tormenting weeks. He remembered every magical moment with vivid clarity, and it had very nearly driven him crazy.

His breath lodged in his throat when her satiny flesh caressed him in ways that boggled his mind and set his body aflame . . . again. "If you don't quit that, I can't be held responsible for my actions," he gasped hoarsely. "I've run short of patience and self-control."

"I was counting on that," Jacquelyn murmured as her hands and lips continued to trek across his masculine flesh, causing his nerves to sizzle like lightning.

Mace broke into a rakish grin as he hooked an arm around the trim indention of her waist and pinned her to the sheets. This was the first time he had made love to Jacquelyn on his own bed. Indeed, it was the first time any woman had laid her head upon his pillow. Jacquelyn was the only woman he had ever wanted in his home, in his room, in his life. Tonight was a monumental first and Mace knew he wanted this feisty nymph to be the only woman who was granted this privilege. But this would not be the last time they shared this bed. They were going to create a lifetime of memories inside these four walls.

"Witch," he playfully teased as he stared down into her radiant face. "I swear you were sent up from hell to taunt me with that shapely body of yours and leave me to burn. I have never been able to get enough of you. . . ."

The mischievous smile vanished from her enchanting features, and Mace marveled at the myriad of emotions mirrored in those dark, hypnotic pools. "No, my love," she contradicted in such a soft, sincere voice that goose

510

pimples raced each other up and down his spine. "I'm the rebel who has found her cause. We may have waded through hell to find each other, but the match must surely have been made in heaven. It feels so right, so perfect." Her bottom lip trembled, as it always had a habit of doing when her body came in intimate contact with his, and Mace was quick to note that fascinating characteristic. "Do you know how much I love you, how much I want to become the essence of all your dreams?"

When her petal-soft lips melted against his, Mace knew he had been granted a love to span eternity. Jacquelyn possessed a unique combination of strength and gentleness that made Mace believe in forever. She had come to mean all things to him. She was his dream come true. . . .